The SIX

Kirk Holland

ISBN: 9781736361023

Cover design by: Kim Sajan
Printed in the United States of America

To Janice, Harrison, and Jones -
thank you for being on this journey with me.
This road has already been such an adventure,
and we have a whole map to explore.

To everyone else on the journey of discovering who you are,
you're in good company.

CHAPTER ONE

Stumped

Charlie hated Texas.

Hated everything about it. The unpredictability of the weather. The ridiculous heat in the summer and the infuriating fact there were only two seasons: hot summer and warm winter. No fall. No spring. It was all the same and it was suffocating.

Or how about the flatness? The brown. The dead brown mesquite trees. Muddy brown creeks. Dead brown grass. Brown dirt roads. Brown.

Wildlife? Fire ants. Buzzards looking for something dead and rotting to eat. Decimated skunks littering the country roads yet still filling the air with their stink as though it were their last vengeful act.

Suffocating.

Yet the most suffocating thing about it was the expectations. If you were a guy, you played sports, particularly football. If you were a dude and didn't play football, it meant you were probably gay and that label took on a whole new set of social complications. To Charlie's knowledge, only one guy ever dared to come out of the closet at Farnsworth High School. The other guys were relentless in their taunting and harassment of the brave kid who dared to claim his identity, it actually gave the geeks a break for a little while. They never laid a hand on the guy, they *wouldn't* for fear of catching *it*. But the daily social crucifixion was hard to watch. *Everyone* just watched. At some point the kid disappeared, moved away to live with his grandmother or aunt or whoever in wherever.

Charlie imagined girls had it just as bad in their own way. Most of them *aspired* to be a cheerleader and those who didn't quite hit the mark, but were still pretty enough, were shuffled into some sort of consolation prize dance team, the *almost* cheerleaders but not really and everyone knew it. But if you weren't pretty enough, strong enough, popular enough, rich enough, you were either a target or a nameless face in the crowd.

Charlie was just a face.

Sweat trickled down the side of his face and he rubbed his cheek on the shoulder of his t-shirt. If his mom had seen him "desecrate his freshly laundered shirt," she would have given him an ear full even if she *did* have to cross the two-acre front yard to where he sat hunched over, knees to his ears, perched on the "waiting stump", something his dad had come up with when he started riding the bus in kindergarten.

Seven o'clock in the morning and it was already hot enough to sweat. Charlie could feel it trickle down between his shoulder blades and down his butt crack.

Texas sucked. Texas was the dull *butt crack* of America.

In reality, Charlie wasn't faceless, people just treated him that way because he required it of them. Coaches had all but begged him to play football since he was in fifth grade. And why not? He was a perfect candidate for it. He'd been taller than everyone else since he could remember. The first time his height really registered was in second grade. It was a class party, probably for Christmas or something, and one of the moms, a pug-nosed woman with gooey red lipstick had asked him how old he was.

"I'm seven," he had told her.

She had scrunched up her face with suspicion and twanged, "You're only seven years old?" Somehow that last word was divvied up into two syllables.

"Yes, ma'am."

"You turn eight this year?"

"Yes, ma'am. My birthday is in March. March 16."

"You're a big boy! You gonna play football? Be a big football player?"

He shrugged.

Later on, he remembered hearing her tell another mom about how young, but how big he was. The other mom swore he'd been held back a grade and whispered how he clearly didn't take after his daddy, short and scrawny. Charlie just sat at his desk drinking his watered-down punch, nibbling his cookies with green sprinkles.

It only became more exaggerated from there. In sixth grade, he was already as tall as some tenth graders and his voice had dropped. By eighth grade he was as tall as a senior and just as broad-shouldered, but still not filled out. And now as a junior in high school, he was taller than all of them and built like a tank. But he didn't shave. No need to. Anywhere. That was embarrassing in the locker room.

Tall, broad, fast, coordinated. Every year, he knew a question mark hung over his head. Would this be the year Charlie Daniels finally figured out he was meant to serve the football gods and would sell his soul to the football team, more specifically Coach Tark? Would he give in and just play?

Coach Tark could shove it. It wasn't happening. Charlie was prepared for another year of the looks, the sneers, the rolled eyes. Some of the guys on the football team ignored him, but most still considered it their job to make their disapproval clear. They referred to themselves as *the Pack*. The Pack roamed the halls like wolves, bigger and stronger than the rest of the team, they all looked as though they should be serving time in a juvenile penitentiary and every single one of them had at least one tattoo, a big black wolf paw on their chest, shoulder, or neck. It was stupid. Only one tattoo shop existed in town, and the Pack must have paid extra for the burly Hell's Angel reject to not check their IDs. Never guys to make actual trouble, they just managed to make you feel weaker, inconsequential. The Pack, of course, was all starters on the team, Coach Tark's little gang. And first and foremost in that gang, was Ben.

Ben was a junior, like Charlie, but had to be at least twenty-one, yet if he were, he wouldn't have been able to play on the team according to state rules. He was almost as tall as Charlie, but where Charlie lacked in the more follicle aspects of puberty, Ben was clearly the alpha in the Pack. Only seniors were allowed facial hair, but Ben insisted he shaved every morning, it just grew too fast, so his face was always covered in stubble. The guy was a beast and Charlie was suitably intimidated. Ben was the only person who outright intimidated him.

And because he didn't play football, he was doomed to be in PE. It was fine, it gave him the opportunity to stretch his legs at the end of a full day of sitting at a desk. The issue, however, was PE ended right before football practice started, meaning the locker room deteriorated into the Pack's den. And the Pack didn't care a shred about decency. They would parade around the locker room howling in all levels of undress. Most of the scrawny or chubby PE guys wouldn't shower and vacated the locker room as fast as they could, adding their unshowered funk to the bus ride home. Not Charlie, he stayed decent, but refused to give up his rightful territory. He took his shower, dealt with the sneers, the disdainful looks from Ben, muttering and laughing, dressed and left.

Decency had always been a big deal to his parents, James and Harriett hammered it into him. The way you treated people, the way you presented yourself, what you talked about, and what you *didn't* talk about. Being shirtless at home wasn't necessarily an issue, but he was expected to be dressed when he came to the table. And "maturing" obviously wasn't on the list of decent topics. Puberty had been hellish, no one talked about any of it. His body was changing, his thoughts were changing, and the combination of a changing body and changing thoughts created situations he didn't know how to deal with. Hoping again hope, Charlie kept waiting for his dad to talk to him about it, have the birds and bees talk, whatever that was, but it never came. He figured things out on his own, well, on his own and Mr. McWhitten's biology class, but he was pretty sure there were gigantic gaps of ignorance that might not ever be explained.

Another element of the whole decency zone was control, and Charlie was always in control. You had to be good, even tempered, and cordial. He only overstepped that one time when he was a freshman. This kid, not a member of the Pack, but desperate to prove himself, was brave, or stupid, enough to get in his face about his refusal to even try out for the team when Charlie had first arrived on the high school campus, but even as a freshman, he was bigger than most of the seniors. That kid had found himself on the ground holding his nose before he knew what hit him and Charlie had found himself suspended for two weeks. "You're bigger than they are, Charlie," his dad said with disappointment. "You have to control that. You could have really hurt that boy."

Charlie went on to learn his strength was the underlying real need for control. Simple brute strength. It's what he spent his free time doing. His dad relied on him to lift big rocks or limbs on their land that most people couldn't. He was unusually strong and he had to control it because if he didn't, his parents constantly reminded him, he would hurt someone. "Be gentle," his mom used to tell him. "Be careful," his dad would say. They didn't have to say it anymore, it was ingrained in him. If he weren't gentle or careful, something bad would happen. Something worse than a bloody nose.

Charlie's absence from any athletic field or court had started when he was going into junior high. He'd actually been excited about trying out for the football team, he knew he'd be a star, the crowds would chant his name and the girls would be lining up. The permission slip was never signed. He gripped it in his hand, waving it at both his mom and dad, pleading until he was furious and in tears. "You just can't, son," his dad begged him to understand, a true sincerity underlying the heartbreaking denial. Charlie looked to his mom, but with tears in her own eyes, she crossed her arms and shook her head. In a rage, Charlie yanked open the front door and nearly pulled the entire thing off its hinges. No one ever had to explain it again. If he had done that to a door as a twelve-year-old, what might he do to another kid?

Charlie took a deep breath and felt sweat drip from his nose. It was like this every morning. The waiting. Sitting on the stump, waiting for the school bus to rumble down the dusty road to his old farmhouse which sat alone on several acres of land. Privacy acres, as his dad called them. They didn't do anything with the land, no farming except for his mother's garden out back, no animals, the land just sat there like a vast guardian against anything that might be moderately interesting or fun. The whole town was like that, like some kind of wall keeping out the murderous hordes of . . . what? Life? Experience? Adventure?

And why exactly was he sitting there? Sixteen and carless. An automotive virgin. "There's no place in Farnsworth, Texas, you can't reach on foot or on a bicycle," his mom would say, pushing a strand of curly gray hair out of her face. "Another car would be nothing but trouble. Headaches and trouble. And your legs are stronger and more capable than any car you could have." *Technology* was nothing but headaches and trouble—period. No television, so Charlie was socially stunted in discussing television *shows*. No video games, so Charlie spent his time in the garage with the weights his dad bought him several years ago and added to regularly. No computer, so Charlie knew the land surrounding their farmhouse like most kids knew the internet. Not even a DVD player, so Charlie dreamed. The only films Charlie had ever seen were the ones shown in class from time to time when the teachers were clearly passing the time until Christmas or summer break kicked in. His home's lack of technology was also why his parents still wrote their books by hand on stacks and stacks of yellow legal pads. The publisher hated it, but the two bestselling authors could have it their way and did.

The books were so popular that film and television producers had been pursuing his parents for the last three years. Always touting it as the next great *fill-in-the-blank*, the blood sucking vampires (his mother's pet name for the money grabbing producers) did their best to sell their big picture visions. Was it going to be a multi-film epic? Would it be the next blood and guts fantasy drama on premium cable? Maybe the next streaming subscription hit? Whatever the case, his mother was sickened by the "obscene" amount of money they wanted to throw at the two authors. Money wasn't their thing and every time a producer called quoting a new amount, his parents dug their heels in that much more. Unfortunately, it wasn't going to be any of those entertainment goldmines. James and Harriett weren't interested, they simply wanted to sell their books. No, he'd been thoroughly corrected over that particular phrasing, they simply wanted "to tell their stories."

One particular media mogul, his parents wouldn't tell Charlie who, not that he would know a mogul from a mongrel, was particularly persistent. At first, the *assistant* made the calls, and despite the fact his dad was going to turn it down, James Daniels was still insulted. What neither of his parents was prepared for, however, was the calls from the mogul's attorneys. They were threatening. Initially, onslaught of legal jargon terrified his mother, and that infuriated his dad. James didn't get worked up often, but this had done it. Their own attorney, some guy connected to the publisher, finally got the legal dogs called off. Things were quiet enough for a couple of months, then the gift baskets began to show up on the first Monday of every month complete with a friendly phone call from the mogul's own *daughter*.

Charlie looked up the empty road. Bestselling authors. They could *afford* to buy him a car. Should the world turn upside down and James and Harriett caved in the great automobile debate, Charlie could never decide between big or fast. Most of the guys in town had trucks, big trucks with big wheels. It may have been one of the only things he had in common with those guys. Their trucks were beautiful and could all be found parked in rows, shining in the sun, like sun bathing beasts. But fast looked like fun too. *Those* cars belonged to the guys in shop class, the self-proclaimed grease monkeys. Vintage Camaros, Mustangs, a T-Bird here and there. Fast and loud, and sometimes late at night, they would scream down the empty road, racing by Charlie's lonely house. He would lay in bed listening, his jealousy growing in bounds.

Big or fast? Not a problem he'd ever have to solve apparently.

Charlie sighed and wiped his sweaty eyes on his shirt. Two years ago, he had started carrying a spare shirt in his backpack because by the time he got to school, he was a slick mess. He may not have gotten any of the body hair with puberty, but he certainly acquired the sweat glands.

He heard the rumbling of the old yellow school bus before he saw the chugging machine. Full of lower class-men and rejects, that bus was the bane of Charlie's mornings and afternoons, even more so than the Pack in the locker room. Obviously, he could ride his bike to school and add a third shirt to his backpack, but that would be giving in and Charlie Daniels never gave in.

Standing, Charlie brushed the dirt off the butt of his long athletic shorts, about the only thing that fit him normally, and hiked his backpack up on his shoulders. The bus came to a groaning stop as though it hated the morning routine as much as its next passenger. With a squeal, the door unfolded and Charlie stepped in.

Man, was there a funk. Which came first: social rejection or poor hygiene? It stood to reason if you wanted to work your way up that social ladder, you might want to do something that would immediately make you more tolerable to others. Shower. Brush your hair. Brush your *teeth*. Wear freakin' deodorant. Were these keys to acceptance so hard to grasp? As it was, this was hands down the worst smelling place associated with school. You'd think the locker room would be reigning champion, but the fact of the matter was the locker room may have started out smelling like body odor and sweat, but at least ended in a cloud of body spray and cologne. This bus was still the dominating victor of funk.

Gladys, the drooping driver, ignored Charlie as he passed her. He knew her well enough to know, though she seemed disinterested and oblivious, Gladys was all too aware of the goings-on of her bus. The woman had been the bus driver as long as Charlie could remember. Year after year, her back bent lower, her hands gnarled more, and the bags under her eyes grew thicker. Her mouth always hung open, making her dangling turkey neck bulge. Gladys the bus driver was a crooked staple in Charlie's life. With every transition, she was there. She'd terrified him the first time the school bus door screeched open when he was in kindergarten. For the first three weeks, his mom had to take him by the hand and lead him past her until he realized if he just looked at the floor he could pretend she was a sweet lady with bright eyes and rosy cheeks. In junior high he thought he'd escaped her, but the first day of school, she was there. Droopy. And surprise, surprise. Gladys "welcomed" him his first day of high school as well.

Working his way to the back, Charlie avoided eye contact with everyone. He found his usual empty bench and dropped his backpack next to him in an attempt to dissuade anyone picked up in the next several stops from joining him. Truth be told, he took up most of the bench anyway. However, to further his subtle demand for seclusion, he leaned his head against the window and closed his eyes.

"I brought my book for your parents to sign!"

Some people wouldn't take the hint.

A heavy hardback book dropped onto Charlie's lap, hitting him squarely where he wished it hadn't. Charlie doubled over with a groan and the book fell to the floor of the bus. The owner of the book, a rotund boy, leaped from his seat in front of Charlie and dove for the book as though rescuing a priceless national treasure. Charlie was too concerned with his current discomfort to help the blundering interloper who was currently burrowing under Charlie's seat as the book slid back due to the bouncing and jarring of the bus.

"There! Got it!" The kid proclaimed triumphantly as he unwedged himself from between the seats with no little effort and exposure of butt crack, to stand unsteadily, intermittently situating his stretched fanboy t-shirt and thick glasses, while clutching the back of the seat beside him.

"Sit down!" Gladys slurred loudly from the front of the bus, her sagging, basset hound eyes watching in the large, overhead mirror.

The kid scrambled onto his bench, but immediately turned around on his knees to focus his attention back on Charlie. "So, here's the book." He made to drop it again, but Charlie, still feeling the echoes of dull pain from the last time, quickly snagged the book and tossed it onto the seat next to him. The kid watched, an internal battle playing openly across his face: a reprimand for the unholy treatment of a sacred text versus gushing thankfulness that the object was one step closer to his idols.

Charlie took the burden of making that decision from him and offered him a sighed assurance it would get signed . . . eventually. The kid beamed.

The kid was Humberto Hidalgo, but he insisted everyone call him Bogart. Most kids called him Bogey if they called him anything at all. He was one of the only Hispanic kids at FHS, one of the very few people of color at FHS aside from a black assistant coach and three of the Pack, two big black guys and an Asian guy. A weird phenomenon in Texas, but it explained the racial slurs the kids at FHS felt were okay to jab at Bogart. Charlie didn't do it, it wasn't decent or right, but he certainly didn't try to stop it. If it bothered Bogart, he could deal with it himself, but Charlie wasn't sure if Bogart was even aware of it.

Charlie, however, was all too aware of Bogart. The kid blathered on and on about everything sci-fi/fantasy related and when he found out who Charlie's parents were, Bogart attached himself to Charlie like a leech to a skinny-dipper. Charlie had attempted to avoid any bus seat near Bogart, but that didn't matter. If he sat somewhere else, Bogart would simply invade the seat in front of him whether it was fully occupied already or not. Soon enough, Charlie discovered resistance was futile and the best defense was monosyllabic responses and neutral grunts.

"I can't believe you finally agreed to have your parents sign my book! You still gonna have them do it? Like you said, right?" the puffing boy said with punctuated spittle. Bogart had begged both overtly and subtly for two years. Yesterday, Charlie snapped and told him to bring the stupid book and he'd have his parents sign it. He was pretty sure it was the most he'd said to the kid in months.

Would you mind remembering antiperspirant, Charlie grumbled internally. "Yeah. Fine."

"Can you get them to sign it tonight?" Bogart asked feverishly.

"Yeah."

Bogart started to say something, but he gagged on the words, his hands kneading the back of the bench. The kid's face was red and sweaty from his excitement, the heat, or his high cholesterol. Probably all three. "Ever since," he choked out, "ever since I looked your house up on the internet and saw who your parents were, I've been obsessed with getting that book signed. I mean, what are the odds the son of James and Harriett Daniels would be on my bus? You know? I mean, what are the odds mi abuela and I would move to this awesome little town and the son of James and Harriett Daniels would go to my school?" Bogart watched expectantly for a response. Bogart lived with his grandma, or his abuela as he called her, and the woman was dropping the ball when it came to teaching her grandson about social normality.

Charlie didn't offer a response.

"I mean . . . you know? Just . . . wow, right?" Bogart panted liberally. His dark brown eyes widened suddenly and his meaty hands doubled their efforts on the back of the seat his bulk leaned against. "I hope you don't think I'm just your friend so I can get that book signed. I mean, you're my best friend and *would* be whether your parents were James and Harriett Daniels or not. I promise. You know? Right?"

Best friend? Bogart thought Charlie was his best friend now? This had to stop. Charlie sighed, "Bogart . . ."

The sweaty kid's eyes lit up. "Yeah?"

"We're not friends. We're —" Bogart began to wilt like a flower planted in the scorching Texas heat. Charlie just couldn't do it. It wasn't *decent*. "We're not friends just because of my parents. We're just friends . . . because." Charlie wanted to cuss, but that wasn't decent either, so he never did.

And that wilting flower took shade and was planted in the stinking compost of false hope and a decent lie. Charlie couldn't ever remember seeing Bogart this energized and that was saying something for the kid with pixie sticks flowing in his veins.

It looked as though Charlie was about to experience the full wrath of Bogart's glee, but the bus came to its usual lurching halt and the rotund boy was thrown back. Charlie had never been more grateful for Gladys and her lead foot. Taking advantage of Bogart's momentary distraction, Charlie snatched up the book and his backpack and darted down the aisle, pushing freshmen aside and leaping out of the door with yet another disapproving slurred bark from Gladys.

The heat hit him again full on, but he didn't give it time to settle in. Charlie rushed past the variety of social groups meeting up on the well-manicured, dead-brown lawn outside the sprawling high school. He dodged groups of skaters, jocks, pretties, and geeks, none of them giving him the slightest hint he existed. And that was fine, he could do without them too. As he reached the doors, he was sure he heard Bogart calling from a distance, but Charlie was practiced at ignoring the nuisance.

Walking briskly through the halls, Charlie made it to a second-floor bathroom that was practically forgotten by the general population since it was so far from the nearest occupied classroom. Apparently back in the 1940s, when the city council built Farnsworth High, it was during a population boom and the projected need was that of a bustling city like Houston or Dallas. Those visions of grandeur never came to fruition and much of the high school was abandoned and used for storage. Charlie had discovered the isolated restroom one morning when an omelet his mom made didn't settle too well and he needed some privacy while his body sorted some things out. It hadn't been anywhere near *decent*. Now he used the lonesome bathroom as a place to change out of his sweaty t-shirt and freshen up before the day began, avoiding the locker room and the Pack who prowled there.

Charlie had just pulled off his shirt and was wiping down his pits when a toilet flushed in the stall behind him and out sauntered Coach Tark. Charlie let off a string of expletives in his head, internal decency forgotten. Of all the bathrooms in all the school, Tark had to be in this one. The looming man in his inappropriately tight coaching shorts and tucked in t-shirt hocked something up in his throat and spit it into the nearby sink. Charlie shuddered. Tark was the only person on campus whom Charlie felt small around. The mustached coach was solid and a solidly terrible teacher. Charlie had endured him as a computer teacher one year and didn't learn a single thing except the fact earwax could be dug out with a pencil and common scissors were good for trimming thick mustaches and nose hairs. But it wasn't his public grooming that made Charlie want to bolt, it was the inevitable coaxing to the dark side.

"You changed your mind yet, Daniels? Looks like you got even bigger over the summer. You a junior now?" The coach knew he was. "What program you usin' to build muscle like that? You usin' HGH, son? *Officially*, I have to tell you we do not condone the use of chemical enhancement on the FHS field." Tark crossed his burly arms, tattoos peeking out of his short sleeves and just up out of his collar, and stood in front of the bathroom door blocking any and all escape.

"No, sir. I just lift, sir." Charlie was suddenly very aware he was being sized up like a race horse or rodeo bull. He quickly pulled his shirt on and fixed his unruly hair. He'd have to endure whatever sweat was left.

"I seen your dad, he's a little fella. Where do you think you get it? You got a grand-dad with your size? Maybe on your mama's side?"

Charlie wasn't sure if that was a slam on his mom, so he avoided the matter by squatting and stuffing his other shirt in his backpack. "Don't know, sir. I've never seen my grandparents. They're all dead."

"Photographs?"

"No, sir," Charlie shrugged, "my parents lost all that in a fire just after I was born."

Tark made a face, "Fire? What fire?"

Charlie refused to make eye contact, so he shrugged as he pretended to be struggling with the zipper of his backpack. "I dunno, when I was a baby."

"Been here a long time and don't remember a fire."

"Maybe it was before I was born, I don't know."

"Huh." Tark stood watching. Examining. What did he want? "This gonna be the year, Daniels?"

Standing, Charlie looked the looming coach in the eye, "No, sir." Charlie wasn't exactly sure what happened next. When he went to pass the coach, he suddenly felt himself pitched across the room, knocking the trashcan over as he slammed against the tile wall, barely keeping his footing. "Holy," Charlie groaned.

Tark was still standing by the door, his arms crossed over his broad chest, no sign he had moved an inch. "I don't know what you're waiting on, hot shot," the hulking man sneered, "but this is all passing you right up. You got the build, and I figure you got the coordination to go with it, but what's it all for? Huh? Damn waste is what it is." Tark gave him one final appraisal and threw the door open, banging it into a paper towel dispenser.

The bathroom was quiet except for Charlie's breathing. His heart was pounding in his chest and his knees were threatening to give out on him. What was that all about? Could the coach get fired for that? He *could* get fired for that, right? The bigger question, could Charlie actually turn him in? His all too vivid imagination had no problem creating scene after scene of gruesome outcomes if he dared to report Tark. In most of them, Tark destroyed him barehanded on his own, in others, the Pack joined in. If the coach was willing to go that far on campus, physically shove him into a wall, what would he do off campus? Charlie knew he'd never say anything about it.

Taking a deep breath, Charlie tucked his hair behind his ears and left the restroom that had once been a sanctuary. The rest of the morning was just as much of a blur as his flight into the bathroom wall. He was intimidated by the Coach before, now he flat out feared him. Charlie couldn't help constantly looking over his shoulder for the big man, rocketing him to the top of the list of daily avoidances, just above Bogart. Worst of all, the fear that kept niggling in the back of his mind wasn't the threat of being murdered, *that* was looming in his frontal lobe, it was the fear the mustached monster might be right. All his time spent working out, running, getting stronger, getting better, was all for what? Was he passing up his best shot at college? While he wasn't an idiot, he certainly wasn't the smartest, therefore it wouldn't be his grades winning him entrance into a good school. And he wasn't involved in school clubs or activities. At all. The guidance counselors had gathered all the juniors into the gym at the beginning of the year and droned on and on about how colleges like to see what you're a part of. Plain and simple, Charlie wasn't *a part* of anything. And now he was shooting down his best chance to excel. What *was* he doing?

The hulking coach didn't get it. The problem was, it wasn't simply that Charlie *wouldn't*, it's he *couldn't*. He wasn't allowed to. What if he got on the field, the adrenaline hit, and he lost control? That kid he punched as a freshman lucked out. *Charlie* had lucked out. Over two more years, Charlie was stronger than he'd been as that freshman and he trusted himself even less.

CHAPTER TWO

A Long Walk

Driving his sudden fears home, Charlie found himself sitting alone at lunch at a table in the corner of the rowdy cafeteria. Were all high school cafeterias the same? Everyone divided and categorized into their preordained places? Rows upon rows of benched tables where kids gathered with like-minded peers to either find respite from the morning, lick their wounds, or inflict new ones upon those deemed lower on the food chain. The food was a rotation of misery: chicken tenders, pizza, Salisbury steak, corn dogs or hamburgers, all thawed and reheated to a tasteless lukewarm. Charlie brought his own lunch, usually a sandwich his mom had made, but they weren't just some sad meat and cheese combos slapped on bread. He didn't know how she did it, but Harriett Daniels could make a killer sandwich. Soft homemade bread smothered in dill mayo. Handcrafted cheeses from her Cheese of the Month club. Veggies born in her expansive garden behind the house. Sure, the meat was just some plain old packaged ham, but that woman could dress it up. And there were always two. He *was* a growing boy after all.

Charlie was moments away from sinking his teeth into the first of his homemade delicacies when his world was disrupted by his curly haired, new *best friend*, "How long do you think it'll take for them to sign it?" Bogart's tray hit the table with such force, it sent a few of his nuggets and fries scattering. "I mean, I know the actual signing part won't take long. I mean, how long could it take to write a few thoughtful words to one of your biggest fans, right? You know? I'm just wondering how long it might take for you to give them the book, for them to find some time in their schedule, and *then* write it. Well, and then get it back to me, of course. You know?" Within the span of those words, the forsaken fried foods had been rescued and consumed. It was amazing to watch the simultaneous outpouring of words and intake of food. Disgusting, but amazing nonetheless. "What do you think?"

Charlie shrugged, "They'll get to it tonight, I'm sure."

The fat kid's nostrils flared in excitement, "I could ride my bike and pick it up!"

"No," Charlie almost choked on his sandwich. "I'll just bring it with me tomorrow. On the bus. First thing in the morning."

"It's really no big deal! It's only two point seven miles to your house and I can easily ride that on my bike. Mi abuela is always telling me I need to get some exercise and two point seven miles isn't that big of a deal because everything is pretty flat. That plus the adrenaline of picking up my book from my two favorite authors ever!" His eyes bulged with a new thought, "Maybe I could even say hi?" Bogart was working himself up so much Charlie was positive he could detect a sheen breaking out on the kid's tan face.

"Listen, Bogart, James and Harriett Daniels do *not* like visitors." That drew the fanboy up short. "Why do you think we live out in the middle of nowhere?"

"I . . . I figured the landscape reminded them of the quaint farming village of Grigginshire where book one started."

Charlie solemnly shook his head, laying it on thick, "No, Bogart. James and Harriett Daniels do not like visitors. *Don't* drop in. The last time a fan showed up on our front porch, it shook them up so badly, it took them months to get back into the right frame of mind to continue working."

Bogart's mouth hung open, a half-chewed nugget cradled in his cheek. "Is that why *Jewel of Blood* is six months late being published?"

"Bogart," Charlie spoke in a hush, "you didn't hear it from me."

Of course, he bought it. Why had the last book taken so long? It hadn't. Their publisher said some idiot threw out a hoped-for release date on his blog and the rabid fan world latched onto it as gospel truth. The fact was, everything was right on schedule as usual. While it *might* not have been true that James and Harriett Daniels didn't like visitors, it *was* true that James and Harriett Daniels were obsessively on schedule. Charlie wasn't sure how that gene was lost on him, because *he* struggled to get *anything* turned in on time, and the broader the assignment's time table, the worse. His sophomore year term paper was turned in almost a month late, because Charlie just couldn't wrap his mind around the whole process. He was terrible at papers. At *school*. Maybe he was an idiot at school.

The hulking coach's words dug a little deeper. Charlie *was* missing his only chance to succeed.

"I read online," Bogart said with a wad of fries in his mouth, "another rumor about the books being turned into a television series."

Charlie rolled his eyes, "They're not. No one is."

"I think it would be incredible. Could you imagine? The world of the United Realms coming to life?"

"It's not happening," Charlie insisted.

"Word has it," Bogart chomped down on a nugget, "that Bull and Badger Pictures is developing it. Paid a hefty sum for it."

"Bogart," Charlie sighed, "it's just a rumor, man. The internet is full of them." Not that *he* would know personally, but that's what people said.

The two lapsed into welcomed silence.

The next thing to drop itself into Charlie's personal space wasn't another lunch tray, it was a body. A body that smelled like wildflowers and made Charlie's thick arms break out into goosebumps. Charlie's head whipped to the right and there sat an actual girl. A girl had come and sat down next to Charlie Daniels. A girl. A cute one. Short blonde hair with what looked like two pigtails exploding out of the sides of her head, vibrantly colored vintage clothing that fit her . . . just right . . . every bit of her. And her big blue eyes . . .

Things stirred.

Charlie tore his eyes from her and quickly looked around the room to see if he could locate the jerks who had sent her over. They'd be easy to spot, heads down, but eyes up, shoulders shaking with stupidly concealed laughter. Probably a bunch of the football guys and their girlfriends, possibly the Pack. Was it Ben? But after scanning the rowdy room, there was no sign of a setup. Ben was holding court with his paw print pals several tables away, paying no mind to anyone but themselves.

Charlie looked back at her. She was still there, her eyes glittering. "That sandwich looks delicious and delightful." She winked.

Across the table, Bogart was just as stunned. A handful of fries was moments away from meeting his mouth, but the girl's arrival had interrupted. "I'm Meg."

"I'm Bogart," he said stupidly. "Humberto Hidalgo, but my friends call me Bogart. Everyone calls me Bogart because that's how I introduced myself to them when I first started school here. Humberto is hard for people to say, oddly enough. Bogart works better. And it's mysterious and eccentric."

Meg gasped, "What a neat name! I love neat names."

"*He* has a neat name," Bogart said stupidly gesturing at Charlie with a handful of greasy fries.

Meg turned those sparkling blue eyes on Charlie expectantly, who in turn lost all nerve to say anything remotely polite or intelligent.

"He's Charlie." Bogart wasn't having a problem at all, though all his sentences were uncharacteristically short and to the point. Except for his introduction. That had been painful.

"Hi, Charlie." Meg giggled, the sound of tinkling bells.

Charlie grunted. At least what came out sounded like a grunt. Internally, the grunt was intended to be an actual word, which word he wasn't completely sure, so it was probably better it came out as a grunt. At least with a grunt he could seem passively cool, but he hated people who tried to come off as passively cool. Did she hate people who tried to come off as passively cool? Charlie couldn't say why it mattered. But suddenly it did.

Meg looked around the room, granting Charlie a reprieve from those adorable blue eyes. *Adorable*? "Do you always sit at this table? Just you and Bogart?"

Charlie was working up an excuse for the fat kid's presence when Bogart jumped in, "No, usually he sits here by himself and I sit over there with the other kids in my computer programing club. But his parents are going to sign a book for me and I was just asking him how soon it might happen."

Meg perked up even more, if such a thing were possible. "Your parents wrote a book?"

"Yeah," Charlie mumbled as he crammed a bite of his sandwich in his mouth. Was he eating weird? He felt like he was eating weird.

"Wrote a book? Wrote *a* book?" Bogart was dumbfounded. "Yeah, duh, they did! A whole flippin' series of them! Well, almost a whole series, it's not finished yet, so it's not technically whole. They're only *the* most prolific fantasy authors of our time! Seriously, they're set to overshadow Tolkien."

"That's incredible! I'd love to meet them!" Charlie couldn't tell if she was genuine, or if she was just humoring him, maybe even humoring both of them. Either way, it *appeared* to come out of a good place. He couldn't imagine her having a *bad* place.

Her eyes were good places.

The bell rang and without a word of excusing himself or farewell, Charlie stuffed the remaining sandwich in his lunch sack and bolted from the table, making a clean exit altogether. It wasn't until he was standing in front of his locker when he realized what he'd done. His mother would have been humiliated by his impoliteness. The only girl who had sat down next to him for two years and he shunned her. He dropped his head none to gently against the wall above his locker. Well, not the *only* girl. His freshman year, the week after his suspension, a few girls who had filtered into FHS from the other middle school across town had tried to break through his shell, but he shut them down quickly and since then no one else of the female persuasion had made an attempt. Even the new ones interpreted his uninviting body language correctly and steered clear of him. All the new girls until this one.

He was going to die an unsuccessful, lonely man. And it was all his doing.

Might as well get to the next hour of confusing humiliation: pre-cal. Math was the worst. Numbers had been bad enough, but letters? Symbols that were neither letter nor number? Ms. Holpher attempted to explain why it all mattered, the theories behind it, but it was a completely different language and Charlie barely held on by just repeating what he saw her do on the board even though he couldn't explain a fraction of it. Ugh. Fractions.

Yanking open his locker, a piece of notebook paper fell to the ground. It was folded a couple of times. While he'd certainly observed notes passed back and forth between people and had even been the temporary courier of a few, he'd never *received* one. Who could it possibly be from? It couldn't have been Meg, could it? Would she have had enough time to slip a note into his locker after lunch? Charlie's stomach dropped at the thought of it being from Bogart and almost kicked it down the hall. But it could have been Meg, right? What if she dropped it off *before* lunch, a stealthy and well-orchestrated follow up to their lunch together. *Lunch together*? Charlie had barely been there mentally. But it could have been from her, right?

Nervously, Charlie snatched it up from the floor, his palms sweating and fingers twitchy. His heart racing, he carefully unfolded the note not wanting to accidentally rip it.

There was no fire.

What?

There was no fire.

That was all. Sketchy handwriting in blue ink in the middle of a piece of notebook paper.

There was no fire.

The nervousness that had once been from the possibility of a note from the girl, was now replaced by— what, fear? His heart was beating faster and he looked up and down the hall. It was empty. "Holy—" it was empty! Hands shaking and face flushed, he slammed his locker and refolded the paper, shoving it into a side pocket of his backpack. Ms. Holpher wouldn't care why he was late.

There was no fire.

Dashing into class just after the bell rang, Charlie tried to slip into his seat without Ms. Holpher noticing as she shuffled through a stack of papers on her desk. Unfortunately, his seat was next to Ben, who scratched his stubbly chin and grinned, "Welcome to class, Daniels." He said it loudly. Intentionally loud. Charlie stared at him in disbelief. A few of the Pack snickered and Holpher looked up, her beady eyes magnified through her bifocals resting on the tip of her beak of a nose.

"You're late, Mr. Daniels. Last one in, first one up." She pointed at the board and held up a marker, "Take us through number one from last night's homework."

He glanced at Ben who made himself comfortable in his desk and mouthed, "you're welcome."

The mysterious note in his backpack was the least of his concerns now.

A distracted blur, a daze of information, a series of confusing equations later, and pre-cal was finished for the day. Charlie took several extra laps around the track during PE in an attempt to run off his anger. All he could see was Ben mouthing those two words and with every lap, Charlie grew more positive he could take him in a fight. Forget decency or control.

But he didn't. The Pack invaded the locker room and Ben strutted, locking eyes with Charlie several times and flashing a toothy smile that never met his eyes. Charlie hated him.

Only one year and eight more months until it was all over . . . and then what? Charlie suppressed the thought as he hurriedly stepped out of the sterile hallways into the Texas sun. He had stopped by Ms. Holpher's room in an attempt to unravel the mysteries of pre-Cal, but the old buzzard spoke only in numbers and letters and even when she spoke to him as though he were a first grader, he still couldn't get it. That tutoring session had put him a little behind getting out of the building, but thankfully the bus was still sitting there with its doors wide open.

A few steps into the sweltering Texas heat and the doors closed, the yellow beast beginning to rumble forward. Startled, Charlie broke into a run catching the bus easily and slapped the grimy door repeatedly. Gladys merely turned her droopy eyes to him and lazily shook her gray head. He knew it was an impossibility to get her to open that door once it had closed, but with a three-mile walk in the scorching sun as incentive, he'd tried anyway.

The bus rumbled on.

Charlie began to sweat. "Crap," he sighed. Decent enough.

"I told her we were going to walk to your place." Charlie spun and came nose to nose, well, chest to nose, with that girl from lunch. That girl with the eyes.

Stunned for several reasons, Charlie could barely get the words out, "You did *what*?"

“I told her we were going to walk to your place.” She smiled brightly, unphased by the suffocating heat. “Where’s it at?”

“It’s three miles away,” Charlie said.

“Neat, let’s go!” Meg started walking, no, skipping down the sidewalk.

He could have just let her go, but he didn’t. “Wrong way.” He grinned like an idiot despite his irritation.

She stopped and spun around like a ballerina lightly tossing her hands over her head and started the other direction. Again, he thought about just letting her go. She *had* screwed this up after all. He could have been riding miserably on the bus with a bunch of funky smelling freshmen instead of walking with a cute girl. He definitely would rather be with the cute girl. “Wrong again.”

The spunky little girl stopped and spun around again, her movement graceful and lithe. Playfully, Meg planted her hands on her hips and raised an eyebrow, “You know, this could go smoother if *you* would take the lead.”

Charlie took in a long breath and let it out. She was a nuisance, albeit an adorable nuisance. *Adorable* again. Charlie hiked his backpack up on his shoulders and gave the straps a tug, tightening them for the long walk. “Come on,” he said as he stepped off the curb, “it’s this way.”

The two passed quietly through middle-class neighborhoods with tall trees and sturdy brick houses. Meg pointed out trees she liked, well-groomed yards, and flower beds colorfully alive with vibrant flowers despite the heat threatening to ruin them. Charlie didn’t say much except to agree here and there. Mainly, he just watched her. She was a little off-beat and he liked it. The slight girl bounced and skipped down the asphalt streets, not once did her pace ever become a simple walk. The sun reflected off her bobbing pigtails and the glitter on her little t-shirt. But mostly he was attracted to something which couldn't be seen yet gushed out of her with every word and movement. Her confidence.

People are attracted to their opposites, right? Wasn't that the saying? She was confident and Charlie wasn't. Plain and simple. Regardless of what people saw on the outside, his stature and his aloofness, Charlie was clueless as to who he was or what he should do in life. That was the gaping wound Coach Tark had jabbed into so abruptly that morning. The coach exposed his deepest fear of not being enough. What if he tried out for the football team and was terrible? Ben and the Pack would rip him to shreds with gleeful ferocity. If he *didn't* try, no one would know if he was terrible and the mystery of it would rescue him. And girls. He had no confidence in that arena at all. Not like Ben. Girls hung on Ben's arms and every word. The rumors of what the quarterback got up to on the weekends and with how many were disgusting. Ben was every bit the animal he claimed to be.

The final neighborhood gave way to dirt road and expansive fields, fields surrounding houses much like his. Older. Spread out. Quiet. And even then, they still had about two miles before they reached his house, and if he were to be truthful with himself, this was the best part of the walk. In the spring these spacious fields exploded with wildflowers to shame those in the suburban gardens, every color imaginable. But what if he were a *product* of this? Of the spaciousness? The distance? His parents always claimed they wanted what was best for him, but he felt shut off from everything. He barely knew how to search the internet for school projects in the computer lab while everyone else clicked and typed away. Was his lack of confidence their fault?

Yet at the same time, he did *like* it. With no one around, he would often be left alone with his thoughts, though after today and Tark's intrusion into those very thoughts, he wasn't sure he wanted to be with them alone ever again. But then, this time he *wasn't* alone. Meg was with him.

The flitting girl floated into a walk. Finally, just walking. And she did it close to him. He could smell her again. Flowery and soft. Whatever her perfume was, he liked it a lot. Charlie found himself *trying* to smell her, turning his head in her direction as though attempting to see something in the distance, but taking purposeful whiffs.

"You like it here?" There was a distinct kindness in her tone, a gentle kindness.

Why he paused before he answered, he wasn't sure. Maybe because no one had ever asked him that before. Maybe because, aside from his parents, no one had ever asked him a question about his thoughts with which he was so often alone. "Not really."

"Why?"

"It's boring. And ugly. Mainly boring." He kicked a rock down the road.

"But you don't *do* anything." She said it gently, but it still stung.

Charlie looked over at her, "Who says?"

"Nobody says," she said with a little giggle as she continued to study the distant houses and land around them, "It's just obvious. You sit by yourself at lunch. You're in and out of school. Most guys that look like you were staying for that football thing after school."

"'That football thing'?"

"Did I say it wrong?"

"It's just football practice," he laughed easily. It felt good. "Where are you from?"

Her eyes never left their surroundings, it was as though she was soaking it all in. More than likely she was just trying to remember how to get back to her house. Where was her house? "Up north."

"What, like Oklahoma? Kansas? Or like New York?" Charlie kicked the same rock a little further down the road.

"New York. Ever been?"

Charlie shook his head. "Never been out of Farnsworth."

"I bet you will someday."

They lapsed into silence. She was . . . what . . . comfortable? That feeling of nervousness to be around a girl had melted away less than a mile into their walk and he found himself at ease. She was easy to be around. Nice to be around, in fact. Suddenly his days of high school gloom weren't looking so bad if this was who he got to be with for the next year and eight months. And the summer! Who knew, maybe that dead end was coming to life. Suddenly Farnsworth, TX, was more bearable.

A bend in the road and a grove of trees to their right gave way and Charlie's house peeked through. "That's my place."

Meg came to a stop. "It's cute! Looks like one of those cookie houses."

"A gingerbread house? I guess." Charlie had never really given his house much thought before. He just lived there. But it was pretty sweet. Dark green trimmed in yellow and two stories with an attic and wrap around porch, it was full of nooks and closets. He and his dad played hide and seek for hours when he was little, much to his mother's dismay. It would start out tame enough, but soon the two would find themselves racing across the roof and leaping through the sprawling trees whose limbs made a network of paths perfect for a nimble chase. They were the only trees of their kind in Farnsworth, big and strong. His mother would pitch a fit, but it only seemed to egg on his dad.

Speaking of his dad, the short, lanky man was sitting on the steps of the front porch looking in their direction. His dad usually only did that when Charlie had forgotten to finish a morning chore and he wanted to be the first to get to him and mercifully give him fair warning. When his mother got to him first, it was a tongue lashing. Standing with a wince, his dad's hip had been bothering him for as long as Charlie could remember. It never hampered him from playing, but he would blame it if Harriet had a chore for *him*. James craned his neck and gave a big wave, probably trying to get a better look at the social phenomenon that was Charlie accompanied by someone, let alone a girl.

"That your father?" Meg returned James' curiosity.

"That's him. My dad. Want to come meet him?" Charlie took a step in his dad's direction.

"No," she said casually, "I'd hate to drop in unannounced."

"Come on," he grinned, "I'll announce you, James and Harriett don't mind visitors," he said grandly. Did he sound stupid?

She laid her small hand on his forearm and rubbed it with her thumb. Her touch was cool and soft. And electric. "Some other time. I should get home." She gave his arm a slight squeeze, "See you soon, Charlie." He watched her as she walked back up the road, always taking in her surroundings, always a slight bounce in her step. Charlie's heart was racing as though he'd just run five miles. She had touched his arm. His arm.

"Who was that?" Charlie jumped at the familiar voice.

"Dad! Holy—" Heart racing for a different reason now, Charlie's legs felt weak, whether from the scare or the hormones, he wasn't sure. His dad came out of nowhere, as he was prone to do. Those hide and seek games usually ended in James' favor. They would start out simple enough, but little by little, his dad would turn on the stealth, becoming completely imperceptible as he and Charlie took on the roles of the hunter and the hunted. Over the years, those skills rubbed off on Charlie until he was just as slick. It drove Harriett nuts when he would creep up behind her and loudly ask what was on the menu for dinner.

"Where's she live?" James asked peering off down the road.

Charlie shrugged, "I dunno."

"Nearby?"

"I *dunno.*"

"Did you pass her house on the way here?" The heat was rising in James' voice, a rare occurrence.

"I—"

The shorter man took in and let out a long calming breath. "Charlie, you don't let a young lady go walking down a country road on her own. Farnsworth is a decent enough town, but every town has its troubled people. I've taught you better than that. You run down there and walk her home. It's the decent thing to do."

There was no arguing with him, especially when he was right. "Yes, sir." James gave his boy a slap on the rear and Charlie dropped his backpack, setting off at a run. Meg had just disappeared behind the slight bend in the road, so she wasn't that far. It felt good to run, his body in motion, doing what it was supposed to do. Legs stretching in long strides down the country road, fields passing beside him. Maybe he should do track this year? He couldn't *hurt* people doing track, right? It could be a start.

He cleared the bend and expected to see her skipping ahead, lost in her own world, but she was gone. Stopping, Charlie looked to the sides of the road thinking maybe she had heard him coming and slipped into the long dry grass as a joke. "Meg?" he called out, his voice strong despite his heavy breathing. "Meg!"

No response. The blades of grass rustled a bit in the slight evening breeze sweeping over the flat land, but there was no sign of the girl. Wiping his face on his shirt, he could hear his mother's rebukes every time he did it, he turned in a curious circle searching the road and fields around him. Where had she gone? Did she break into a run herself to get home faster? As much energy as she had it wouldn't have surprised him, but with the road as flat as it was, he should still be able to see her. And if she had cut across a field, he'd be able to see her there too. Panic welled up in him for a moment at the possibility that someone may have picked her up, *grabbed* her and took off. Even then he was sure he would have seen the vehicle.

Charlie returned to the house and, much to his relief, his dad had already gone inside. Charlie snatched up his backpack where he had dropped it and headed in. As the screen door slapped behind him, the cozy living room and smells of dinner welcomed him. Everything in the house was old and comfortable, "well-worn and experienced" his dad would say. "Practical and meaningful," his mother would correct. The furniture was nothing special, bought from a catalogue around the time Charlie was born, but the crocheted blankets were Harriett's touch. Filling the shelves were copies of their books in all the many languages of their publications from around the world. And stuffed here and there were a few of their numerous awards. His mom and dad appreciated them, but they valued the gifts their readers sent them over the many years. Fan art, hand-carved statuettes of characters, costume pieces. It was all weird to Charlie, but he didn't dare say anything.

Fried chicken, green beans, mashed potatoes with gravy, and fresh biscuits. It was a good thing he exercised as much as he did or he would be bigger than Bogart. Harriett stuck her head around the corner from the kitchen and swept her curly steel gray hair out of her face. "Get changed, you're a mess. Dinner's in a few minutes." Charlie dropped his backpack. "Take that up to your room!" Charlie scooped it back up and hauled it up the stairs to his room.

It was small, but he liked that. Most rooms, he assumed, had a theme of some sort. Posters of girls, cars, or sports heroes. Trophies. Deer heads. Charlie's room was simple and neat. Everything was within arm's reach and his too short twin bed was tucked up underneath a window that let him out onto his favorite place, the roof over the back porch. It was there he would often lay at night, watching the stars, looking out over the woods, and listening to the coyotes call. He didn't actually spend too much time *inside* his room, it was more like a gateway to the roof. When it was warm enough, which was most of the time, Charlie would slip out his window in his sleeping shorts and spend the night on a blanket with his pillow. Harriett hated it when she first discovered his new habit, going on and on about rolling off in his sleep and breaking his fool neck. True, he could have, but he never did. His dad just said boys were boys and if this was the peak of his rebellion, leave him to it. Harriett eventually conceded, but the huff she woke him up with in the mornings spoke clearly of her lingering disdain.

That rooftop was his sanctuary. The place he would attempt to sort out his feelings, his confusing ideas about his life, and what he hoped were the normal riddles about girls, his body, and growing up. But a few minutes outside at night, the breeze tickling his skin, stars twinkling overhead, and his head would clear and things would seem fine for the moment. Until the next day when he'd be thrust into it all over again. Tonight would be different though, a new idea would have to be contemplated and that idea had explosive pigtails and smelled like wildflowers.

A few minutes and a clean pair of gym shorts and tank later, Charlie ran down the stairs and into the kitchen, a sprawling room full of restaurant grade appliances and farm knickknacks, especially roosters. His mother called them cocks and he struggled to keep a straight face every time she said it. Charlie gave his mom a slap on the butt as a distraction from the biscuit he stole. She swatted at him with a hand towel, the phone tucked between her ear and shoulder, ". . . was a very nice basket this month. Yes, I love the local honey and candles. Mmm-hmm. I'm sure." From the tone and the mention of the basket, he knew it was someone calling on behalf of the persistent media mogul. "Can you guess what my answer is, sweetheart? That's right, it's still no. Well, you can keep waiting. I can't wait to hear your lovely voice next month. Buh-bye, hon." She flicked the phone shut and tossed it down on the kitchen counter where it clattered to a stop.

Charlie took a bite of the biscuit, "Who was that?"

Harriett engaged evasive maneuvers. "You couldn't wait five minutes until I got the food to the table?"

"Nope."

"No, ma'am." He had known the correction was coming.

"Nope, ma'am."

She sighed.

The table was covered with a southern feast. Charlie wasn't sure how she kept the house like she did, stayed on top of their laundry, and delivered banquets worthy of cooking magazines, but she did it without missing their publisher's deadline. And always without complaint of pain or exhaustion. Unlike his dad. "Women are just made of sterner stuff," she would say self-righteously. "A man gets a head cold and he's down for a week. A woman gets a head cold and you'll never even know it."

Charlie knew better than to press his luck by reaching for a piece of chicken before his dad arrived and they had said grace, Harriett did have limits. But it smelled so good. So good and he was starving. Thankfully, he didn't have to wait long. His dad entered, wiping his hands on his pants, earning his own glare from Harriett. It seemed everything earned a glare from his mother, but it was mostly all in jest and certainly all in love. She wasn't mean. There wasn't a mean bone in her little body. She just liked things a certain way and when the men in her life at times tiptoed over that line, and at other times belligerently barreled over it, it would earn them anywhere from a casual eye roll to a good tongue lashing.

"Sit down," she fussed, "everything is getting cold."

It wasn't. It never got cold. Harriet's meals were *always* perfection.

James collapsed into a chair as though he'd been doing back-breaking work all day. Charlie didn't actually know *what* he did all day. Well, there was the books, but did he do that *all* day? Much to their publisher's chagrin, they didn't do interviews or make appearances when a book released. "Who'd want to see us?" his mother would fuss. "We're just a couple of old crows. Nothing interesting. We're not even pretty." Of course, his dad would refute that by going on and on about her aesthetic *giftings* and she would protest and deny it until she found herself in his arms and Charlie was disturbed to the point of excusing himself from the room.

Those two loved each other. Immensely. Charlie didn't know anything about girls and dating, really, but he knew a lot about love and commitment. Maybe they never outright talked to him about it, but they showed it all the time. That's what counted, right?

As soon as amen left James' lips, Charlie made a reach for the chicken.

"Mom, would you please pass the chicken?" she chided him.

"No," he said grabbing a leg and a breast, "I got it."

Leg and breast. Pigtails. Sparkling blue eyes. Not now. His face flushed.

"Muscles walked home with a girl today."

The chicken was almost to his mouth, but that stopped him short. Charlie looked incredulously at his dad, but the man was busy buttering a biscuit as though he was completely unaware of the furor he had just caused. Charlie's hand was frozen an inch from his gaping mouth and Harriet's was stuck in mid green bean scoop. Though he had just prayed, his dad was the devil incarnate.

"Who is she?" Harriet asked pointedly.

Charlie shrugged, "Nobody." He shoved the chicken in his mouth and his other hand had just reached the serving spoon for the mashed potatoes when a flash of silver whipped through the air and his knuckles were suddenly throbbing. The chicken was now the last thing on his mind. His face felt like it was on fire.

"Ow, woman!" Charlie shook his hand vigorously. For a scrawny old woman, she could deliver a good thwack.

Harriet wielded her silver spoon like a saber, leveling it at him. "*Who* is this girl?"

Charlie looked at his dad who just shrugged and took a bite out of his biscuit, crumbs tumbling down the front of his shirt. "You're the worst, you know that?" Charlie grumbled through a mouthful of chicken, grease dripping down his chin.

James shrugged stupidly again.

His mother was fixed on him like a hawk on a mouse and Charlie knew it. There was no getting around her when she was locked in. It was always easier to just give up. "She's just a new girl from school."

"*At* school. She isn't *from* school. She doesn't *live* there. School isn't her point of origin." The woman was ruthless.

"Holy crap! *At* school! Meg is just a new girl *at* school. Crap." Charlie whirled the chicken leg in the air with gusto then ripped into it.

"Language." That was his dad's warning voice. *Crap* was across the decency line. They would both *crap* themselves if they walked five minutes down the halls at school and heard what language Charlie refrained from using.

"Sorry," Charlie sighed. "It's *your* fault."

Harriet scooped up a heap of mashed potatoes and delivered them to Charlie's plate. It was her version of a peace offering. She knew when she had pushed him and she knew how to appease him. Food. The gravy she slathered on top was an extra measure of apology. "So . . ." she led.

"*So,* she's cool."

Harriet scooped up some green beans and put them on his plate. "And . . . ?"

"And . . . she's cute."

"She *is* cute," his dad affirmed around a mouthful of chicken.

"Are you going to court her?"

Charlie's chicken slipped out of his fingers and landed in his mashed potatoes. "Mom!"

"What?" She asked, busying herself with delicately buttering her biscuit. "This is new territory for us too. You've never had a female companion before and we're not entirely sure what the protocol is. When your father and I courted, he asked my father first. Are you going to ask her father?"

"Oh, for the love," Charlie shoveled a load of mashed potatoes into his mouth. "And no one uses the term *court.*"

"I for one," James chimed in, "think it's honorable to ask the intended's father. It speaks of strong moral fiber and removes all mystery from your intentions."

"It's weird," Charlie muttered.

"It isn't *weird,*" Harriett chided, "it's noble. Noble shouldn't be weird."

"How about I just ask her dad when I propose to her?" Charlie said sarcastically.

Sarcasm which was obviously lost on the both of them. James choked and Harriett almost spit out the iced tea she just sipped. "You're going to marry her?" Harriett dabbed her mouth with her napkin.

"I don't know!"

"So, it's an open possibility?" Harriett pushed further.

Charlie slammed on the brakes and changed lanes fast, "I have a book from a friend for you two to sign."

James was still coughing.

"Are you going to marry—" Harriett pressed on.

Charlie raised his voice, "I have a book for the two of you to sign!"

James coughed.

“Raise your arms over your head,” Harriett threw at her choking husband. He complied. “Take a drink of water.”

“I can’t do both,” James wheezed.

The table lapsed into silence as James regained composure and Charlie grabbed a chicken thigh and another drumstick, had he already eaten two? Harriett pouted glumly. “Well,” Harriett broke the silence, “at least we know now you like girls. Your father and I were beginning to wonder which direction you were headed.”

“Mom!” When would this meal be over?

She shrugged simply and took a bite of green beans. “Who is this *friend* we’re signing a book for? Is it her? Autographs for your girlfriend?”

“His name is Bogart. He’s not really a friend . . . he’s just . . . he’s . . . he’s Bogart.”

“You’re little friend on the bus?” Harriett asked coolly.

“There’s nothing *little* about him,” James added, enjoying his own joke.

“That was rude,” Harriett admonished. “How should we sign the book?”

Charlie shrugged, “I don’t know. I’m sure anything you write in there would make him crap his pants.”

“Charlie—”

“Just sign it. He’ll be thrilled.”

“I wish *you* would take this much interest in our books.” It had been almost six months since they had this conversation. Was it already time again?

“I know.” Charlie zeroed in on his plate, his mission: clearing it and getting out.

“I just think you would *enjoy* them if you would *try* them. Millions of readers around the world can’t be wrong, Charlie.” She was buttering another biscuit and the poor thing was crumbling in her hands.

"I know," Charlie mumbled.

James set his fork down, "Harriet."

"No, James!" Charlie could feel her eyes boring into him. "Charlie, I wish you would take some pride in *us*. In what *we do*. We're your parents, Charlie. *Your* parents. I don't even expect you to read the whole series, just crack open the first one! Who knows, Charlie, you might actually like it and *want* to read the others. You already enjoy the *fruits* of our labor. A nice house, plenty of land to run around on and explore, nice things."

"So why can't I have a car?" Charlie asked quietly, but pointedly. If she wanted to go there, so would he.

Silence.

James wiped his mouth with his napkin.

Harriett took a long, deliberate breath.

"Son," his dad said with a firm gentleness, "I think it best if you went to your room."

"Why am *I* in trouble for—?"

James held up his hand, "To your room, please. Do your homework."

Charlie shoved his chair back, banging it into the window shutters behind him. He was livid. This was completely unfair, *she* started this. As he passed her chair, she grabbed his arm tightly, "We've done all of this for you, Charlie. All of this. We wrote those books for *you*. I just wish you understood how much we've done *for you*." Deep sincerity hid behind the frustration and anger in her teary eyes. She let go of his arm but held him with her eyes.

He mustered up what courage he had left and let the next words fly, knowing they would hit home. "Well, if the books are for me, then I'm selling the film rights when you die and getting out of this hell hole." With effort, Charlie broke her gaze and left the room, pounding up the stairs and slamming his bedroom door behind him.

CHAPTER THREE

Moonlit Encounters

It was unfair. It was all *incredibly* unfair. *He* hadn't started it. *He* hadn't chosen the topic of books and affluence and . . . and . . . he *hadn't* started it. So why was *he* the one lying face down in his bed, the heat of the battle raging in his forehead? Screw his homework. The conversation played over and over in his brain while he explored other avenues it could have gone down, some alleviating the situation, but the majority leading to far more dire outcomes. It just wasn't fair.

Neither one of them had any idea what they were doing to him. When a kid turned sixteen, he got a license and a car! That's the way it was! When Charlie turned sixteen, he got a cake, a song, and a new pair of shoes, and those were only out of necessity because his other tennis shoes had worn out.

Two Marches ago he just knew it was going to happen, he would wake up the morning of his birthday, his fifteenth birthday, they would discuss driver's ed, and he'd earn his permit. Nothing. The day passed, he had his cake and song, and his dad gave him more weights for his bench. That's when the car conversations, or battles, had started. It was clear by June he wasn't getting his permit any time soon.

Last March, he tried not to get his hopes up, but he couldn't help it. Maybe a birthday miracle had happened. Maybe they changed their minds and he would wake up that morning with a big, glossy, black truck in front of the house. Or Mustang. He'd even take a little Toyota. But there was nothing. Just new shoes.

And those last words . . . why did he have to say it? Of course he didn't mean it, he just knew it would hurt.

When he first threw himself into his room, everything was silent for a few minutes. He imagined she was crying and his dad was stunned. But it didn't last long, soon he could hear the conversation, maybe not the words, but certainly the tone. Of course, he couldn't hear his dad at all, but Harriett was coming through loud and clear. Pots clanged in the sink, eating utensils clanked, and he was almost positive a plate met its fate on the floor, sacrificed to hurricane Harriett. Before too long, the voices faded, feet climbed the creaky stairs, and the two retired to their bedroom for the night. Not even a word to clear the air.

It was in times like this Charlie felt terrible for his dad. The two of them, his mom and dad, couldn't be more opposite, his dad always so calm and patient, his mother a volcano always on the verge of eruption these days. The time would come and Charlie would be gone, living his own life in a city far more interesting than Farnsworth, with a car, and away from the emotional roller coaster that was his mother, but James was never getting off that ride.

Charlie pulled himself up and sat on the edge of his bed. He still had homework to get done, but quickly decided to stick it to Harriett by not doing it. Sure, it would only ignite another explosion, but at the moment, he just didn't care. But then . . . he actually did. Suck at school as he did, he still didn't want give up. He pulled his backpack over to the bed and yanked out his pre-cal book. It seemed stupid to try to solve the riddles of the mathematical world in his current emotional state, but maybe it would give him an edge. Nothing else worked. Checking the pockets of his backpack for a pencil, his hand came in contact with something he'd forgotten about entirely. The folded piece of paper with those words written on it: *There was no fire*. His homework officially got the shaft for the night.

Sitting on the edge of the bed, he just kept reading over and over those four words scrawled in blue ink. It had to be Tark. He'd already cast doubt on the subject before throwing Charlie into the bathroom wall. Now he was just being a complete . . . jerk about it. But past *the who* of it, was the *what.* Was it true? He'd never doubted the fire before. It was an event that happened when Charlie was a baby. Or before. He was fuzzy on the details. When he was in elementary and he was tasked with creating poster boards or reports about his family, he never had pictures of his grandparents or even pictures of himself as a baby. "I'm sorry, sweetheart," his mom would say heavily, "It was all lost in the fire." Just *the fire* and that was always enough.

Obviously, all he had to do was swallow a bit of pride and walk through two doorways to get confirmation about the event, but that bit of pride felt like a whole meal. It could wait until morning.

Changing out of his clothes and into his sleep shorts, he opened his window, grabbed his pillow and a blanket, and slipped outside onto the roof. The shingles were rough under his feet, but the night breeze felt good on his skin. The moon was bright and bathed his backyard and the surrounding trees in silver light. Spreading out the blanket, he lay down and stared up at the stars above. This time, *she* was in his head. Meg. He felt himself grin stupidly, but he couldn't help it. He was into her and he'd never felt that was before. Yeah, she was cute, but she smelled so good and she made him feel important, *wanted* for the first time in his life. Charlie whispered her name a few times to the stars and his stupid grin grew into a very content smile.

Down below, a small grey fox slipped out of the shadows and into the open yard amidst potted flowers and lawn furniture. Charlie had seen the little guy a lot more in the past few days. He assumed it was the same one. It would show up every now and then, peer up at him for a moment and be on its way. He'd seen the sleek night visitor for years, ever since he could remember. It wasn't possible for it to be the same one, according to his dad, they didn't live that long.

The little fox approached a bed of rosemary, sniffing. Charlie scratched the shingles with a finger and it grabbed the critter's attention, its ears twitching. It locked eyes with Charlie for a moment before it ducked back into the shadows of the nearby trees.

Charlie let out a deep breath and laid back, the night air tickling over his skin. "Meg," he whispered.

It hadn't always been like this between the two of them—Harriett and him. He and his mom had gotten along so well when he was a kid. She would explore the woods with him, pointing out plants and berries, teaching him names of birds and how to make their calls. He remembered crawling up in her lap and her humming songs over him as she rocked him, his head laying on her chest, listening to her heartbeat. So why was it like this now? What happened? Why was she suddenly so cold toward him, always ready to correct and rebuke? Now, a day couldn't go by without her chewing him out or at least giving him a disapproving glare. He told himself she stilled loved him, but sometimes convincing himself was near impossible.

Charlie rubbed his eyes with the heels of his hand, squashing the emotion threatening to break loose, then crossed his arms over his bare chest. It would all be better when he moved away to college. They would get space and she would miss him. If he could even get into college.

"Meg," he whispered again.

Charlie took another deep breath, this time to enjoy the smells of the country around him, he could smell *her*. While his need for a more exciting life wanted to pull him away from this boring country town, he couldn't deny the beauty of it all, even in its current dry and dusty form. Somewhere down below he heard a rustling. Probably an armadillo or possum scavenging for a late night snack. All sorts of wildlife snuck around Harriett's garden at night. Maybe his little fox had returned. His favorite was the coyotes, calling to each other in the dark, their cries pitched high like a baby sometimes.

"Charlie!" That hushed call wasn't an armadillo. "Charlie! It's me, Bogart!"

Charlie bolted upright, his peaceful sanctuary shattered. Unbelievable. "What are you doing here?"

Bogart stepped out into a clearing so that the moonlight could identify him. "Did they sign it yet?"

Charlie stood up on the roof. Did they sign- "Are you serious?" The anger, which had dropped to a low simmer, flashed into a full boil. "Are you freaking serious right now? You stupid—" His mind couldn't even get enough traction right now to let Bogart have it. "You know what?"

"What?"

Charlie slipped into his room and grabbed his backpack off the floor. Finding what he was looking for, he slipped back out on the roof and chunked it at the fat trespasser with his full strength. As the large hardback book rocketed through the air, Charlie immediately regretted his rash behavior. Bogart obviously couldn't see the projectile and took the hit from the heavy book directly in the chest sending him to the ground. A moment passed into eternity as Bogart lay on his back and the full realization of what Charlie had done sunk in. Charlie sagged. "Charlie," he whispered to himself, "you're such an ass— a jerk." Tonight sucked.

Clambering off the side of the roof, Charlie found the porch column and railing, his usual way down to the backyard when he felt like wandering the woods at night. Bogart had rolled to his side, one hand clutching his chest and the other searching for his fallen treasure. Berating himself again in his head, Charlie stooped down and gripped Bogart by the arm to help him up, but the other kid quickly pulled away with a grunt.

"I'm sorry, Bogart." He really was.

The other boy rolled over onto his hands and knees and pushed himself up. Even in the moonlight, Charlie could see the tears behind Bogart's crooked glasses, the tears and the hurt. "Bogart, I'm sorry." With effort, Bogart bent over and picked up his book, brushing off the cover and tucking it securely under his arm, cradling his baby. Silently wiping his eyes, he crossed the backyard to his bike waiting in the shadows and laid his treasure in the metal basket hanging from the handle bars. Charlie didn't make a move to the other kid, it was pointless, that much was very clear. He felt like such a turd as he watched Bogart make his way to the road and disappear.

Gripping the porch column, Charlie pulled himself up onto the railing to climb back up. He felt heavy, drained. He stood there for a moment, his chest pressed against the column, head resting upon it, the breeze blowing his hair. What was his problem? Why was *he* acting like this? This wasn't him, he was a *good* guy. Wasn't he? And among these thoughts, that constant sense of dissatisfaction came slithering back in accompanied now by Tark's admonishment. And if Tark was right? What if he had been wasting all this time, how much greater could he have been if he'd just bit the bullet and started playing ball when he was a freshman? In middle school? Earlier? He and his parents could have figured something out, some way to control himself so he would hurt anyone but still get to play. What if it was too late now and he'd never actually amount to anything and joining the team would just be a way of appeasing Tark and the Pack, yet not actually gaining Charlie anything because scouts would be completely uninterested in the arrogant kid who finally gave into the pleas?

Arrogant. That's what he was. Aloof and arrogant. No wonder he didn't have any friends. Who'd want to be friends with that? And the one kid who was making an honest effort, Charlie just treated like trash.

Charlie sunk to the railing under the weight of all of this. Easing himself down, chips of paint flecked off onto his hands and back of his legs. He slumped and leaned on the post, closing his eyes. What if he just dozed off right here? He'd probably wake up in the morning with Harriett looking at him curiously over a cup of coffee. She'd glare at him and chalk his odd behavior up to being an emotional teenager. Was *that* all this was? Was he just an average emotional teenage guy and it would all blow over and he'd emerge as a well-adjusted adult? God, he hoped so.

Just on the verge of falling asleep, a cool hand rested on Charlie's shoulder. At first he tensed from surprise, but it gave way to relief. Harriett must have found him earlier than he thought she would. He'd have a time explaining himself to her, maybe he would just leave out the whole part about Bogart and tell her his pillow had fallen off the roof and he came down to get it. The hand squeezed his shoulder reassuringly, her silent way of apologizing. For being a bestselling word-smith, she was terrible at actually *saying* words.

But it kept squeezing, harder, fingers beginning to dig in painfully.

Charlie pulled away, "What are you doing?" Charlie slid off the railing and turned around, gripping his bare shoulder, "that hurt." And who, or what, he saw was not his mother. It was a *woman*, all right, had *been* a woman, at least. Wispy, lank hair floating in the night breeze on a head that was gaunt and gray. The woman's mouth hung open and eyes sagged, staring at him with focus and determination, but devoid of life. Even though he didn't watch TV or movies, he still knew what she was. Zombies were all the rage at school. It was one thing that every student sect agreed upon and loved. Charlie felt like he'd seen every episode of the shows because it was all anyone talked about in U.S. History on Monday mornings. And this decaying woman, slouching in a faded floral dress, was living, as it were, proof that all fiction seemed to have its roots in truth.

The woman lurched toward him, gripping the porch post in one hand, coming around it and taking each porch step in simple stride. No clumsiness, no stumbling, just a predator hunting her prey, her eyes never leaving him.

The sound of his own shouting and yelling filled Charlie's head, but it felt like his throat had betrayed him and he couldn't get a single one of those sounds out. Instead he heard himself making unintelligible grunts and moans, like those sounds you make when you wake out of a terrible nightmare. His whole world was moving in a sickening and terrifying slow motion as he slipped past the thing, shoving it off the steps and throwing himself against the backdoor and, to his increasing horror, it was locked. Of course it was. It was night. The doors were locked at night because at night everyone was inside and safely asleep. Everyone but him. Charlie turned to see the dead woman walking toward him, no rush, a consistent flowing pace.

Behind him, he heard the click of the door unlocking and it opened. With renewed hope, Charlie spun around and ran headlong into an overweight man in a baggy dingy suit, his skin gray and waxy. The two fell and Charlie found himself face to face with it, the smell coming off it putrid, making his eyes water. The dead man's arms wrapping around Charlie's waist, squeezing him so tightly his back popped several times. Survival instincts kicked in and Charlie hammered two fists down into the face of his attacker and felt just enough give in the crushing embrace to pull his way out of it, almost losing his shorts. Scrambling to his feet, Charlie felt a hand claw down his back, the dead woman from outside, the sting of it burning bright.

The front door was open, more of them were stumbling through, their unseeing eyes focused on him. Too many of them between the stairs and him, he couldn't get to his parents. "Mom!" he bellowed in the dark, finally finding his voice. "Mom! Dad!"

Immediate clamor above him, the sound of feet hitting the floor and a door being thrown open. A light came on in the upstairs hallway, "Charlie?" It was his mother, "Charlie, where are you? What's—" Half of the undead crowd that had gathered through the front door turned their faces up into the soft light and began a new pursuit while the rest continued their slow march toward Charlie.

As Charlie ducked into the kitchen, he heard his mother scream his dad's name, true terror in her voice and Charlie's heart clenched. He'd never heard that depth of fear from her before and it instantly broke everything within him.

Broke and released a fury to action. If there was one thing Charlie had gleaned from all the pointless conversations about zombies and how to deal with them, it was they could be taken down by head trauma. Running to the counter, Charlie yanked open the knife drawer and pulled out the biggest, sharpest looking knife he could find. His chest heaving, he turned and lunged himself at the woman in the floral dress who had been on his heels the entire time. Raising the knife high, he brought it down onto the top of her head. As strong as he was, it barely went in an inch. Charlie was panting and the woman wasn't even stunned, instead her hand took Charlie by the bicep and pulled him to her. Charlie's free hand swung wildly behind him for the drawer, his hand searching desperately for another blade, getting poked and jabbed by the contents in the process. And as he finally found a handle, the drawer slammed shut, catching his hand inside. Shooting pain ran up Charlie's trapped arm met by the burning pain of his other arm being squeezed by the dead woman in flowers. The newcomer was a teenager, Charlie's same age, but shorter, dressed in a tailored suit, and he was using all of his body weight to crush Charlie's hand in the drawer.

Upstairs, the sound of scuffling continued, but there was nothing he could do about it, there was nothing he could do about any of it. He was cornered as more of the undead oozed into the kitchen cutting off any and all means of escape. It was hopeless. As hard as he'd worked for that great moment in his life, all the strength and endurance he had accumulated, it was all useless in the face of something he had never expected to be possible. Fear overwhelmed him and tears choked him as more bodies crowded the kitchen, hands reached for him, grabbing his shoulders, his hair, shorts, chest. The free hand of the dead teen wrapped itself around the front of his throat and dug in, cutting off Charlie's air. Desperate to breathe, Charlie reached up to pull the hand away, but the woman held his arm so tightly, he was sure it would snap at any moment. All hope of survival dissipated and in humiliation he gave up fighting and surrendered to his death.

The room swirled and black specks filled Charlie's vision as his mouth gaped for air and he sank into the crowd of dead. And just before he lost consciousness, he glimpsed the light.

CHAPTER FOUR

Gone

Charlie was cold. Cold was nothing new, his parents cranked the air conditioner down to sixty-five every night and it was the perfect temperature by which to sleep, when he slept inside. He'd always rather be cold than hot because when you're cold, you can always put more on, snuggle down deeper into your blankets. When you were hot, you could only strip down so far, then if you were still hot, you were just sweaty and out of luck. He reached over for his blanket, but his fingers found nothing but smooth . . . tile? Had he gone to the bathroom in his sleep and laid down on the bathroom floor again?

A breeze tickled over his body giving him goosebumps all over. All over. All. Over.

Wait. Am I-?

Forcing himself to push through the muddiness of his sleepy, groggy head, Charlie willed his eyes open. Stars twinkled above him, watching him with their distant curiosity. Stretching, Charlie slid his arms and legs over the smooth glass-like ground beneath his bare skin, and then he pulled himself up to sit, the ground cold under his butt.

He was naked. He was outside.

He was naked outside.

Charlie jumped to his unsteady feet, his hands immediately covering himself out of instinct. His foggy brain began working overtime trying to solve the riddle of why he was naked outside and exactly where outside he was. Nothing around him was recognizable, just flat, smooth ground and a ring of trees about a hundred feet away. This had to be a dream, one of those weird naked dreams, but it felt so real and he felt in complete control. But he also felt sore.

Stiff and sore, like he'd had the workout of his life. And a stinging fire ran down his back.

"You okay?" a girl's voice came from somewhere behind him. Whirling around, the world spinning even more wildly in his head, threatening to send him to the ground, he eventually focused on Meg standing in the shadows of the trees. Out of instinct, his hands lunged down in front of him again, attempting to salvage some sort of decency. She looked away quickly. "Bogart's over by the road keeping watch. I would have dressed you, but I was kind of afraid to touch you. I wasn't too sure if you were okay. I told him to bring a blanket too, but he forgot in his anxiousness to get back here." She walked toward him, eyes averted, and holding a backpack out to him.

With one hand attempting to hide things, the other one snagged the bag from her. Hurriedly, he turned away from her and squatted down so that he could use both hands to rummage through the contents. A huge Hawaiian shirt, a giant pair of cargo shorts, some well-worn white briefs, and tube socks and tennis shoes.

Meg was standing over him regarding him with . . . what? Concern? Inquisitiveness? "Um, do you mind?" Charlie asked a little harsher than intended.

Meg's eyes widened, "Oh, of course. Sure thing." She turned around with a hop.

Charlie focused his attention on getting dressed. No chance he was putting on the other kid's underwear, so he pulled the shorts on quickly. Unfortunately, even though Charlie was a big guy, he wasn't big *enough* in the waist to keep the shorts up without holding onto them, but rolling the waistband helped a bit. They still made getting the Hawaiian shirt buttoned tricky.

"Where are we?" Charlie asked as he sat down to pull on the socks, a pair of tall tube socks with colored stripes around the top. They were like something he had seen in eighties health class films.

The old pair of Converse wasn't much better and his toes had to scrunch to fit, they were almost a lost cause.

Thinking that the girl hadn't heard him, Charlie looked up to ask again, but found that she had turned and was simply watching him with that look again. Her mouth opened as though she were about to say something, but softly closed again.

"We're at your house." Bogart tromped up heavily behind him. "Well, we're at your house, but not. I mean, Dios mio, it's not here. This is where it used to be, but it's not here anymore. Just gone! BOOM! Destruida! Obliterated! I was—" Bogart reached into his pocket and yanked out an inhaler. After a couple of puffs, his rant continued. "I was on my way home after . . . you know . . . after *that* happened with the book, you know. I was on my way home and there was this massive flash of light and . . . and . . . I thought lightning had struck somewhere, but I knew it wasn't lightning because, well, it wasn't storming. I mean, I know this is Texas and all, and thunderstorms just come out of nowhere, but it wasn't lightning. So, I—"

Charlie stood up with some difficulty, gripping the shorts in his hand, his dizziness threatening to pitch him back to his knees. And that searing burn down his back. Why did it hurt so bad? He felt like he should remember, but couldn't. Turning slowly, he took it all in. The road. The houses in the distance. The trees . . . well, most of them. Most of most of them. The trees. He walked toward the edge of the trees, his legs sore. The trees. Most of them were whole, the ones to the back. But those that stood up front were sliced, as though a giant knife had shaved off the front of them, every branch, every leaf, and through the trunk. Sliced through like a block of cheese, and left smooth as glass. Like the ground. And what was cut away was simply gone. Turning, Charlie followed the tree line with his eyes. A perfect ring cut into the trees, some shallow, some deeper depending on where they stood in proximity to where his house had been. And inside the ring? Nothing. Dirt. No grass. No rocks. No trees. No . . . house.

When Charlie was a kid, his dad had shown him pictures of the land before the house had been built. It had always felt silly to him. The house was there and it always would be. Nothing could bring it down. Even those nights when lightning and thunder fought in the skies and Charlie was hunkered down in his bed, his comforter pulled up to his eyes, he knew that the house would stand strong.

Now it was *gone.*

Charlie turned to see Meg and Bogart side by side watching him with a mixture of pity and curiosity.

"What happened?" he asked, his throat sore. He rubbed his neck. It was tender, it felt bruised.

"Well, your house disappeared." Bogart was no help as usual.

Meg laid a hand on Bogart's arm before he could be of any more uselessness. "I don't know, Charlie."

Now that the shock was beginning to ebb, a list of questions started to flow. "Bogart said there was a flash of light, did it explode?"

Meg shook her head, the moonlight glimmering off her blonde hair. "I don't think so. The trees would have been pushed out, debris scattered around, and you . . . well, you probably wouldn't be here."

"No, not like explosion, 'cause there'd be, like, concentric rings of furniture and house and all kinds of pictures and books and stuff everywhere. It was a huge flash, Charlie. Huge. Like, think of the biggest flash of lightning you've ever seen and multiply that by, like, a gazillion." Bogart's excitement seemed to be growing as much as Charlie's fear and confusion.

Charlie headed off Bogart the only way he knew how, "There's no such thing as gazillion, Bogart."

"Technically, there is if you add enough numbers."

"Technically, shut up, Bogart."

Meg stood watching the interaction with her usual interest, almost as though she'd never seen two people converse before.

Charlie walked a few feet toward the center of where his house used to be. "Have you seen my parents?"

Meg shook her head, "You were the only one here."

"Wait, they're dead?"

"We don't know that," she said with an attempt at reassurance.

Charlie took a deep breath and ran his free hand through his hair. He winced, his scalp was sore. Why? "What do I do?"

"I think getting away from here is the first step," Bogart chimed in. "Someone always comes looking after something like this happens in the books. Like police, or worse, some mysterious guy waiting in the shadows. When his plan doesn't go through, he tries again, harder. I bet the next person here is the one who did it. Yeah, we should get out of here, you know?"

Charlie was about to reject the idea out of habit, but Meg jumped in before he could, "I think that's probably a good idea."

"Breaking away from the two of them, Charlie trotted to the center of the circle, scanning, hoping. They had to be here. If he had been thrown away from the house like that, maybe they had been too. He gripped the shorts and some hope and ran to where the trees were still thickest, darkest. Moving from tree to tree, trees he knew so well, he searched and hoped, "Mom? Dad? Can you hear me? Mom?" Panic was settling in, his stomach churning. "I'm here! Dad! Mom!" He didn't know how long he roamed among the trees, calling out to them, but he eventually made it all around the eerie, glassy circle, Meg and Bogart watching from a distance the entire time. At some point his calls had dropped to mumbles, then whispers. Finally, nothing.

"They really aren't here," Charlie numbly. "I don't know what to do. Where do I go? Town? The police?"

Meg's pigtails bounced as she softly shook her head, "No, somewhere else."

The sun still wasn't up, but it was threatening to rise. Already the horizon was beginning to glow. Charlie walked through the brush, following Meg closely, and Bogart trailed somewhere behind. They both tried to persuade Bogart to go home, but the fat kid wouldn't hear it. He kept going on about how he wanted to be a part of this adventure and neither one of them could make him see reason. Truth be told, Charlie didn't try very hard. He just didn't care. He only cared about his parents and the further they moved from the house, the more he felt like he was abandoning them. So what if the fat kid wanted to trail along? He'd eventually pass out and they could just leave him.

Desperately, Charlie tried to piece the evening together. He remembered the argument with his parents, the roof, the stars and the fox. Whispering her name and the rush he felt. Bogart had shown up and Charlie had behaved like a complete jerk. It was a wonder the kid came back at all, flash of light or not. Then he couldn't remember. Did he do this? Was this his fault? He had heard of people going crazy, losing their minds and setting their house on fire or killing their family, but surely *he* wouldn't have done this. And *what* was it he might have done? How does anyone just make an entire house and the people inside vanish? Or, whatever it did. Those trees. The ground. How did it happen?

As they walked, he assessed how he felt. Like . . . Crap. There was another word he wanted to use, but knew he shouldn't. So, he felt like crap. He hurt. His back burned, his arms hurt, his neck and scalp hurt. He felt beat up. But he couldn't see anything yet, it was just too dark. He had been sore after workouts before, but this was different, it wasn't deep, it was surface.

“How much further?” came the puffing question from behind. This was the fifth time he had asked in the last couple of hours.

Meg’s response was always the same. “Not much further,” she would say with a chirp, as though they were walking down the sidewalk to the park for ice cream. Bogart’s reply had become less and less accepting and more often in Spanish. At first the three words would comfort him, but by now he recognized the empty promise for what it was.

“We’re almost there,” she said this time, her voice quieter, focused.

“Are we really?” Bogart whined.

“Yes.”

Charlie looked around. It didn’t seem like they were almost anywhere. This dry as bones field with scruffy brush and mesquite trees wasn’t any different than the other dry as bones fields with scruffy brush and mesquite trees they’d trespassed through previously. Fence after fence had been crossed and slipped under, Bogart’s shirt ripped twice now after getting hung on barbed wire. And with every fence, Charlie became that much more apprehensive. He’d heard the stories in the halls about students getting shot at because ranchers assumed they were poachers and they had every right to shoot first and ask questions later. This was Texas, after all, it seemed most people slept and grocery shopped with a gun at their side. His dad never had one. Maybe if he had, things would have turned out differently.

“Can we stop for a minute?” Charlie could hear the earnestness in Bogart’s voice. “Just for a minute. I just need a breather.”

Ahead of him, Meg’s head dropped a bit, but her tone was still kind, “Sure. Just for a minute.”

Instead of catching up, Bogart stopped right where he was, doubling over, his hands on his knees. After several attempts at a deep breath, he pulled out his inhaler and took a couple of puffs.

Charlie turned his attention to the world that was waking up around him. His mom would have already been awake making breakfast and his dad would be nudging him any minute for their morning run, the hip suddenly good enough. Of course, he would resist and eventually give in, but he loved it. And he'd miss it.

"Bogart," Charlie called out.

"Yeah?" the boy wheezed.

"Can I try your phone again?" He'd already tried calling both cell phones, his dad's and his mom's. It was the only bit of technology they had, but even then, they were just simple flip phones. He had the numbers memorized because he didn't have a phone of his own. If he ever called them, it was on a rare occasion from school when he didn't feel well or had left homework at home. The latter only ever earned him a tongue lashing from Harriett.

His dad's number was already in the phone from the previous calls, so he just tapped it. He wished he had a phone . . . now was not the time. It went straight to voicemail again, "This is James Daniels, leave a messa—' Charlie hung up. Calling his mom produced the same result. He knew it would, but he had to try anyway.

Calling home was pointless.

It didn't matter how many times he tried, it was going to be the same. He knew that. He walked the phone back to Bogart, handing it to him in defeat.

"Are they somewhere?" Charlie asked Meg hopefully. "Will we find them?"

Meg shook her head. "I don't know, Charlie. I didn't expect this."

"You didn't *expect* it?" That was new. "So there was an element of this you were *ready* for, but *something* caught you off guard?"

"Right. I didn't think this would happen . . . with your house and . . . parents and all." The words seemed to be difficult for her.

What? "So you . . . you had a plan and it somehow involved me?"

"Yes." That at least came out with confidence.

He felt his anger rising again, his forehead filling up. "What was the *plan*?"

Meg considered him for a moment with those sparkling blue eyes, then shook her head, her pigtails bobbing. "Not yet."

That came as a slap. Charlie marched up to her, her diminutive size overshadowed by his above average height. "Tell me!"

"No." She was solid.

He wouldn't get any further and it only stoked his rage. Turning away from her, he yelled at the top of his lungs at the surrounding, empty countryside. Almost as bad as swearing, was losing your temper. At least that's what his parents had taught him to believe. *Work* through it. *Talk* through it. *Think* through it, but don't *lose* yourself to it. Charlie had never seen his parents lose control. James and Harriett's arguments could get quite heated, but they had always had the appearance of control. The only time Charlie had lost control; he had found himself suspended from school. That kid had it coming.

But yelling had felt good. It *was* good. No one had gotten hurt. It was just sound. Why was it wrong?

Sheepishly, Bogart tromped up to them, his breathing heavy, his odor ripe. Maybe he thought the yell was because of him. "I'm ready." He lifted his backpack, "Would you mind carrying this, Charlie? I might last a little longer without it."

Charlie slung it onto his back. No wonder Bogart was having so much trouble keeping up, it felt like it was full of bricks. "What's in this thing?" Charlie dropped it to the ground and Bogart winced.

"Be careful with it, please!"

Charlie yanked open the zipper and immediately wanted to unleash another yell at the curly haired, fat kid. "Books? You brought all your stupid books?"

"They're your parents' books!" Bogart whined in a weak defense.

"Why the— why did you bring them?"

"I . . . I don't know! I didn't know where to leave them and they're important to me! I didn't bring all of them! Just the first four! Well, five. I thought that maybe if your parents had signed the first one, maybe they could go ahead and sign the others. I just . . . I didn't know where to leave them and they're important to me," he repeated and wilted. Bogart obviously knew it was stupid, but couldn't help himself.

Charlie took a deep breath and let it out slowly, trying to cope with the mounting pressure. Everything in him wanted to yell again, but he couldn't. He had to hold onto it. Meg was watching and as frustrated as he was with her, he still wanted to . . . please her? Impress her? "This is stupid, Bogart."

"I know," the other kid mumbled.

Meg knelt down by the backpack and peered inside. "These are the books your parents wrote?" She plucked one out, by chance, the first in the series, the one Charlie had knocked Bogart to the ground with. But this time, unlike the hundreds of times he had looked upon that book in the past, the sight of *The Road to Hope* made something tighten in Charlie's chest. He watched as Meg opened the cover and flipped through the first couple of pages. He knew what was coming.

The dedication page.

"To our son, Charlie. May this book help you on your path." He could hear his mother saying it even as Meg read it tenderly.

"All of their books start with something along those lines," Bogart chimed in, his spirits lifted at the sight of his most prized possessions.

Meg flipped through several more pages. "What are they about?"

Thankfully, Bogart answered for him, though unsurprising. "They're brilliant, you know? They follow the lineage of a man named Crawford Billingshound. I mean, generations of characters and stories and intrigues and . . . and . . . and, oh man, they're just so good." Bogart glanced at Charlie. A quiet moment. "He hasn't read any of them."

The slight girl kept sifting through the pages. "Why, Charlie?"

Now it was Charlie's turn, "I don't know." Regret. So much regret. What would it have hurt if he'd just cracked the cover and forced himself through the first book? He hated reading. He had never told his parents that before. Honestly, all the little words hurt his head. They swam around and it was hard. He could do it, but it took so much effort. He never let on that anything was wrong, but he figured it wasn't normal. If this is what went on in Bogart's head, he'd hate reading too, but he didn't. Charlie knew about dyslexia and figured he had it, but self-diagnosed as mildly. When he had to, he could force his way through reading for school. It's why he put things off. No one knew. His parents didn't even know. Two author's whose kid struggled to read? It's why he wouldn't get into a good college. However, college seemed like the least of his concerns now.

Meg made a pass through the pages one more time and as she did, she stopped at a map. Her eyes seemed to pick it a part, scanning over every city name, country, mountain and river.

"Those are the lands of the United Realm," Bogart said. "You can see all of the countries and places where the story happens.

Meg looked up, "The United Realm?"

"Yeah," Bogart shrugged, "that's the name of the land."

"Why is it called that?" Meg had returned her attention to the map, a finger tracing one of the large rivers that seemed to cleave the whole thing in two.

"Oh, lots of reasons, it's kind of misleading, but I think that's the point!" Bogart's enthusiasm was mounting, "Intrigues, genocide, natural disasters, wars, enslavements of entire nations. It's all . . . it's just so . . . beautiful."

Charlie had had enough. He pulled the book out of Meg's hands and slipped it back into the pack, zipping it up and closing it off, effectively ending the conversation. Standing, he slung it over his shoulder, shifting the weight into place and gripped his shorts. "We should probably be going, right?"

He wasn't too sure where he was going, other than forward, but he started walking and let the other two catch up as they would.

CHAPTER FIVE

Traveling

Charlie kept tromping through the tall grass. The heat was beginning to get to him and the baggy shorts and the lack of protection between them and his bare skin were rubbing him the wrong way, quite literally. And the Hawaiian shirt was drenched in sweat. He would have taken it off if it weren't his only protection against the burning sun. His exposed skin pulsed heat.

Now that the sun was up, he could see why he hurt so bad, his arms were covered in bruises, purple, green, and yellow. He had lifted his shirt and his torso was covered in them as well. If he had to guess, it was the same with his neck. His back was another pain altogether, fiery and the backpack pressing against it didn't help the situation. As they walked, he tried to piece together what had happened, why he was covered in bruises, but he just couldn't. Nothing made sense.

As bad as Charlie *felt*, Bogart *looked* worse. The poor kid slipped further and further behind, his inhaler and misery his only companions. Charlie was worried about what might happen when the inhaler ran out in the middle of nowhere. The fat kid's normal waddle had turned into a full-blown straddle as Charlie was sure that he too was feeling the rub.

This was the thing about Texas, it was huge. You could walk and walk and never see anything. Sure, there were the cities, like Austin or Dallas or Houston, they were regular cities, *big* cities. This was the country, though, and in the country, you could walk forever and never see a soul.

Meg was a very different story. Chipper was the best word Charlie could come up with and he mildly begrudged her for it. The further they walked, the lighter her mood. He considered mentioning it, but realized in his own misery and fear for his parents, he couldn't possibly care less about her *indecent* chipperness.

And that left Charlie alone with his thoughts. The more he poured over the last night his parents existed, the more lost he felt. The words he launched at his mom about selling the film rights to the books haunted him, he'd never spoken to her like that and now he could never take any of it back. And even though he didn't direct it at his dad, Charlie knew James been collateral damage. No hope of redemption. Charlie failed them both.

"We're here!" Meg clapped her hands giddily, hopping up and down, her pigtails bouncing. "Well done, everyone!" Her exuberance was strange; he couldn't read her. His dad said that was normal with women, you never knew from one moment to the next who you would get. His mother proved his point daily.

Charlie stopped. Holding his shorts up with one hand, he used the other to wipe the sweat from his face with his shirt, *Bogart's* shirt rather. A futile action, as it only succeeded in smearing the new sweat with the old. Before him stood a huge dead tree, its insides hollowed out and around it, the evidence of a neatly kept campsite. "What is this?"

Meg looked about proudly, "This is home."

"It took us hours to get here. How do you get to school in the morning?"

She shrugged, "I usually run. You two slowed me down . . . a lot." She smiled.

She ran? Charlie shrugged off Bogart's backpack and this time gently set it on the ground before he collapsed onto the ground against the tree, though he immediately wished he hadn't as searing pain shot up his back. Bogart had finally straddle-shuffled his way to them, but instead of collapsing in a fat heap, he stayed on his feet, though threatening to topple over any second. "Okay, what now?"

Charlie leaned forward, but that hurt too. "I need you to look at my back. It hurts. Bad." He unbuttoned the soaked Hawaiian shirt and pealed it away.

The moment Meg saw it, she gasped. "Oh, Charlie. Why didn't you say anything?" She touched it lightly. Charlie winced, but strangely her touch was cool and soothing.

Bogart shuffled over to him and took a look too as Meg leapt lightly to the hollow of the tree, "Those look like . . . claw marks. What did that? And your arms, your *neck! Y*ou're covered in bruises."

Meg returned with a little jar in her hands. Not a jar like his mom would pickle okra in, but more like a little ceramic pot. She dabbed her finger in it, "This should help." Her touch was light and comforting. Almost immediately the angry burning he'd dealt with for hours, agitated by the heat and sweat, calmed. She started up between his shoulder blades and ended near the waistband of his shorts. "Let that dry before putting your shirt back on."

Charlie sighed. Finally, relief.

Meg knelt by the tree and crawled halfway into the hollow. "Bogart," her voice muffled in the empty tree, "you need to rest and then head home once the sun starts going down. Thank you for your help this far, but you just can't go the rest of the way. Besides, your grandmother will miss you."

"I'm not going anywhere. I mean, I *am* going somewhere, but that's with you guys." There was an edge of panic in his voice. "You can't just leave me. This is the most exciting thing that's ever happened to me and I don't want to be left out!" Charlie saw the fear in his brown eyes and the threatening tears. "Charlie, you can't leave me out! Please, don't let her kick me out!"

"Bogart, *I* don't even know what's going on and if whatever happened last night happens—"

"Shells," Meg interjected from within the tree. "You were attacked by Shells. Five claw marks down your back. Five fingers," she scooted out and wriggled her own fingers. "Shells tried to kill you last night."

And the fog began to subside.

Zombies on the porch. In the kitchen. One had him around the neck, his hand had been trapped. His throat tightened as the memory unfolded. The terror. "If they come again," Charlie managed, "how do I kill them?" He remembered trying to plunge something, a butcher knife, into the head of one and it didn't do a thing.

Bogart took a deep breath, calming himself, and crossed his arms, "How do you kill a *Shell*?"

Charlie sighed and pulled his hair back out of his face and behind his ears, "I don't know, man, bash them in the head or something? That's why I'm asking."

"What?" Meg pulled herself out of the tree, incredulous.

Bogart shook his head smugly, "You *don't* kill them. You *contain* them or *bind* them."

"Why would you do that?" Charlie asked, his irritation mounting at Bogart's smugness. "They'll just keep coming after you if you don't."

"They'll just keep coming after you if you *do*. There's a lot of debate on the subject in the fan forums, but most agree that it's best to tie them up. While they can open doors, they can't do things that require fine motor skills, they can't even *run*. Your best bet is to tie them up, but if you can't, *lock* them in a room, because they can't use keys. Last resort, fire, but then you risk burning everything down around you, duh. How many different kinds of knots do you know?"

Charlie rolled his eyes, "I don't know." Feeling stupid, he struggled for an answer, "What's the knot you make when you don't tie your shoes right?"

"Crow's Knot, Wayfarer's Knot, Prince's Knot, Keeper's Knot, Viper's Knot." Bogart's tone had gone from desperate to smug and now to arrogant. Charlie decided he liked him better puffing and whining. "Should I go on?"

Meg was smirking, her eyes sparkling. "Where'd you learn all of those?"

Bogart waved her off, "Those are only a few of them. While some geeks are wasting their time in the Boy Scouts, I was learning the practical arts of the United Realm from your parents in those books."

"I think the Boy Scouts would disagree with being called a waste of time," Charlie mumbled.

"Well, the *next* time you're faced with a *cluster* of Shells, maybe you'll thank me."

"Okay, smart guy," Charlie was past annoyed by the other boy's high and mighty attitude, "if I lock them in a room, why don't they just crowd the door and break it down or break a window and climb out."

Bogart snorted and shook his head, "Oh, Charlie. If they did that, it would hurt their Host. You really should crack one of those books soon. You'd save yourself a lot of embarrassment."

Meg giggled, but with a glance from Charlie, returned to her business inside the tree. "Okay, you two. Our next move is moving on."

"'Our' as in . . .?" Charlie didn't like the sound of that.

"'Our' as in you and me." Meg set a woven knapsack outside the tree and stood, dusting off her knees. "I'm sorry, Bogart," she shrugged sympathetically, "if you got hurt, or worse, I couldn't forgive myself and your grandmother might not ever know what happened."

Bogart's jaw dropped, "Are you serious? Are you . . .? I *know* stuff! I know *a lot* of stuff! I can be helpful!" The arrogance vanished and he was almost crying again.

Meg fished inside her bag, obviously avoiding eye contact with the distraught fat kid. "You just *can't*, Bogart. You've been so sweet and helpful, but you just can't. I'm sorry. Rest here and walk home as soon as you feel like you can." Meg pulled something out of her bag, a fist-sized ball of something, it looked like a giant green marble.

"All right, Charlie, this is a—"

"Transport Orb!" Everything happened so fast. Bogart, with unprecedented swiftness, reached out and snagged the green ball from Meg's hands. He cradled it in his own as though he held the very essence of life.

"Give it to me, Bogart." Meg's voice had lost all cheeriness. "Give it to me *now*."

Bogart paused a moment and looked up at her, the ball beginning to shimmer. "I'm *going* to help."

"Bogart, stop! Give me the Orb *now*!"

Charlie was on his feet, Bogart was being an idiot and if she wasn't going to take him before, this was sealing the deal. "This is actually *not* helping! Give it to her, you moron!"

Bogart grinned. "Read the books, *moron*."

A flash of green. A yanking pull forward. A shove backward. And Bogart was gone.

The glittering, green ball thudded to the ground in a cloud of dust.

"Shit."

Black smoke belched out of the exhaust pipe of the rumbling yellow bus as it idled on the side of the road. Its driver stood in the middle of nothing, her head low between her drooping shoulders. As she limped around the circumference of the clearing and took in the trees sheered cleanly by . . . something, Gladys could hear the excited chittering of the stinking rejects on the bus. Even *she* knew they were all losers and smelled like stale dog shit.

Unsteadily, Gladys bent down and ran her gnarled fingers over the smooth ground then raised her index finger and licked it. Tasted metallic, coppery. Like blood. She spat it out and wiped her mouth with the back of her moth-eaten sweater sleeve.

"Shit."

She would be blamed for this. Of course she would. From the moment the baby was brought to the house, *she* had wanted to do away with the parents and put him in the direct care of his Pair. But no, he had outvoted her, talked her out of it. The boy would grow up and they would keep an eye on him as they had been charged to do. Sentenced to do, more like it.

She *would* be blamed for this.

When she turned, every curious eye on the bus was watching her through the dirty windows.

"Shit."

As the dust cleared, for a moment, Charlie and Meg stared at the green ball, the Transport Orb as Bogart had called it. Maybe it would do something else. But as they watched it, it did nothing but fade, its shimmering life dulling in the Texas sun. Meg was the first to move and scoop it up. She held it in her hands, feeling it, turning it, and fingers tracing. Charlie had no idea what she was searching for, but it was clear *she* did. "What just happened?"

Meg shook her head, "He knew. How did he know?" He was sure she wasn't talking to *him*.

"*What* did he know?" Charlie demanded.

"He knew how to use a Transport Orb."

"What in the world is a Transport Orb?" The heat was rising, the pressure in his forehead.

"It's this," Meg held the dusty, green ball up.

Charlie clenched his jaw. "Right," he said as steadily as possible, "but what's it *do*?"

Meg's eyebrows scrunched in confusion and if he weren't so angry, it might have passed for cute. "It *transports* you." There was a silent *duh* trailing the end of that.

He erupted before he knew it, roaring into the clear sky again, his throat straining. Everything, all he had held in, his frustration with her, with Bogart, the loss of everything, his parents, the pain of not being able to do anything about it all, erupted out of him and he couldn't control it. He wanted something to hurt as bad as he did, and it wouldn't be Meg. So Charlie unleashed his rage on the hollow tree and gripped it in his big hands. With every shred of strength, he pushed against the tree, willing it to hurt, to *scream*, and in his imagination, the gaping hole was like a mouth howling agonizing pleas for mercy.

But Charlie *wouldn't* stop, he kept pressing, pushing, until he heard the first creek of wood giving under pressure. It only urged him on and he redoubled his efforts, pressing all of his weight and strength into the tree, until the breaking creeks turned to moans and snapping and finally the pathetic thing was out of his grasp and collapsing to the ground, its few limbs snapping and rebounding off the dusty, hard ground.

Chest heaving, Charlie stood there with cramping hands and shaking arms and legs. It felt good. *Really* good. He felt drained but so very good. Charlie picked up the colorful, dirty shirt with trembling hands and wiped the sweat from his face.

And then he was embarrassed. Humiliated. He'd lost control, lost all decency. Charlie shamed his parents again. He turned away from Meg and covered his face in the shirt, willing himself to disappear. It was that rage his Dad had always warned him about. His size and strength mixed with anger was a terrible combination, exactly why he could never play ball. And right there in front of the girl he so desperately wanted to like him, he had lost himself. Charlie started shutting down. He allowed his emotions and mind to slip into numbness. Not cold. Just nothing. He simply stood, his eyes losing focus as he looked at the ground.

"So," Meg's quiet voice said from somewhere to his right, "I see you're angry." She laid a cool hand on his back.

He didn't respond.

Her hand resting on his back, her touch so soft, it didn't mean anything, he couldn't *let it* mean anything. "You have every right to be angry. In fact, I was surprised you lasted this long. But that . . ." she looked to the fallen tree, its broken trunk jagged, "that was even more surprising. You push over a lot of trees at your house?"

No response. Sweat dripped from his long hair. The sun beat down on his bare shoulders, his back.

Reaching up, Meg ran her cool hand across his shoulders. Any other time, he would have loved it, but it didn't do anything.

She stepped in front of him and looked up into his eyes, forcing him to look at her, but she was just a fuzzy silhouette.

"Charlie, we're going to go now." She placed the backpack in his hands, Bogart's shirt crumpled in the handle, and he gripped it instinctively. With the same reverence as before, she picked up the green ball, cupping it in one hand and directing Charlie's other limp hand to cover it with hers. All her movements were measured and cautious, like a trainer with an unfamiliar beast.

"This is going to feel strange," she said slowly, "but it'll be over soon." She added quietly, "make sure you keep your hands, feet, and head inside the swirling colors."

Charlie didn't care. He really didn't care about anything right then.

Green light flashed.

CHAPTER SIX

Farnsworth's Finest

Tark trotted down the locker-lined empty hallway, his cleats clacking with every step. Adrenaline was raging and he was sure he could charge through the cinderblock wall ahead of him.

Gladys had found him in the weight room. The moment he saw her bent frame silhouetted in the open garage door, he knew something had happened. Of course, he assumed *she* was responsible for whatever it was. "The house'd been destroyed by unnatural means," she had explained through slow, slurred words.

"Did you do it?" he asked, sitting on a weight bench. Tark had barely held her at bay all those years ago when all of this had first started.

Time after time, she made attempts to sway him to her side. "It would be easier to guard him," she insisted around the cigarette dangling from her wrinkled lips. "You could have a stronger influence, train the boy as he *should* be for what he *is*. Those two aren't doing him any favors."

The old woman looked him squarely in the eyes, "I did not do it." That was all he needed to hear from her. The woman could not lie. It was impossible for her, part of her sentence, as though this place weren't enough. But that's the price she paid for the things she dabbled in.

"Marrs! Hawkins!" Tark shouted. Two younger men rushed from the coach's office nearby. Marrs, a quiet, olive-skinned young man with dark short hair, barely taller than the other, and Hawkins, his skin darker still, frame thicker and eyes always bright and ready.

"Coach?" Hawkins asked lightly. That was always his disposition and why Tark liked having him around. The men he collected had the tendency to be dark and brooding, but when he could find one who's heart was still light enough, he kept him in close company. Marrs was quite the opposite, but his judgment was keen. The mostly silent man only spoke when it was important or had a differing perspective than Tark and wanted his head coach to consider it before moving forward. Tark had won several championships after Marrs had succeeded in changing his mind.

"Gather your squads from whatever mundane *educational* beating they're taking, call the network, and meet me at the equipment shed. We leave in half an hour."

Without a word, they sprinted through the open garage door. Good men.

Tark and Gladys parted ways and he went to collect his own squad. While most might surround themselves with the more experienced, Tark insisted on taking the new recruits under his wings. That meant underclassmen— or those who could pass for underclassmen. The coach yanked the door open to one of those mundane educational beatings. "Ben, grab the Pups and—"

"Coach Tark," a woman with a nose like a crane's bill screeched at him, "I am aghast at your inexplicable interruption of my calculus class."

Tark hadn't the slightest notion as to what her name was, he never bothered to learn them. Every year he managed to dismiss himself from the in-service teacher training at the beginning of the term. Having a state champion football program for eleven years running afforded him certain favors. As a result, he didn't know any of his 'colleagues'. So dismissing the beak-nosed woman was simple enough. Again, he directed his attention at Ben and the other members of the Pack in the crane woman's classroom. "Let's go. Now!"

The woman flapped her arms and squawked, but the boys, men really, abandoned their desks and stampeded from the room, leaving only two lanky boys behind whom Tark recognized as basketball players.

Letting the door swing shut behind him, Tark took a deep breath and let out a howl that echoed down the hallways.

This is what he'd been waiting for.

Within the hour, the Pack was trotting down the lonely country road to the place where the Daniels house had been. Gladys' bus sat idling and belching. Nearly two hundred of them had to go by foot because the bus could only hold thirty plus equipment. Almost two hundred and fifty strong. Tark led the runners with Marrs bringing up the rear guard and Hawkins on the bus with Gladys. The younger players had been forced to ride the big, yellow beast at the insistence of the senior players, who wanted the honor of the run. Tark was all too happy to oblige them, though he could tell Ben was crushed by the realization he'd be on the bus. The boy, because he was only sixteen, was too easily offended by things like that. Sensitive.

Most of the men running and several on the bus were no longer students, but members of the Pack who had graduated and, out of loyalty to Tark, stayed there in Farnsworth. Mechanics, carpenters, a barber, and all manner of other trades, made up the legacy Tark had been pouring himself into for the last fifteen years. He'd been a young man, thirty-two winters with quite the reputation when he had been sentenced. Now he would be forty-seven this winter and his current reputation was something else altogether.

A squad car was parked at the side of the road in front of the bus, two officers standing near the clearing on either side of Gladys. With a signal to those behind him, Tark peeled away from the Pack and trotted over to the trio.

One of the officers, a fair skinned, chubby man, was drilling Gladys with questions. Having been in enough conversations with the little woman, Tark knew how easily she evaded topics she didn't wish to discuss with mumbled responses and questions of her own. It could be maddening, and by the look of the chubby officer's pink face and wide eyes, he was on the brink of a Gladys induced seizure. The other officer, a young tanned man with well-groomed hair, watched the conversation passively through a pair of mirrored aviator sunglasses. The young man's arms were crossed and the muscles in his forearms twitched now and then, a sign of frustration.

The pudgy officer squinted at Tark as he approached, "What the hell are you doing here, Coach?"

Tark glanced at Gladys, but the woman was no help, "We were on our way to a game in Waco."

"Where's your other bus? Why are your boys running?"

The other officer looked on coolly.

"It broke down a little ways back," Tark offered tightly, "I phoned Gladys and she pulled over to wait for us. The district will be sendin' us another one shortly."

Officer chubby turned his scrutiny on Gladys, "That right?"

Gladys blinked slowly, "I don't keep no phone."

Damn it. "Gladys is just foolin' ya. Aren't ya, Gladys?"

The old woman shrugged, "I don't keep no phone. Ain't got no one to call. Ain't no one callin' me."

Tark took a deep breath and released it. Why of all people had he been Paired with her?

Officer chubby crossed his arms over his puffed-up chest, matching his partner, minus the intimidation factor. "*So*," he said slowly as though he now meant business, "*why* have the two of you *really* shown up in the middle of the school day with a third of the football team on the bus and another third running behind it on foot to the location where the house of Farnsworth's most famous family stood until some point overnight? And don't give me that Waco crap. It's Tuesday and you don't have a full team." The chubby man squinted past Tark, "And is that Wade? I just saw him at the barbershop. What the hell is going on, Coach?"

Sweat trickled down Tark's face. Where was he supposed to go with this? And what if the chubby little man looked *in* the bus and saw the 'equipment'?

Click-click-click-click-click.

Officer chubby's eyes widened and his body stiffened and shook, a second later and he was on the ground in a heap, piss spreading across his lap.

The young officer holstered his taser, "Sorry, Coach. I should have done that earlier. God, that felt good."

"It's fine, Karsark." Tark dropped the Texas accent and turned on the little woman. "Why the hell couldn't you just go along with it?"

She shrugged her stooped shoulders, "Can't lie."

He took another deep breath and released it slowly.

Karsark nudged the fat officer in the ribs with the toe of his boot, "What are we going to do with him, Coach?"

Gladys tapped him in the belly with her own dingy orthopedic shoe, "Gut him?"

"Damn it, we're not gutting him, Gladys. Stick him in the back of the squad car and turn the air conditioning on. We don't want him to roast. You coming with us, Karsark?"

"Yes, sir, it's what I've been waiting for." Karsark squatted and hooked the unconscious officer under the arms and began dragging him to the squad car.

Tark started walking toward the Pack. "We have extra equipment on the bus, Karsark!"

"I got mine in my trunk with the spare, Coach!" Karsark called back.

Tark grinned to himself, "Good, boy."

CHAPTER SEVEN

Street Smarts

"Don't you look over here at me like that, boy!" Maze yelled down the block at the scraggly white man with his dog and piece of cardboard. "You know this is my spot! Yeah, you wave your hand at me! Oh, you gonna use the finger now? Well, I got two of them!" She gave him the double bird. "You know why? Because my ass didn't lose an arm in Desert Storm! And guess what? Neither did *your* ass! You got it hidden under your shirt, asshole!"

This was *her* spot. *Her* territory. Right outside Grand Central station. It was her spot every morning. Maze had seen him trying to edge into it yesterday morning, but she gave him the eye and he walked off. But this morning when she got there, his dirty white ass and dog was sitting there. "You don't disrespect like that!" She yelled at him again for good measure. "You lose an arm for real if I find you here tomorrow morning! You hear me?"

Maze finished eating her bagel and downed her juice. At the moment, she was just a big black girl sitting by the wall. People passed by and didn't give her a second look. That was fine. She didn't need them to right then. Wadding up the bag, she tossed it down the sidewalk, but she kept the cup. You always need a good cup. Reaching into her backpack next to her, she pulled out her blanket and folded it, making a cushion for her ass. She removed her earbuds and iPod and slipped them into the bottom of the bag.

Now, which sign to use? "Help me feed my babies"? "My grandmother needs her medication"? Or would it be the blind act with the sunglasses and "please help" sign? She used the "Let's be honest, I just want liquor" sign yesterday and did well with it. Tourists thought it was funny and she would even let them take a picture with her for another dollar. She didn't ask for it, but they gave it to her anyway for playing along. And she didn't actually use the money for alcohol, she didn't drink, just like she didn't *actually* have a grandma and she didn't *actually* have kids and she wasn't *actually* blind. She just bought what she needed. Food. Clothes. Tampons. New earbuds when she got tired of the ones she had. Just the necessities. Sure, the shelters gave out some of that stuff, but the tampons felt like cardboard toilet paper rolls and the clothes were usually ugly and outdated. She was homeless, but she wasn't *desperate*. She did take a few pieces of the shelter clothes, they made for a good begging costume. Wearing her nicer clothes meant getting less money from the sucker tourists who passed by.

Since she used the liquor sign yesterday, she decided upon the grandma sign. Being blind was exhausting, but it could make good money. She wasn't feeling it though. You couldn't look at anything directly and that was weird, but you always had to be ready to grab your cup in case some asshole tried to snatch it. And the moment you grabbed it, the act was over for the day.

Maze pulled out the grandma sign and zipped her backpack up, slipping it between her and the wall for security. Always know where your shit is, always be alert. Coogey had taught her all he knew. Told her about different signs, taught her how to look beat down, and taught her it was just a numbers game. It all depended on how long you were willing to sit and be ignored, rejected. Because all those people who coolly passed on by didn't matter. "It's the *one* who matters," Coogey would say, the gaps in his teeth showing. "The one who feels sorry for you. The one who takes pity on you. The one who just wants you to have a meal that day." If Maze had had a granddad, she'd have wanted him to have been like Coogey. The old man would reach the end of the day, and his fingers that had been gnarled with arthritis for hours on end would straighten out and slip his pearly dentures into his mouth. He was a master. He had it all as far as people in their condition were concerned, which is why his death was difficult to swallow.

People walked by.

Word was, Coogey got drunk and ran onto the tracks as a train was racing up to the platform. She saw the footage on the news that night from the security cameras. Everyone thought he'd lost his mind and done it, but Maze couldn't help but feel like he was running *from* something. Something real. Maze remembered the anchor woman warning the viewers that the following footage was graphic and might be too much for some. The pretty white woman sitting in her pretty clothes had no idea just how hard it was for the people gathered in the shelter around the little TV. Coogey was like *all* their granddads.

Whether he'd been on the bottle or not, Coogey gave her one last gift when he died: a hate for booze. Her sign might joke about it, but that was just a trick. Her real self would never touch the stuff.

People walked by.

Her phone vibrated in her backpack, but she wouldn't answer it. Probably Lola. Bitch knew not to call her right then. She was at *work*. Pull out a phone and the money would dry up, not that she was having much luck yet. "Wait for the one," she heard Coogey say.

People walked by.

"What's wrong with your grandmother?" It was an Asian lady in a pantsuit.

"Lymphoma."

The pantsuit woman winced, "I'm so sorry. Is it Hodgkin or non-Hodgkin?"

This was the danger of the Grandma sign. Some people wanted to interview you before they stuck money in your cup. It was cool, though, she had her answers ready. "Hodgkin."

"When was her diagnosis?"

"About three months ago."

She was looking through her purse. Pantsuit lady was going to be the first *one* for the day. "That's awful. What stage is she in?"

"Six," Maze said confidently.

The woman paused and narrowed her eyes, "There's only four stages. My mother had Hodgkin's lymphoma. Stage four before we knew what was happening. Are you . . .? Is this just a . . .?"

Really? Right outta the gate? "Bitch, please, just go on with yourself. Go give to one-armed-Wally down there."

Her honor, the pantsuit princess closed her purse with a jerk. "You should be ashamed."

"Lady," Maze rolled her eyes, "my shame went dead a long time ago. Right after my give-a-damn broke and my shits-to-give ran out. Bye now!"

The woman opened her mouth to say more, but Maze held up her hand and wiggled her fingers at her, "Bye now! Bye-bye! Move along!"

And she did, thank Jesus.

Nobody bugged her again. The morning passed and while most people passed with the morning, several stopped and tucked bills into her cup. You never kept the bills in there, that would signal passersby on the edge of giving that you didn't need it. It was all about the illusion. An act.

Her workday came to an end and she clocked out, putting her sign and blanket in her backpack. If she was keeping track correctly, she made fifty-three dollars and some change in a little over five hours. Ten dollars an hour. Not bad.

The shelter was on the other side of Times Square, closer to the Hudson. Lola would be there by now waiting in line and saving her a spot. You weren't supposed to do that, but Lola's give-a-damn was just as busted as hers. Lola. Somebody had called. Pulling her backpack around, she opened it up and rummaged to the bottom for her phone. It *had* been Lola. She hit the return call button and held the phone up to her ear.

"Hey, May," Lola answered.

"Hey, you know you can't call while I'm at work, the boss don't like it. Gets all mad and says he'll take it out of my paycheck." She laughed and so did her friend. "What's up, bitch? Why you call me?"

Maze crossed 5th Avenue with a crowd of tourists. A guide was walking ahead of them with a pink umbrella in the air so they could keep track of her. More than individual tourists, Maze hated *groups* of them. Like a herd of swivel headed idiots. "George dropped by my spot this morning in Battery and said some dude was looking for you."

"He hot?"

"Not unless you think dirty and white is hot."

"Depends if he has a good ass. I don't mind me some grunge on a fine ass."

"Maze," Lola said flatly, "George said the guy was all kinds of crazy. Scraggly red beard, wide-eyed and talking to himself."

"A'ight, I'll be careful," she said trying to appease her friend. "I can take care of myself."

"George said he was wearing a sweatshirt, big pocket in front."

"Sweatshirt, big pocket, dirty, white, and scraggly beard. For real, did he have a nice ass? Cause I might be willing to look past the other shit if he does." Maze tried to lighten the mood, but Lo wasn't having it.

"Be careful, girl."

"I will, Lo. Promise." She flipped her phone shut.

Eight million people in New York City. One and a half million in Manhattan alone. She wasn't worried.

But she should have been because crossing 6th Avenue coming her way was a scrawny white guy with a scraggly red beard wearing a nasty hoodie sweatshirt with a big ol' pocket.

"Oh, shit."

CHAPTER EIGHT

The Problem with Bus Drivers

The entire Pack now trotted ahead of the coach, Marrs in the lead. The man was a damn good tracker, almost as good as Karsark, who had run on ahead. Most of them had either ripped the sleeves from their shirts or taken them off. Now the eighty men could be seen more clearly for who they really were—not a football team or regular Joes from town, but a mass of brutes whom Tark had been collecting for nearly thirteen years and passing off as a state champ football program. Many of them had come and gone, like Officer Karsark. A few had married, though Tark constantly spoke against it. "Have a woman to take care of your needs, but don't marry them. It's not what we're here for." But hearts did what hearts did. Those were the men absent today. Marriage had muddied the waters and judgment.

Within the first year of his sentence, Tark bought the house where the drop-off happened, at least in this area. As a Pair, He and Gladys had been sent with limited resources, but it was just enough to buy the old house and raise a privacy fence around the backyard. Gladys had spent hers on the bus and a trailer home. People were easy enough to intimidate, and he soon had the head coaching position as the former coach suddenly decided to move to Oklahoma and retire.

Karsark was one of the first to appear in the high fenced backyard, naked and angry. He had ideas those who sentenced him didn't agree with. Labeled a rebel, he simply had a thirst for real justice. Tark took him in, gave him shelter and vision. Karsark, though nearly twenty, enrolled in FHS as a sophomore. The paperwork was easy enough in a small town like this, you could find people to get you the papers you needed to prove a man was just a boy. And the Pack was born.

For years now, young men appeared and he recruited them. He couldn't keep them all at his house, so as they graduated and found jobs, they would in turn open their houses to new recruits, who would graduate, get jobs, and open their homes. Thirteen years.

Tark only passed on two types. Those who were too old and those who had committed murder. You couldn't trust murderers. If they'd done it once, they'd do it again. It was a risk he wasn't willing to take. He would invite them in, clothe them, feed them, and give them a bed for the night. The poison Gladys supplied him with mixed well in a good, cold beer and a man never turned down a beer. Before sunrise, Karsark would help him with the body and Gladys would do away with it. Tark never asked what she did them.

The Pack was now fulfilling its purpose, albeit earlier than he'd expected. Tark knew the whole business was going to be ugly and that he and Gladys wouldn't be able to handle it on their own. They all took the task of watching the boy with due gravity and pride. It gave them all purpose again. The Pack watched him grow up, and here recently, many of them watched him in their classes and in the hallways. The younger members of the Pack, the Pups, those still in school, were developing a different opinion of the boy than those who came before them. They thought he was arrogant, a dick. And truth be told, the Daniels boy was an arrogant bastard. The Pups knew their duty and would do it, but they didn't hold Charlie in the same regard the older men did.

Gladys drove the bus behind them, the yellow beast bouncing along the uneven terrain. She wouldn't abandon it as Tark and Marrs tried to convince her to do, but Hawkins thought it was hysterical and, flashing a toothy smile, sided with her to bring it. She was attached to the belching monster and she knew better than to get attached to anything. To say that Gladys was a mystery to him would be a serious understatement.

The two of them had been picked out fifteen years ago and placed in this small town to keep an eye on the boy. They were the boy's Pair. His adoption on this side of things had come as a surprise and Tark had been determined that it would be the last surprise they experienced on the mission. Tark was just as frustrated as the rest of the Pack at the boy's refusal to join the team. It wasn't about having another player; it was about molding the boy into what Tark knew he needed to be. Charlie was a perfect specimen, far better than the young men who ran ahead of him now. What could he have turned that boy into had he been able to get his hands on him?

Karsark stood up ahead waiting. He was a talented scout, always had been, so it was natural for him to join the Farnsworth police force, small as it may have been. He stood with his arms folded across his police uniform, badge gleaming in the setting sun. He was proud of what he'd made of himself.

As the Pack approached, Karsark held out his hands and they slowed to a stop several yards away. An old hollowed tree laid on its side near what could have been a campsite. "He was here," Karsark said quietly, but they could all hear him clearly.

The bus rumbled to a stop, the door squealed open, and the Pack parted to allow Gladys through. "Show me," she mumbled.

Karsark turned and cautiously stepped around the small clearing in order to not disturb the footprints. "The three pairs of footprints stop here. Over there, the heavy one's disappear. And right there, Charlie's and the girl's disappear."

Gladys snorted. The old woman stumped through the campsite, not paying heed to any of the other prints, but keeping the final pair in her gaze. Finally, she squatted and ran her finger through the dirt where Karsark had indicated the girl had stood last. After licking her finger, she nodded. "It stood here," she mumbled.

It. It was always the worst. *Him* or *her*, were doable. *Him* or *her* came with a typical set of rules that if studied enough could be strategized against and defeated. *It* was *always* unpredictable.

"What's the *it* we're discussing here?" Tark probed.

Gladys pursed her lips, "I'd say Gohlem by the taste of it. Earthy. Touch of herbs and flowers. For scent, I assume."

"You can taste it?" Karsark chimed in. The eager officer stooped down and ran his finger through the print just as Gladys had.

The old woman shrugged, "Creature made of dirt and clay leaves dirt and clay wherever it walks."

Gohlems were tricky creatures. Housing the heartsoul of a victim or volunteer, the rookies were dirt clods with arms and legs, the more experienced Gohlems were harder to distinguish and could shift on a whim.

Damn it, why did it have to be a Gohlem?

"Anything else?" Tark grunted.

Gladys stood, several joints popping in the process, "They Transported from here by orb."

"Damn it. Where to?"

She shook her head, "Two directions west is all I can sense of their trail." She pointed at a pair of footprints, "The fat one Transported first. What does *he* know and why?" She shrugged and waved a hand at the other two sets of footprints, "and the Gohlem took the boy elsewhere."

Tark looked away to the west, "Do *you* have an Orb?"

Gladys snorted, "You know I don't. They wouldn't let me bring anything with me, you know that." She shrugged her drooping shoulders, "Even if I did, it wouldn't work properly anymore. Whatever the Gohlem is using is fresher."

"So even if we could get to them in the blink of an eye, we still have no idea as to where that is. Just that way somewhere?" Tark said with an aggravated sweeping gesture.

“I said they didn’t let me bring anything with me. It doesn’t mean I don’t have anything now.” Gladys pointed a bent finger at the Pack, “You’ve been preparing for a day like this and so have I.” Turning from them, she squinted into the sky. Karsark looked at Tark and raised an eyebrow. Tark, in turn, folded his burly arms and watched the woman carefully. The old woman began making a series of croaking chirps followed by whistles. Bird calls. Tark searched the sky around them and sure enough a single bird, a grackle, drifted close. Gladys repeated the call and held up her hand, her crooked index finger extended. The bird, a glossy black male, circled and after a few more coaxing calls, landed on the offered finger, its beady yellow eyes watching the humans around it.

“And how does that help?”

Gladys stroked the head of the bird, calming it. Then in a swift moment snapped its neck and wrenched off the head.

“Holy shit!” Karsark jumped back nearly tripping over the hollow tree behind him.

Taking a deep breath, Tark calmed his center, “You aren’t allowed to use those ways.”

Gladys grinned, a dark and menacing thing, the bird’s blood dripping over her hand in pulses. “And you weren’t allowed to assemble an army, *General* Tark, yet you did. Now, decide who of your men will follow which trail. We camp here tonight and travel at sunrise.”

CHAPTER NINE

West Coast Trespassers

Something *had* felt weird, but Charlie really couldn't say what it was. So much of him felt numb now and he wasn't willing to reach out past it. The numbness felt good, comfortable, soothing. His eyes were in a perpetual state of fuzzy focus, like when he would zone out in class— any of them. Light shifted around him, sounds came and went, and Meg was in it all somewhere. Now and then he would feel her touch on his arm, even a concerned squeeze trying to pull him out, but he wouldn't take the bait. In the empty recesses of his head was where he wanted to stay. It felt good.

What was he supposed to do now? Where was he supposed to go? How would he live? His parents were dead and he was impossibly pathetic. If he was concerned for his future before, he grieved it now. He didn't have anything or anyone. Everything, *literally* everything, was gone. Was he an orphan now? Would he end up in an orphanage? Was that even still a thing? It seemed to him that orphanages were something in Dickens books he was supposed to have read in school. No, now he'd probably just end up 'a ward of the state', or something like that.

You could always sell those rights now.

He was impossibly pathetic and a horrible human for even having that thought pass through his consciousness.

Meg's cool hand was on his lower back. He *did* like it, even in his self-inflicted emotional quarantine.

"Charlie?" Her voice was as soft as her touch. "Charlie, are you there?"

For the first time since he mentally disappeared, he turned his head to her in response. She was frightened, he could see it in her eyes that sparkled even now, and he added that to the list of things he felt terrible about.

"There you are." Meg smiled sweetly. "I thought I had lost you." She turned and the moonlight highlighted her cute nose and firecracker pigtails. "It's pretty here."

Charlie looked up and focused for the first time in . . . he had no idea how long he'd been "away". It *was* pretty. Tall leafy plants, blooming flowers that looked silver in the moonlight, the smooth surface of the pool, and a nice cool breeze tickled his skin. Where'd his shirt go? Bogart's shirt. He could hear the soft wind rustle the leaves of the palm trees standing vigilantly over them. Palm trees? The sight of them pulled him out a little further. "Where are we?"

"California. Beverly Hills to be precise."

A weird mixture of emotion coursed through him, forcing the mental fog away. On the one hand, a spark of life awakened. He'd always wanted to get out of Texas and now he was. Then there was the other part. He'd always imagined visiting California with his parents, and now they were gone.

Charlie took a deep breath and let the breeze soothe that away. "Why are we in California?"

"There's another one here."

"Another what?"

A brief pause. "Let's get you inside."

"Inside where?"

"A little cottage. There hasn't been anyone here all day. I watched it for hours while you laid on a bench in the park. When the sun went down and no lights came on, I figured it was safe." She did all that while he was in mental limbo? Wait, he walked?

"Hold on." It took him a moment to piece it together. "You broke in?"

"It was hardly a break in," she stood and pulled on his hand, "the gate was unlocked."

Charlie stood, his body felt heavy. “Then we’re trespassing.”
“Only if someone catches us,” she winked.

Hot water ran over Charlie’s body, his muscles wanting to relax, but his heart holding them tight for protection. In all that had gone on, he didn’t realize how tense he was. It made sense though. Who wouldn’t be this on edge with everything he’d been through? It was an indication that maybe he wasn’t as much of a monster as he thought he was. As the water ran over him, so too did his self-loathing. Hateful thoughts working their way to his lips, his lips moving to give them shape quietly in the steady fall of the shower, “I’m such . . . I’m such an asshole.” His head hung and the water cascaded down him and so did the shame of even saying that word, but he owned it, “I’m such an asshole.”

Meg had insisted he shower, she said he looked greasy and he’d feel better after. The idea of showering in someone else’s place was weird. Weirder still was the idea this *someone* didn’t know he was here. Meg didn’t think they’d be back anytime soon and by the looks of it, they hadn’t been here for quite some time. It didn’t make the shower any less weird.

Growing up, Charlie never went to anyone else’s house. From an early age, his parents had always taken a stance opposing sleepovers on the basis they could never be sure about the hosting parents. As he grew up, invitations became rarer and eventually dried up altogether. He heard about parties and guys getting together on the weekends, but he was never a part of it. When he was little, he resented it immensely, but over time, he surrendered to it. His world was his house and school, and now the one was gone and the other wouldn’t be missed. And more than likely, neither would he.

Charlie thought the whole pool house had an odd vibe to it. Simple lines, gray walls, and sleek furniture, someone knew how to decorate. Or at least they knew how to order furniture sets from catalogs. It was very different from the farmhouse full of knickknacks he grew up in. And as nicely dressed as the little house seemed, there were the other touches slapped on top. Posters hung crooked on those gray walls, posters for bands who made a witch's coven look like a librarian club. The fridge was stocked with all kinds of alcohol and there were strange pipes and bowls on bookshelves that caused Charlie to believe that if he looked hard enough, he might find something illegal in a hidden baggy. Charlie wasn't going to look hard enough.

Kids did drugs at school. On the far side of the football field, under the trees that marked the edge of campus was where they did it. He'd watch them skip PE and wander over there. Tark and the other coaches saw it, but they didn't seem to care. So the stoners burned out some more brain cells? What did it matter? As Charlie would take his laps around the track, though, he couldn't help but wonder what it was like. Add that to the list of things never discussed at home. Puberty, sex, and drugs.

Charlie decided the little pool house was Cape Cod Punk.

Looking for shampoo, Charlie sorted through the hair products piled in the darkly tiled shower. Half of the bottles he picked up didn't seem to have anything in them and the other half he couldn't find any labels identifying them as shampoo or conditioner, and one of them would have knocked his socks off if he had been wearing any when he took a whiff of it. It had to be liquor of some kind, but he had no idea *what* kind. Another taboo word on the list of avoided subjects and ignorance: alcohol. Finally, he came across one that looked promising and it lathered well . . . and smelled nice. Surprising. He almost expected anything found in this place to smell like that booze hiding in the shampoo bottle. The actual shampoo smelled so nice, he lathered up a couple of times just to make sure his long, thick hair was clean enough. His hair was one of the things his mom constantly praised him for. She would always come up behind him and run her fingers through it when he was sitting at the kitchen table doing homework. She would then pull out pictures of him when he was little (was he ever actually little?), about four or five, and talk about how she couldn't bear to take him to get a haircut. It was his dad who finally insisted upon it when a lady at the store told him how precious his daughter was.

As he was about to turn the water off, he glanced at that one shampoo bottle again, the one that certainly wasn't shampoo. He'd never had alcohol before. Every now and then his mom and dad would share a bottle of wine after a book hit the shelves, but it wasn't a *regular* thing. When he was a kid, his dad let him try a sip, much to his mother's dismay, but he choked and said he hated it, much to his mother's pleasure. And after that, they never talked about it again. He could feel his anger bubbling up. *Why* didn't they talk? Why was everything so maddeningly taboo? Sure, he recognized that in some twisted way, they were attempting to protect him from things, but all they succeeded in was turning every unmentionable into a mystery, and mysteries were meant to be solved.

Now? His parents were gone and he was alone with his mysteries. Besides, a sip might help him relax a bit, that's what his dad always said upon his second glass of celebratory wine. And that's why the stoners smoked out. And this was just alcohol, it wasn't even illegal.

As though he were about to grab a power line, Charlie reached timidly for the bottle. His heart was beating fast in his chest as he unscrewed the cap and he felt a little stupid for it. Placing the bottle to his lips, he decided to close off his nose and not inhale. He took a small sip, the liquid burning like the marks down his back when it hit his throat, but other than that, it wasn't too bad. Another sip, this one bigger than the last. It burned and he coughed, but he liked it. It felt alive. And before he turned off the water, he took another drink, this one a gulp. He coughed immediately and almost gagged, but he recovered. He was good. Really good. The burning liquid warmed his belly, liquid calm. Mystery solved and there was nothing to it. Bonus, whatever it was he drank numbed the shame.

With a towel wrapped around his waist, Charlie walked into the little living room/kitchen combo, his legs and head feeling the effect of his little secret. Meg was sitting on the couch under a lamp, pouring through Bogart's books, the backpack discarded on the floor. She had changed into a little pair of shorts and a tank top with a kitten on it, hair now pulled to one side in a single short braid. She looked him over and grinned slyly, "Very nice."

Old *asshole* Charlie felt a little exposed, but new bottle-emboldened Charlie couldn't help but like it. "Cut it out," he giggled as he pulled the towel tighter around him. Giggled? He took a deep breath hoping to help clear his head.

"What? I'm a girl. I can look. Besides, I already saw you naked. *Nothing* left to my imagination. But the wet look is pretty hot." She winked. That's right, she *had* seen him naked. Totally naked. He didn't have anything to be ashamed of, being in the locker room around the Pack had proved that. To hell with decency.

He smirked. Meg didn't seem to notice his growing unsteadiness, and if she did, she probably chalked it up to exhaustion and the relaxing shower she had insisted upon, not the treasure he had found *in* the shower. And, truthfully, he liked her flirting. He'd never had a girl hit on him like that. It was awesome. He let the towel relax a bit as he turned looking for Bogart's baggy shorts.

"I tossed the shorts, they were huge on you. I couldn't find much that looked like it would fit. You're kind of a big guy, not Bogart big. Beefy big. Tree Wrecker." She giggled to herself. As refreshing as the shower had been for his body and the booze for his anxiety, her laugh had the same effect on his heart. "Anyway, the shorts I found are there on the chair. All the t-shirts are black and look small, but I pulled out the least heart-of-darkness-and-soul-eating one and those underclothes are . . . well, I don't want to make you blush. Whoever lives here has a colorful sense of taste underneath it all, like the lovechild of a vamp and a unicorn with lots of . . . straps."

Unexpectedly, Charlie laughed—a deep honking thing. His dad had always given him grief about it, making him out to sound like an over-caffeinated goose. On the rare occasion when something really struck him as funny, the honk just wouldn't stop and eventually his mom and dad both would be laughing just as hard. He'd miss that.

One hand holding the towel, he picked up the pair of briefs. Striped, colorful, and not a whole lot to them. "Are you kidding me?"

"You're welcome to pick through that drawer over there, but you're not going to find much better than that. Although I did almost choose the tiny pair with Technicolor teddy bears dancing up the straps."

Straps? A fancy jockstrap? "I'll deal with stripes over straps, thanks. The last thing I want to do is go poking through some guy's underwear drawer. I'm starting to get an idea of what this guy is into, and I don't want to go digging any deeper."

"It was an adventure. I did find some little plastic bags with herbs in them. Weird place for herbs."

"Perfect place for *those* kinds of herbs." If he kept liquor in the shower, weed in the underwear drawer wasn't all that strange. Charlie realized he wanted to slip back into the bathroom for another sip.

Meg's confusion was clear and he didn't feel like going into it any further if she was truly that naive about herbs in baggies. While Charlie didn't have any firsthand experience, life in public school had taught him enough. Health class felt like a Nancy Raegan "Just Say No" marathon for an entire six weeks in eighth grade. Charlie was positive that's when most of the stoners got started once they knew what to look for.

Still being a bit of a prude, Charlie took the opportunity to excuse himself to the bathroom. Locking the door behind him, he took a quick nip from the bottle, pulled the clothes on, and another swig. The running shorts were short, the t-shirt tight, and the underwear . . . well, he was trying not to think about where they'd been and prayed to God they were clean. Anyway, it was all a hell of a lot better than Bogart's tent sized cargo shorts.

Bogart. Charlie hoped that kid was all right.

Laying his hand on the knob, Charlie glanced at the bottle one more time, the temptation pulling at him. His head was already swimming and it felt so good, but he was afraid that too much more and he would lose control. He'd been afraid *so much* in the last twenty-four hours, the pain of it all building up, and the few small drinks just . . . helped.

He lingered. And after he lingered he took another deep drink and headed out the door, steadying himself with the wall.

Meg's attention was on the books again, which was great since Charlie wasn't sure how *normal* he was at the moment. He dropped down next to her and saw the first five books of his parents' series displayed on the table in order. Instantly, a pang of regret hit him in the gut. Charlie took the first book in his unsteady hands, a heavy hardback book with some sort of nobleman in vibrant, flowing robes drawn in powerful detail on the dustjacket. According to his dad, the publishers gave his parents grief about the length of the book, said it was too big and would cost too much to print and bind, especially for their maiden publication. James and Harriett had insisted, and as usual, got their way. Ever since then, the publisher hadn't argued with them, because ever since then, they'd been at the top of the *New York Times* bestseller list for months after every release.

All that was dead now.

Emotion threatened to overwhelm him, unexpectedly amplified in his current state, his throat tightened and he had to fight to hold it back. Crying would feel really good, cathartic. But if he started, would he be able to stop?

"Cute shorts." Meg winked. "Nice legs."

Charlie forced a smile and flexed a quad. "I'm starting to feel like I'm just a piece of meat to you."

She grinned like a cat, "Nothing wrong with meat, unless you're a vegetarian." Her voice dropped a little, "I'm not a vegetarian, Charlie."

Did that mean what he thought it meant? Was she coming on to him? Or was he just drunk and she was earnestly talking about meat and vegetables? Even *that* sounded like a come on. Where did he go from here? What was he supposed to do?

She laid her small, cool hand on his knee and his entire body tingled immediately. He wasn't sure if that was normal and didn't care. He liked it. He liked it a lot. Charlie's heart was beating against his rib cage and his hand was begging to hold hers, so he let it. It felt like fumbling at first, but when their fingers intertwined, all was good. Her hand felt so incredibly small in his, and cold. And that tingling sensation he felt before was now a steady buzz giving his booze-buzz a run for its money.

"Hey . . ." Meg narrowed her eyes. "Charlie, what's wrong with you?"

He watched her out of heavily lidded eyes. What should he tell her? Should he tell her about the bottle in the bathroom? Would she be disappointed? Angry? Would she even care? Would she have some too? He sighed, "I don't know. I think I'm just bushed. All the . . . all the stuff we've been, you know, doing . . . and shit." His eyes closed and it felt so good. What had he said? Somewhere disapproving echoes of his parents swirled and warped in the background.

Cool, soft hands nudged him over and he felt his head slide and lay on the armrest of the couch. His long legs were lifted and stretched out, feet dangling over the other end. And before he could put a thank you together, he passed out.

Charlie rubbed his eyes as he woke. The room was dark except for the moonlight. His head throbbed thickly and he realized he was still somewhat drunk, but he had slept well, like he'd been sleeping for ages. Guilt began to wiggle its way into his thoughts. His parents would have been so disappointed in his choices, the indecency. *No*, he told himself firmly, *they don't get to have a say*. Collecting his thoughts, he lay studying the ceiling, following the circling of the fan, his eyes adjusting to the silvery darkness. Sleep had never meant that much to him. He could take a quick nap and feel completely rejuvenated, a thing his parents had always accepted. So nights were always long and he spent most of them on the roof thinking or in the garage lifting weights.

Meg stood by the French doors, her arms crossed under her chest. He unabashedly drank in the back of her. The fit of her shirt, her short shorts, tiny waist and long legs. She was barefoot, tiny feet. They had held hands and if he hadn't passed out, he might have gotten to kiss her. How do you kiss a girl? Well, he hadn't known how to hold one's hand, so he figured the kissing part would come naturally too. The thought of it made him smile. Drunk smile.

"Hey," he mumbled in a rumbling, sleepy bass.

"Sorry," she replied softly, "did I wake you?"

Charlie turned onto his side, pulling the blanket up to his chin. "I guess. I don't care. I don't sleep much."

"Yeah," she said simply.

He wanted to touch her, put his arms around her. Was that too much too soon? Holding her from behind seemed romantic, he could see it in his head and it looked good to him. Would she even want him to? He kind of thought she would, but even these *thoughts* were new territory for him.

"I heard something." Her attention was acutely focused out the window.

Charlie stood unsteadily, the room threatening to lurch and topple him over if he moved too quickly. Definitely still drunk, but not like he had been before. The room and his brain agreed finally and he blinked. He'd had a few too many swigs from that bottle, that much was clear. Next time he'd have to be more careful. Next time. Those words touched off a pang of guilt. *You don't have to feel bad about it*, he told himself. *They're gone. This is you now and you handled it like a champ. No more mysteries. Face things head on. It doesn't matter. You're in charge.*

Approaching the French doors, he positioned himself closer to her than he ever had before, his right-hand brushing against her arm. She was so much shorter than him, he felt like a giant. Thankfully, she didn't seem to mind, or she didn't notice. The latter was worse than the former. Was she feeling the same way about him? He hoped so. The haze of memories last night suggested she had been strongly flirting with him, or had he misinterpreted all of that because he was drunk? Whatever the case may be, the back of his hand was still touching her smooth, cool skin and he liked it. Strange to say, but he felt a rush from the touch. Energized. Was it always like that when a guy touched a girl? If that's what a touch of her skin was like, what would a kiss be like? Or more?

He ran his fingers up her forearm. Her head turned toward it and she sighed, leaning back into him. A couple of hours ago, he might have toppled with her added weight, little as that might be, but he was able to account for it and stay vertical. Taking the cue, he wrapped his arms around and she let them entwine with her own. She was always so cool to the touch, which was great because Charlie was so hot natured.

He dropped his head and rested his lips on the top of her head, inhaling. Flowers and herbs. Reminded him of the garden in the back of his house. In the midst of that Texan flatland, full of dust and brown, his mother had managed to cultivate a lush garden exactly like the ones in her magazines collected on the coffee table. The few ladies his mother had befriended remarked on the explosive colors her green thumb had coaxed from the dust every time they came over for tea.

Willfully, Charlie kissed her on the top of the head, inhaling deeply as he did. Her hands caressed his arms and he responded in kind, feeling the shirt that separated him from her skin. He bent lower and kissed her neck and she tilted to the side to allow it, exposing her shoulder. His body was alive with the rushing energy he felt when he touched her. Was it because more of him was touching her? Was it because it was a longer amount of time? Whatever it was, he wanted more.

Meg stiffened in his arms and it took Charlie a moment to put the pieces together. Just as he was gathering the boldness to slip his fingers under the hem of her shirt, a gate opened on the other side of the pool, the same gate they had snuck through earlier that evening, and a slender silhouette stumbled through.

Someone was home.

And they were *in* the home.

And they shouldn't be.

Charlie instinctively took a step back, more of a wobble, but Meg's small hand grabbed his wrist and held him still. The buzz of energy was pulsing through his veins mixed with his hunger for her and the adrenaline coursing through him from the fear of being caught.

The figure came closer. Last time he saw stumbling figures, his world changed completely. "It's okay, it's not a Shell," she whispered as though he had spoken his fear aloud. Her hushed voice was calm and soothing, her grip on his arm loosened, but she didn't remove it and Charlie didn't mind, he felt like he was gripped by an electric fence. Blinking, he tried to clear his head, but he'd made his choices earlier that evening and was now dealing with the consequences of it. If this came to a fight, he wasn't sure he could defend either of them in his current state.

They both watched as the person maneuvered the pool, knocking into furniture, and swearing and raising a mostly empty bottle threateningly as though the inanimate objects had been the offenders. Charlie could tell the guy was a mess the closer he came. His pale skin almost glowed in the moonlight and was in stark contrast to the tight, black clothes he wore. Short hair spiked in all directions from his head and a chain swung from his hip. Maybe the odds just swung in Charlie's favor, maybe this guy was in a worse spot than he was. If Charlie was putting the pieces together correctly, this was the mess who lived in the pool house.

Behind the skinny guy, the gate opened again and this time *several* stumbling bodies came through, the stumbling bodies Charlie had definitely encountered before. The fear was immediately at war with the pure energy pulsing through him. Meg let his arm go and threw the French door open, the sudden movement causing all stumbling bodies, wasted and decaying, to stop in their tracks.

"What the hell?" the spikey haired guy slurred, his shoulders thrown back, completely unaware of the danger lurking behind him.

Meg ignored him as she swept passed on her way to the Shells. She was pure confidence, no hesitation. The guy swung his bottle at her sloppily, but she was already out of his long, lanky reach. "You take care of *him*, Charlie," she ordered.

"My name's not Charlie, bitch! I'm Spencer!" he said belligerently. "This is my house, bitch! *I'll* take care of Charlie!"

Charlie gathered his focus and forced himself to step out the door and when he did, the guy turned his hazy attention to him. "You Charlie? Charles? Chuck?" The guy raised his bottle to him in a toast, "Charlies are big. Hey, big fella, you gonna man up to me? Huh, you think you can handle all this?" Spencer raised the bottle, and when he did the contents sloshed out. "Shit, man! Look what you made me do now! I'm gonna kick your big, stupid ass!" Charlie's size had always protected him from moments like this. Well, his size and his parents. No one messed with him. It had been that way ever since he was in elementary. Because he was always at least a head taller than the other kids, no one ever messed with him. Mostly. But when the other person was clearly out of his mind, that created an unpredictable situation, and Charlie seriously hated unpredictable.

The skinny guy squatted down, steadying himself, and smashed the bottle on the concrete. He barely made it up again after a couple of staggered attempts, but when he did, he was holding a jagged bottleneck in his left hand. This was getting worse than unpredictable. "Meg! He's got a weapon! Kinda!"

"You can deal with it, Charlie!" He heard her grunt.

Charlie allowed himself to take his eyes off of the immediate danger long enough to see that at least five more Shells had shuffled through the gate and Meg had picked up a pool lounge chair, herding them together. They pressed against her, but she held them at bay.

"I've never fought anyone before!"

"Sucks to be you," the guy slurred and lunged.

"Shit!" Charlie dodged to the side. The guy didn't waste any time and lunged and swung at him again and again, each time Charlie moved reflexively, his adrenaline pumping. They kept this dance up, but something had to change. Charlie caught glances of Meg with the herd of Shells, their arms reaching out passed her to them as though she wasn't even there. She had managed to guide them toward the pool. Everything in him wanted to forget this guy and rescue her. Did she need rescuing?

A flash of pain across Charlie's chest brought him back to his own struggle. He instinctively put a hand to his chest and felt a gash in the shirt and his fingers were slick with blood. Charlie was sobering quickly and panic was starting to take control.

The guy grinned sloppily, "Gotcha, Chuck."

Charlie could feel warm blood dripping down his stomach. This guy was going to *kill* him, or least try to. Skinny guy lunged again and Charlie jumped back, his foot catching on something, and suddenly he was crashing to the ground amid potted plants and pool furniture. With the jagged glass over his head, skinny guy rushed him. Instinctively, Charlie wrapped his big hand around the nearest flower pot and threw it. He watched in slow motion as the clay pot flew through the air, the long greenery like the fiery tail of a missile, and connected with skinny guy's forehead, the pot exploding. Charlie hoped the hit would stop the guy, and it did, but what he didn't expect was that the guy would flop backward and unconsciously plunge into the pool.

Spencer's splash wasn't the only one Charlie heard; one by one, Meg was using the long pool chair to force the Shells to topple into the deep end.

Leaping unsteadily to his feet, his chest searing, Charlie watched as the dark shapes of the Shells who'd been fighting against Meg, now turned their underwater attention to the sinking dark shape that was Spencer and were slowly wading toward him.

As the last Shell fell in, Meg lowered the chair. "Where is he?"

Charlie held one hand to his chest and with the other pointed at the pool.

Meg's eyes widened and she took a small step toward the pool, then back. "You have to get him!"

"He tried to kill me!"

"Get him!"

"With broken glass! He tried to kill me!"

The Shells were walking along the bottom of the pool, not swimming, their advance slowed considerably, and skinny guy had already hit bottom. Charlie could still feel the cold, hard hands pulling and squeezing him in the kitchen that no longer existed. What would they do to the skinny guy?

"Charlie, we *need* him. You have to get him out! Now!"

Charlie dove. Within seconds, he had the guy in his hands and pulled frantically. He wrapped his arms around him and started working his way up, the weight in his arms surprisingly light. Breaking the surface, he lifted the guy and rolled him onto the concrete. Meg stood at a distance, watching with clear concern.

Just as Charlie gripped the side of the pool to lift himself out, a hand gripped his ankle.

And another.

Charlie kicked, but couldn't shake the tight fingers and another hand grabbed his leg further up, the fingers digging into his skin. Panic flared and he opened his mouth to yell, but he was pulled under, his mouth filling with water. Charlie kicked down with his free leg, his foot connecting with what felt like a head. Opening his eyes, he saw the gaunt faces of dead men and women in the eerie underwater moonlight staring back up at him, their eyes empty of life, mouths slack. With everything he had, Charlie kicked back up to the surface, his hands reaching for the edge of the pool and thankfully finding it.

Meg was there, her hands clenched at her chest, "Come on, Charlie, you can do it! I know you can!" With renewed effort, Charlie yanked his leg toward him and shoved it back down with all his strength. His foot caught something solid and he tried again and again, each time connecting with something. The Shells' grips loosed just enough and Charlie pulled free, heaving himself up and out of the pool. Coughing, Charlie rolled over onto his back, gulping in air, the pain across his chest reestablishing itself.

Quietly, Meg stepped to the edge of the pool and looked down, her eyes seemingly taking in all of the Shells, scanning them. A small ball rested in her hand, the ball giving off a faint blue glow. Gently, she tilted her hand and the ball rolled down her fingers and dropped into pool. With effort, Charlie raised himself onto his elbows and looked. The pool, so warm a moment before was now solid ice, the Shells below now grotesque statues.

CHAPTER TEN

A Grande Entrance

Maze ducked into the coffee shop, her heart chugging. Outside, the busy New Yorkers went about their business, not noticing a homeless black girl running from a crazy white boy. After all, this was New York City, a city full of homeless and crazies. No one had time to take note of two more.

Standing in a crowd of people waiting on their lattes and fraps, Maze took a good deep breath to clear her head and slow her heart rate. That boy came out of nowhere. How did she let him get that close? Where'd he even come from?

A pretty NYU sorority girl glanced at her out of the corner of her eye from behind designer sunglasses. Maze cocked her head to the side, the beads on her braids clacking, "What?"

The girl's manicured eyebrows shot up, "What? I didn't—"

"What?" Maze struck her perfect college girl pose, "I didn't . . . I didn't mean to look at the black homeless girl. What? I didn't mean to acknowledge her existence. I didn't . . . I didn't . . . I didn't . . ."

"Hey! Enough!" A big, bald Middle Eastern guy in a green apron shouted from behind the counter. "You going to buy something or just harass the *paying* customers?"

Others were looking at her now and the skinny college girl was emboldened by the big guy's support. She was openly looking at her now, hands on her hips as though she were posing for the fiftieth selfie of the day. Maze looked out the window, the throngs of people walking by. Stupid. She should have kept watching for him out that window. Had he already passed? Did he see her scurry into the overpriced coffee shop and he was now biding his time out there somewhere? Lurking?

Everyone was watching her now.

Ugh. Typical bullshit. "Yeah," she shot back with all the boldness she could muster, though her insides were quivering from the chase, "I'm gonna buy something. I ain't poor. I *got* money." She did too, she did the blind girl trick in Midtown that morning. Tourists always went for that. Tourists were the stupidest. College girls were the next stupidest. At some point, college girls always turned their backs on their purses. The trick was to pick one out who had just started a phone call. Sit down next to her on the bench and when she turns away from you for privacy, slip a hand in the purse and snag her designer wallet. Take the cash and put the wallet back. Don't go for the cards. Cards can be tracked. Coogey always warned her about the cards.

The big man stood behind the register, "What do you want to drink?"

"Man, give me a sec. I'm lookin'." She could look at that wall full of drinks for hours and have no idea what she wanted. Some of her people drank this kind of stuff, but she didn't. Maze could think of better ways to spend her money. What was cheap? "How much is a cup of coffee?"

The man blew out his hipster mustache. "What size?"

"How big do you think I want? Something small. Cheap." Someone nearby snickered. She looked around but couldn't see who it was in the sea of java heads.

"A small coffee is two dollars and fifty-six cents."

"For a lousy cup of coffee? Damn." Again, the hidden laugh. Was it *him*? The guy? Had he slipped in here when she was busy with the white girl? "Just give me the coffee, man." She slipped her purse off her shoulder. *Purse*. Lola said it was luggage. It probably was. Big enough for her clothes and the rest of her things, but the retro floral print was cute. Sassy and practical. Like her. Counting out the change, she regretted it the moment hipster-stache swiped it off the counter in exchange for her lousy cup of coffee.

Maze shoved her way through a few chattering kids with their nanny and maneuvered her way to the counter by the window. Looping her arm in the handles of her purse, she perched herself up on a stool and relaxed. She took a sip of her coffee, it *was* good, better be for two dollars and fifty-six cents, and for just a moment she *felt* good. Just a girl sitting in a coffee shop having a cup of coffee like all the other girls. For a moment, she could pretend that she'd spent her day shopping, having brunch at a cafe in the West Village with the Lo, and now stopping for a cup of coffee before she went home to her studio in Chelsea to get ready for a date tonight. Just for a moment.

"You are *funny.*" Someone pulled out the stool next to her and sat down. Immediately, her defenses went up, they had to. You didn't last long if you're defenses were slow as molasses, Coogey would say. But then she smelled the newcomer and those defenses faltered. Apprehensively, she looked at the man who had just invaded her space. First of all, it wasn't *him*. That was good. But she knew that, because *he* couldn't smell that good. Secondly, this man was gorgeous. Radiantly dark skin, she always had a place in her heart for dark, dark men, and a beautiful face. And he knew it. He gave her a moment to take him in, and just as she was getting used to it, he turned and looked at *her* and her heart caught again. Those eyes. Palest blue. What was this ebony angel doing next to her in a coffee shop at the corner of Washington Square Park?

He laughed, the laugh she'd heard before, he obviously enjoyed the effect he was having on her. Sweet Jesus, his teeth were beautiful too. And still, the smell of his cologne. "Who are you running from?" His voice was rich and velvety.

As best as she could, she turned her attention back to her coffee, "Who says I'm running?"

"You bolted in here like the cops were on your tail. Wait, is that who it is? Is it the cops?"

Maze shook her head, "No, it ain't the cops."

"Isn't."

"Excuse me?"

"Isn't the cops. 'No, it isn't the cops.' You might be street, but you don't have to talk like it." He took a sip of his own drink as his eyes turned to the passersby on the sidewalk outside.

Who the hell *was* this guy? He was nice on the eyes, but it didn't give him a right to correct her like he was her daddy or something. She was about to tell him as much when the *other he* walked by. Maze all but stuck her head in her purse acting like she was looking for something important. Her friendly neighborhood grammar officer caught the signal all too clearly and peered out at the flowing traffic of pedestrians keenly. "Who is it?"

"That dirty lookin' white guy."

"A little more specific?"

"Red hair, scraggly beard and mustache. Green sweatshirt. I think it's green, maybe it's gray." She couldn't remember. Her hands were shaking, rattling the contents of her purse.

"Doesn't matter what color, he's wearing a sweatshirt in Manhattan in August. I see him."

"He lookin' this way?"

The handsome man shook his head, "No, he's pretty fixated ahead of him. Few more seconds and he'll be gone."

Maze took a good long deep breath. Well, as deep as she could doubled-over with her head under the counter. Her boobs were about to suffocate her. Designer Sunglasses chick was watching her curiously. Maze bared her teeth. Give college girls a little crazy and they steer clear. Her glasses are probably Canal Street knock-offs anyway.

"He's gone." Ebony Angel helped her sit back up, his grip strong but gentle. "Are you okay? Is that guy bothering you?"

What could she say? Honestly, he hadn't *done* a thing to her, he just wouldn't leave her alone, kept showing up. "No, not really. He's just around."

"Is he *stalking* you?" This guy seemed earnestly concerned. "You could report him if he is."

"Man, ain't no cop gonna care if some crazy white guy is following a homeless black girl. Oh, I'm sorry," Maze lifted her chin snootily, "An officer of the peace isn't going to mind if a lunatic is casually shadowing a young lady of color without residence."

The guy barked a laugh so loud the whole shop seemed to jump. "You *are* funny."

Maze smiled to herself and took a sip of her coffee, coffee that was losing its heat while this guy was getting hers up.

"Where do you know this guy from?"

Maze shrugged, "I don't really *know* him. He turned up yesterday."

"Turned up where?"

Here it went. "Down by Grand Central."

"A Midtown girl, huh? Those are *my* stomping grounds. You don't look like the type who would put up with the tourists. Wait. Oh, wait." The light turned on in his pale eyes. "You *rook* the tourists, don't you!" At her bashful response, he barked another laugh. "Oh, that's beautiful! What do you use? What's your scam?"

What was it about this guy that pulled her defenses down so easily? She knew what it was, those eyes, that face, that cologne, and the body wasn't bad either. She'd gotten a glimpse of his ass and it was nice. "Blind girl is my best one, but feed-my-babies works pretty well too, 'specially when you put a little groan into it."

He looked at her for a moment, his eyes looking firmly into hers, but not invasively. She liked it. "Tell you what . . .", his hand slipped into a leather messenger bag hanging on the other side of his stool. "Take this," he slipped her a folded piece of paper, "and I'll see you after." Before she could open it, he was up, throwing his bag over his shoulder. "Oh, and here . . ." he slipped his hand in and out of his pocket in a smooth glide and, with a very practiced move, took hers. "I'll see you later." With a quick kiss on the forehead, he released her hand and left the shop, setting his sunglasses in place as he did.

It was a moment after he left when she opened her hand to discover a wad of cash, big-billed cash. If she thought her hands were shakes before, it was nothing compared to the high-octane spasms she was having right now. "Oh my Jesus!"

Taking deep breaths, she unfolded the other piece of paper and out fell a ticket.

Philip de Grande just entered her life.

CHAPTER ELEVEN

Rags to Riches to Rubbish

"I'm telling you, he's a pimp and your big ass is being recruited." Lola was upset and suspicious and had been from the moment Maze blurted out the story at the McDonald's on 9th. Every Thursday they met for lunch at that McDonalds, scratched enough money together for two Happy Meals and let it do its work. The Crazy Cuss Lady was always there swearing at people in line, separating the locals from the tourists or new NYU students. The locals and seasoned students ignored her no matter how in-your-face she got. Tourists and new students, especially sorority bitches, got their shit spooked and usually hit the door pretty fast. Lola shouted back with every inch of her wiry little black frame. She loved it and Maze loved watching her do it.

Two years ago, Maze met Lola at school. The skinny girl was new and sat right next to her in math. A month later and they both dropped out, opting to play in the city instead. Maze's foster mom had no idea what was going on until they got caught by a cop who wrote her up for truancy. She didn't even know what the hell truancy was, but she did then. Her foster mom beat her for it, the charge had cost her money. Fosters hated it when you cost them money. Their own kids were one thing, but *she* was an extra and unnecessary evil. Maze put that foster mom through hell until she kicked her truant ass out.

Lola didn't pull shit like that on her. She was up front and loyal. When Maze turned eighteen in February, she aged out of the system and could do what she wanted. What she wanted didn't include school, that was for damn sure. Coogey had already taught her enough and she started begging and picking full time.

Her best friend dipped a french fry in her little cup of ketchup and popped it in her mouth. "You better listen to me, girl, I have fifth sense about this kind of stuff. He's recruiting you."

"Sixth sense," Maze sipped her tiny Coke.

Lola stopped mid dip. "*Fifth* sense."

Maze laughed from down deep, "You have *five* senses, stupid," she held up a finger for each, "see, smell, taste, touch, hear. Those are your *five* senses. The psychic one is your *sixth* sense," Maze punctuated it by adding the middle finger from her other hand. "So unless you tastin' him recruitin' me, you're usin' your sixth sense. And I wouldn't mind him tastin' me to recruit me," Maze added under her breath.

The other girl just rolled her eyes and crammed another french fry into her mouth. "*You're* stupid. And you're even stupider if you go to that show tonight."

The two slipped into an uncomfortable silence. Lola had pressed her point as far as she would go. That was her way. Say it heavy and leave it. And it usually worked. Usually. But that *money*. That *ticket*. Back at the coffee shop, after she let herself take a breath, she looked at the ticket more closely. Fourth row, center section. Orchestra level. It was perfect. And if she were all dressed up, her hair and nails done, for one night she could just forget and act like she was somethin'.

And she wouldn't have to be on her own the *entire* time.

Looking over her tiny cheeseburger, she caught Lola's eye.

The other lowered her chin. "What?"

Six hours later, after finding the perfect outfits, enjoying manis and pedis, and getting their hair (Maze let go of the dreads and got high-dollar extensions) and makeup did, they were sitting at a very different table in a very different part of the city. A very different table with too many forks and a table full of food she couldn't even pronounce. But it didn't matter. Apparently when you go to a fancy restaurant, you don't get to choose what you eat, the cook does that. Rather, the *chef*. You just get told what you're going to have. And that was fine, because it was all delicious. Lola wouldn't try the fish, said she hated fish, but Maze tried it and loved it. She loved it all.

"Girl," Maze politely wiped her mouth with her napkin like she'd seen white women in movies do, "if I'm being recruited, then I'm all in."

Lola shook her head as she picked another strawberry out of her salad. "This is how they get you. Give you the money, give you the tickets, show you the life, then they *got* you."

"He's an actor, Lo. An *actor*." She took a sip of water. When they first sat down, she had tried to order a bottle of wine, but the waiter carded her and that venture ended quickly.

"You think he makes his living off that? Actors in this city are almost as poor as we are."

"He's a famous one. I seen his face on posters in the subway all the time."

"So what's a famous actor want with you? Huh? You need to get your head outta the clouds and get your poor big black ass back down here on earth."

"She says as she takes a bite of steak worth more than a *year* of Happy Meals."

Lola stopped mid-bite. "Shut up, May."

Maze grinned, "It was fun though, right? Bein' rich for a day?"

Lola, her hair freshly cut short, her eyes bronzed, her lips glossy, smiled back. "It was fun." Then she looked down, searching for something internally. "I'm just . . . scared for you."

Reaching across the table, Maze took her best friend's hand in hers. "I'm a little scared too. I'm scared of all the people in that theatre who might figure out I'm a fake. I'm scared of just trying to get through the door. What if my ticket ain't real? What if it's all a joke, like something you see the mean white kids do to the poor white girl in the movies?" Maze traced the edge of her water glass with a newly painted purple nail, "I'm scared of what he might want after the show." She took a deep breath and let it go, doing her best to smile. "But I'm more scared of not tryin'. What if this is the start of something amazing? What if it is and I don't even try?"

And the rest of their meal was spent a little more superficially. Talking about the food, their clothes. She had to admit, they pulled it off. They looked and acted like they belonged there with all the others. They'd seen enough movies to know *how* to pull it off. *Pretty Woman* had nothing on her. No one gave them a second glance, and when Maze tipped the waiter generously, he escorted them to the door and told them he looked forward to waiting on them in the future.

What if this really was the start of a brand-new life? One of her favorite things to do, something she never even told Lola about, was to walk the streets of the West Village as the sun dipped below the skyline. It was quiet and the homes were old and gorgeous, brownstones that hadn't been cut up into twelve different apartments. At night, she could walk in silence and look through the windows from the other side of the street. Pausing for a moment, she would soak it in and imagine what sort of a life she would have to create to be the woman on the other side of that window enjoying a movie with her husband on the couch and drinking a glass of wine. This evening could be the first step to that life.

Cars raced by as they walked down the sidewalk.

"You make it back to the shelter okay?" Maze reached into her little clutch purse.

Lola grinned drunkenly, not from anything a bottle could hold, it was the euphoria of the whole experience. Lo felt it deep. "Yeah, I'll be good. I'll make sure Rusty has your stuff at the office for you. Get there before midnight and he'll save you a cot."

Maze felt the wad of cash in her pocket and slipped her thumb in it, cutting it in half. She still had plenty of it. "Here," she said quietly as she pressed that half into Lola's hand.

Lola's eyes widened, her breath caught. "Girl . . . I— I can't . . ."

"Shut up and take it." Maze knew just how she felt. Even at half, it was more money than she was ever likely to see. It was a lot. A. Lot. With a struggle, she pressed down those questions that persistently came up from the moment Philip slipped her the cash.

Maze turned and left her friend still struggling for words. "You're welcome, bitch!" she hollered over her shoulder with a smile the likes of which she'd never felt before. That felt good. Real good.

Her heels clicked down the sidewalk to the rhythm of her city.

The audience erupted in applause. Men and women stood around her, calling out their approval for the actors taking their bows on stage. The story, *A Raisin in the Sun*, had been merciless. She got it. The need, the hunger, the passion, the fear, and the drive. Maze got it and it got *her* to the core. From the beginning of the whole thing, she wept. Not just sniffles, nor a tearing up, but body wracking sobbing. She kept it quiet, but it caught the attention of the beautiful Asian woman with golden eyes sitting next to her who slipped her a handkerchief and patted her leg in comfort. By the time Lena Younger clutched her little plant to her breast and walked boldly out of that apartment, the first handkerchief had become accompanied by another from the kind gentleman on the other side of the first handkerchief donor. And so at the end, when everyone around her was standing with praise, Maze didn't trust her legs to hold her up.

As the house emptied, Maze folded the two handkerchiefs in her lap, her kind neighbors urging her to keep them and remember the evening. Philip had been amazing, bringing Walter's pain and need to a gut-wrenching reality. This play had been written for *her*. Glancing at the tear-stained Playbill in her hand, she thanked

Lorraine Hansberry for listening to the Muse who whispered this play to her.

And there it was. That glimmer. Calling to her so softly it was almost missed, but in the quiet of an almost empty theatre, it was clearer. The ultimate message of the play: hope. Every so often, after finishing a book on a park bench, sitting on a subway bench looking at a graffitied Broadway poster, or when standing at a window on the Staten Island Ferry and watching the Statue of Liberty as the boat passed by, she would hear the soft whisper.

Hope.

It was time to go. The ushers were giving her looks. Putting her handkerchiefs in her little clutch, she gathered herself up and headed for the nearest exit. A few patrons were making their way out of the bathrooms, but the foyer was mostly empty, and as she stepped outside, the noise of the city greeted her. The best chance to see Philip would be at the stage exit. How many times had she stood outside those exits waiting to see a celebrity? She had never tried to get close, it didn't feel right since she hadn't spent the money to watch them perform. Not that she *could* spend it. But this time was different. Well, she hadn't spent the money, but she'd had the ticket fair and square. The awaiting crowd was electric, everyone a critic discussing every detail of the performance, their likes, their dislikes. How could anyone have a *dislike*? It was a different crowd from those she had seen outside of musicals. Those people were crazy like they were waiting to see rock stars. That time Daniel Radcliffe had come out of *How to Succeed* was laughable, all those girls falling over themselves. This crowd was eager but smart and calm.

Maze stood at the edge of the crowd. Finally, the stage door opened and several of the actors stepped out. She imagined the actors waited on the other side of the door until there was enough of them to make it less awkward as they passed through their fans. Everyone offered their praise and congratulations, a few of the younger, and older for that matter, women took selfies with their favorites. And those actors soon wandered off down the street to be lost in the crowds of tourists milling about in Times Square. Now the anticipation had grown, the crowd was eager for their star. The stage door opened again and Opal Brannigan, the woman who had played Lena, the brave and compassionate matriarch, came out much to the pleasure of the crowd. Autographs were signed, pictures were taken, and the large woman who seemed much older on stage laughed her way from the crowd to an awaiting car. That sent a third of the hangers-on away, Opal had fulfilled their expectations. The rest, like Maze, were waiting for Philip.

Time passed. Sirens wailed somewhere in the city. The crowd began to thin as anticipation waned. A few of the last patrons grumbled as they surrendered to the fact that Philip would not be coming out that door. Grumbled and complained as though he owed it to them. He had just given them two and half hours of his soul. Maze was indignant as they walked past her, their words of praise now soured to undeserved criticisms.

And it was just as she had resigned *herself* to not seeing him and began walking down the sidewalk, that Philip came around the corner of the theatre. He smiled and any disillusionment that Maze was fighting dissipated. Eyes bright, he embraced her, then held her at arm's length. "What did you think?"

What did she think? About the play? His performance? The hug? His gorgeous eyes? Muscly arms? His ass? Which circling, dreamy thought was he asking about? "It was good." What? *Good*? That was it?

He barked a laugh. "Good? I saw you at curtain call, you were a mess. 'It was good'." He mocked and laughed again. The power from that laugh was intense, invigorating. "Well, *you* look *good*. Quite a change from the girl I had coffee with this afternoon." He said it like the two of them had met up, as though it were an agreed upon event. "You take a stroll down Fifth Avenue and find that dress?"

She laughed too, "Please, I seen *Pretty Woman*. I ain't gonna be looked at like a hooker. I'm a black homeless girl, we have higher expectations."

"*I've seen* Pretty Woman. *I'm not going to* be looked at like that," he said with a touch of irritation in his voice.

"Right," she said with her own heaping scoop of irritation.

Philip grinned, teeth sparkling, "You have to learn to represent yourself better than that."

Represent yourself? Wait, was Lola right? "Represent myself in what?"

That grin was disarming, "In . . . life. Just *life*."

She wanted to accept that, but the seed Lola planted had just been watered. "Mm-hmm."

Philip's voice dropped almost to a whisper, "Do you still have any of that money I gave you, or have you blown through it already?" That last bit delivered a smirk.

"I still have some," Maze said awkwardly, "I know how to shop goo— well. I know how to shop well."

The self-correction earned an approving smile and Maze was irked by how good it felt. "Here." He reached into his pocket and pulled out another roll of cash larger than the first. "I was able to get more. I hope it helps."

Maze's heart leaped into her throat again. What *was* this? It felt bad. Wrong. And it must have been all over her face because he pressed it further. "Just take it. You need it."

She stepped back as though he were waving a knife at her. "I don't need your money. I'm good on my own."

Philip pressed forward. "No, you're not. Look at you."

She smoothed her dress over her curvy, full frame and took a deep breath. "I'm just fine, I'm not gonna be one of your girls."

He flinched as though she slapped him, "One of my girls? You think . . . wait, you think I'm a pimp? That I'm, what, trying to buy you? Employ you? Is that what you think this is?"

"I don't do that. I won't live like that. I'm gonna make a living, but not like *that*." She could feel the dream, the fantasy of the evening crashing all around her. New tears were making their way to the surface and before they broke free and humiliated her, Maze turned and began stomping her way to the lights and sounds of Times Square.

Philip grabbed her arm and yanked her around. "Maze, take the money."

"No!" She swung at his hand and the result was an explosion of cash. Large bills hit the air and fluttered, the gusts from the city picking them up and carrying them away. They were close enough to the main thoroughfare that taxis sent the green cloud swirling down the street to the delight of pedestrians.

Both Philip and Maze were frozen in place. The look on Philip's face was a mix of shock and pain. Why had she done that? Why didn't she just take it?

Because she wouldn't be bought. She *would* become the woman sipping wine on the other side of the brownstone window, but not like that.

Amid the confusion of hands grabbing for fluttering cash, the homeless girl in a pretty costume made her exit from the scene.

Maze ran for blocks through Times Square. '*Ran*'. There was no actual running in Times Square, especially at night. It was a toilet bowl full of all kinds of stank. Whether it was the Comedy Show guys sticking their cards in your face and trashing you if you ignored them, the creepy short stacks in ghetto cartoon character costumes, or the newest addition to the madness, the topless showgirls in body paint, it was all trash. This part of the city and its smell was on the express train to hell.

And she was trapped in it.

Pushing her way through a group of selfie happy tourists, Maze finally made it to a less crowded street where she could move freely. Now that she could think, regret surged forward. She should have just taken the money. It didn't mean she *owed* him anything. If he was stupid enough to hand it over, that was his own dumbass fault. With as much as he was offering, she could take it, jump on a plane, and leave this place behind. Start over. She had always heard that California was nice and Texas was cheap.

Pedestrians thinned out more and more the further west she walked. Tourists didn't care about west of Times Square, especially at this time of night, businesses were closed and sealed off by security gates. This city was home. Well, home for now. Home until she could do something about it. And with that money she could have.

Shit.

"Stop thinking about it," she muttered under her breath, like Crazy Al at the Columbus Circle station. Is that who she was destined to be? Some crazy woman moaning for change on the steps of a subway entrance? Hell no.

Maze crossed Tenth Avenue, the shelter in sight. Lola would be waiting for her and Rusty would have her things in a locker in the office. Everything would just return to normal.

Except *he* was sitting on the stoop, running his shaking hands through his greasy red hair, and in the exact moment she saw him, he turned his head at that weird, crazy ass angle and saw her. In an awkward, jerky motion, he jumped to his feet and began running full speed at her.

"Oh, hell no! Jesus, help me!" she shouted, calling out to the only person she could think might be listening. Kicking off her heels, she turned and ran. Despite her size, she was fast. Always had been. Buildings blurred past her, lights flashed past. All regard for running barefoot through the city and its littered sidewalks was dismissed. It didn't matter. She might step on glass, she might break a toe on uneven pavement, but the threat of whatever this crazy asshole was intending to do to her was putting the hush on reason. Maze was sure he was still behind her even though she couldn't hear him. He never seemed to make a sound, he was just there. Never called out to her. Never said a word. Just followed her with that shifty look in his beady eyes.

Maze had no idea how many times she'd turned, how many streets she'd crossed, she was just praying to whoever might be listening that she was fast enough to get away. Now and then she would think to look over her shoulder, but she was more afraid of running into scaffolding or an enormous pile of garbage heaped on the sidewalk and allowing him the chance to close that much more ground between them.

Shit, this is starting to hurt. Her boobs were bouncing and her feet were slapping the pavement and metal grating, the pain beginning to push through her fear. And despite her strong start, her side was cramping and hurt like hell. Somehow she had to lose him.

With a little extra push, Maze took a fast turn onto 42nd Street, the glitz of the theaters giving her a renewed hope. If she could make it to the Square, she could get to the police station standing like a beacon in the middle of the chaos. And the cops didn't even have to do anything, 'cause they wouldn't. She could just sit and be safe until morning. Everything would be fine in the morning. She chugged on, her side screaming at her, her feet throbbing.

WHAM!

She was flying sideways through the air, everything was slow, buildings whirling and the street and Square passing out of sight. With a muffled crash, she landed in a pile of reeking garbage bags, a heavy weight on top of her. Gulping for air, she was in a daze, the world around her shifting and wobbling. Reality wouldn't steady. Above her, a shape moved.

As her eyes began to cooperate, fear began to flood her. The shape laying on top of her sharpened, two images becoming one. Through greasy red hair, manic eyes stared down at her.

Like a trapped rat, Maze lay paralyzed with fear. The sweating maniac raised a shaking, filthy finger to his lips.

Maze began to cry for the second time that night.

CHAPTER TWELVE

A Grande Explanation

The red-haired man hadn't budged from the moment he tackled her into the alley. His hollow eyes shifted, his breathing heavy, but he kept her pinned in the pile of garbage. It was easy to pick out his stench from the trash engulfing her, and both were enough to make Maze puke. Or was it her fear that made her feel like vomiting? Had he started beating her, choking her, even stabbing her, it wouldn't have been as terrifying. But the guy just lay there on her, holding her arms to her side.

Tears trickled down and dripped onto whatever was beneath her head. How long would this go on? What was he going to do? Maze knew she should at least scream, but she couldn't even figure out how to start, her brain was so screwed up with fear. What if she did start screaming and it provoked him to begin wailing on her? What if she screamed and he slit her throat? It was the what-ifs scaring her the most.

His eyes shifted. His head turned slightly away. Was he waiting for someone? Was this going to be a team up? Would her face plaster the papers as another victim of gang rape? Would she just disappear? Her kind too often just disappeared in this city. No, *people* just disappeared in this city.

"I has her . . ." the red-haired man mumbled.

The fear flared again.

"No, she's okay," he mumbled, "I tried not to hurt her. She was fast."

Maze did her best to look around, see the person he was talking to, but with the man on top of her and garbage bags piled around her, she couldn't see anything. She couldn't even *hear* the other one.

Was there actually someone else or was this insanity? *Oh, shit. He's a schizo.*

New tears surfaced.

And then in a rush and a shriek, the man was lifted into the air and disappeared. Maze, still addled by fear, struggled to figure out what had just happened and even more to decide whether moving was in her best interest. Like a turtle on its back, she pushed and fought to get out of the heap of trash and when she did, she saw why the man flew off. The red-haired man was pinned against the nearby brick wall by the throat, eyes bulging and mouth working in an attempt to breathe. Her liberator held the man inches off the ground with one hand, and by the cut of his clothes . . . and his ass, she knew exactly who it was. Philip held the man, strangling him to the death.

Immediately, a fight awoke within Maze. On the one hand, the greasy man who had been following her for several days now was being dealt with. She could slip away and, by the looks of it, never be bothered by him again. Then there was the other side. A man, a person was being hurt and it was because of her. He wasn't just being hurt, he was going to die. Philip, solid as a statue in Central Park, held the man firmly despite his kicks and thrashing. All she had to do was walk away.

She couldn't.

As the red-haired man's body fell still, Maze shook Philip's free arm, "Hey man, you're killing him! You gotta stop!"

Philip's face turned to her, his eyes distant and void of the life she had seen so beautifully on stage earlier that evening. Did he even see her? Where was he? She pulled on his arm again, pleading, "You have to stop! He's gonna die! You can't kill him!" Nothing.

Something on the ground brushed by her feet and Philip's eyes flashed to life, sudden explosive life. Yelling profanities, Philip dropped the man's limp body to the ground and grabbed his ankle. Maze fell back against a dumpster. Philip raised his hand and in the moonlight, she could see the wet glisten of blood. "What happened?"

"Something bit me!" he hissed. "Something bit me on the back of my ankle. And I swear if my shoes are ruined, I'll skin it for new ones!"

Maze turned her attention to the ground and the trash bags around them, but the target of their search wasn't *there*, it was perched on the still body of the red-haired man. She screamed. A rat, a large rat even for New York City standards, sat on the man's chest, nudging his cheek with his pink twitching nose, it's tail lashing back and forth. "Holy Daughter of Idris," Philip swore, "that's . . ." and then he was on his knees beside the boy, feeling for a pulse despite the snarls of the rodent. "I didn't know! You have to believe me; I just didn't know! It didn't look anything like him. He was a baby last time I saw him. A very small, bald baby."

The unconscious man coughed and both man and beast appeared to relax. The large rat gently placed its paws on the red-haired man's chin and peered at him with beady eyes. Philip stood, favoring his bitten foot. "Come on, help me get him up." He didn't look at her, but Maze knew he was talking to her.

"I'm not going anywhere near him or *that*," she said with a nod to the rat.

"Mazonne Marie Archambeau, help me get him up. Enough is enough. The games are over."

No one had called her by her full name her entire life.

She helped.

The red-haired man wasn't a man at all, he was a boy. He might have been seventeen, but sixteen was more likely. Time hadn't been kind to this . . . kid. It had been a struggle to get him to Philip's apartment. Three cabs had passed them, probably assuming he was wasted and didn't want to risk cleaning up puke in their backseat.

Finally, one pulled over and Philip convinced the driver their friend was in need of his meds and wouldn't be a problem. With the flash of a few extra presidents, the cabbie relented and the three, with a rat hidden in the boy's sweatshirt, slid into the backseat.

Philip's apartment was a condo in a building on the south side of Central Park. Maze had watched them build this new skyscraper and always wondered what kind of person would live here. Now she knew. She also knew she should have taken that money because Philip de Grande wasn't hurting. Philip went to work attending the boy like he was a trained nurse. Before she knew it, he was clean enough and resting peacefully in a sleekly decorated guest room, the rat standing watch on the nightstand.

The entire apartment was sleek. White, clean, rich, and sleek. She flopped down on the sofa. Maze always thought that rich people stuff looked uncomfortable and now she knew it for a fact. It looked like it was made out of white wood and it felt the same way. A tea pot whistled on the stove and Philip slid into the room, now wearing a pair of comfortable looking loose white pants and pulling on an equally comfortable looking light t-shirt. But not before she noticed the scars. Dark lines crossing his lean chest and torso. Where had those come from?

"Tea?" Philip gracefully prepared a cup for himself.

"No, thanks." The look he gave her suggested that her answer had been wrong. But as soon as it had come, it dissipated.

"You'll need to learn."

"Learn what?"

"Too much." A little cream. A leaf of some sort. "How long has Adelaide been dead?"

"Who?"

"Adelaide. Pretty woman. Beautiful eyes. Thick white hair."

"I don't know no Adelaides."

He rolled his eyes. "You don't know *any* Adelaides?" The graceful man took a deep breath and a sip of his tea, the saucer held gently in one hand, the cup in the other. "Ad? Addie? Adele?"

"Wait, Addie? Scrawny sister at the welfare office?" Maze remembered *her*. Always worked Maze in between other people, pried into her business. Lola said she didn't do that to her. She was nice enough, except for where it mattered. Woman never could get her with folks of her own, not even into a decent foster home. Kids with way more problems than her found homes, but Maze could never get a break and she always had the suspicion it was Addie's doing.

"Adelaide wasn't scrawny. She was *lithe*."

Maze couldn't hold back a laugh. "Then you hadn't seen her in a *long* ass time. That girl needed a sandwich and a helping of fries. And a shake. And that hair. Lord, those thick dreads and thicker glasses. She was somethin'."

"Was?"

Maze took a deep breath and let it out, "Something happened to her. About a year ago. Two? Yeah, two years ago, I was still in a home."

"What happened to her?" Philip's eyes were locked on her.

"I don't know for sure. Somebody said she was jumped near her apartment in the Bronx. Like I said, I don't know for sure. I knew her, but I didn't really *know* her. You know?"

Philip held her in his gaze, she felt like she was being watched by some crazy person on a subway train. Except you knew that most of those crazy people weren't really looking at you, just looking toward you. What they were actually seeing was somewhere else and that might have been the case now. Had she traded one crazy for a sleeker, nicer model of crazy? "Mazonne, we have a lot to talk about."

"Call me Maze."

He took a seat in a high backed white chair, a king on his throne. "I'll call you *Mazonne*."

"Listen," she sat up straight and it was her turn to lock eyes on him, "I been puttin' up with your shit since I ran into you at the coffee shop."

"You think—"

She threw up a hand, "Ah, ah, ah, ah! You hush. You been throwin' your money at me, show tickets, and then you straight up throw more money at me before you tackle that dude in the alley and choke him out. I been puttin' up with your crazy. I'll tell you when you can call me Mazonne, which, by the way, will be hella never. It's a shitty ass name." She crossed her arms and leaned back into the uncomfortable sofa. "I'm Maze, damn it. And if you correct anything I said, I will pick your skinny but nicely tight ass up and throw it through that window."

He smiled.

She boiled. "Are you—?"

"You are just like your mother." He sipped his tea.

And she was silent. Words had never failed her before, but they surely abandoned her now.

"Interested in listening now, *Maze?*"

She was.

He considered her for a moment. Maybe trying to decide where to start?

"You're one of the Six. Six babies smuggled out of our world, the First. That boy in there? He's another. There are four others and we have to find them because all of this is going down much earlier than any of us thought."

CHAPTER THIRTEEN

The Spirit of the Bronx

Philip stood out in the Bronx no matter how hard he tried not to. People didn't wear designer shoes in this part of the Bronx, they sold knockoffs of them. And on this block, they sold them after they had pulled them off a body. Maze followed Philip at a generous distance, he wore his hat pulled low and his designer shoes clicking on the sidewalk, announcing to anyone in earshot that this fool didn't belong here.

"You're gonna get jumped if you keep pulling that phone out."

Philip tucked it back into his pocket, "How else am I going to know where we're going?"

"You figure that out while you're still on the train, get it in your head. Pullin' your phone out like that is gonna get you jumped. Well, the phone *and* the shoes. And the hat. That hat is a dead giveaway."

She wanted him to toss it into the next trash can, he only pulled it lower.

Streets like this were nothing to Maze. This was how she'd grown up. Don't use your back pockets. Don't walk too closely to alleys as you pass. Don't make too much eye contact, but don't avoid it. Coogey taught her well, but she clearly forgot the alley rule last night.

Blocks like this weren't too scary in the morning. Most people who were up to no good were asleep until late in the morning. They'd been up all night getting into trouble and were now trying to sleep it off or lay low. Maze always turned in early and got busy with life, or what *she* called life, when the sun came up.

Philip came to a stop in front of a building just as ugly as the rest. He took the stoop two steps at a time, settling into business mode with a shrug of his shoulders and neck pop, but stopped short at the callbox outside the front door. Twice he looked ready to press a button, then faltered.

"No doorman here, Mr. de Grande. In these parts, we push our own callbox buttons. What's your problem?" Maze asked.

"The numbers are . . . uh . . . well, they're not . . ." the slick man was perplexed.

Maze nudged him out of the way. The callbox had their usual two rows of buttons with little slots next to each one for apartment numbers and names. However, only a couple of the buttons had any sort of identification and those had been scratched out with something illegible written over it. Maze thought for a moment, then boldly pressed one that looked as though the word *daddy* was visible under the scribble.

Philip's eyes grew. "What are you doing?"

"Just how long you wanna stand out here?"

A click. A groggy voice, "What?"

Maze took a deep breath, "It's me, baby, let me in."

"Who this?"

Maze planted her fists on her curvy hips, "My feet hurt and I'm hungry, you open that damn door!"

They waited. Philip chewed his thumb nail. Maze's heart was picking up pace. Her cool on the outside was only skin deep.

The door buzzed and clicked. She let out the breath she hadn't realized she was holding. "You shouldn't bite your nails, it's nasty. You can get butt worms." Pushing past the stunned man in fancy ass shoes, she opened the door before their moment had passed.

The two stood in the cramped entryway of the apartment building. Dying fluorescent lights flickered over mailboxes crammed with ignored communications. Coupons, fliers, 'final notice' bills, porno mags. Maze shook her head. Who still ordered those things? Everyone knew pervs could get their kicks online and the magazine business was in a pinch. But these poor pervs probably didn't have the internet. Nasty.

"This where Addie lived? Smells like . . . like . . . hell, I ain't never smelled somethin' this bad. Crazy white boy smelled better than this."

Philip drew an annoyed breath.

Maze held up a finger, "Don't you do it, damn it. I talk how I wanna talk."

He let the breath go and ran a hand over his face. "Apartment number 701."

Now it was Maze's turn to take in a breath. What the hell? The seventh floor? Really? "Old lady didn't get jumped, she died from climbing seven floors every day."

Philip stretched like he was about to go for his daily run through Central Park. He looked like the type who would do that. Tiny little running shorts, expensive running shoes. Yeah, he was that type. "Come on, let's go up," he said confidently and started taking the steps two at a time.

"Shit," Maze huffed and started up *not* two steps at a time.

Pulling herself up to the fourth floor, she was sure she was going to die. "What—" she took a deep breath. Gulped. "What do you think we're gonna find?"

Philip wasn't even breathing deeply or sweating. She was doing both. "Something to help us out," he said with a shrug.

"Like what?"

He rubbed his strong chin, "Like something useful."

"Every time you open your mouth I feel less and less confident in you. You make a good sugar daddy, but you ain't worth shit as anything else."

He grinned wryly, "Adelaide used to say the same thing."

"Then it looks like we lost the wrong one." Maze took a deep breath and flung a hand at the stairs leading up, "Come on, let's get this done with."

Climbing those damn steps was the worst. And why was that? She walked the streets of New York City day in and day out. She was a curvy girl, but she wasn't big. *Mostly*, she wasn't big. She was bigger than Lola, but that was Lola, she was a twig.

Fifth floor.

The flights of stairs had to be growing longer and she was positive gravity was fighting against her more than usual. Her feet felt heavy. It was three in the morning and she was climbing to the top of the damn Empire State Building.

Sixth floor.

One more.

Philip stood at the top with his hands on his narrow hips.

"What? Go on up," Maze waved a hand at him, "I've got momentum."

He cocked a pretty eyebrow and stepped to the side.

It was a wall. "What the hell?" Maze turned around expecting to see another stairwell leading to the seventh floor. Some of these old buildings, especially the pre-war buildings, were pieced together and unpredictable. But there wasn't another stairwell. 601. 602. 603. 604. 605. 606. "You sure you got the apartment number right?"

Philip pulled the yellowed slip of paper from his pocket, "701."

"There ain't no 701. There ain't no *seventh* floor! What the hell, man? Did you take us to the wrong building?"

"*You* brought us here!"

"'Cause you gave me this address!"

Philip crossed his arms and looked around, "Maybe we should ask someone."

Maze's eyes went wide, "Are you insane or just stupid? You go knockin' on one of these doors and we could get popped right here!

And the cops would say we had it comin' if they even bothered to show up!" She threw herself against the wall next to the stairs, the place where stairs should keep going up to the ain't-there seventh floor, and as she leaned into it, she felt as though she were melting into a thick wall of butter. Losing her balance, she kept sinking, Philip's face reflecting the shock that must've been painted all over her own. She felt out of control, like a kid who'd been warned not to lean back in her chair and then chair cruelly betrays her. The *butter* got thinner and thinner until she was moving full force to the ground where her ass found the first step and the back of her head found another. Her head rang and she rolled onto her side. "What the hell just happened?" she moaned.

"You just found the stairs, Maze. Good girl." Philip climbed a few stairs and helped her to her feet sending her head into another round of throbbing.

Maze balanced herself on the railing and squeezed her eyes shut, "Why couldn't we see them before?"

"Good old Adelaide must've hidden them."

"With what, like magic?"

Philip barked a laugh, "Yeah, 'like magic'. Oh, Mazonne, you have so much to learn."

The stairwell hidden beyond the wall was dark and only became more so once Philip stepped through the hole and it closed up behind him. Maze let her eyes adjust to the darkness before she started climbing the stairs behind Philip who had stepped in front of her cautiously. It only took a couple of steps up before soft, lavender lights began to flicker to life in sconces previously unseen in the darkness. The sconces themselves looked like they were from another world, polished silver seashells curving up around a bulb that was very clearly not from the drugstore down the street. As more light spilled into the stairwell, it was obvious this part of the building had been safeguarded from the rest of it. The walls were clean and clear of graffiti and the air didn't reek of piss, booze, and weed. Someone had taken good care of it.

When Maze stepped onto the seventh floor, her breath caught. Unlike the other six floors, there was only one door to one apartment, and on either side of it were sculpted sconces like tentacled sea creatures, but these didn't hold bulbs. As soon as Maze had set foot on the floor, flames leaped from the mouths of the creatures, the color of the fire a bright aqua blue. Maze pursed her lips, "Bitch must have liked the ocean."

"Honor the dead, Mazonne," Philip warned.

Maze raised an eyebrow, "What she gonna do?"

"Honor the dead."

Philip stepped up to the door and tried the crystal knob. It turned and the door swung open.

"No wonder she dead, leavin' her door unlocked like that. She had it comin'."

Philip glared at her.

"Okay. *Honorably,* she had it comin'."

The interior of the apartment lit immediately, just like the hall. Warm light mixed with more of the bright blue flames bathing the room. And it was quite a room. The ceilings were like nothing she had seen in any apartment in this part of the Bronx. Crown molding carved like ocean waves wrapped around the large living room and in the moving firelight, they seemed to heave to and fro like the tide. Books covered shelves and tables and stood in stacks in every corner of the room. And between books were all sorts of strange knickknacks; skeletons Maze didn't recognize, contraptions made from shells and bronze, jars with dried plants and jars with preserved creatures. And the furniture, it was gorgeous and opulent. Who had this woman been?

Maze was about to crack a joke about it all when the look on Philip's face stopped her. He stood in the middle of the room, tears trickling down his cheeks. Quietly, he pulled a handkerchief from his pocket and touched it to his nose, folded it, then smoothly returned it. He took a deep breath and let it go evenly but with effort. "This was Adelaide, Maze. *This* was Adelaide." The man acted like he was in church.

But church was about to get wild. A book flew across the room and caught him on the side of the head, throwing Philip into a nearby chair. "What the hell?" he yelled, holding the side of his head.

Maze's eyes went wide.

Another book launched at Philip from the other side of the room, but the pretty man had time to duck. Maze threw herself behind the sofa as three more books rose from their places around the room and took aim at Philip, one catching him in the shoulder. Then all hell broke loose. Books floated into the air, one by one joining a tornado of movement around the opulent room. Philip dove underneath the sofa Maze was hiding behind.

"You think I can't get you under there?" a woman's voice cried out from everywhere and nowhere. "I've been waiting for this moment for the better part of the last two years, you son of a bitch!" A few books broke free from the swirling storm and zoomed along the floor, catching Philip in the balls and forehead. He doubled in on himself with a groan.

"Adelaide?" Philip grunted feebly over the flurry of pages. "Is that you?"

"Adelaide?" Maze shouted, "I thought she was dead?"

"I am!"

The tongues of blue flames stretched from the sconces on the wall and swirled counter to the books, the light dodging around the debris. Tighter and tighter the aqua light spun into the center of the gale then stretched up and down until, little by little, it took the form of a spinning woman, a woman Maze recognized from many visits to the social services building in Brooklyn. There, hovering in the middle of a tornado of old books, was the blue form of Ms. Addie in her large glasses, full dreadlocks pulled back and hanging down to her waist, and that chunky, clacking jewelry.

The books came to a sudden halt and hung in the air. Addie cocked her head to the side and gave a small flick of her wrist causing the sofa to fling into the air, exposing both Philip and Maze. Maze was ninety-nine percent sure *she* was safe but didn't want to draw any attention to herself by making any sudden moves, although every bit of her was screaming to run across the room to the door and get the hell out of the Bronx. It was her usual reaction to the Bronx anyway.

"Stand up, traitor," Adelaide boomed. "Get up!"

Philip did as he was told without protest, though Maze could see he was still in a good amount of pain from the book to the balls.

"I'm dead because of *you*."

"I didn't know you were—"

The woman, still a shape cast in light, flared brighter momentarily. "You didn't know because you didn't give a good goddamn about anyone else but your own damn self, you worthless little bitch."

"Adelaide, please—", Philip took a pleading step forward, but Addie would have none of it. A book flew from its place and caught him squarely in the back of the head, sending him to his knees.

"You stepped into this world and disappeared. Lured by its lights and wealth. You had a responsibility, Philip, to the girl and to me. You failed, Philip. You failed so damn miserably."

Philip stood to his feet quickly, if not wobbly, "That's not fair, Adelaide! I found the girl! I'm taking care of her now!"

Adelaide swooped in inches from his face. "And why is that? Sudden guilt? Shame?"

Philip took a measured breath, "Because I was approached two days ago by someone wanting to . . . purchase her whereabouts."

Maze, who hadn't been able to move from her place on the floor, was suddenly on her feet. "Wait, what? Me? Why?"

Both Philip and Addie turned their attention to her, but neither said anything, it felt like they were measuring, weighing her. "Uh, hello? I want to know."

Addie's ghost crossed her arms and the room began to clean itself up, like that scene in Mary Poppins. Books returned to their places, the sofa slipped back down to its place, the fireplace returned to a normal color and crackling. Addie drifted to a large armchair and settled herself onto it, if such a thing were possible for a ghost. "You two make yourselves comfortable. Tea?" The change in tone was obvious.

Philip said cautiously, "Yes, please."

"Tea, baby doll?"

Maze was about to answer no when Addie answered for her, "Of course you do."

"I really don't want any."

Addie clucked, "You'll need to learn."

A tea pot hovered to the fire and situated itself onto a hook while bags slipped into cups waiting on saucers. Now she thought about that scene in *Sword in the Stone* when Merlin's house shit would prance around like it was alive. One of her fosters was sick on Disney. Maze hoped Addie was controlling the stuff moving around and that she wasn't surrounded by furniture and knickknacks that could move on their own like that one with the white girl and hunky beast. The thought of sitting on a sofa that might have an opinion about her weight was unsettling.

"Why are you still standing? Sit down, baby doll."

Maze settled herself onto the other end of the sofa from Philip, apologizing to the sofa in her head as she did so, giving plenty of space in case more books, or something more lethal, flung themselves at the man who had so royally pissed off the blue ghost.

Addie's image came into focus more and more the longer she sat in one place. The ghostly woman eyed both of them through her large glasses making Maze wonder if she really needed the glasses as a ghost or if it was just part of the look.

Philip was the first one to speak. "You've been here for two years?"

Addie narrowed her eyes at him. "Yes, no thanks to you. I'm confined to my sanctuary, well, to an Anchor I had planted here. I was afraid of something like this happening, so I tied my spirit to an item in *here* in case I was killed out *there*."

"How'd it happen?" Maze heard herself asking before she thought the words through.

Addie rolled her magnified eyes, "Baby doll, I have no idea. One minute I was walking home with groceries ready to watch celebrities dance on TV and the next I was being pulled through the air and plopped down here. Never saw who did it, never even felt it. Just *dead*. I spent the first year of my death trying to figure it all out and the second year fretting that you were next."

"I'm sorry," Philip muttered.

The ghost eyed him, "Mm-hmm. Who approached you?"

Philip shook his head, "It was in a letter brought by courier. No name, no address."

The tea pot whistled then helped itself to the awaiting cups.

"When?"

"Couple of weeks ago, I was in my dressing room getting ready for the performance. It was typed. No name, no address."

"You said that," the ghost chided. "How were you supposed to respond to the anonymous letter?"

Philip shrugged, "I don't know. It was a nonissue. I wasn't going to be giving her up, so it didn't matter."

Something in Maze's stomach tightened and her eyes met with the glowing eyes of Addie, "And that's when you started looking for me?"

The man spread his hands, "Exactly. And I found you! So it's all good."

"Shit," Addie hissed. She zipped into the air and over to a window.

Philip jumped to his feet, "You think they followed us here?"

"That's exactly what I think." Addie studied the street below. "I don't see anybody, but that doesn't mean a damn thing. They've probably got eyes on your apartment, Philip, so you can't go back there for now. At least you're here. I can keep you safe while we figure out what to do next."

"What about rat boy?" Maze blurted out.

Philip swore under his breath.

Addie turned on them both, "Who?"

"The Speaker, Stephen," Philip sighed, "he's at my apartment."

"Why is he *there*?" Addie demanded. "Why isn't he *here*?"

"Philip laid him out cold 'cause he was attacking me."

"I didn't mean . . . I didn't know it was him. He was on her, had been following her and he jumped her earlier tonight. I thought he was just some crazy white guy and I knocked him out."

Addie's light grew with her anger and a few nearby books began to shift, "And you just left him there by himself?"

"He ain't by himself," Maze offered, "There's a rat with him."

"Jacob," Addie sighed. "So whoever sent you that letter could still get their hands on one of the Six." Addie floated within inches of Philip's face. "You neglect your duties, you let me die, and you basically hand one of the Six into the hands of some invisible threat. I see why *I* was killed now."

"Why," Philip mumbled dejectedly.

"Because *I* was a threat. You're just a *tool*."

CHAPTER FOURTEEN

Naked, Clean, Full, and Sleepy

Right hand.
One.
Two.
Three.
Four.
Five.
Left hand.
One.
Two.
Three.
Four.
Five.
Right foot.
Left foot.
Penis.
Right butt cheek.
Left butt cheek.
Chin.
Nose.
Tongue.
Right ear.

Left ear. No. He still couldn't make that one move. Left ear. Left ear, wiggle. Nothing.

Right eye open.

Left eye open.

Darkness.

Breathe in and out. Breathe in and out. Breathe in and out. Sniff. Cough. Sit up.

Stephen sat up in the soft bed and the room took a moment to catch up with hisself. But not too long. Not as long as the other day. That was good.

The sheets were soft. Softer than those at the home. They felt good on his skin. All over. He looked down. He was naked. Naked in bed. And so skinny. He could see all of his ribs. So skinny and still dirty. Very dirty. Too dirty. He wasn't supposed to be this dirty. They would have made hisself clean hisself if he was still with them. But he wasn't with them. He hadn't been with them for . . . how long? Since the other day.

And it was so quiet. He sat for a moment. Naked in the bed. Dirty. He felt his face. Scruffy. No, not scruffy. He pulled at it. It was a beard now. Hair on his face. Hair on his chest. Hair everywhere. They had made hisself cut the hairs on his face, but not bald. But not since the other day. And it was a beard now? He could pull at it. It must be a beard.

Slow, he moved out of the bed and stood to his feet. Slow. If he did it slow, the dizzy wouldn't know as much and would leave hisself alone. Slow, he stood all the way up. His toes liked the fuzzy rug. They crinkled in it. Soft sheets. Fuzzy rug. Beard. Quiet. Naked in his bed.

Alone.

"Hello?"

Dark in the room, but he could see good. They never knew that, but he did. He looked around hisself. Nothing. Empty room with pictures of lines and splatters of black paint on white paint. Big bed with dirty white sheets. His fault. Big windows with long curtains. Door shut. Hard floor with big fuzzy rug.

"Hello?"

Quiet.

He walked naked to the door and opened it. Big room. Couch. Table. Windows with long curtains. White. Very empty. Pictures of lines and splatters.

No one here.

He walked naked to the kitchen. Hard counters. Silver things that cooked. Refrigerator?

He opened the big door. Light. Bright. Food. Lots of food. Vegetables. Fruit. Raw meat. Milk. Juice. Cheese. He reached for the vegetables. Celery? He saw his fingers. Filthy. Nails long. Dirty.

"Clean before you eat or you *don't* eat," he heard her say in there. She wasn't there, but he heard her. He heard her a lot.

"Hello?"

Nothing. She wasn't there, but he heard her a lot.

He walked naked back to the bedroom. To the bathroom. He turned on the light even though he didn't need to. "It's what people do," she said. She wasn't there, but he heard her a lot. But the light was on now because that's what people do.

And now he saw hisself in the mirror. All of hisself. His naked self. His skinny, naked, dirty self. He touched his bones on his side. His bones at his hips stuck out too. Too far. Too much bones. He touched his hair on his chest. Orange. All of it orange. Orange like the hair on his face. His beard. Was that a beard? It was down his neck too. On his arms. His legs. Just like the hair on his head, except for the one place all over the left side of his head that was white. White like snow on the cartoons. All white on the left side of his head where his ear was that wouldn't wiggle.

Left ear. Wiggle. No.

He was too dirty. He could smell himself. Strong smell. Like cheese. It was good. If he smelled bad, the person in the dark wouldn't do that to him. But he couldn't smell bad for long because she would make him wash hisself. Then the person in the dark would be there.

He took a long breath. In. Out. He was by hisself. No one. No one since the other day.

If he washed, he could eat. And there was lots to eat. And if he ate, the bones would go away and he would get big.

The water felt good running over his body. His naked body. His hairy body. Made his thoughts quiet. Stilled his hands. His shaking hands. They were shaking again. Not all the time, but right now they were.

"Moi . . .moisturi . . .zing. Moisturizing. Body. Guh-el? Moisturizing body guh-el?" He didn't read good. It was okay. He did other things good. Things in the dark. He heard good. He saw good. He hid good.

The moisturizing body guh-el smelled pretty and made his skin tingle funny. He used it all over. He used it all over until the heavy bottle was empty. "You wasteful idiot, you've used up your ration and someone else's," she said.

"Hello?" his voice echoed in the big glass shower.

She wasn't there.

Neither was the person in the dark because the lights were on.

"Mint sham . . . poo. Mint shampoo. Hair. This is for hair," his voice echoed again. He covered hisself in it and it tingled too. Tingled more that the guh-el. She wasn't there to get mad. To hit. He liked the tingle more than the hit.

"Hello?"

No one.

Stepping out of the shower, he walked naked and dripping in front of the big mirror again. Clean. Clean all over. Fingernails. Long. Too long. He opened drawers and found many things. Brushes. Razors. Clippers for hair. Cream for shaving. Fingernail clippers. Deodorant. Lotions.

With calming shakes, he clipped his nails. Hands and feet. With calmer hands, he put on deodorant. With calm, still hands, he shaved his neck and cut the hairs on his beard smaller. He combed his hair and lotioned his face.

He put the things away and wiped up the water on the floor, she had taught hisself that and he knew it was good. "Put things back the way you found them. You might be sick, but you can clean up," she said.

"Hello?" he said softly.

Nothing.

He was alone. Now that he was clean, he had to stay in the light so the person in the dark wouldn't find hisself. He took a deep breath and let it go. In. Out. Quiet. The lights are on. The person in the dark is not here. Not since the other day.

He walked naked and clean to the kitchen. He opened the refrigerator and started to eat. He started with the vegetables and ate his way through most of the fruit. He gulped down juice and water. Five bottles of water. He ate cheese of all tastes. Smooth. Crumbly. Sharp. Mild. No meat. He didn't want the meat. Cooked or not cooked, he didn't want it.

Looking down, his belly was full and sticking out. He could still see the bumps of the muscles under his skin, but his belly was sticking out now. He patted his belly. Happy belly.

He cleaned up after hisself and walked to the bedroom naked and clean and full. He pulled off the dirty bed sheets and put them away in the basket in the bathroom. He found clean bed coverings in the bathroom closet and made the bed. "Put them on straight and right, or do it again," she said.

"Hello?" he muttered.

No one.

He crawled into the bed naked, clean, full, and sleepy. He fell asleep with the lights on so that the person in the dark couldn't find hisself.

CHAPTER FIFTEEN

The Warriors of Dree

Hedy hopped down out of her parents' RV into the ankle length green grass and took a deep breath. An almost sugary sweet scent met her, accompanied by bird song and a lovely breeze. The girl adjusted her full, long skirts and shifted her bodice, aware of the daggers hidden in just the right places, and headed toward the chain link gate. Passing row upon row of RVs, she knew most of her friends were still sleeping off the night. That was one perk of being a teetotaler, she never had to worry about the day after and fear the sight of the sun. Her Pap was the worst of them all, standing on the table, stein in hand, bellowing one of his songs, but they all egged him on, especially her Mam. Smiling to herself, she knew she wouldn't have it any other way.

"Top of the morning, Hedy!" Old Millie called from an open RV door, pipe smoke curling out in clouds.

"Morning, Mil!" Hedy waved.

Hedy stumped on toward the back gate, a couple of big mastiffs barking their own greeting, their big heads poking through Millie's door. She had been terrified of those brutes for years until they got off their chain one day and instead of devouring her, they covered her in slobbery kisses. Now she considered Polly and Brutus two of her best pals.

Three final steps and she laid her hand on the chain link gate at the back of the property, the hardware that separated her two homes. With a push and one short step through, she was transported to another world, the Cougan County Renaissance Faire. Breaking through the trees that masked the RV parking lot full of merchants' and entertainers' homes, Hedy felt the same thrill she felt every day when she entered the faire grounds and it didn't matter which faire or which state she was in, the rush was always the same, rain or shine. Oh, the layout varied from grounds to grounds, but the faces were always the same with a few adjustments here and there. Not everyone traveled the circuit year-round, some preferred to stay north or south, or some swore they wouldn't pass Kansas one way or the other. But her Pap and Mam had been following the circuit ever since she could remember and she wouldn't have it any other way. Especially being the way she was.

She was a little person. Proudly. And while she was sure she would wear the same badge of honor no matter where she was, within the faire circuit she was a bad ass and proved it every weekend at 10:00, 12:00, 2:00 and 4:00. The *Warriors of Dree* was the most popular show at every stop. Their skills with blades, long and short, one-handed or two, melee or thrown, couldn't be rivaled. At every stop, there would be audience members who clearly hadn't seen their act. The three of them would take the stage, she and Mam in their colorful bulky skirts and Pap in his leather breeches and high boots, and inevitably someone would bark a laugh. Truthfully? That sort of a reaction used to be painful, angering, but come the end of the performance, every patron was clapping wildly and the tip hat overflowed. This was truly what she wouldn't have any other way.

"They only see what they want to see, Hedy," her Pap would say over a foamy stein of beer. "It's up to us to help them *interpret* what they see the proper way."

Many of the faire grounds had permanent buildings designed to look like something out of a fanciful medieval village. The Cougan County faire ground in Oregon was one such place and it was Hedy's favorite. Whoever had designed it had poured quite a bit of cash into the cozy, faux hamlet and the county worked at keeping it clean and in good repair. Every now and then, the faire's corporate arm would have another building or three created expanding the territory and imagination. What had once been a small collection of plaster and stucco huts was now a sprawling village with three taverns, several stages, and more storefronts than a mall. Hedy found it easy to disappear into another time and realm when she walked the streets of the Cougan County Renaissance Faire.

It was only three years ago Hedy understood there was a business to the faire outside of the shows, shops, and food stalls she saw every day. Until then, she naively assumed the entertainers and craftsmen led their own lives and handled their own affairs. A new corporation bought out the previous owners at a pretty price and had caused quite a commotion of fear in the faire for several weeks. But when wages rose, struggling buildings were repaired, and the territory expanded, the faire folk couldn't have been happier with their new employer. The Bull and Badger Agency was doing right by them and Pap was their loudest champion.

Smells of fresh baked goodies caught her nose, the precise smells her nose was seeking out. With a skip, she pushed her way through the swinging door of the *Headless Whore* and a chorus of "Hello, Hedy!" met her like a hug. Marla, her dress colorful and low-cut, swept out from behind the counter and enveloped Hedy in a tight squeeze. "How's my birthday girl?", the olive-skinned woman purred.

"As Pap says, 'pain in the knees, hurting hips, but happy heart and miles to go.'" Hedy climbed her usual stool, one of three made specifically for her and her parents, and took her place at the bar, which at this early in the morning was spread with pastries of both sweet and savory varieties.

"Pick your poison, birthday girl, it's on the house." Marla grinned.

"I'll take a ham and cheese, please."

Marla slid a hot roll oozing with stringy cheese onto a wooden plate and then another with a wink.

"You're the best," Hedy giggled.

Big Matt, his dark, tattooed arms the size of both of Hedy's legs side by side, delicately set a cup of coffee in front of her and followed it up with a stein of chocolate milk. "Happy birthday, Miss Oakenroot," his low voice said softly. The big man was a picture of contradictions. This beast of a man used to babysit her when her Pap and Mam needed a break. There were pictures of him cradling her in his muscly arms while pouring stout beer for rowdy customers. He was her Uncle Big, or Ubby, as her toddler's brain had somehow worked out. And Ubby wore a variation of the same thing every day: a rough leather vest, a thick belt, and loose plaid pants tucked into his calf high boots. The colors might change and were generally bright, but the uniform always looked the same. "You feelin' eighteen yet, sweet girl?"

Hedy took a sip of her coffee, prepared just the way she liked it, sweet and creamy. "Yes, Ubby, as a matter of fact, the moment I woke up, I felt eighteen." She giggled to herself and Ubby grinned, his teeth brightly white in contrast to his rich, black skin. "What a child I was last night," she said with her dramatic flair, "I went to bed a wee babe and awoke the curvy woman you see before you."

Marla leaned against the bar, "Finally, another woman to walk the streets with at night. I was getting tired of taking all the men on myself." She winked and nodded toward Ubby who had suddenly become very busy with cleaning a mug that had seconds before been hanging with the other clean mugs. "What's the matter Ubby," Marla purred, "your face is as red as your pants."

"Don't like that kind of talk, especially when it comes to—," he broke off with an indistinct head nod toward Hedy.

Hedy let out a loud, raucous laugh, a thing that sounded much more like her Mam, a boisterous woman who easily held her own next to her rowdy husband. "Ubby," she took a bite from her pastry, cheese stringing everywhere, "I promise you no boy is interested in me like that. I think my people are supposed to go to those conventions and Pap and Mam aren't going anywhere that won't allow them to throw a knife at the other's head."

Ubby grunted, "Heard there was another dug up hole." The change in subject was anything but subtle.

"Where at?" String from the pastry clung from her mouth to the treat in her hand and back to the plate. She chugged down some chocolate milk, a trickle finding its way down her chin.

"Wipe your mouth, sweet girl." Ubby slid a napkin across to her just as she ran her sleeve over her face. The big man groaned. "Close to the wishing well. Street stones were out of sorts this time."

"How does no one hear or see anything?" Marla asked in a hush. "It's so stealthy and peculiar."

All across the grounds large holes had been discovered every morning for the last two weeks, usually somewhere on the outskirts, but the last three were more central. Her Pap blamed Polly and Brutus, probably digging up buried treats. Old Millie had them in her crosshairs too at first, but claimed the two were inside every night since the initial holes were discovered. And the holes were too big, even for those two massive beasts.

Everyone had their theories. Because dirt wasn't misplaced, just churned, it looked as though mole tunnels had collapsed, but those would be gigantic moles. Others more logically assumed the holes had been dug out and filled back in, but Ubby pointed out there would be a place where the dirt had rested before replaced. And *why* was it happening? What was being looked for? And of course, the questions always came back to *who*. Whatever the *reason*, the *who*, or the *method*, the fact that something mysterious had been happening for the last several nights was fuel for new stories and hushed conversations.

Ubby shook his head, "Denny set volunteer patrols, but hasn't come up with somethin' so far." Denny was the grounds manager. The old, quiet man was kind enough, but something told Hedy that anyone who crossed him would regret it. Hedy imagined he was a war veteran and had seen his fair share of violence. Denny never said much, but when he did, people were all ears.

Hedy shrugged, "But no one's been hurt, right? So no harm, no foul. Someone's just making a bit of a mess and giving people something to talk about."

"S'pose that's true," Ubby admitted.

"It's only a matter of time," Marla said resolutely, "you watch. Started on the outskirts, moved into the midst of us, now it's messing things up. What if a hole opens under a trailer or right here in the middle of the *Whore*?"

All three glanced at the open floor near the cold fireplace.

"We're fine," Hedy said before she shoved the rest of her pastry into her mouth followed by a gulp of coffee and then one of chocolate milk. "Can I get that wrapped up?" she asked, sliding the other pastry across to Ubby.

The big man took it gently in his big hand, "Certainly, sweet girl."

And with that she was out the door and back into the cool morning air.

The rest of the morning passed in the usual way. Hedy made her rounds, visiting friends as they prepared shops and rehearsed acts. Today, however, every stop included a birthday well-wishing and most often a gift. Most times it was a candy, a bag of cinnamon almonds, or some small token, like a ribbon for her long, thick hair or pewter figurine. Eventually, her short arms were so full, Dave the Weaver took pity on her and gifted her with a basket, an intricately beautiful creation and just as practical. "Like you," he said with a wink.

It was now the final visit, the one where she knew a magnificent gift was waiting, the one Hedy had been looking forward to all morning. *Sunnie's Slender Silhouette*, a charming two-story building with soft, curving walls reflecting the shape of a woman, stood at the edge of the faire grounds. Ivy crept up the soft pink walls, luring the building to join the rest of the woods.

Hedy slipped inside and took a deep breath. Fresh flowers hung on the walls, their fragrances filling the air. Sunnie was pulling a linen blouse over the top of a mannequin, glasses perched on the tip of her thin, pointed nose and a cigarette hanging from her lips. Hedy knew she was at the end of her twenties, but something about the woman felt ageless. Full black hair framed a lovely face, her almond shaped eyes twinkled from morning to night. Physically, she was the very opposite of Hedy; soulfully, they were a perfect match.

"Hey, bug, you ready to see it?" Her cigarette bobbed in her lips.

Butterflies exploded in Hedy's stomach and she knew exactly why but didn't want to give it a second thought. She set her basket of birthday goodies on the ground and clapped, "I was ready when you took my measurements three weeks ago."

Sunnie gave the blouse a final tug on the mannequin and twirled around to disappear behind a beaded curtain. When she returned, she carried a bundle in her hands wrapped in tissue paper and tied off with roughly spun yarn and a decorative stalk of lavender. The tall woman laid the gift on a nearby stool with a wink, "Happy birthday, bug."

The time for ceremonious cherishing was over and Hedy ripped into the tissue like a wolf into a kill. Paper flew and the lavender stalk vanished. Sunnie laughed musically and took a drag off her cigarette.

Hedy gasped and held up her prize, or part of it rather. It was a dark green brocade corset; the kind the women wore around the faire. The kind the men liked to look at. The kind Pap had refused to allow her to wear on stage, or off for that matter. Oak leaves subtly made up the pattern of the brocade, silver thread running throughout. It was gorgeous. And as gorgeous as the corset was, it was the next piece that might draw the most attention.

Pants.

Made of heavy cotton and dyed a dark brown, they would be just as snug as the corset and tuck into her thigh high leather boots. Pap was going to throw a fit. Hedy wasn't sure how her Mam would react.

Sunnie pulled back the curtain of a fitting stall, "Get in there, you know you want to."

"He's going to kill me." The butterflies were a tornado now.

The other woman shrugged, "Probably, so enjoy it while you can."

Hedy took a deep breath and gathered her things, determined to see this through.

Things were squeezed, others were lifted, and her strong legs and hips looked good in the mirror. Sunnie whistled when Hedy pulled back the curtain, "At least you'll be able to outrun him in those breeches, bug."

"I hope it doesn't come to that."

"Your boobs look great." Sunnie adjusted the blouse at her bosom and shoulders. "Knives fit well?"

Hedy nodded and shifted, two daggers suddenly in her hands and the third still safely tucked away, the third that only came out when necessary as her Pap had taught her. "They move well," she said as she deftly returned them to their hiding places.

"Well, happy birthday, bug, it was nice knowing you," Sunnie stooped and hugged her tightly, a kiss on the cheek.

"Thank you, Sunnie."

Timorously, Hedy stepped back out onto the faire grounds, but this time was different. She was aware. Aware of every sound, every movement, and most aware of herself. As she crossed the grounds, her basket hugged to her emphasized chest, she didn't know whether she was imagining the reactions of those who took notice of her or if the gasps and smirks were reality. It wasn't until she passed the *Whore* that she knew it wasn't her imagination. The woman spun fluidly from the window she was cleaning and dropped the rag, "You, my little lady, look like quite the saucy tart."

"Marla!"

"What? Sure I can't put an apron around those hips and put you to work here? Has your Pap seen you?"

Hedy could only shake her head.

"Oh, sweetie . . ."

The little woman wilted.

Marla snatched up her rag, "No, sweetie, you'll be fine. Your Mam will have your back . . . what's left of it once he's done with ya."

Hedy hugged the basket tighter and hurried on her way.

This time of the morning, Pap and Mam would already be at the stage warming up, so she could get to the RV without setting off that explosion quite yet. Two hours ago, this same walk was soothing and cheery. Now her heart quickened with every step. She was afraid it would detonate by the time she reached the stage, which might not be a terrible thing.

Denny stood outside Millie's trailer, Polly and Brutus gnawing on giant bones. The argument was hushed, but it was clearly an argument all the same. Denny was shaking his head as he used the tip of his boot to make lines in the dirt path leading to the road and Millie was jabbing at the air with her pipe, her head jerking like an aggravated chicken. Denny took notice of Hedy first, a quick, soft smile greeted her from a distance, but even from a distance she could see the effort it took for the man to make the kind gesture. The old woman glanced her way but didn't give her customary wave. The two were involved in something and it was clear Hedy should keep her distance.

Hedy made it to the RV without further incident, and just as she thought, her Pap and Mam weren't there. She put her things away quickly, straightened her snug outfit, took a deep breath, and with as much confidence as she could muster, made her way to the stage in the center of the grounds.

As she neared the stage, Hedy could hear the *thunks* of axes hitting targets. That would be her Mam. The woman couldn't miss and taught Hedy everything she knew. And as her Mam was the expert thrower, her Pap was the expert juggler. Sharp, heavy, flaming, or alive, her Pap could juggle it. The crowd favorite was when he would uncover a butcher's knife, an unlit torch, and big, slippery tuna. The crowd went wild as the three items flew through air and a ball of flame spewed from the stocky man's mouth lighting the torch. By the end of the stunt, the fish was fileted, cooked, and caught on plates. Some audience members insisted there was some sort of sleight of hand at work, but there wasn't. Her Pap was just that good.

Hedy couldn't remember her training anymore. She knew she hadn't always been so adept at the short blades in the same way she knew she couldn't always walk and talk. Dolls and daggers. She played with them both and was sure it wasn't *normal*, but it was *her* normal. And should the day come when she had children of her own, they would know the trade of the *Warriors of Dree*.

But before that day came, she had to survive the next five minutes.

The storm of butterflies was raging in her belly, but she used the same calming techniques her Pap had taught her years ago when she was still afraid of stepping up on stage. With faux confidence, she walked down the center aisle of the audience benches. Thankfully, her Mam saw her first, her eyes widening momentarily before she caught herself, swallowed, and smiled warmly. "Well, look at you, missy. Who is this fierce woman approaching our stage?"

Her Pap looked up from a blade he was sharpening and froze. Immediately, his face began turning purple, his eyes bulged, and his thick knuckles whitened around the hilt. Just as his lips managed to part behind his thick graying beard, her Mam's hand raised a sharp finger, deadlier than the ax held in the other. "Beloved, say one word out of place and it could be your last. So help me, you know I'm not jesting."

Silence hung thick in the air, and with obvious force, her Pap's lips closed and he turned his attention to the blade in his trembling fist.

Her Mam smiled sweetly, took her skirts in her hand, and hopped off the stage to embrace her. Though there wasn't much height to them, the two women measured the same, eye to eye. And now, more than ever, they were seeing eye to eye. "You, my lovey, look every bit the woman I knew you would. Is this Sunnie's work?" The little woman stepped back and ran her hand over the sides of the corset. "What am I saying, of course it is. Look at that detail! The leaves!"

The butterflies had begun to slow down, but they still weren't at rest.

Mam took her by the hand, leading her up the wooden steps to her Pap. "Darling, acknowledge the woman standing before you."

Pap's head didn't move, his trembling hands kept moving stone and blade.

"Braeden Oakenroot . . ."

His hands stopped moving and he looked up, but not toward his daughter. "Grounds open in ten minutes, first show in twenty. Check the props and warm up." He stumped off the stage and down the center aisle.

Every butterfly in her belly died.

Her Mam's hand squeezed her arm. "He doesn't do well with change, especially when it comes to you. Boobs almost put him in the grave when you were twelve."

The comment was meant to lighten the mood, but it couldn't happen. Hedy had never seen him so disappointed. From the moment Sunnie took her measurements, Hedy knew it would be a battle, but she never thought it would be like *this*. Yelling and shouting she could handle, but that look on his face was more than she could bear. "I can go change real quick."

"Don't you dare, Hedy Oakenroot. You're a woman and a warrior. Bulky skirts slow us down."

Hedy flicked her Mam's skirt with a finger, "You're in skirts."

Mam smirked, "I wear skirts for a very different reason. With your Pap's hunger, it's a lot easier."

Hedy's face burned red. "Mam!"

Mam laughed loudly and slapped her girl on the back, "There it is! When I point out to that stubborn jackass just how *binding* breeches can be, he'll come around fast as lightening. You might be putting your goods up for sale, but you've locked the shop up tight." This time her Mam slapped her on the bottom and the flames in Hedy's face burned hotter. "Now, go do as your Pap said."

Hedy was all too happy to leave that talk behind. Sara Oakenroot never shied away from topics. They talked about everything. When Hedy had her first period, they went into the woods and talked all about sex and how to please yourself when you felt like it. No mysteries, no secrets, just the honest truth about life and how things worked.

The grounds opened promptly as they always did, a flood of people in their own costumes mixed with those in street clothes who came to enjoy themselves by watching shows and combat as well as gawking at their fellow costumed patrons. As always, the benches for their show filled up quickly. Their fans were loyal and many of them had been coming for as long as she could remember. So faithfully, in fact, she recognized most of the excited faces filling the rows and knew many of their names. Hedy loved watching through a knothole backstage as the crowds poured in, she'd done it for every show since she was a little girl, the little girl she had left behind this morning.

This would be the first show in her new costume. What would the audience think? Would they react the way her Pap had?

Only a moment remained before her Pap would take the stage and welcome the crowd, but she hadn't seen him since he walked away. He would be back, wouldn't he? He wouldn't do that to their show? To them? Or maybe that was how he was going to make his point? The litter of dead butterflies in her belly feebly flittered their wings.

"Are you ready, lovey?" Her Mam came up behind her, slipping one of her axes in its loop at her belt.

"Yeah, where's Pap?"

"Ladies and Gentlemen, people little and big, are you prepared for the biggest show put on by the littlest of people?" The crowd roared as her Pap triumphantly marched down the aisle, his presence demanding their attention and filling the space. "Is that all you have?" he shouted over the thunderous audience. "Because if that's it, then—" her Pap stumbled as he was shoved aside by an out of breath curly-haired, chunky boy trying to make his way to the front row. "Piss and shit, boy! Take your seat before I throw a dagger between the cheeks of your ass!" her Pap roared much to the delight of the crowd.

It looked as though the boy mumbled some apologies, but did as he was told and squeezed into the nonexistent space between two audience members on the front row.

And that's how the first show of the season began. Hedy always entered a focused state the moment she stepped on stage. The details of the audience disappeared, but she heard their gasps, their laughter, their applause. She even heard a man in the back of the crowd yell, "Marry me, Hedy Oakenroot!" Her Pap volunteered the man to be part of his next act, the one where he juggled blades between the '*volunteer's*' legs. The audience loved it.

Her knives flipped and danced, her hands flowed. Now and then, as she would step aside to give the stage to her Mam or Pap, she would survey the crowd and breathe them in. Faces glowed and eyes twinkled. This is what she lived for.

Hedy's eyes passed over the sea of faces, then locked on one in particular. The only face that was still glued to *her* while the rest of the audience watched with bated breath as her blindfolded Mam threw axes at her Pap who stood against a wall holding all manner of vegetation as targets. The face belonged to that curly-haired boy on the front row. Did he just give her a little wave? The crowd burst into applause and her Mam bowed as her Pap transitioned to his most dangerous routine, juggling three double-bladed daggers, no hilt to catch them by, and a trout gulping for water, all eyes were on him. All eyes, but that one pair. She glanced at him again and he waved again. Hedy had hoped boys would flirt, but this didn't seem like the right time and she certainly wasn't going to return the gesture.

Forcing her attention back on her Pap, she turned her eyes on him just in time to see it happen. His leg buckled and he collapsed to the ground, the trout slapping the ground and the blades clattering down around him.

Gasps and silence.

CHAPTER SIXTEEN

Date Interrupted

For the first time in her memory, the *Warriors of Dree* had canceled a show. And not just a show, all shows for the rest of the day with those scheduled for tomorrow pending.

Pending.

Pap's *leg* was pending. Denny and Old Millie had come at once to the Oakenroot RV once Pap had limped all the way there. He refused to be carried on a stretcher, to be wheeled in a chair, or even given a crutch or shoulder to lean on. He limped the entire way, pausing here and there to rest against a tree, and then limped on. By the time he reached the threadbare green sofa in their den, he had broken out into a noticeable sweat. Outwardly, nothing appeared to be wrong with the leg, but Denny and Old Millie could barely touch it without Pap gripping the sofa and muttering colorful combinations of swear words.

"You knew something like this was bound to happen, Brae," Denny said softly.

Pap mumbled something unintelligible.

"It's the effect," Denny went on, "You can't escape it. No one can. Just hitting you and yours harder than some others. You've seen how it is among your people all throughout this God forsaken place."

Pap nodded and Mam patted his arm comfortingly.

Old Millie passed Pap a coffee mug, one Hedy had painted him for his birthday one year. "Drink that down," she ordered crisply.

"It ain't gonna kill me, is it?"

Old Millie squared her shoulders, "Braeden Oakenroot, if I was going to kill you, I wouldn't do it right here in front of your wife and girl. Besides, I've gotten used to your bullshit. I'da killed you years ago, in the woods, and fed you to the mutts."

He smiled through his beard and pain, taking a chug like it was a Friday night— any night really, at the Headless Whore. Pap never did anything small. His eyes narrowed, "Is that . . ."

Old Millie nodded, "Ayup."

"Where'd you get it?" Pap took another drink.

She waved him off. "Never you mind, Dree. Just drink it down. We've done what we can and you'll heal up, but it'll take longer. The effect and all."

Denny stretched his skinny frame, a few joints popping. "We'll adjust the schedule and have others cover your slot while you heal. When you're ready, when you're *actually* ready, things will go back to the way they've been."

Old Millie snorted at the last bit. Denny shot her a look and something unmistakable passed between them.

The old woman was the first to slip back into her pleasantries, as pleasant as she could be. Giving final instructions to Pap to stay put and Mam to keep him put by any means necessary, some of the means suggested making Hedy's cheeks catch fire, Old Millie clicked her pipe between her teeth and waved a farewell.

Mam held the door for them both, said her thanks. As Denny walked out, he paused, looking at Hedy. She felt like he was going to say something, but he simply stood there watching her, weighing her it seemed. And just like with Old Millie, his countenance shifted and he smiled warmly. Well, warmly for Denny, "Having a pleasant birthday, young lady?"

Hedy shrugged, "I suppose so." She had so much more to say than that, but she couldn't. It had been the worst so far. Sure, it started out perfectly, but the business with her Pap before the show and now this, she felt responsible.

Denny nodded and stepped out, bending low and giving Mam a peck on the cheek.

"Take care, Denny," her Mam said and let the door close. The short woman planted her fists on her strong hips and took in the room with Hedy sitting on an ottoman and Pap laid up on the couch. "All right, young woman, you get on out of here and enjoy the rest of the day. A girl only becomes a woman once in her life and today is your day. I'll take care of your Pap."

How could she go out and celebrate when her Pap wasn't just laid up, but he wouldn't talk to her? Hedy was about to say as much, but her Mam pulled her up by the arm and directed her to the door. "Mam!"

"Get out! Don't get a whoopin' on your birthday, Hedy. It wouldn't do. Unless it's a whoopin' by a boy, then be my guest." Her Pap coughed loudly, or choked, she couldn't be sure.

And Hedy found herself outside, the sky blue, birds singing, fanciful melodies riding on the breeze, and faire goers laughing and playing in the distance. But Hedy couldn't reflect on any of that. There was far too much going on inside her. Far too much *pending*.

Hedy pushed the little gate open and stepped back onto the faire grounds.

"Hi!"

The sudden greetings startled her out of her ruminating. It was the curly haired boy. The one who had squeezed himself onto the front row and waved at her in the middle of her Pap's act.

Wait. Had it been *his* fault? Had her Pap seen the gesture and taken a misstep because he was distracted?

"Go away." Hedy shoved past him, her shoulder catching him in his soft belly.

The boy wheezed but adjusted his glasses and came after her. "I think your show was incredible, I mean, you know, aside from the part where Braeden Oakenroot fell and dropped everything, but other than that it was amazing! Everything I thought it would be! I mean, the Dree! *The* Dree!"

Hedy had no idea where she was headed, but she kept going there, doing her best to ignore and discourage the boy from following.

"And you! Look at you! Just like in the books! The breeches and . . . and . . . I mean, you have knives and stuff . . . hidden, right?"

"You're about to find out," she growled.

And then he said it, "You're prettier than I ever imagined."

Hedy stopped dead in her tracks. Fireworks went off in her head and the world spun. Goosebumps. "Huh?"

She heard a spray like from an aerosol can and a quick inhale. "Yeah," he said weakly, "you're super pretty."

Slowly, Hedy turned around. The pudgy boy was fumbling with an inhaler and drawing in the dirt with the toe of his sneaker. He was cute. Latino, she thought. She had thought that when she saw him during the act. His eyes were dark, his hair nearly black, and his lips full. He was *very* cute.

"Um, anyway, I was thinking of getting some clothes like yours. Well, not just like yours 'cause yours are for girls and all. For women. You're *clearly* a woman. A lady. I'd like to get something. Maybe, you know, boots and stuff. A cloak. For a boy. A man. I'm a man . . ." he trailed off.

Was this a date? Unofficially? Was he asking her on a date? You get a boob-boosting corset and a pair of tight breeches and suddenly the boys are flocking. "Sure, I can show you a few good places. Do you have money?"

He pulled out a couple of credit cards. "I have these. They're mi abuela's. She's going to kill me anyway once this is all over, might as well make it worth it." He grinned goofily. "I'm Bogart. Actually, I'm Humberto Hidalgo, but my friends call me Bogart. My one friend. Two now if you count Meg and I think I can. The jerks call me—".

She put out her hand, "I'm Hedy."

Bending low, he kissed the back of her hand, it was very old-fashioned, and perfect at a renaissance faire. "My pleasure, Hedy."

And they walked. He asked all sorts of questions about the faire and her parents. The boy had clearly done his homework on the Cougan County Renaissance Faire because he already knew so much about the *Warriors of Dree*. But he always had more questions.

They stopped at a men's clothier with a sign depicting a rooster wearing a crown, the *King's Cock*, and Bogart picked through the wares. At first, Hedy sifted through the less expensive items, but the boy wouldn't have it. With his arms full, he slipped into a dressing room. She was having a wonderful time. Briefly, the concerns for her Pap and the show tried to intrude, but those thoughts were immediately snuffed by images of his eyes and lips tickling through her mind. Those lips that had kissed the back of her hand. She could still feel it.

"What do you think?" He stood posed like Robin Hood, his chest out and fists planted on his hips. He looked every bit the hero in his black buckskin vest laced up over the linen shirt that hung open at the neck, two or three chest hairs showing. Dark blue breeches were tucked into polished black cuffed boots. And fastened around his neck, a beautiful, dark green cloak that made his skin glow, and his eyes . . . those eyes that were currently unimpeded by his glasses. He did look every bit the hero and the fitted clothes had a slimming effect on him.

Hedy beamed, "You look very handsome. Extremely handsome."

Bogart turned toward the mirror and ran his fingers through his messy black hair. "It looks okay? I can't really see myself too well without my glasses. I was going to get some contacts, but the thought of touching my eyeballs freaks me out, you know?"

She laughed, "I do know! But don't you need them?"

"I've seen the most beautiful thing I'll see all day," he smiled and she blushed. "Besides," he patted a leather pouch hanging from his belt, "They're safe." Turning to her, he put his arm out for her to take, "M'lady?"

She was too short for hers to fit through comfortably, so she simply laid her hand on his forearm. "Thank you, kind sir."

And they walked.

That's how the day went. The gallant young man and the little lady walked every inch of the Cougan County Renaissance Faire several times. It was awkward at first, she didn't know him and it felt as though he knew all about her. Bogart kept referencing things about the *Warriors of Dree*, their legendary skills with blades and nimble movement, and how he never thought he'd actually ever get to see them, let alone spend time with Hedy. The boy could talk. It was the questions about the faire that drew her out of her awkwardness, that was a subject she knew all about and could match his motor mouth word for word. The pair had lunch at the *Headless Whore* and she introduced him to Ubby and Marla, the latter giving her eyes that made her blush clear down to her corset. They visited Sunnie's hut, so Bogart could meet the woman who had crafted her new garments. With every introduction, his excitement grew. Hedy loved the fact he was as passionate about the faire as she was.

And at some point in the day, between the jousting tournament and the second round of ale she was given in secret by a friendly tavern keeper, Bogart casually took her hand. Her heart had never raced like it was in that moment and she didn't know what to do. What was there *to* do? Was she holding his hand, right? Was it comfortable for him, or did their height difference make it strange? Could he sense how nervous she was? Were her palms sweaty? Should she say something?

It was night. They were near the heart of the faire, a square with a well-kept English garden, its flowers allowed to grow in planned disarray. Lamps had been lit around the perimeter bathing blooms in soft light, their shadows swaying under the moon. Bogart sat on a bench pulling her down beside him. "My feet hurt."

"Is it the boots?"

He shrugged, "I just don't think I'm used to walking this much. I mean, I'm not a very active guy. This is probably the most I've walked willingly." He laughed a little at himself.

She rubbed a hand over her right knee. It was sore. But she was used to it. It came with being a little person. Joints hurt at times. Nothing unbearable, just a nuisance. It made her think of Pap and wonder how he was, both physically and relationally.

"Your leg hurt?"

It was her turn to shrug, "Not really, just a little stiff. It happens."

"It shouldn't."

She barked a laugh, "Why do you say that?"

"Well, you're a warrior of Dree, your people are the toughest. Everyone knows that."

"That's very kind of you and flattering," she sighed, kneading her leg above the knee. "But we're little people and it all just goes with the territory. What happened with Pap today was bound to happen. In fact, it's a miracle it hasn't happened earlier. People like us tend to start struggling with this sort of thing around my age, he and Mam are a bit of an anomaly. Mam's started a couple of years ago, but mainly just in her lower back. Nothing strange for a middle-aged woman, you know?"

Bogart was grinning, "Say that word again."

"Which one," she giggled.

"Anomaly."

"Why?"

"Because most kids our age don't even know it exists."

She giggled again, "Okay. Anomaly."

"Exquisita." His hand found hers again and he raised it to his lips. He was in the middle of pressing his pink lips to the back of her nervous hand when the first scream cut through the night. They both turned in the direction of the startling sound, waiting. And then another broke out, followed by more and finally a full out commotion.

Regardless of her sore knee, Hedy jumped to her feet and Bogart was quickly on his as well. At first the noise seemed to be coming from the rear of the grounds, but soon there was a cacophony of fear and panic surrounding them. Patrons ran through the square from all directions heading in the other where they probably hoped to find safety, only to nearly crash into other patrons and employees running from the other direction. But from what?

And then Hedy saw the first one. A skeleton, its bones brown from dirt and decay, raced into the square and jumped high into the air landing on the back of a fat woman in a red velvet ladies gown. The woman crashed to the ground, her face bouncing off a cobblestone, blood spurting. The thing raised a bony hand, a stone gripped in it, and brought it down into the back of her skull. Several times.

More of the filthy skeletons came swarming into the square, taking down men and women, and even more horrifically, children. Each time was just as brutal, the creatures made sure the dead were dead.

"We need to run," Bogart said in a hush. Hedy knew he was right, it was foolish not to, but running hadn't done the dead any good. She was about to suggest they find a place to hide when something grabbed her attention. The skeleton that had been perched on the back of the woman in the red dress collapsed to the ground with a clatter. In fact, they all did, one after another. For a moment, the garden seemed to sigh in the stillness. The entire faire had grown quiet.

"Is it over?" Hedy whispered, daring not to move.

"Hell no," Bogart whispered back, "it's about to get worse."

"How could it poss—"

And that's when the woman in the red dress stood to her feet. Brains slipped down her back and splatted on the cobblestones. One by one, the freshly dead stood to their feet, their eyes unseeing, their wounds bleeding freely. As one, they turned to look at the only two living things in the square. "Child of Dree," they spoke in unison, "I see you."

Bogart grabbed Hedy by the arm and they started running. It was a good thing too because fear had gripped her coldly and wouldn't let go. She had no idea where he was taking her, everything was a blur. Colorful lights flashed by as he led her down the faire roads and the screaming had started again. Another sound was added to the cacophony. War cries, blasting horns, and the clanging of metal. Somewhere, people were *fighting*.

Suddenly, the wind was knocked from her and she was tumbling on the ground, coming to a hard stop against a stony wall. She could hear Bogart swearing and struggling to pull himself to his feet. A hand grabbed her by the hair and yanked her into the air, it was the fat woman in the red dress. Her dress was bathed in blood and her head tilted at a strange angle. "Child of Dree, I see you," she slurred and gurgled. With the kicking prey in hand, the other dead stood in place.

Bogart had gotten to his feet, his cloak twisted around him. "Let her go!" His bravery was short lived as a man in a blood-soaked University of Oregon hoody took the stout boy's throat in his grip. Bogart's eyes bulged and he fumbled to pull the hand away, but couldn't.

Deftly, Hedy's third dagger was in her hand, the dagger she was only supposed to use in emergencies. Mustering her courage, Hedy plunged the dagger up into the woman's thick neck, cold blood spilling down her hand. The woman, who's empty eyes had been turned on Bogart, redirected her gaze at Hedy. "Child of Dree," she gurgled, the dagger blade visible in her mouth as she spoke, "your little weapons are no good on the Vacusai."

Then a flash of steel and Hedy was falling to the ground.

Another flash and Bogart landed beside her coughing and gasping for air.

People, living people, formed a wall around her. "Get to your feet, sweetie." Slender fingers helped Hedy to her feet. It was Sunnie. She pulled Bogart up as well. Ubby stood over them with a gigantic ax in his hands and Marla held a simple staff at the ready. Other members of Hedy's faire family were just as armed and alert. Jugglers, fire breathers, blacksmith, jesters, glassblowers, and bards.

A thick cloud of the recently dead stood facing the band of entertainers as though sizing up the new challenge.

"Are you good enough to run?" Sunnie asked with an edge Hedy had never heard before.

Hedy could only nod.

"Good enough." Pulling the dagger from the bodiless head of the fat woman, Sunnie wiped it on her skirt and handed it to Hedy. A twin pair of cloth sheers twirled to the ready in Sunnie's hands, "Aim for the legs. Bodies without legs don't go far. Take hands and arms as you need to and heads as a last resort. Keep your eyes open. These are quick. Someone has put an extra punch to them." The group affirmed the orders either verbally or with a gesture. "Joe, clear us a path."

One of the fire breathers stepped forward, the dead turned their attention on him. He pulled a squeeze bottle from a pouch and sprayed the ground before him for many yards. Then turning the bottle to his own mouth, he filled it to capacity. The fire breather raised a torch to his mouth and spewed. A great ball of fire bloomed, first directed into the air and then brought low to the ground. Fire sprung from the ground consuming anything within it. Immediately, the dead sprung backward, a single bellow rising from the many slack mouths.

"Whoever's behind them will feel that," Marla purred.

"Aye," Ubby nodded, "let's give their Dominosk more."

Ubby pounded down the open path swinging his ax low. Bodies fell to both sides, arms reaching out as legs abandoned them. The troupe followed behind the powerful man knocking outreaching hands to the side, in some cases lopping them off altogether.

Hedy was struggling to comprehend what was happening, as she ran within the heart of the group, Bogart tightly behind her, she would catch glimpses of faire patrons who once filled the audience, *her* audience, and applauded her family's feats. She could feel her heart beginning to break and she knew she had to resist it. Right now was about surviving. Grieving could happen later. *If* there were a later.

And who were these people with her? She knew them, but never like *this*. Sunnie spun and whirled, slicing with her sheers at everything that came too close. At the head of the troupe, Ubby and Marla worked as well with their deadly weapons as they did with a rag or spatula in the tavern. The staff stunning and tripping, the ax toppling. At times, someone's timing would be miscalculated and a creature would grab them, biting into them. A bard who had no business fighting was the first to be lost. He swung a fist, missing his target and taking him off balance. The creature, a gangly teenage boy, wrapped his arms around the bard and sunk his braces into the neck of the surprised bard.

They lost a fire breather.

A juggler.

Then Marla.

As the group ran forward, she slipped in a puddle of blood and lost her footing. One of the dead, a huge sweaty man with arms as thick as Ubby's, grabbed her by the arm and yanked her from the troupe. Before she could drive her staff up into his nose, his hands were on either side of her head, and in a moment that Hedy would never forget, Marla's neck cracked and her body fell limp to the ground.

Ubby bellowed like a mad bull and swung his ax at the other big man, catching him across the belly and spilling his bowels. But the dead had found their inlet, the wall of protection broke around Hedy and the horrors began to work their way in. She felt hands grabbing at her and she couldn't say if they were friendly or not. It was all chaos. Ubby kept swinging his ax madly, what had been Marla's killer was nothing but a pile on the ground, the peaceful barkeep bathed in blood and gore. Sunnie and Joe did what they could to fend off the attackers, but there were so many of them. Even Bogart was kicking out against the dead.

Somewhere to Hedy's right, a horn blew. Predators and prey alike paused. Hedy couldn't see the source of it, but a rumbling could be heard, like thunder.

"Down!" Sunnie shouted, and shoved Hedy and Bogart to the ground just as the horses charged by, the jousters lowering their lances and clearing the surprised dead from the group. Hedy raised her head in time to see the horsemen turn around to make another sweep. The living clambered over the writhing dead to clear the path. Again, the lancers swept by, the gruesome creatures trampled and mangled under hooves beating anything standing, thrown, or struck down.

Sunnie stomped forward, "You fucking idiot! You could have killed us all!"

One of the men on horseback turned around; it was Shane, a beautiful man, his long blond hair pulled up into a knot on top of his head. He smiled and his white teeth shone in the night, "Aye, but you're still alive. And a good thing too, because I'll need someone with all their pieces intact to fuck when this is all over."

"Go fuck your horse," Sunnie growled, her almond eyes flashing.

He laughed, "I've tried, but he's just not into it."

The rest of the troupe stepped cautiously onto the cleared road. Ubby dropped to his knees beside Marla, her eyes open and empty.

Scooping her into his big arms, he gently carried her body to a bench outside a carver's booth. He lay her down delicately and crossed her arms across her chest and closed her eyes. "We'll come back and take care of her proper, big man," Joe said soothingly. "Aye?"

Ubby ran the back of his bloody arm over his eyes and nodded.

"Where are you headed? The boys and I—"

"Hey!" A woman's voice rang out from those on horseback.

Shane rolled his eyes, "And Rachel. Rachel and the boys and I will clear the way for you."

Hedy spoke up, "We have to get to my Mam and Pap."

Sunnie agreed, "Get us to the RVs."

Shane pulled his mount around, "You heard the pretty titties, boys! This way!"

Sunnie swore, "Regroup around Hedy, we're going to get her there. No more losses."

It was physically easier this time, but Hedy's fear was reaching new found levels. That moment was the first she had been able to think outside of her survival to what might be happening to her Mam and Pap. The horsemen, and Rachel, did as they said they would and made the way easy to travel. Every now and then, a creature would lurch out of the shadows of a storefront or booth only to be solidly put down by the grieving and raging Ubby.

Hedy noticed the bodies of the creatures never quit moving. No matter how much they had been mutilated, they still fought to move toward the group, toward *her*. Arms, fingers, lone heads, parts Hedy couldn't identify because she was sure they should be *inside*, all appeared to futilely continue the fight.

Finally, they cleared the gate separating faire from private grounds. The fight looked to have been just as ugly here. It was dark and where it wasn't dark there was fire. However, unlike the grounds proper, this place was quiet. Shane led, his eyes shifting from one side of the road to the other. Soon, they came upon Old Millie's RV and the door swung open. It was Denny with a shotgun in his hands. He peered about and stepped down, "Is it clear?"

"Looks to be," Shane conceded.

Denny slouched in relief. "The Vacusai rampaged through here on their way to the grounds. Took several of our people with them."

"Did you see my Mam and Pap?" Hedy blurted out.

Denny shook his head, "I didn't see much, I took Millie and the dogs inside and locked them up, stood guard in the living room here."

Bogart laid a hand on her shoulder and squeezed comfortingly, "I know your parents are fine. I mean, they have to be, right? They're the warriors of Dree."

"Of course." Hedy wanted to believe it, but in her Pap's state, she couldn't be sure.

"We'll go on down the road and find them," Sunnie suggested. "Hedy, you stay here with Denny and Old Millie." That last part wasn't a suggestion.

Fury exploded in Hedy, "No! I'm going with you! They're my Mam and Pap, I'm going with you!"

Sunnie's eyes blazed like her namesake. "Young woman, I'm not arguing this with you. Someone is out for *you* and they more than likely know your Mam and Pap are your weak spot. I will not have gone through all of this, the loss of my family members, only to lose you too. We'll come back for you the moment we know they're safe and your home is clear."

Hedy wanted to fight, but she knew the other woman was right. Those things had spoken to her directly. This was all about *her* for some reason and it might not be over yet. Every precaution had to be taken even if she didn't like it.

"Fine," she muttered and stomped off to Old Millie's RV.

"We'll leave Ubby here with you and Rachel can—," Sunnie was saying, but was cut off by Denny.

"The two of them will just draw attention. I can hold things down here with Millie and the mutts."

The inside was musty and reeked of tobacco smoke among other things Old Millie was rumored to puff on. Trinkets of all kind covered shelves and wall space. Mostly porcelain cattle and chickens. Here and there a crystal sphere would stand amongst them, beautifully colored and shiny, almost alive.

Hedy dropped herself onto the sofa in resignation sending up a cloud of yellow dust. Behind a closed door at one end of the RV, where the kitchen was, she could hear Brutus and Polly snuffling and sniffing through the gap at the floor. The bedroom door at the other end was closed as well, probably where Old Millie was hiding. The rattley front door opened and Denny shuffled in with Bogart right behind him.

"The others are checking on your parents," Denny sighed. "They'll be back soon enough with good news, I'm sure."

Bogart's eyes were taking in the old RV with its treasure trove of junk. "Where's Old Millie," Bogart asked as he looked at it all.

"Sleeping," Denny said in his usual soft voice. "The whole affair was a bit much for her and I urged the old bird to rest in her room."

"Why'd you lock up Brutus and Polly?" Hedy asked with a glance at the kitchen door where she could still hear the active dogs.

Denny shook his head, "They kept trying to break through the front door to get to the creatures. They'll protect her at all costs. It was for their own good."

Hedy nodded. It sounded exactly like what those two would do. She'd seen them turn savage when an insurance salesman had once made his way onto the private grounds and wouldn't take no for an answer from the old woman. Brutus had pulled the jacket from the man and Polly was left with a pant leg. The salesman never returned.

"Can I use the bathroom?" Bogart asked suddenly, "I really need to go."

Denny craned his neck and looked down the short hallway of the trailer home, then nodded, “It’s fine, boy. It’s just right there on the left. Quiet though, don’t wake her up.”

“Thanks.” Bogart left the room pulling at his belt buckle before he made it to the bathroom’s door.

“Guess we know what’s been comin’ out of those holes now.” Denny collapsed into a large recliner, the old chair creaking as it rocked, the shotgun across his lap. “You’re okay?”

Hedy shrugged, “Scared. Scared for my Mam and Pap.”

Denny sighed quietly, “They’ll be fine. Like the boy said, they’re the *Warriors of Dree*. If any two people can come out of this unscathed, it’s those two.”

Hedy shook her head, “Marla was killed.” She could still see the beautiful woman’s empty eyes staring up at the night sky.

“No telling who all we lost,” Denny ran a hand over his face. “Tomorrow morning will be just as hard as we tally the dead.” He leaned over the arm of the recliner to one of Old Millie’s cabinets and pulled out a crystal whiskey decanter and a couple of glasses. He poured a glass and took a sip. “Something to calm you?”

Hedy shrugged, “Couldn’t hurt.”

Denny poured her a drink and handed it to her. “Marla is gone,” he said as she took the glass. “Marla, countless patrons, any others?”

Hedy stared down into the drink, “Aaron was . . .” But she couldn’t finish. The picture of blood gushing down the young bard’s neck was too much and threatened to break her.

Denny pulled himself to his feet and walked over to the front door, looking out, presumably to see if the others were returning yet with news of her Mam and Pap.

Hedy heard movement to her left. Bogart was slipping out of Old Millie’s bedroom, his eyes wide. How did he get in there? She cocked her head at him and he drew a finger across his throat and thumbed at the closed door. She mouthed the word dead and he nodded slowly in the shadow of the hallway.

"What your fat friend is telling you is that I slit her throat and threw her limp body onto her bed." The voice wasn't Denny's, but it was coming from him. It was the voice the others had spoken with as one. Deep, measured, cold.

Denny turned, his eyes not seeing. "Child of Dree, I see you." Bogart ran into the room, throwing himself between her and the possessed grounds keeper. Denny didn't raise the gun, just a hand and Bogart was suddenly flung into the wall, porcelain figurines and other tchotchkes clattering down on top of him. "Veneficos are wonderful, are they not? Generally, takes one to kill one. The power in these old hands. How did they come by it?" There was a touch of awe in the sinister voice.

Hedy was barely able to get to her feet, fear threatening to throw her back down onto the sofa. "Denny, please, let us go."

The slack face smiled strangely, "Denny surrendered long ago. He's always blamed the Six. That level of resentment makes for simpler followers."

Denny stepped toward her and she screamed. That sent the dogs into a frenzy behind the kitchen door, claws against the thin plastic, thick bodies heaved against it. Hedy could feel the whole trailer shake with their combined force.

Hedy used the distraction to snag her daggers, whipping two of them free and throwing them into the eyes of the man before her. Her aim was on point and he reeled back for a moment, tottered, then balanced himself again. Sickeningly, a smile spread across his face as blood trickled down like morbid tears and he looked right at her. "Child of Dree, I still see you."

He lunged for her.

She screamed again, truly terrified by the sight of her old friend hurtling at her, blood now spilling down his pierced face.

All at once, the vinyl kitchen door shattered and a flurry of movement knocked Hedy to the ground, a beast on top of her. The other, it was hard to say which in the tumult, barreling into Denny and shoving him backward against the front door, his neck in its toothy grip, ripping and pulling. Denny fought against the beast, hands thrashing, but the giant mastiff couldn't be shaken. It was Polly, Hedy could see that now. Brutus still stood above Hedy, his teeth bared at the aggressor.

As Denny struggled, Bogart stood to his feet, something in his hand. "Get off him!" Bogart shouted. The dog obeyed immediately and dropped to all fours, hair a bristled ridge on her back and bloody muzzle snarling. Bathed in the yellow glow of Old Millie's living room, Bogart confidently raised a white crystal ball above his head and with all his might threw it to the ground at Denny's feet.

The room filled with a flash of white light.

All was silent.

CHAPTER SEVENTEEN

Honesty Here

Sunlight was breaking through the palms, a soothing breeze blew over Charlie as he laid comfortably in a lounge chair by the pool. The scene of the struggle had been cleaned up, Meg had insisted on "putting everything back the way they found it." The blood from skinny guy's head rinsed off the concrete easy enough, a little could still be seen if you looked hard, but who would? Pool chairs had been up righted and the broken pieces of terra-cotta pot had been swept up. It all looked normal again.

Mostly.

Frozen Shells at the bottom of the pool reached up in their icy casing. Meg assured him they weren't going anywhere, but after she sewed him up—the gash across his chest had been deep—Charlie insisted on keeping an eye on them while *she* kept an eye on her patient clad in black. Thankfully, as daylight began to bring clarity to his surroundings, Charlie discovered the pool had a cover that was easily operated by the flick of a switch. Prying eyes wouldn't see anything, but the pool boy was going to get quite a surprise.

After everything went down the night before, Meg had seen to skinny guy's— *Spencer's* head wound. Spencer. His license said his name was Spencer Carrington. Nineteen. Pasty skin. Black hair dyed blacker. Gaunt. The guy was an absolute mess. And according to Meg, they *needed* him.

The whole time she was stitching Charlie up in the bathroom, he was grilling her. "What do you mean, 'we *need* him'?"

"He's part of all of this," she said vaguely.

"Part of *what*?"

“This whole *thing*. It’s why the Shells were after you and him. Why I’m here.” She pulled at the string to close the cut in his chest and deftly knotted it off.

His building frustration at her vague answers and the electricity that coursed through his body every time she touched him caused him to only be mildly aware of the needle and string she had been maneuvering through his skin.

“So, what, we’re stuck with this *addict* who tried to gut me with a broken bottle?” She put her finger to her lips. “He can’t hear us,” Charlie said quietly anyway, “he’s out cold still.”

Spencer was stretched out on the couch under a blanket. Meg had seen to his head and when he wouldn’t stop shivering, she cut the wet clothes off him and added a couple more blankets. It didn’t help, though, he kept shivering. If Charlie had learned anything about drugs in health class, this had to be withdrawal from whatever was in his system and Meg’s reaction was equal parts horror and heartbreak. That’s what was in the drawers, he explained. Drugs. Lots of drugs. And if he had his guess, there were little baggies and bottles hidden all over the pool house.

That’s when she ransacked it. Through every drawer, under every cushion, inside anything that could hide what someone didn’t want found. The same determination that herded the Shells into the pool, Meg now turned on a *new* enemy. Charlie watched her find stash after stash, all of them flushed the moment she found them, and he quit counting after seventeen. The entire time Spencer just laid on the couch, shivering under the blanket. Withdrawal mixed with a decent concussion couldn’t be the healthiest of combinations. How long would they be stuck here waiting for more Shells to come knocking?

While she was on her rampage, Charlie took the opportunity to shower and wash off the blood. The cut had bled all down the front of him. Was that truly the reason he showered? No. He did it to protect his own secret. If she came storming through the bathroom, she might find his liquid secret in the shower and he didn't want her to. The bottle was more than half full, but he had already learned about limitations. While he wanted to drink the whole thing, he knew he'd be passed out next to Spencer if he did. So he took a few swigs and left it at that. Just enough to knock off the edge, chill him out. And it worked, by the time he finished showering, he was in a nice buzz, and that's where he intended to stay.

Charlie managed to find a new pair of athletic shorts, the previous ones had been stained with blood. Arms folded, he stood by the French doors, the sun beginning to make the sky glow through the tall palm trees.

"What do we do about our friends in the pool?"

"You can't do *anything* about them."

"So what happens when someone sees them? Because they're going to, you know."

For the first time, Charlie saw uncertainty in Meg. "I don't know, Charlie."

The California sun was beautiful and the blue sky was just as good; and had it been under any other circumstances, Charlie would have been blown away by the sprawling mansion he could now see in its entirety. Currently, the opulent building felt like nothing more than a wall, protecting them from the eyes of the outside world. Well, most of the eyes. A woman whom Charlie assumed was a maid of some sort, it was her uniform that gave her away, peered at him from one of the backdoors of the main house. When she cracked it open, he just said he was a friend of Spencer's and that seemed to be enough for her. She nodded and closed the door. Charlie turned his attention again to the covered pool. Well, not really. He just looked at it as thoughts rolled over and over in his head. His buzz was wearing off and he started to feel pissed off. For the second time in as many days he'd been attacked by those things, the Shells. Why? Why were they after *him*? Why did they need a wasted junky? How far was all of this going to go? His house was gone. His parents were gone. The entirety of his life was simply gone. Why?

Never being one to be confrontational, Charlie hadn't pressed Meg for answers. He supposed he hoped she would offer them willingly when it was time. Now they were so far down the rabbit hole, he didn't know if there were enough answers in the world. He couldn't remember much through his haze the night before, but he remembered the books being important somehow.

The French doors opened behind him. "He's stopped shivering."

Charlie shrugged. He didn't care. The idiot shouldn't do drugs.

Meg sat on the edge of the lounge chair next to him and leaned in with her elbows on her knees. "You're angry."

He shook his head.

That was a lie.

He sighed moodily.

"Yeah, I'm angry." He ran his fingers through his hair and refused to look at her. "What the . . . *hell* is all of this? Why is this happening? I mean . . ." He sat up, his legs straddling the lounge chair, and threw a hand at the covered pool. "What *is* all this . . . shit?"

He still couldn't look at *her*.

Out of the corner of his eye, he saw she looked over at the pool too. "Those are Shells. I told you that."

The anger flared. "I *know* they're Shells, but *what's* a Shell?" he asked as steadily as he could.

"This world calls them zombies. Living dead. They aren't dead. They're still alive, kind of. The technical term is Vacusai. *Empty*." Meg took a deep breath. "What makes a person a person has been . . . extricated, pulled out and stored in something like this." Charlie looked at her, still not at her face, and saw she held another one of those little balls in her hand like the one she used to freeze the pool last night . . . or early this morning. It was all running together. This particular little ball was a pulsing yellow. "Their souls, for lack of a better word, are kept in something like this so that someone else can tie themselves to a cluster of Shells and control them."

Charlie looked back at the pool. "So someone is puppeteering those things?"

Meg nodded. "A Dominosk. A *host*."

"And that someone is trying to kill me?"

She nodded again. "And Spencer. I think you and I being here was a surprise."

"Who is it?"

"I don't know."

He looked up at her sharply, directly into her eyes, "Seriously, Meg. I'm over evasiveness."

Her hand moved as though she was about to reach across and touch his leg, but she settled it back on her own. "Charlie, I really don't know. I was sent to bring you home."

His guts started to squirm. "A moment ago, you said something about 'this world' and now you're trying to bring me 'home' . . ." his guts were doing more than squirming now. He felt like he was about to jump off a cliff. "Where's home? Where are you from?"

"Charlie, your parents have been writing about it for years."

In an instant, the pulsing yellow ball was gone and in its place was the first volume of his parents' series. If he hadn't already been so baffled by his current circumstances, he would have been incredibly impressed by her sleight of hand skills.

Taking the book from her, the weight of it took on a whole new meaning.

Charlie struggled emotionally as he flipped the cover open and recognized the map of the United Realm that welcomed the reader in the front of every book and gave a final farewell in the back. Agalon,

Inglind, Umyrika. They were all words he'd grown up hearing but didn't know what any of them had meant, and here they were on the map. Places. They were all places, countries it seemed. Countries with cities and mountains and rivers.

Meg slipped over next to him. "Do you have any idea how they knew about all of this?"

Charlie shrugged. "They always had big imaginations," he mumbled. "Dad would take me on dragon hunts on our land when I was little. We'd camp out and he made everything seem so real, telling me stories of great dragons and the hunters who caught them."

"Caught them? You didn't kill them?"

Charlie shook his head, "No, dad always insisted it was better to catch them and train them than kill them. 'What use is a dead dragon?' he would ask as we lay next to the campfire. 'If you train one it can do all sorts of things for you. Protect you, carry you, keep you company, boil your water. Dead dragons can't do any of that. How do you think I got your mom?' The first time I saw my mom boiling water on the stove after he said that, I broke down in a honking laughing fit. Mom thought I'd lost my mind." Charlie took a deep breath, holding back the emotion. "He was a good guy. Couldn't hurt anything."

Softly, Meg reached over and turned the pages. Title page, table of contents, the dedication. It was almost the same in every book. Some sort of a variation on, "To our son, Charlie. This is all for you." He turned past that one quickly, his fingers fumbling with the pages.

"What's that?" A poem lay in the middle of the next page.

> Like scattered leaves in a raging storm,
> The six have left and await return.
> Darkened sun and radiant moon,
> Obsidian and fire, will meet none too soon.

A property lost, will in chains be bound,
Gnarled small tree, its truth not found.
All six will join and journey home,
Else one will fade, second enthrone.

Meg looked spellbound by the poem. "It's in all of them," Charlie said, a touch of pride in his hushed words. "Only part I ever read, right after the dedication page."

"Charlie . . ." Meg looked at him, a certain surprise in her eyes. "*How* did your parents know all of this?"

He shrugged his big shoulders, "They just made it up. Like I said, great imaginations."

Meg looked back at the books. "Charlie," her surprise had turned to awe. "Charlie, this isn't made up. This is all *real*. The robed man on the front is Billingshound, the Father of the United Realm."

Charlie snorted and waited for the punch line.

Meg's shock hung in the air.

"Charlie," she gestured with a shaking hand, "this is all about you."

Immediately, Charlie wanted to reject the idea. After all, it was completely ludicrous, wasn't it? Magically he was from this land, this world his parents had created on paper? All this time he had been living under the same roof with his history and his actual story? All this time, the feeling he had harbored of being intended for more was actually true? Every day when he rode that bus to school and vaguely knew this wasn't what he was supposed to be doing, wasn't his reality? Every single moment he sat on the roof outside of his room and looked up at the stars wondering how to ease the aching in his heart, the possibilities filled the bookshelves of the house he couldn't wait to leave behind? No, it was too much.

But it all came back to potential. Back to purpose. Back to his mom pleading with him to just crack the first one.

What an absolute arrogant asshole he had been.

Now it was potential and purpose deteriorating into regret.

"Bogart knew . . ." Charlie said, the revelation blooming in his brain while at the same time filling his belly with guilt. "Bogart knew what that orb was. He knew how to use it because he's read these books over and over." That's what he meant when he told Charlie to read the books. Seeing that orb must have confirmed it all for him. Wherever Bogart went, was he okay?

"This was very irresponsible of them."

"Of who?"

"Your parents." The look on Meg's face read of equal parts indignation and wonder. "If Bogart could do what he did as a casual reader—"

Charlie chuckled, "There was—," No, Bogart was still alive. "There *is* nothing casual about Bogart's obsession with these books. He's voracious."

"Whatever the case, these volumes could be dangerous."

"And what exactly do you propose we do about that? They're all over the world. It's not like you can hop on a global news channel and recall them like a malfunctioning baby swing."

Meg sighed, "Right. Of course." Perhaps sensing the tension between them had melted, Meg slid her body up against his and laid her head in the crook of his arm. It felt good. Right. Lightly, she touched the wound across his chest, "Why didn't you just read them? Your parents' books?"

He sighed. Here he went. "Okay, honesty here. I don't read well. It messes with my eyes. You know what dyslexia is?" By the look she gave him, he could tell she didn't. "It's this thing with my head where the words get kind of jumpy and jumbled up. It's not too crazy, I can do all right, but it's still hard."

"I'm sorry."

"Yeah," he went on, "I looked at them," he laughed, "but they're huge! It would take me a year to get through that. I never told my parents about the dyslexia thing, if that's even what it is, figured it would be insanely disappointing for the son of two bestselling authors to suck at reading. What I didn't count on was the fact that when the son of two bestselling authors refused to read their books, that would hurt worse." Emotion threatened to overwhelm him, but he took a deep breath and kept it at bay.

"Okay," she ran a hand over his shoulder, "So, don't read them. You've got me. I'll tell you what you need to know."

"What I need to know?" He took her hand and gave it a kiss, "Can we start with: why me?" He glanced toward the pool house where Spencer shivered and slept, "why him?"

"Of course," Meg nodded, "the Six of you— there are Six. You, him, and four others. The plan, as I understand it, was to get the Six of you away from the chaos seeping through our world, keep you safe while you grew up, and eventually bring you back when the time was right. And now is the time."

"What happens when we're all scooped up?" He watched perfect white puffy clouds drift across the rich blue sky.

"You go home. Your actual home." She traced a finger over his belly, making it flex involuntarily. "Okay, honesty," she said in a soft voice. "I really want you to kiss me."

"Yeah?"

"Yeah."

"I really want to kiss you too." He shifted to the side of the lounge chair, the wound across his chest pulling uncomfortably, and she slid up beside him. Placing a hand on her waist, he leaned in and felt her lips touch his. The electricity was real and it lit him up. He loved it. He refused to take his lips away and he was sure he could feel the same from her. Her lips were as cool as the rest of her, soft and cool to the touch. A touch of saltiness, flowery. Her hand was tracing his jaw. He didn't know how long the kiss went on, it felt like it revived every time it seemed to be drawing to an end. At some point, his hand had slipped up the back of her shirt and he was running his fingers up and down her spine.

Charlie took a deep breath and leaned back. That kiss was everything he had always hoped a kiss would be. And he wanted so much more. He was drunk with it, a totally different kind of drunk, but drunk all the same. By the look of it, her experience was much the same. "Okay, honesty here. I've never done that before."

"Could have fooled me."

"You?"

"I can't say the concept is foreign to me, but it hasn't happened too often," she grinned slyly.

He watched her for a moment and decided to take the plunge. "Okay, honesty there?"

She made a cute confused face, "Okay, honesty here. What?"

"What are you?"

Charlie felt her stiffen beside him. Her eyes were suddenly distant. Had he just hit a bullseye he wasn't even aiming for?

"Why are you asking me that?" She sat up.

He propped himself up on his elbow, the cut across his chest stretching painfully. "You took on— what, seven Shells on your own when I was almost killed by, like, four? I love the way you feel. You're soft and kind of, cold to the touch." He laughed, "I'm so freakin' hot natured, I'm in shorts and a t-shirt on a cold day. And also, when you touch me, it . . . it sends this energy through me, like, every muscle vibrates and pulses." He heard himself and laughed again, "I'm sorry, I'm rambling. I sound like Bogart. But, I really want to know, what are you? I know you come from some other world, so I'm not going to be shocked if you're, like, a goddess or something."

Meg studied his face for a moment, looking from eye to eye as though she was trying to gauge his sincerity. She ran her finger over the cut again, then nodded.

Standing up from the lounge chair, she turned to face him. "Okay, honesty here." She hesitated, then shrugged, "I'm a girl." She must have clearly read the disappointment on his face because she pressed on, "and at the moment, I'm also a Gohlem."

Charlie sat all the way up, he'd heard of those. His dad would tell stories of them. Creatures made of . . . of . . . well, of anything, really. Dirt, metal, ice, it didn't matter. What mattered was they were brainless, will-less slaves. *Cool to the touch*, of course, like clay or dirt when you dig deep. Earthy, flowery, the smell of fresh herbs. "You're a Gohlem?"

"You know about Gohlems?" she asked tentatively.

"Kinda . . ." He swallowed hard.

"I'm a . . . I . . ." The girl before him, generally so spunky and confident, was genuinely struggling, her hands pulling at the hem of her frayed, denim shorts. "It happened to me a long time ago. Kinda. All this stuff, the other world, the things happening there. They were . . . there was a lot of human experimentation going on. It's awful, everything has turned awful. You want to know something about our world? *Your* world Charlie? It used to be perfect and now it's not. When the Choice happened, that's when you were sent away, the Six. And since then, really, really bad things happened. And it happened to me. This is me. I'm a Gohlem for now."

Charlie's mind was spinning and he was trying to grab onto one of the hundreds of thoughts whirling around. "Okay, so . . . you keep saying, 'for now,' this is *temporary*?"

She swallowed and nodded vigorously. Was that real? Do Gohlems swallow? Why would they swallow? Meg pointed at the pool. "It's why I don't hurt them. Somewhere out there, someone has their heartsoul. In something like this." She held out her hand palm up.

Pushing out through the skin in the middle of her hand emerged the small, marble-sized orb, glowing yellow she had shown him earlier. "That's *me* in there."

CHAPTER EIGHTEEN

On the Road Again

The little yellow marble was only the beginning of it. Meg showed him how her body changed and moved and shifted. She didn't necessarily have to be what she was, but it's what she knew best. "And this is really you?" Charlie had asked her.

She bit her lip and nodded, "This is me. This is what my real body looks like. But it doesn't have to." Without warning her features shifted, her whole body shifted and she was a faceless, featureless Meg-sized gingerbread cookie. Charlie fell back off his chair and somehow managed to end up on his feet without making too much more of a fool of himself. He couldn't possibly have had a worse reaction, not a shred of decency, and he knew it. He'd been raised better than that and his dad would have said as much. By the time he had recovered, she was back to what he was accustomed to, but her hair was out of the braid and back into the explosive pigtails, her shirt and shorts were the ones she wore yesterday.

"You're freaked out."

He nodded, "I'm suitably freaked out."

She started backing away, "I'm sorry, Charlie."

In way of reassuring her, he stepped over the pool chair, wrapped his arms around her and kissed her. He felt her body relax under him and hoped in the back of his mind that she wasn't relaxing too much. In his mind's eye, he saw himself holding an armful of fleshy goo. Was that possible? He pulled back and smiled. "I'm suitably freaked out, but you are mind blowing in so many ways."

That made her smile, "Glad you think so. Yeah, I can do and be a lot of things, but I'm looking forward to having my body again. This has its drawbacks. Can't taste food, don't really sleep, can't smell. I haven't bathed in years. Water is a big no-no. Obviously."

"Right. Obviously. I'm sorry."

She shrugged. "But I can feel. I've figured out how to concentrate my surface to simulate feeling. So when you kiss me, I feel it." She kissed him lightly and smiled. "I'm gonna go check on our sleeping host."

And that's when he laid back down in the chair. The girl he was into was a creature from his parents' books. His parents' books weren't fiction. Charlie didn't belong here. Not in California or Texas or . . . Earth?

"Wake up, man. Get it together and let's go."

Charlie blinked, the afternoon Californian sunlight was warm and comforting. The booted toe nudging him in the side was not.

"Wake it up, big guy." Spence was hovering over him with a cigarette hanging from his lips, its ash threatening to fall at any moment. After being whacked in the head with a flower pot last night, the skinny guy seemed to have made a full recovery. His hair was freshly spiked at all angles and he smelled like he'd scrubbed off all the filth in the shower. There was a bruise in the center of his forehead, but not near as bad as Charlie thought it should be. As well as the other guy was functioning, Charlie couldn't help but assume Meg had missed a well-hidden baggie or five.

Charlie sat up and stretched, "Where're we going?"

Spence took a drag off his cigarette, "No idea, but we can't stay here. Those bitches'll be back." He exhaled as he nodded at the frozen pool. "Ever been to a beach, big tits?"

Charlie wasn't sure which caught him more off guard the disturbing nickname or the idea of seeing a beach for the first time in his life. A real beach? Charlie had never been out of Farnsworth, Texas, until Meg whisked him away. He just shook his head.

"Perfect, we'll go to the beach and figure it out from there."

"Wait, how are you okay with all this?"

"Your girl and I talked while you snoozed out here. I'm down. I'm always up for a party, road trips, and hotties. Scoot over." Charlie made room and Spence dropped down next to him. He was so light, the chair didn't even seem to respond. "I always knew something was weird, right? I mean, I'm adopted and I'm Asian as hell, but I have these." He raised his sunglasses to nest in his hair.

In the dark, Charlie hadn't noticed them last night, but now he could. They were light gray. No, they were glittering silver. "Are they contacts?"

Spence laughed, a very melodic thing and slapped Charlie on the leg, "No, dumbass, they're my legit eyeballs." He took a long drag off his cigarette and flung it onto the pool cover. "My sister's are golden." Smoke curled from his nostrils. "Her agency— my *dad's* agency, Bull and Badger, heard of it? Anyway, the agency loves them, her eyes, and so do the photographers. She's shit as a model, I mean real shit, can't walk worth a damn, but daddy's money and those eyes opened all kinds of doors. That and she plays the game." He turned his silver eyes on Charlie, "You could make it in the business with your size and build." He squeezed Charlie's arm with his long thin fingers. "Fitness mags would eat you up for sure. How long have you and your girl been together?"

The question came out of nowhere and Charlie felt the heat in his face, "I don't really think she's my girl."

The other raised a well-manicured eyebrow, "Really? Cause the way your tongue was down her throat sure looked that way. Good to know there's no commitment though." Spence slapped him on the leg again and squeezed it, "Get your ass up and let's go. I packed us a duffle. Tried to find some of my biggest workout stuff. Shut up, I work out, I just can't bulk up. We're not all gifted in that area, big guy. But I'm gifted in another area, if you get what I'm saying." He grabbed his crotch through his tight black jeans.

Charlie *got it* all too clearly.

"Spencer Carrington," he held his hand out.

Charlie took it, but wished he hadn't based on where it just came from, "Charlie Daniels."

"Nice titties, Charlie. Let's get them bouncin' out of here."

Spencer was exhausting. He seemed to run from one subject to another without taking a breath. Parties, beach life, parties, Hollywood gossip, parties, hookups, parties. He ran through it all. Meg listened politely, but Charlie could hardly stand it. The silver-eyed junky was easier to stomach when he was passed out shivering on the couch.

Despite the new plus-one, this was how California should be experienced, Charlie thought to himself as he rode in the back of Spence's Mustang convertible. The engine hummed under the hood of the old vintage beast, the black paint job sparkled in the sun. He took up the entirety of the back seat with his arms stretched out over the head rests. Spence had loaned him a pair of aviator sunglasses which he claimed cost more than the totality of Charlie's possessions. Since Charlie no longer had any possessions, Spence was more correct than he knew. The sound of the wind and thumping music was welcome as it drowned out Spencer's constant blabbing.

Meg sat up front in a pair of huge white-framed sunglasses and a floral scarf over her hair. She looked like something out of an old magazine and Charlie couldn't help but grin every time he looked at her. The coolest part was she let him watch as she "put it on." Spencer had run to his room to grab a few things, so she took the opportunity. The scarf was the first to materialize, then he watched as her eyes bulged and the glasses took shape. It was incredible, *she* was incredible. She changed her shorts to white and her shirt lost its sleeves and went bright floral. What else could she do?

At first, Spence pointed out house after house where this and that celebrity lived as they drove through his "neighborhood." It wasn't a neighborhood; it was a series of walled-off monuments to wealth. Charlie was getting a glimpse of what his parents thought they were protecting him from. Once he realized neither Meg nor Charlie recognized the names, he gave up and just turned up the radio, which was fine with Charlie, all he wanted to do was spend time with his thoughts and soak in the sun.

Bogart's bag sat on the seat next to him, the books inside calling to him. It wouldn't do any good though. The thought of reading them made his head hurt. Besides, he had Meg, they had an understanding. The revelation of her being a Gohlem proved he could trust her, and the more he thought about her and the possibilities, the more into it he was. Plus, even if reading wasn't an issue, he couldn't do it in the car. He tried to do homework on the bus several times before and almost ended up puking all over his algebra binder. It would have been an improvement.

As the car purred past palm trees, Meg would look over her shoulder and grin. Was the adventure going the way she had expected? She'd found two of her Six and with the Traveling Orb, Charlie hoped the other four would be just as easy to come by. Charlie had pushed to use the orb right there in the mansion's backyard, but Meg insisted they had to use it in an open space, hence why they'd walked so far away from his house in Texas to use it the first time in the open field. Spence just kept repeating the word *beach* over and over.

The walk through the fields in Texas. His home. His parents. It felt like the longer he kept those thoughts at bay, the less important they were, which only made him feel guilty. Riding in the back of the car under the Californian sun, Charlie could almost convince himself this was simply some sort of vacation, as though home still existed in the middle of nowhere Texas.

Spence glanced at him in the rearview mirror. "Hey, big guy," Spence shouted over the wind, "why don't you check that duffle and make sure you're cool with what I brought you? If not, we could always stop and buy you something at a surf shop. Some sweet board shorts, one of those tanks with the gaping arm holes. Take a look in the bag first." Confused, Charlie pulled the black duffle over to him. "I think your stuff is close to the bottom."

Unzipping the bag, Charlie dug through the clothes. His hand came in contact with something familiar and when it did he shot the rearview mirror a look. Spence was watching him with a wicked gleam in his almond shaped silver eyes. Charlie glanced back down at the object nestled against his hand. The shampoo bottle. And it was full. Not only was *it* full, but so were the other three and the baggies with who-knew-what in them. Charlie's heart was beating hard and fast before he knew it.

"All that work for you, big guy?" Spence called out over the wind noise.

Charlie zipped the bag back up and pushed it away from him, but nodded all the same. "Yeah, it's all good," he stammered out. Spencer knew. Spencer knew, and worse, they were in on it together.

The convertible slowed and Charlie realized the roar of the wind had been traded for the roar of the ocean. As the car rolled to a stop in an empty public parking lot, Charlie stood up and looked out over the vastness that was the Pacific Ocean. The brief panic of being found out Spence had just ignited was soothed by the sight of the sea and cry of the seagulls. Meg slipped off her sunglasses—*now, how did she manage that?* — and smiled to herself.

"Impressive, yeah?" Spence leaped over the side of the car and peeled his snug t-shirt off. "I don't care much for the outdoors, but this shit is magical and you can't help but submit." Instantly, he lit a cigarette and took a long drag off of it. "You guys getting out or what?"

Meg let herself out and Charlie stepped over the side of the car.

"Get the bag, big guy." Spence grinned and took another drag. Charlie's stomach clenched and he grabbed the duffle and Bogart's backpack.

The parking lot was at the top of a rocky cliff, one that looked as though it were puzzle pieced together with giant boulders. Seagulls cried out over the white sand and shifted their attention to the three newcomers in obvious hopes of food. An old wooden staircase zig-zagged back and forth down the side of the cliff face and creaked and swayed as Spence led them down.

Meg took a few steps toward the water, but stopped well away from it, drawing in a deep breath.

Spence flicked his cigarette into the sand.

And Charlie stood silent. He'd seen pictures of beaches and the ocean, but the real thing was something he struggled to comprehend. All that water. All that life *beneath* the water.

The water.

Before he knew it, Charlie's feet were racing him to the water. He threw off his shirt, shoes and socks in an awkward dance, and met the water with total abandon. Meg laughed melodically from a good distance behind him in the dry sand. "Come out with me!"

"No! I *can't swim*," she called back with a rueful smile.

Damn it, that's right. "It's beautiful, isn't it?" Charlie swept the hair out of his face, his body bobbing with the tide.

She waved him off, "Gorgeous! I'll enjoy it from here!"

Charlie saw it happening before he could stop him. Spence came up behind her and wrapped his arms around her, lifting Meg off the ground and hauling her toward the water. She screamed and when she did, Charlie's instincts kicked in and he fought his way back to the shore as quickly as he could against the current. Meg was kicking and Spence only laughed. He only laughed for a moment, however, because just as Charlie reached shore, Spence was doubled over on the ground, his hands holding his crotch.

"You kicked me in the nuts, you bitch! I was only messing with you!"

Charlie reached out to Meg, but she jerked back just before he touched her with his wet hand. "Are you okay?"

Meg was rattled. "I'm fine. I'm just . . . I'm sorry, I didn't mean to hurt you. I just don't like to swim, is all."

Spence groaned and rolled in the sand.

"But you're okay?" Charlie wanted to touch her, but he knew he couldn't. What would even a few drops of water do to her?

Straightening her scarf, Meg looked off down the beach toward a more secluded area. "I'm going to go . . . um . . . I'm going to go find a place to use the orb. You two just stay put."

And she was gone.

Charlie watched her go and felt completely helpless. Was he supposed to go after her? Comfort her? What would his dad have done if his mom was in a similar situation? What was the decent thing to do?

Spence was finally still but kept his knees pulled up to his chest.

Charlie looked down at him without a shred of sympathy, "You shouldn't have done that."

"No shit," he groaned. "She kicked me in the balls, man. You don't ever kick a guy in the balls." He stretched his legs hesitantly as though he were trying out the move for the first time and was unsure of whether or not something would fall out of his pant leg. Taking a deep breath, he coughed and raised his hand. "Help me up, big guy."

Charlie bent and took Spence by the hand, and pulled him to his feet. "Just leave her alone, okay?"

"No problem there." Spence staggered. "You put up with that shit? She's raw, man. Issues. I know a good therapist. I mean, hasn't done shit for me, but the quack is good."

The bags lay between them and Charlie could feel the pull to the duffle. It wouldn't be like last time. Last time he had lost control because he didn't know how much was too much. Now he knew. With a look down the shoreline to make sure Meg was out of sight, and he out of her sight, he knelt down beside the black duffel and unzipped it. "Yeah, man," Spence smirked, "get what you need." The shampoo bottle was buried under clothes, clothes Charlie hoped were clean. When he pulled the bottle free, a couple of orange prescription containers rattled into view. Charlie eyed them cautiously, "What are those for? Are you sick or something?"

Spence grinned and threw his head back, "Or something, man. Or something." Like a lunging snake, the skinny guy grabbed one of the containers and popped a pill in a practiced motion. "Want one? They're good. Really makes everything settle. Like, most people do this shit for crazy colors and stuff. Naw, not me. I gotta settle all that shit down. Too many colors. Too many sounds. Doctors told my dad it was some kind of, what, sensory sensitivity shit? Had me on meds when I was a kid, but I found other stuff that worked way, way better."

Charlie glanced at the shampoo bottle in his hand and shook his head, "No, this is fine." Unscrewing the lid, he took a gulp, the liquid burning its way down to his belly. "What is this?" he coughed. It was stronger than before. A lot stronger.

"Whiskey, man. Aged real good. Took it from daddy's stash."

Charlie knocked off a couple more swigs before recapping it and burying it back under the clothes. Spence dropped the pills in and Charlie covered those too before he zipped the bag up.

"You saw mine, so show me yours," Spencer grinned.

Charlie bolted to his feet, "What the hell?"

The other guy laughed, "Relax, what's in your backpack? Like, secret plans or some shit? Or what, you got some homework to get done before tomorrow? Book report? 'Who I did last night in California' by Charlie Douglas."

Charlie's face flushed at the suggestion, "Daniels."

"Who the hell cares?" Spence squatted over the backpack. "Let's see what you got. Probably some wine coolers. I bet you were a fuzzy navel guy before you hit my stuff, huh?" He unzipped the backpack, but his reaction wasn't what Charlie expected. His mouth hung open and for once he was silent. It didn't last long though, "Hold the fuckin' phone. Charlie *Daniels*? Like, *Daniels* Daniels?" He pulled one of the books out. "James and Harriett, *United* fuckin' *Realms* Daniels?"

"Yeah," Charlie shrugged. "You've read them?"

Spence made a face, "Not a damn page, but every time one is released, people blow their loads all over themselves. Why didn't you say so? People lose their shit over these books! And, oh man, would they make a killer new cable series. I mean, could you imagine it? All the special effects and shit? Like, tons of fantasy titties and shit? I mean, they'd have to add a lot of sex and shit, because your parents are hella prudes, but that's easy." Spencer stood and his hands went to his head like his brain was trying to explode, "*Charlie Daniels*! Right here! This whole thing got way more fucking sweet!"

"Hey, Charlie!" It was Meg from a good distance down the beach. "I've found a good spot! You two come on!"

Thank God. Charlie was seconds from picking the guy up and throwing him in the water.

Scooping up his shirt, shoes, and socks, Charlie knocked the sand off them as best he could, and walked down the shoreline, the tide creeping up over his feet before rolling back out. Spence grabbed the bags and trailed behind him, humming some melody to himself, it might have been *Hotel California*, and giggling periodically in combination with "Charlie fuckin' Daniels" and ". . . we haven't had the spirit here since 1969 . . ."

Yeah, it was *Hotel California*.

The sips from the shampoo bottle were settling in and he was feeling that warmth and peace that was becoming familiar. His muscles and mood relaxed as water lapped his feet and the breeze licked over his shoulders and down his back. His chest stung, but he could handle it here. This is why people love California. When this was all over, this is where he would find himself.

The quirky, little blond had found a grove of palm trees secluded from the rest of the beach and the road above. The sound of waves crashing and gulls crying penetrated the little sanctuary. Reluctantly, Charlie slipped his t-shirt back on, but stuck his shoes and socks in Spence's bag, feeling the soft pull of the hidden bottle.

Meg produced the green marbled Traveling Orb and held it out in front of her. "Ready?"

Charlie placed his big hand over it. Secretly, and desperately, he hoped his buzz would help him relax and avoid retching up his toes upon their arrival to wherever it was the green ball was taking them.

Spence looked perplexed. "What's that?"

"A Transport Orb," Charlie said with a serious lack of enthusiasm. "Just stick your damn hand on it."

A frown slipped across Meg's face and Charlie mumbled something like an apology.

"What's it do?"

"It takes us where we need to go next," Meg chirped quickly.

"Like magic or some shit?"

Meg shrugged, "Something like that."

Spence slapped his hand on it, "Sweet. Let's do this."

"It might be a little disorienting."

"Honey," Spence smirked, "I live in realms of disorienting you couldn't even put words, colors, or imagination to. I got this."

Spence gave Charlie a silvery wink and blew him a kiss.

Charlie glared at him.

Meg placed her other hand over both of theirs, "Okay, just make sure you keep your hands, feet, and head inside the swirling colors."

Spence raised a lazy eyebrow, "And if I don't?"

"Feel free to find out," Charlie muttered.

Green light flashed.

CHAPTER NINETEEN

To Hell with It

Charlie's addition of alcohol to the Transport Orb's disorienting nausea didn't go quite as he had hoped. While his mind hadn't fought the twisting, yanking, and shoving sensations as it had the first time, his stomach was so relaxed that when his feet hit the ground, it immediately ejected its contents onto said ground. Well, into the *water*. The low tide rolled in and lapped his puke away. He took a deep breath and almost emptied his stomach again, but managed to hold things together. Charlie straightened up to see Spence ankle deep in the water lighting a cigarette and scanning the place. Meg was standing on the shore, wide-eyed and visibly shaken.

"Where are we?" Charlie asked as he wiped his mouth. How was the other guy okay after that psychedelic rollercoaster?

Spence hefted the bags on his shoulder, "Looks like Coney Island. Damn freak show." He took a drag off his cigarette and let it seethe from his lips as he spoke, "My dad used to bring me and my sister here all the time. He loved it. He'd make us go to these . . . shows where dudes would drill things up their noses and hang weights from their nuts. Unbelievable. The man was— is? The man's— my dad's a monster. The world loves him, but he's a real piece of shit." He took a longer drag off his cigarette and ashed it into the water. "I hate this place. He owns it now. This and—" another long drag, "a bunch of other crazy little entertainment pockets. You ever go to those renaissance faires? He owns like six of them. Two in Nowhere, Texas, a couple in Who-the-fuck-knows, Wisconsin, and now one in Oregon. I say *now*, but it's been, like, a year or something." He flicked the spent butt into the water, "Hella waste of money."

There was a weird moment where a bit of sympathy started welling up in Charlie for the skinny guy dressed in black. Charlie knew *he* had some issues with his parents, with James and Harriett, but they never pulled anything like that. Maybe they weren't perfect, but they were a far cry from monsters. They loved him and went out of their way to make sure he knew it.

"Your girl/not-your-girl looks like she's about to pass out."

"She's my—" Charlie said quickly, but didn't know where to go from there. They hadn't discussed it.

"No label? Just checking again," the other guy said with, what? Charlie couldn't place it, but he felt it and it was awkward.

"That was close," was all Meg could say for several minutes. "That was super close."

The brave little blonde girl's fear of water was on full display and their Travel that time had nearly pitched her right into it. The boys were fine. Both had their shoes off, so no harm. In fact, Charlie puking in the water was a hell of a lot better than on solid ground. At least this way his humiliation was washed away without a trace.

"I knew we'd end up some place like we were, but I thought we were far enough away . . .", Meg said.

Spence threw his arm around Charlie's shoulder, like they were old buddies, and leaned in, "So that green thing has rules?"

Meg looked down at it and nodded, her breathing starting to calm, "Yes. Generally. It knows where you need to go, even if you don't totally know yourself. Like, I knew I was coming to find one of you when I first got here, I just didn't know which one. Could have been any of the Six of you." She took another settling breath and let it out, "You can manipulate it a little, I think. The more you focus on a thought, a need, the more you can press it, hopefully, in that direction. It's like moving an elephant. Your little pushes might move it where you want it to go—"

"Or," Spence cut in, "It could get tired of your shit and squish your insides out." Spence squeezed Charlie's shoulder.

"Yeah," Meg said uncertainly.

Charlie shrugged Spence's arm off, only to feel his hand reach up and hang onto his shoulder. Whatever this was, it was going to get old. "So," Charlie said, "we're in New York? Coney Island is in New York, right?"

"Yeah, home away from home, or some shit like that. I take it we're here for my sister?"

Meg slipped the orb into her little flowery backpack, "They're all here now."

"All?" Charlie asked. "As in all Six of us? How do you know that?" This was big. Charlie could feel it.

"Yeah, you got a radar for us in that bag of yours, Ms. Poppins?" Charlie hated the way he said it, but he was wondering the same thing.

Meg looked like she was struggling with an answer. She glanced at Charlie, a plea for help in her eyes. But the mixture of booze, Transport nausea, and Spencer's handsiness was cutting Charlie's patience short. He could tell she was evading again and he hated it. *Just answer. Just say it. We've come this far.* "I just . . . know. I mean, I can feel it?"

Spence pressed, "Oh, so you're psychic or something? You can pick up on our vibes?"

Meg bit her lip and kept looking to Charlie for a rescue, but he didn't want to give it. He wanted to know. He wanted her to just give a straight, clear answer. "I just, know. I can feel it. That's all I can really say."

Charlie watched her. So much wasn't being said, so much she knew and just wouldn't say. Why? What was going to happen if she did? Charlie wasn't sure if it was her evasiveness that was bothering him so much or the fact that he was beginning to side with the guy groping his shoulder. Charlie shook his head, "You know what, Meg? I thought we were past this. I thought I *knew* it all by now or you'd at least just answer whatever the hell I needed to know. Guess I not, right? Just figure out where we're going next and point me in the right direction like a damn dog when you're good and ready as usual." He pulled the black duffle off Spencer's shoulder and nodded at a bench a brief walk away, "I'll be over there getting my shoes on."

He was pissed and he was becoming more so. They'd had that conversation at the pool house, she knew he was over the evasiveness. He knew she was a Gohlem. That was the depth of it right? Could it go any deeper? Get any 'worse'? Just answer the damn questions. Just be *clear*. Enough with the weird little pauses. When someone asks you something, answer.

But it was the secrets. That's exactly what it was. Not *her* secrets, but secrets in general. Mysteries. The ones his parents held, the things they never talked to him about and thought they were protecting him from, but they weren't! He was sick of it all.

There was no fire.

Dammit, he hadn't thought of that at all and it whispered in his ear, hissed, stoking the fire in his belly, the pressure in his forehead mounting. Making matters worse, he knew he'd never get an answer. They were gone and the truth with them. Charlie's hands shook as he yanked on his socks and shoes, he fumbled with the laces and it only served to piss him off all the more. He was far more furious than he thought he could be over something like this. But it wasn't simply *this*. And it was deeper and more painful than secrets. It was *lies*. His parents had been *lying* to him. His *parents*. Were they his parents? That thought hit him hard and he didn't have the capacity for it. He loved them, but he clearly hadn't *known* them. And he was angry. Livid. Pissed. And on top of it all, his own new lie was hidden at the bottom of the bag at his feet.

By now his chest was heaving as though he'd been running for miles, and the cut across his chest stung. His own secret. That bottle. Those bottles. They called to him. And he was fuming with Meg and his parents for *their* secrets and lies, but was he growing his own right here?

No.

Reaching into the bag, he pulled out the shampoo bottle of whiskey, uncapped it and took a serious gulp. It burned and he wanted to cough, but he closed his eyes and regained control. The whiskey's heat burned and settled in his belly like resolve. He took one more drink and capped it, then zipped up the bag and slung it over his shoulder.

With the bottle boldly and openly in hand, he returned to the other two. Spence had lit up again and Meg was standing at a good distance from the shoreline, her own bag gripped tightly in her hands. Charlie tossed the duffle to Spence, "Your shoes are in there." Eyes on Meg, Charlie uncapped the shampoo bottle and took another drink.

Meg's eyes narrowed, "What's that, Charlie?"

Charlie took another drink, his eyes locked with hers. "In the name of openness, I'll tell you. It's whiskey."

"Really damn good whiskey, I might add," Spence chimed in.

"Shut the hell up, Spence," Charlie snapped.

"You got it, boss."

Meg's eyes narrowed. "Liquor? Where'd you get it?"

Charlie took another drink. "The first time, in the shower at Spence's place. I like it. I like the way it makes me feel. It calms me."

"You don't seem calm now," she said quietly.

"I'm *not* calm now," Charlie fired back. "I'm pissed. But it's fine. This is apparently the game you play. Give just enough information, string me along, seduce me, get me to follow you like a . . . a . . ."

"Like a dumbass," Spence offered.

Charlie was on the brink of biting the other guy's head off but stopped himself when he realized how apt the word was. "Yeah, like a dumbass. Followed you like a dumbass. And you know? Everything was fine before I met you. The day I met you things really went to hell. No, they went to shit. Pure, unadulterated shit. How do I know this isn't all *because* of you? How do I know it's not *because* of you my parents are dead and my home was obliterated?"

"Charlie, I didn't do that. You know that."

"I *don't* know that!" Charlie bellowed. "And now. And now!" He took another gulp from the bottle, "And now I'm in New York City chasing down four other people who could be worse than this guy," he flung a hand toward Spence who simply shrugged, "while being chased by zombies sent from some Host from behind a curtain somewhere! Shit!"

He was done.

She didn't say anything.

Spence had frozen while tying his second shoe and waited.

The gulls cried overhead.

The waves lapped lazily at the shore.

But she still didn't say a single word.

Charlie raised the shampoo bottle to her in a toast, "To all *your* little secrets and *shifty* lies and evasiveness, may all that shit serve you well." He put the bottle to his lips and guzzled down an obscene amount, his throat burning, his brain screaming at him to stop, but his fury barreling on recklessly. He drained it, capped it, and turned to the ocean and hurled it with everything he had. "Let's get this over with."

Spence stood to his feet awestruck. "You're a god."

"Shut up, Spence."

"You got it, boss."

Meg turned and walked away.

Of course, a piece of Charlie wished he hadn't guzzled the shampoo bottle of whiskey. It was the same piece of him who knew exactly how 'disappointed' his mom and dad would have been in him. Completely indecent. *But here's the thing,* he told himself, *they aren't your parents, right? So who gives a damn?*

So who gives a damn? That's what he began to cling to as he walked down the sidewalk as soberly as he could pretend. He played the words over and over in his head, *who gives a damn?* How angry was Meg at him? *Who gives a damn?* How hurt was Meg by him? *Who gives a damn?* Where was all of this going to end? *Who gives a damn?* Was he even interested in getting to the end of it? Some stupid ass quest. He was over it. *Who gives a damn?* Shells? Let them keep coming. From here on out, he was ripping them apart with his bare hands. And you know what? Since he was off the quest, they'd probably quit coming. The little girl would go find someone else's head to screw with. And Bogart . . . Bogart . . . *Who gives a damn?*

At some point Spence had taken the lead and was taking the two of them to God only knew where. They rode a subway, a thing Charlie had always wanted to do, but due to the amount of alcohol he had swimming in his bloodstream and his current state of melancholy, he wasn't really *experiencing* it. His world was hazy at best. People were present on the train with him, strangers moving through the city. A man sat opposite of him with a bottle in a brown, paper sack and stared into space, his lips giving shape to unspoken words. Charlie felt him, knew what he was experiencing. Hopeless. For a better part of his life, Charlie had judged those people. Now he felt for them. The whiskey felt good, it put the apprehensive parts of his mind to sleep and allowed him to just be.

The train came to a stop and an arm pulled him up, guiding him out. More stairs he stumbled up, more sidewalks, more streets to cross, more people Charlie bumped past guided by the hand on his lower back.

And eventually, at some point, there must have been a couch, because that's where he woke up in the dark.

"I don't mind him being here, Spencer, but we have a lot going on in the next few days and don't have time to host a guest." The man's voice was older, firm. A warm light was on down the hallway. "Where did you find this one?"

"Dad, it's *Charlie Daniels*."

Silence.

"Am I supposed to recognize that name?" The older man sounded confused, tired.

"Charlie *Daniels*. The books. James and Harriett *Daniels*, dad!"

Silence again. "That man out there?"

Spencer laughed, "He's barely a man. He's a kid, like, 18."

"Where'd you find him, Spence?" It was a woman, her voice a purr.

"We met on the flight here," that was Spencer, "hit it off, flight attendant assumed he was legal and gave him some drinks. The guy clearly can't hold his liquor worth shit—"

"Spencer," the man rebuffed.

"Sorry, dad. Anyway, I didn't know where he was staying, so I just brought him here."

"Helps that he's hot, right Spence?" The woman again.

"Shut up, V," Spence shot back.

"What?" the girl said, "It's what you do, right? Grab someone hot and bring them home? It's not your fault they don't stick around once they've realized how utterly useless you are. Does he know who your daddy is? Did you tell him that?"

"Seriously, V, shut up."

"Because if you told him, *that's* why he's here. You do know that, right? He's not into you, he's into your daddy?" She giggled, "Sorry, that sounds horrific, daddy, but you know what I mean."

There was a brief silence. Then, "*Did* you tell him who I am, Spencer?"

"No, sir."

"You're sure?"
"Yes, sir."
"Did you tell him who *I* am?" the girl interjected.
"Nobody gives a shit who you are, V," Spencer spat.
"Everyone gives a shit who I am, Spencer," she laughed. "Don't project yourself onto me."
"Children," the older man said with a hint of exhaustion. "Spencer, did you tell this young man who your *sister* is?"
Again, an uncomfortable silence. "Kind of, I think."
She laughed, "So he knows who *you* are, daddy. God, Spence, you're such an imbecile. You know that, right? You're *literally* brain dead. And I don't mean that as an insult, I'm stating fact. You're medically brain dead. You've shoved so many pills down your throat and fumes in your head, you can't help but be this stupid. It's sad."
"Veronica," the older man chided gently.
"I'm sorry, daddy, I just can't help it," she sighed. "I know it's not *nice*, but it's the *truth*. *You've* said it before. *I've* said it before. His *therapists* have said it before. If you didn't give him a roof over his head, he'd be lost and dead in a gutter somewhere."
Seconds of silence passed. Charlie lay there waiting for the rest of the conversation and grew more uncomfortable the longer nothing was said even though he wasn't in the room, for that he was grateful. He couldn't imagine what Spencer was going through. Even though Charlie wasn't sure he liked the guy, he didn't think anyone deserved this.
"Spencer," the man finally said, "I'm happy for you to be here. Thrilled. When I saw you sitting in the living room watching TV, my heart leaped. The day I adopted you and your sister, I made a commitment to care for the two of you until the day I died. You're my treasures, my most prized possession."
"I know, sir. I thought bringing him here . . . you've been trying to reach his parents . . ."

"You did well, son," Charlie couldn't tell if he was placating his son or not. This man didn't sound like the controlling tyrant Spence had made him out to be. "How long are you staying?"

"I don't know."

"That's fine. Stay as long as you like or need to."

"Thank you, sir."

"Veronica, help Spencer get his friend to his room."

"Okay, daddy."

Footsteps approached in the dark room and Charlie closed his eyes as though he'd been asleep the whole time. When fingers pulled on his arm, he feigned waking up. The room spun. Spence was standing over him pulling. "Get up, man." The woman stepped in and slipped her hand around his other arm. Charlie couldn't make out any features, but her silhouette was slender and tall. The twins pulled him to his feet and led him down a couple of dark hallways to a back bedroom. Lights came on and revealed a colorful, lavish room with modern furniture and vintage rock posters. It was like Spencer's cleaned-up self-expressed in a bedroom. Where his California pool house was a wreck with things stashed in every corner, this was polished and clean. An image of what he could be.

Charlie was deposited onto the bed and he finally got a good look at the girl. She looked so much like her brother, just in girl form. But where his hair was jet black, hers was so blond, it was almost platinum, and her almond shaped eyes glowed gold. No wonder the camera liked her so much. Charlie was struggling to take his eyes from her as well.

"I see why you snatched this one off the flight, Spence. He's gorgeous. Were you trying to get in his pants before or after you found out who he was?" She reached down and traced a finger down his jawline. "Georgia would love to use him. A little too muscly for Daney," she said as her hand brushed over his chest, "but *Georgia* likes them like this. Young and fresh-faced, but built like a man. He's what, seventeen? Eighteen? How old are you, puppy?"

Her voice was soothing, liquid. Charlie couldn't help but answer her. "Eighteen." He lied, going along with the story Spencer birthed in the kitchen earlier.

She laughed musically, "Just barely legal, are you, puppy?"

"V . . . ", Spence muttered.

She held up a hand, "I don't care what you do with him, Spence. Have fun with your little toy, but I think you may have actually stumbled onto something here. This could be really good for B&B. Daddy might even sign him with the agency. Let him be in his parents' movies when the rights are all wrapped up. Fans of the books would salivate over that little tid-bit. Might even have him walk one of the shows tomorrow. We'll see how he walks in the morning after he's had a chance to sober up." The slender girl touched the tip of Charlie's nose, "Night, night, puppy."

Spence closed the door behind her and neither of them said anything. It felt like trillions of thoughts were stumbling over each other in Charlie's head, but the first one that verbalized itself was, "Does she think we're. . . ?"

The other guy sighed, "Yeah. It was the easiest way to explain you being here."

That had a lot of implications Charlie wasn't sure how to deal with. "Oh."

"Relax, I'll sleep on the floor, man."

"You don't have to do that," Charlie shrugged, "this bed is huge."

"You sure?" Spence's shoulders sagged under defeat.

Charlie shrugged again, "Yeah, I guess."

Spence nodded and went about the business of getting ready for bed. Charlie watched him. His abundance of ego and arrogance had deflated entirely. The guy who advertised himself as a living

California stereotype had disappeared and this thin, broken man, boy really, took his place. It was crushing.

Charlie unsteadily stripped down to his underwear, then slipped under the expensive covers. It was the first time he'd been in a real bed since his own bed disappeared with his house. Spence slid into the bed with his back to Charlie and turned off the lights with the click of a remote.

The two lay there in silence. Charlie couldn't help but feel Spence's suffocating depression.

"Hey, Spence?"

"Yeah?"

"Where's Meg?"

"I don't know, man. You effectively shut her down. Damn, that was brutal. She took off when we got to the building," he yawned. "Told me to give you something and took off."

"Give me what?"

"I don't know, man. It's in a box in the duffle."

"And the duffle . . .?"

Spence groaned, "It's over by the damn door, man. I want to go to sleep and forget I exist."

"Okay, sorry."

"S'cool, man. Night."

Charlie slid out of the bed unsteadily and could see enough of the room by the moonlight. He was still very drunk. Digging through the bag, he found the other two shampoo bottles and pulled one out, setting it to the side. The box was small and covered in velvet like the ones on the jewelry commercials. Curiously, he opened it. A thick cuff bracelet lay in the middle. In the moonlight, he could tell it was plain, no markings or designs, just a thick band of metal, possibly silver. He squinted. It was hard to tell the color in the moonlight. Was this an apology? A peace offering? He almost stuck it back in the box and tossed it in the corner. But why not just take it? It didn't have to be anything but cool. Laying the box back in the duffle, he slipped the cuff onto his thick wrist. Instantly, his body hummed with life and energy, his mind sharpened, and the room's details came into focus even though it stayed as dark as it had been. He could hear Spence's slow breathing, already asleep. But more than anything was the hum through his body, from head to toe every fiber of muscle alive.

The same hum he had felt when Meg touched him.

He yanked it off and tossed it in the bag. Picking up the bottle, he guzzled a good portion of it and recapped it. With a final look at the cuff laying on the bag, he tossed the bottle down on it and crawled into bed.

CHAPTER TWENTY

A Single Arrow

Ben hated waiting. Waiting was always the worst part. Everything was moving so slowly, slower than Coach had expected and it was driving their impatient General to the edge. And when Coach was on edge, everyone was on edge, even Gladys in her own drooping way.

After Coach had decided upon the squads, Karsark and Hawkins would follow one path with a handful of the Betas, that's what the younger guys called the older ones, the men who had graduated, and Coach and Marrs would take Gladys and the rest. Spirits had been high and eager on that Texas plain. Then time wore on. Several fires had been built for the men to gather around and cook what field critters they could catch. Marrs had come back with several rabbits and a badger and Hawkins with a squirrel. It gave the Pack a moment of levity, that's what Hawkins was good for. Ben had always been partial to the charismatic man.

The Barber gathered several of the Pups around and taught them the art of skinning. A few took to it naturally, understanding the lines and intricacy of it, others did what they could. Ben tried his hand at it. He never wanted to give off the impression he wasn't willing to try. It was important, right? At least giving something a shot? It's what sold him on football. That sort of aggression hadn't been in his bones; he wasn't accustomed to it. His Da had been a farmer, so Ben worked fields. When his Ma needed help in the kitchen, he'd cook. He was skilled around the house and fields and never had a heart for the fight. But Coach had changed that. Or at least taught him how to unleash it when the fight was necessary.

Ben was only fourteen when he'd been sentenced, had just *turned* fourteen. His voice still squeaked and he barely had a hair on his body aside from those up top. The light flashed white and there he was in the middle of a yard of some kind behind a brick homestead with fences built high around it. It was night and raining and cold, he was naked as he was told he would be, soon shivering. The fence had been shrewdly built so that the climbing parts were on the other side, and even if you could climb it, sharp metal wire had been fastened to it high up. Not high enough so it could be seen from the other side, the wire hung just below the top, about a foot. Invisible to anyone outside. Covering himself with his hands, Ben timidly approached the door of the homestead. He was still crying. Should he knock? Before his knuckles made contact with the door, a light came on inside, a hand pulled the curtain aside, and a mustached, hard face appeared.

Coach had taken him in that night, clothed him right away and fed him. Once the daze had worn off, Ben spent most of the night crying, even while trying to eat the food out of gratitude, because he wasn't hungry at all. Wasn't sure he'd ever be hungry again. All he *wanted* to do was die. Curl up in a corner and die. Coach wouldn't allow it.

A couple of nights later, Coach questioned him.

"Where'd you come from?"

"Umyrica."

"What'd you do there?"

Ben wasn't sure what he was asking.

"Your family, what'd your family do there? What was their trade?"

"Oh, yessir," Ben nodded. "Farmers, sir."

"Farm what?"

"Um, the normal stuff. Vegetables mainly. Lots of potatoes and radishes. Some corn."

"Pa and ma?"

"Yessir, my Da and Ma."

"Siblings?"

"Um, two. Two sisters, sir."

"You're the only boy?"

"Yessir."
"And you're fourteen . . ."
"Fourteen *summers*, sir."
They were sitting at the kitchen table and it was late. The other Pups living there, five in all, had been sent off to bed once their homework had been completed and approved. Coach took the fulfillment of responsibilities seriously, just like Ben's Da. The big man leaned back in his chair and smoothed his mustache with one hand, then crossed his thick arms across his chest. He was wearing a t-shirt with the letters FHS across it and the head of a snarling wolf. FHS Wolves.
"What'd you do?"
"Farming, sir . . .?" Ben was confused, they'd already been over that.
He shook his head, "No, son, what'd you do to get *sentenced*?"
Ben's heart immediately started pounding. He had finally managed to gain control of it over the course of the conversation. He thought it'd explode when Coach had sent the other boys off because he knew what was coming. But when the conversation had been about farming and his sisters, those were all *good* things, comfortable things. Now was the part he'd been dreading since he saw Coach through the window two nights ago.
Ben looked down at the table and followed the woodgrain with his eyes.
"Son, what'd you do?"
It wasn't that simple. He wouldn't say it.
Coach took a deep breath and let it out, "Okay, from a different direction." Ben didn't know what that meant. "Did you kill a man?"
The boy's eyes went wide, "No, sir!"
"A woman?"
"No!"
"Did you kill anybody?"

"No, sir, I didn't kill no one." His hands were shaking and tingling. Why were they tingly?

"Did you steal something?"

"No, sir."

"Caught with things you shouldn't have had? Relics, weapons, substances?"

Ben shook his head, "No, sir."

The big man rolled his eyes, "I'm running out of things here." He ran his fingers through his hair, "Were you found out?"

Ben wasn't sure what his outward reaction had been, but inside his stomach tied into six different knots.

"Found out," Coach repeated to himself. "But for what? Rebellion?"

Ben looked back at the table and shook his head.

"Found out . . . Silentmarket?"

Ben didn't even know what that was, but shook his head.

"Found out . . . love?"

Ben's chin trembled and he couldn't make it stop. In fact, the harder he tried the worse it happened and soon, his eyes betrayed him and the tears leaked down his face, but still he wouldn't look up. He wanted to run, but the big man had strategically positioned himself between Ben and the nearest way out of the kitchen.

Coach nodded and looked down at the table too. "Found out for love. Teenage boy, found out for love, but won't talk about it." He sighed. "Get to bed."

Ben went to bed that night not knowing what to expect the next morning. But when he awoke, there was bacon and eggs on the table with biscuits and honey. Everyone ate and joked, and Coach gave them all the run down for the day. The guys were all older than Ben. He ate and laughed at their jokes, though he didn't understand most of them. This world was strange, but he got the hang of it pretty quickly. A month later, Coach took him to the school and registered him. No questions asked. Football practice began. They were long days and Ben wasn't sure he liked it, but he tried it. And he was *good* at it. Good at throwing the ball, making quick decisions, encouraging the other guys. They liked him for it, so he got better at it.

School was strange at first, it wasn't the lessons he was used to and he had to go in for extra 'tutoring.' But with enough time he was passable. The math with the mix of numbers and letters was unnecessarily complicated and he couldn't grasp what it was all for, but he did it anyway, the guys at home helped him with it at night. He liked history and the stories. School was fine, he was quick enough.

Within the first week, Coach had pointed out Charlie, the whole reason for the Pack. The tall boy seemed like a good enough person and Ben made several attempts to befriend him, but the other boy was closed off. Over the next two years, Ben had quit trying, even though he sat next to him in several classes. Charlie was arrogant. Aloof. None of the Pack liked him, and many were resentful of him. Why should they train and give their lives in preparation for someone who didn't give a damn about them? Ben tried not to adopt their cynicism, but it wasn't easy.

"Did you have a chance to look through the big house?" Ben was snapped out of his thoughts. Marrs gripped his shoulder. The older man was like a big brother to him. Lost in thought, Ben had been standing by the pool looking down at the Shells entombed in ice. How the hell did that happen? It was one of the first things the Pack found when they landed in the luxurious backyard. *Luxurious*, right? It was a word he'd learned in his English class last year. Luxurious seemed right. The house was gigantic and the grounds were unbelievably huge, like a farm, but all for frivolity. Opulent would work too. And when one of the guys retracted the cover from the pool, even Coach had been stunned.

It was early evening and hard to say how long Charlie and the Gohlem had been gone, but they'd added a third to their number, Marrs could tell that much. Their tracks had taken them to the warehouse of a garage and a few parking spaces were empty. It was impossible to tell where they had gone from there. Marrs was good, but he couldn't track cars.

"No," Ben said, "I haven't been inside yet." Gladys stood on the other side of the pool chewing her lip and observing the Shells as well. Her bus was parked where it had landed on the tennis court.

Marrs nodded. "Give it a look. You have good eyes for detail. You might see something we've missed." The serious young man glanced at the pool, "Too bad about that, huh? Would have been nice to have a swim."

Both houses had been swept for anyone inside, the big one and the one by the pool. Both were empty, though it was obvious the party of three had more recently occupied the little house. Discarded clothing, a shirt with a large rip across the front stained with blood and a pair of shorts also stained with dried blood. With no real evidence, Coach was certain it was Daniels' blood, an assumption on his part really, and the idea only served to darken his already stormy mood.

Ben didn't even know where to start in the house. Places of information seemed the most obvious. That would dismiss living areas, the kitchen, dining rooms, and entertainment rooms. So, maybe an office? He combed the house looking for a room that might serve as an office. Kitchens were generally at the heart near the largest living room. Dining rooms off that. Up the stairs? At his farmhouse, growing up, the bedrooms were upstairs, so he imagined the same might hold true here. When he wanted quiet to do his homework, he slipped away to the furthest place in the house, in the back. Ben took a hallway that ran along the backside of the sprawling estate. A bathroom. A bedroom. Another bathroom. Closets. An office.

Bookshelves covered the walls, framed pictures of family hung where there was space among award plaques and animal heads. A large desk dominated the far side of the room and Coach sat behind it, his left-hand resting on a book. One of *the* books. The first if Ben was seeing it correctly.

Those books were just as much part of the Pups education as Chemistry and English. They all knew them cover to cover, but the problem was they were mainly rubbish. Many of the facts— the tools, the relics, places— were true enough, but the stories surrounding them were a strange mixture of truth and fabrication. The Daniels, James and Harriett, were just as much on the Packs radar as Charlie. Coach didn't trust them, but insisted it was best to not disturb them until it was necessary. Well, clearly it had become necessary and now they were gone.

A giant flat screen television hanging on the wall was alive with a news report, ". . . in this small town in central Texas." A woman with well sculpted black hair was saying. "Again, authorities came here when Officer Chad Littleton was found by a civilian. The officer was unconscious in the back of his squad car. The officer's partner, a Jonathan Karsark, is still unaccounted for and it's unknown whether he was another victim of the house's disappearance. Residents nearby are confirming a flash of light very early in the morning, though some say it could have been late the night before. Experts are ruling out a gas explosion as there is no sign of debris. What we do know is this, Mike and Julia, the disappearance of the Daniels house, and all three Daniels themselves, is a mystery that will put this sleepy Texas town on the map for years to come. This is Denise Arbola, for CNN. Back to you, Mike and Julia."

The TV turned off. Coach shook his head, "I was wondering how long that would take. Longer than I expected. Guess no one really misses Littleton when he's not around."

"Marrs sent me in, sir."

Coach nodded, "They find anything in the pool house?"

Ben shook his head, "Nothing new."

"Gladys' Traveling took too damn long."

"Yes, sir."

Coach had erupted in front of all the men and for a moment Ben had been afraid for Gladys's safety. The diminutive . . . another word he liked . . . the diminutive woman only watched him with her drooping eyes, no sign of concern. The Traveling had taken too long, he railed, it was too slow. He could have caught a flight on an airplane and made better time.

Ben wanted to ride on an airplane someday. Would it be like riding a dragon? He had always wanted to ride a dragon too.

Gladys had simply shrugged her shoulders, "Do you have the resources to fly eighty men in two different directions on an airplane? I don't know about you, but a bus driver doesn't earn much. I've heard rumors that coaches do better. Do you have that kind of money?"

Coach had stormed off.

"She's right," Coach muttered from behind the desk. "Too many of us and it takes too much time. A relic would be better, but *again*, the witch is right, damn it. Even if we could get our hands on one, it wouldn't be reliable enough and could spin us off into God knows where . . . or worse. I *hate* using the blood."

Ben took a few steps into the room and looked for more details, following Marrs' direction. Among the framed items on the walls were newspaper articles. Mainly centered around B&B's purchases of different pieces of the entertainment industry. Pictures of an older gentleman standing proudly in front of various buildings, shaking hands with other rich people, his arms around two beautiful young . . . Chinese models? The slender young man looked pissed off in the picture as though he'd rather be anywhere else. The woman on the other hand was gorgeous. Tall, slender, pale blond hair spilling down her shoulders and her golden eyes were captivating. Ben scanned the articles and many of them started with something to the effect of, "Word from Bull and Badger headquarters in Manhattan has it . . ." or "The B&B building in NYC confirms their newest acquisition . . ."

"Why would the Gohlem come here, sir?"

Coach sighed, "To gather another of the Six, I'm assuming."

"And . . ."

"And it found the twins," he flung a gesture at the picture Ben had been admiring. "*One* of them according to Marrs. The boy."

"And the girl?"

"Not here. Marrs doesn't think she's been here for a while."

"No, sir." Ben pulled one of the framed articles off the wall and laid it before the Coach. "Because she's there." The article told of the new head of the B&B talent agency in New York, an astounding, but brilliant move by Eric Carrington, placing the reigns of one of his strongest ventures in his daughter's hands, Veronica Carrington. At only nineteen, she's the youngest member of his leadership team, but had already proven herself a shrewd and cunning business woman able to magically close deals with the most stubborn of the entertainment industry.

In a frenzy, Coach howled and launched himself over the desk from the high-backed chair and ran from the room. Ben hoped he was right about New York. He was already asking himself the logistical questions: If they'd had to wait until dawn in order to make it to California from Texas, would they have to do it again? Would travel time be faster for forty as opposed to eighty? What kind of bird was Gladys going to pop the head off of this time?

The others who'd been searching the house were running out to the back of the estate where Ben presumed he'd find Coach. As soon as Ben threw open the door, he heard the yelling and swearing. "What the hell do you mean you can't get us there 'anytime soon'? I don't care what the hell kind of bird you bleed out to get us there. Take a whole damn flock of flamingos, for all I care. That's what they have around here, isn't it?" His finger was inches from Gladys' face, his own beat red, veins bulging in his neck. Ben had only seen him like this when the team wasn't playing the way Coach knew they could. It didn't take long under that form of aggressive encouragement for them to pull around and play the right way.

Gladys, however, was unmotivated. "I don't know *exactly* where they've gone and with this many bodies, it would be like throwing a handful of gravel at a target. Some of you would hit, but most would end up scattered. And it would be highly likely that more than a few would end up in pieces flung over the Atlantic Ocean. I got you *here*," she slurred, "because I could follow the lines of the Orb, like a trail left by a jet. But that isn't the case now. They left on foot, or rather, by car. Correct?" She paused a moment to let it sink in. "So, General, unless you can find the ends of those fading Orb lines . . ."

Coach was pacing around the pool, his face returning to its normal color, but no less agitated. The Betas and Pups dared not speak, they only waited for instruction. Even Marrs was giving Coach distance.

"Now," Gladys slurred with a shrug of her shoulders, "If we wanted to shoot a *single* arrow at the target, there *might* be a way."

"I'll do it!" Ben leaped forward, "I'll be the arrow!"

Coach's head jerked up and the others looked his way. Marrs was shaking his head subtly with a finger against his lips.

"You don't know what you're volunteering for, boy." Coach shook his head, "Too many variables involved."

"Please, can I try?" he begged. Ben ran to Gladys. The woman made him nervous, she was Venefica after all, a Blood Sister, the people in the village near his father's farm had called them. They were capable of any number of atrocities; sacrifices, mutilations, and some said cannibalism. However, this particular Venefica had been chosen as the other half of Coach's Pair. There had to be honor in her somewhere, right? "Gladys," he said respectfully, "*one* can travel fast, right? Like an arrow, like you said?"

"Not as fast as an Orb, mind you, but fast enough."

"Faster than forty men?"

She nodded.

"And if we knew *exactly* where to aim, how fast could I get there?"

Her puffy, drooping eyes glanced at Coach, "With certain *ingredients*, I could have you there within two hours."

"And once I was there, I could give you a read on where to send everyone else, right?"

Coach waved his arms, "Everyone, head up to the big house and make yourselves comfortable." He pointed at Ben and Gladys, "You two, in the little house." He clapped his hands, "Go!" The Pack scattered and trotted up the steps. Some were laying claim to rooms they had found, while others were shouting their dibs on food. A few of the Betas laughed at the Pups and vetoed their claims. Ben hurried to the little pool house, but Gladys took her time.

"I'm letting you do this, boy, because out of all the minds here, yours is the sharpest," Coach told him when they were inside the pool house. "You're sure you can do this?"

"I know I can. And I want to. Most of the guys, they don't care for Charlie much. He's not *my* buddy or anything, hell, we never talk, but he's *important*. And if the Gohlem is set on collecting the Six, then it has to go for the girl twin eventually. And if it has the boy twin, why wouldn't she be next? I find this B&B building, keep an eye on it, and I'll find Charlie eventually, I know it." He was getting excited as the plan rolled out of his mouth. It felt so right. As a quarterback, he was used to strategy and thinking on his feet. This was just a bigger game, higher stakes. But it required strategy all the same.

An hour later at dusk as the sun was setting and the sky was bleeding red, Ben stood in the middle of the tennis court with Coach at his side and Gladys across from him on the opposite side of a small table they had brought from the pool house with a large glass mixing bowl at its center. The only other Pack member present was David, a year older, but shorter than Ben, yet built as solid as a wall. He watched on with concern in his green eyes. David had voiced his opinion of the whole matter quietly to Ben as the latter was preparing himself. Ben wouldn't look him in the eyes as he tried to assure him everything would be all right.

The quarterback didn't like the look of the curved knife or the empty glass vials Gladys had pulled from a purple fanny pack buckled around her waist. The clouds caught every color of the setting sun and cast everything in a weird pink glow. Ben was wearing the black t-shirt with the cut across the chest and the shorts with the blood spilled down them. Both articles of clothing had soaked up enough blood and Ben theorized they could only assist in the pinpointing of Charlie, if Coach's assumption that it was in fact Charlie's blood. Gladys confirmed the theory had merit and, if Ben read her correctly, she'd been impressed. Her raised droopy eyebrows spoke volumes.

"Well done, boy." Coach said as Ben had pulled the shirt on. "Your Da would be proud."

Ben took a deep breath. Words like that still caught him hard. He'd learned to control his trembling chin and tears over the last two years but the lump in his throat was still an untamed beast. *His Da would have been proud*. Prouder still had he never found Ben in the barn with the blacksmith's apprentice in such a compromising way and dutifully had to hand him over to the proper authorities. But his Da was an honest man and Maker fearing. If the Listeners said it was an abomination, then that's what it was. Ben didn't fight him, but he wept and so did his Ma and sisters.

Looking down at the cut in the shirt, he could see the large paw print tattooed over his heart. All the Pack had them, Betas and Pups, even Coach. Ben *had* a family now. He had a new Da and Ben wouldn't disappoint him.

With the others looking on from the house, and David on the other side of the tennis court's fence, Ben presented his hand palm up to Gladys, as she instructed. She drew the knife across it, cutting deeply, blood spilling immediately. Three of the vials were filled. The vials were to track Ben. One for Coach, one for her, and one for Marrs, standing to the side, ready to take it to Hawkins and the other half of the Pack through the same ritual once Ben was away. She held the blond boy's hand over the bowl, filling the bottom with his pulsing blood. All the while she mumbled words Ben couldn't make out, they didn't sound like anything he recognized and it gave him chills. He was nervous, of course. He had no idea what this was going to feel like, the cut was nothing compared to the unknown. Having gathered enough in the bowl, she smeared a paste on the wound and wrapped a gauze around it. Taking the torn shirt in one hand, she cut off a large crusty piece that had been saturated. The black tattooed paw print was clearly visible now. She dropped the stained piece into the bowl where it soaked in Ben's blood. She mumbled a few more words and as she did, Ben realized his vision was clouding . . . a hazy red . . . drifting . . .

CHAPTER TWENTY-ONE

Hume with Sun Hair

Wake your eyes, my lord.

Right hand.

One.

Two.

Three.

Four.

Five.

Left hand.

One.

Two.

Three.

My lord, please, wake your eyes.

"You stopped hisself. Don't stop hisself."

Yes, my lord.

He could tell there was afraid in the voice.

But he had to do it.

Right hand.

One.

Two.

Three.

Four.

Five.

Left hand.

One.

Two.

Three.

Four.

Five.

Right foot.
Left foot.
Penis.
Right butt cheek.
Left butt cheek.
Chin.
Nose.
Tongue.
Right ear.
Left ear. No. Wiggle. Left ear. Left ear, wiggle. Nothing.
Right eye open.
Left eye open.
Light. They were on because he left them on. The person in the dark couldn't hurt hisself.
Breathe in and out. Breathe in and out. Breathe in and out. Sniff. Cough. Sit up.
Stephen sat up in the big clean bed. The room swirled and tilted a little. The sheets still felt good on his naked and clean skin. He felt new.
Your eyes are awake, good, my lord.
The big rat on the bed was bigger than the others he heard. Smartest too. The others talked in stuff they needed. Jacob Tailong talked like all the other people who was real and actual. Jacob was real and actual and what he said was real and actual. No one believed Stephen when he screamed to make the doctor know it was real and actual. He was sent to the house to live with the people with broken heads. Now his head was broken too. That was real and actual also.
You should put on body coverings now.
"I need to pee. Poop also."
You fed? Jacob was happy.

Stephen nodded and rubbed sleepy out of his eyes with his clean hands. They still smelled good from the shower. Minty. They were shaking again.

The large rat sat up on its back legs. *And you cleaned? You are getting healed?* Jacob walked up the bed coverings slow, curious, nose twitching.

"My head is dizzy still and my hands shake kind of, but I'm feeling gooder." Stephen yawned.

This is good. This is very good, my lord. Please, get up and get your body coverings. Jacob took the covers in his mouth and began pulling them backward.

"I need to pee and poop." Stephen stretched and pulled hisself up. He walked naked to the bathroom. He had to hold the doorway to stop the dizzy. Sat on the toilet. "Why are you in a hurry? Is something wrong? Where is Maze? You left me alone. Where did you go?"

Jacob jumped off the bed and ran into the bathroom. He was bigger than tiny dogs. *You were sleeping. I needed to go look.*

Stephen smiled at the rat. The big white patches around his little black eyes made the big rat look like it had googly eyes like in cartoons. The cartoons at the home were a happy thing. "I like your eyes."

Thank you, my lord. That is very kind of you. You need to leave this place.

Stephen rolled up some toilet paper.

"No more than three squares," she said. Stephen remembered what happened when you used more than too much. The water spilled out. The hitting happened.

"Hello?"

Jacob laid a paw on Stephen's naked foot.

My lord, she isn't here. It is you and myself. That is all.

Stephen focused back in and looked down at his friend. "You and myself."

You and myself, my lord. Please, finish and get covered.

Stephen did. He found some jeans he liked and they fit good. A t-shirt. Jacket. Nice thick socks and boots. A dark green toboggan hat like the kids wear when it snows in the cartoons. It all felt so good. New. Clean. Tight. Tight was safe and good. His inside felt good and he smiled big when he saw hisself in the mirror. The jacket was black and long, down past his knees, nice big pockets and Jacob got inside one. Stephen stuck food in two other pockets. Walking food. He ate two bananas and drank some milk. Not too much this time.

"Where is Maze?"

Maze and Philip went on the . . . suv-way? . . .

He knew this one from the cartoons. "Subway. It's a train and a sandwich. Underground." Stephen breathed in hard. "I won't go underground. Too loud. I can't think good when it's too loud."

Yes, my lord. We will not go in the underground.

"Where did Maze and Philip go?"

The others said in the way of the Great Green Woods. And the others at the end of the Great Green Woods did not see Maze or Philip.

Stephen drank more milk, "Will Maze be back?"

I do not know, but we must not be here.

Stephen drank all the milk and burped loud.

"Say excuse me, boy," she said.

"Hello?"

My lord, just you and myself.

"You and myself," Stephen said also.

That is right. That is good. You and myself. We need to go.

"Why? You're afraid?"

Yes, my lord.

"Why are you afraid?"

They are gathering in the dark places underground and the empty high up places. So many of them. Too many of them. More than you can count.

"I don't count good."

I do and I cannot count them.

"Who is them?"

The Hollows, my lord. Countless Hollows.

Stephen nodded to the man in the uniform holding the door for hisself. He stepped out of the big, shiny building. The man was looking at hisself, that was real and actual. The man didn't know hisself and he didn't know the man. "I'm a friend of Philip's," Stephen said just like Jacob showed him how to.

The man's eyes got small at hisself.

"I slept in his bed naked," Stephen said, "And showered naked in his bathroom. I'm wearing his clothes, but no underwear. His underwear went between my cheeks and felt bad."

The man at the door made a funny sound in his throat, "Sir, what Mr. de Grande does in his apartment is his business and his alone."

"Okay," Stephen shrugged. He could tell the old man was bothered, but didn't know why. What he said was real and actual. "I won't be back. It was a one-time sleep over." He saw sleepovers on cartoons too. Stephen didn't get to have a pillow fight. Maybe next time.

The man just held up his hands and walked back inside.

It was early morning now; the sun was lighting the sky. Right across the busy street was the Great Green Woods Jacob had told him about. The trees were really big and the look of them next to the giant buildings was confusing to Stephen's head. After many starts and stops, afraid of being hit by one of the fast, yellow cars, Stephen ran across the street with Jacob bouncing in his pocket making funny sounds. Stephen stood at the front of the Woods, his eyes not knowing which tree to look at.

My lord?

"It's going to be loud in there. Too many voices."

Yes, my lord, but they don't say anything useful. Let them be like the winds and rain. Just sound. Remember? You and myself.

"You and myself," he said also. Stephen breathed in through his nose and out through his mouth. All fingers. All toes. All parts. Right ear. Left ear. No. That one would not wiggle.

Runners passed Stephen. He didn't know what they were running from, but he looked for it. A man on a bicycle yelled, "fuck you" at hisself after yelling "on your left!" a lot. Stephen was bad at left and right. He tried to tell the "fuck you" man that, but he went too fast. It didn't matter to hisself, the big woods was too beautiful. Jacob was quiet also. The big rat rode in the pocket with his head out, his black eyes blinking and watching. Stephen turned onto a sidewalk that led more into the woods. The longer he walked, the less he saw people.

But the more he heard the others.

Their talk was little more than talks about needs. It wasn't real and actual talks. Not like Jacob.

Must be finding food.

Must be finding mates.

Must be feeding the babies.

Must be hiding.

It was this talk that had made Stephen broken when he was little. They didn't turn off. They wouldn't hear hisself tell them to stop. They wouldn't listen to *his*self.

Jacob had been different and had been able to sooth hisself, but when they moved hisself to the other place with people whose heads were broken, Jacob wasn't there at the beginning. They had been away from each other. They had never been away from each other. Stephen didn't know how long he was without his friend, but by the time Jacob found hisself again, the medicines had already hurt hisself and Stephen was just like the other broken people. But he could still hear the others. No medicines made that stop.

Jacob had tried to break Stephen free many times, but even though he was bigger than the other rats and mouses Stephen saw, there wasn't much he could do to get a human boy out of "the home." The big rat had also tried stealing the medicines, but *she* was smart and knew something was going on and Stephen swallowed every medicine from then until the escape since the other day. Since the other week? It was hard to keep clear in his head. Most things were hard to keep clear in his head.

You and myself, my lord.

Stephen walked off the path to a big space of green grass. He laid down on the grass and looked up. Squirrels ran through the trees overhead. *Stupid things, squirrels*, Jacob often said. *They say so much and never say anything at all. They try to talk more than rats and mice and possums.* Possums almost never talked and when they did, it wasn't nice. Squirrels never *stopped* talking.

Hume on the ground near my hiding foods.

Hume looking up. Sleeping? Dying?

Hume with sun hair.

It was always like this. They saw so much and said so much, but they never said anything real.

Jacob crept out of the large coat pocket. *My lord, what are we doing? Truly, we must be on our way.*

"Being still. Listening."

A few more fluffy-tailed squirrels were jumping from branch to branch far up in the trees.

Hume with sun hair.

Hume with sun hair?

Yes. Hume with sun hair.

It went on and on like that.

Stephen stretched out in the grass, his shirt uncovering his skinny tummy. The cool air felt good on it.

More squirrels gathered overhead until the trees were full of them.

Hume with sun hair.

Hume with sun hair.

Where hume with sun hair?

There hume with sun hair.

Stephen lay still and looked up at them all. Their black eyes watching him, noses twitching. He twitched his nose too.

Jacob crawled out of the pocket and looked up at the crowd of squirrels. *What do you think they're doing, my lord?*

Stephen shrugged. "What are you doing, squirrels?"

That set off an explosion of speaking.

Hume with sun hair spoke to we?

Hume with sun hair is speakings to we? We hears.

We knows.

Hume with sun hair not like other dumb humes. He knows how to speak good.

Find Nightfeather.

Yes, Nightfeather.

I will go and find Nightfeather.

I go too!

We goes with!

Several squirrels disappeared into the trees.

Stephen scratched his skinny tummy, pulled at the hair on his belly button. Orange. Sun hair.

Little by little, squirrels trickled down the tree trunks and surrounded the young man laying on the ground with the sun hair. Their noses twitched and tails flicked.

Jacob looked about. *My lord?* He sounded a little afraid.

"They're nice. Silly and nice."

The curious squirrels got closer, noses tucking into his hair and sniffing. Some sniffing his hands and legs, his beard. A small reddish one crawled up onto his chest and put its paws on Stephen's sun-haired chin, looking in his eyes.

Hume?

The surrounding squirrels froze. Waiting and watching.

"Yes?"

You can hears we? Speaks we?

Stephen smiled big. "Yes."

The little squirrel's tail flicked happily.

Why?

Stephen thought for a moment. "Because . . . because my head is broken."

There was more silly talking from all the squirrels around and above him. He felt tiny paws pull away the toboggan hat and pick through his unruly hair. One ruffled and picked through the white hair around his left unwiggly ear. Stephen felt his nose poking and sniffing. *Yes, smells broke here.* Other squirrels picked, pulled, and sniffed the white hair.

See here! Jacob yelled at them, *claws away and to yourself!*

No break, the squirrels chattered. *Broke, no blood.*

Stephen grinned, "It's *in* my head, sillies. You can't see it. My brain is broke."

That made them chatter even more and Stephen just listened. They were too silly to try to make to understand and Stephen wasn't smart enough to make them hear hisself good. But when a *caw* was heard, everything went quiet.

A black crow, landed on a branch way above. It cocked its head side to side, black eyes looking at Stephen.

Nightfeather!

Nightfeather is here!

Nightfeather, we has found the hume with sun hair!

The hume with sun hair!

Nightfeather spread his wings and glided to the ground below, keeping away from Stephen. The crow cocked his head, black eyes always looking at Stephen. He hopped closer and watched. Stephen watched back.

The small squirrel on Stephen's chest sat up. *This is the hume with the sun hair, Nightfeather. He speaked to we and we to he.*

Nightfeather turned his head, hopped closer, then spoke, "Prove it." The words were clipped and croaked. And unlike the squirrels, and even Jacob, the crow spoke from his beak. "Little squirrel, tell a color."

The small squirrel did as asked, *leaves.*

Jacob shook his head, *stupid thing.*

Stephen smiled, "I like her." He ran a finger across the small squirrel's head then lifted her, placing her on his shoulder as he sat up and crossed his legs. "She said 'leaves.' Leaves is her color, Mr. Nightfeather."

Nightfeather bobbed his head. "Fine then. That be the one Addie did charge you all to look for. Your finding be complete. You can all go."

And with that the crowd of squirrels immediately dispersed in a flurry of *we is done! Find foods! Where is mate?*

Jacob walked to the black bird. *This Addie you speak of, do you mean Adelaide?*

The crow bobbed its head, "Addie. Adelaide. Yah, the very woman. You be acquainted?"

Stephen could feel Jacob's excitement. It didn't happen a lot, the real feeling of feelings, but when they were really strong feelings, he could feel them. *Acquainted, yes. Very acquainted. I am with her. What I mean is, I am . . .* the rat moved his little claws like Stephen did when he couldn't think right or couldn't find the right words. *I'm one of them. One of the . . . the Lookouts, Pairs. There are eight of us. The Elyfs chose not to send one, well two. There are always two.*

Nightfeather cocked his head, "Where be your two?"

She . . . Jacob looked at Stephen, *She . . . we forsook her.*

Now Stephen was confused. "Who did we leave, Jacob?"

Not now, my lord. Not now. The large rat looked back to the bird. *Can you take us to Adelaide? Is she nearby?*

Nightfeather flapped his wings and hopped, letting out a croak. "The woman be dead. Hit over the head and dragged into an alley where she been stabbed many a time. Many, many a time. I watched it all. I watched her day and night. I watched it all."

Jacob's excited feelings went away and was turned into sadness. Very, very sad sadness. *Then we are lost?*

The crow shook his head, "Never. Addie knew a thing had been beginning, happening. We talked about it at length. Expecting you would be coming through Central Park, liking all the tree and wood, Addie put the squirrels watching. She knew. She felt it. Many a terrible thing be out there, but many a very good thing too. We will find all the other or they will find us. Keep both eye looking for the odd and different."

This whole city is full of the odd and different.

The crow croaked, "Odder and more different."

Stephen laughed happily and shot his hand in the air like at school in the cartoons.

The two creatures looked at hisself, *Yes, my lord?*

"I have saw something odd and different."

And what would that be, my lord?

Stephen pointed through a bunch of trees, "A house popping out of the air where there wasn't a house."

The two creatures looked where he pointed and saw something odd and different. A real and actual house with wheels that hadn't been there a moment ago was there now.

CHAPTER TWENTY-TWO

A Wise Woman

The light had blinded Hedy for a moment, like when someone uses a camera flash in a dark room. And it was while she was blinded that it felt as though she went on a rollercoaster ride, well, what she imagined that was like. She had never actually been on one. She wasn't quite tall enough. But the world around her lurched and lunged, twisted and toppled so much she was sure when she could see again nothing in the house would be where it had been.

The problem is, she was partially right. When she *could* see again, nothing in the house was where it had been, though everything in the house was still right where Old Millie had put it. None of it was still in Oregon. Rubbing her eyes, things cleared and she could see outside the open front door through the blue tint of her clearing vision, skyscrapers peeking up from behind the tree line. Skyscrapers. Behind the trees. Skyscrapers. Hedy had no clue how long she stood there attempting to make peace with the jarring picture, but it was interrupted by a dog licking her hand. Polly. Brutus was busy sniffing over Denny's body. Half of it anyway, the half lying inside the door.

Hedy rubbed Polly's broad head. "I'm okay, girl." Then after a moment of shifting her gaze between the baffling scene outside and the one lying in the floor before her, "I think."

"You're okay." A hand rested on her shoulder. It was Bogart. The sight of the boy in his faire clothes was comforting.

"What happened?"

"We Travelled. The orb took us to . . . uh . . . here."

"And where is here?"

Bogart stepped up to the door careful not to step on half of Denny. "By the looks of it, I'd say New York City. That's the famous

Essex House sign poking up over there, so I think we're somewhere in Central Park?"

"Have you been here?"

Bogart shook his curly head, "I watch a lot of movies and television. A lot. Mi abuela thinks I watch too much."

Hedy looked at the body Bogart stood over and Brutus was snuffling. "And Denny is dead."

Bogart rested his hands on his hips and nudged one of Denny's legs with his toe. "Well, I would say this half of Denny is dead. The other half is probably still laying on the ground bleeding out through the neck thanks to this brute."

Brutus looked up, his tongue lolling out of his mouth and wagged his tail.

"Denny was a Shell," Bogart sighed, "so the other part is fine—ish?"

Hedy looked down the little hallway to Old Millie's closed bedroom door. "And she's . . .?"

Bogart shook his head, "Not fine—ish. You don't want to go back there." Bogart had slipped back there to go to the bathroom, or so he'd told Denny. Whatever happened in that bedroom, Bogart had seen the result of it. "It's— she's a— um . . . it's messy. Really, really messy."

Hedy felt her knees weakening and she eased herself to the floor before she went down involuntarily. Denny. Old Millie. Her Pap and Mam? And she remembered Marla too. The sounds and the smell of smoke and blood all came back to her, and though the morning sunlight and blue sky through the door was beautiful with chirping birds and swaying trees like her home in Oregon, her insides were a writhing mess. Bogart sat down beside her and rubbed her back. Polly laid down, resting her big head on Hedy's little lap. Brutus took watch out the door with a snort.

"I need a phone," Hedy said finally. "Do you have a phone?"

Bogart shook his head, "No, it was in my other clothes and those are, well, they're in Oregon, I guess. I lose my phone a lot. Mi abuela is used to it. But that's probably the furthest I've ever lost it."

"I need my Mam and Pap to know I'm okay. I need to know *they're* okay. I need a phone. I can't just leave them in the dark. I'm sure they're worried to death." Hedy crawled over to half of Denny's body and felt his pockets. "Ah-ha," she brightened, as much as she could after searching half of a traitor's stiff body, and slipped her thick hand into his pocket. She pulled out an old flip phone, the kind no one used anymore. Except Denny. Flipping it open, she skimmed through the buttons trying to find stored numbers. Surely her parents' numbers would be in here somewhere. There. Oakenroot. Braeden Oakenroot. She pushed the call button and waited. It rang, but not for long.

". . . It's Denny's phone," she heard her Pap say on the other end. Strong and gruff. "Hello?"

Hedy almost couldn't get the words out, "P-Pap?"

"Hedy? It's you, thank the Maker."

The relief in his voice was only matched by the same flooding through Hedy. Then it puckered up just before the next words came out of her mouth, "Is Mam okay? Is she with you?"

"Yes, yes, sweetheart, your Mam is good. We're all a little bumped and bruised, but we're all right. All of us." Except Hedy knew it wasn't all of them. Marla. But her Pap and Mam were enough for now. "Where are you, Hedy? Are you with Old Millie? In her trailer?"

Hedy nodded as though he could see her, "We're here. Me and Bogart, the boy from the faire. Polly and Brutus are with us, but Old Millie . . ." the words started breaking apart.

"Shhh . . . you don't have to say it, sweetheart. She's fine," he was saying away from the phone, "The boy is with her and the mutts. Mil didn't make it." His voice came back strong, "Denny. The . . . uh . . ."

Hedy took a deep breath, "Lower half?"

"Aye," Pap exhaled. "What's it doing?"

Hedy shook her head, "Nothing, just lying there."

"You need to get away from it. It's like a—"

Bogart chimed in, "A homing beacon?" She shot him a look for listening in, "I'm sorry, I have good ears."

"Aye, that," her Pap said. "Get away from it. Can you tell where you are?"

Hedy scanned the buildings like towers reaching for the white, pillowy clouds, "Bogart says we're in New York."

"City?" Pap said with more than a hint of disbelief. "How'd it—"

"Orbs," Bogart blurted. "I found a Transport Orb and used it."

Then there was silence. A very pregnant silence. "The boy," Pap said to someone on the other end, "he knows about Relics. I don't *know* how." He returned to her, "Hedy, that boy. Is he all right? You think he's all right?"

Hedy eyed Bogart for a moment. His pudgy face, tan skin, eager eyes. Those lips. He saved her from Denny. "Yeah, Pap. Yeah, he's all right."

A pause. "Okay, Hedy. I trust you. You're a wise woman."

And that's when the resolve settled in. Those words. That affirmation. It was all she needed. She *could* do this. "Thank you, Pap."

"Hedy, Old Millie had cash, loads of it under her bed in shoeboxes. Old bitch never spent a dime and always complained of the economy." Hedy glanced back at the closed bedroom door with dread, but Bogart held up a hand and mouthed, *I got it.*

"Okay, Pap. Bogart is getting it."

"Good. Get out. Buy some ordinary clothes and hide in the city. Get a hotel room or something."

"Isn't the Bull and Badger headquartered in New York?" That was Sunnie. Hedy teared up all over again at the sound of her voice.

"Aye, that's good," her Pap said resolutely. "Find the Bull and Badger building. Get there. Tell them you're from the Cougan County Renaissance, we're a subsidiary of theirs. They'll take care of you until we can get there."

"All right, Pap."

"And keep that phone on you."

"How are you getting here?"

"We'll get there," Pap's voice was firm with determination, "We will get to you."

"Okay, Pap," she matched his determination. "We'll be fine."

"I know you will be. You're my girl."

And this time she didn't mind the term.

CHAPTER TWENTY-THREE

Truths and Tunnels

Maze had fallen asleep on the overstuffed couch that was now firmly in place, not hovering at a ghost's whim. The shouting had stopped. The hurling books through the air had stopped, though several times a heavy hardback would adjust itself on the table if Philip stepped in a direction Addie didn't like. But the two had sat down, well, Addie floated, and they talked quietly as Maze drifted off to sleep.

When she woke, things were very quiet. Dust swam through sunlight spilling in the windows and Maze lay watching it. She couldn't remember the last time she'd slept in. The shelters always kicked your ass out early and before that, the fosters made her get up and do chores before school. No one was bugging her here.

Thoughts of Lola drifted through her head. The two met up every day and Maze felt the tug to find her friend. But with everything happening the way it was, it didn't feel safe to contact her. Was her best friend truly better off without her? For the two years she'd known her, they'd never spent a day apart. They were like sisters.

Maze pulled up the quilt laying over her and turned onto her side. She nearly threw herself over the back of the couch at the sight of a lavender ghost hovering over an armchair with a cup of tea.

"Morning, baby." Addie took a sip of her tea.

Wait, how was she . . .?

"How are you drinking . . . anything?" Maze rubbed her eyes.

The ghost turned the teacup over. It was empty. "Can't. But going through the motions of it is comforting. How'd you sleep? I've got beds. Could have moved you onto one of those."

"It was fine," she yawned. "Don't remember waking up any."

"You didn't."

The girl raised her eyebrows, "You been watching me all night or something?"

"Baby," the ghost smiled, the wrinkles around her eyes scrunching up, "I watched you sleep from the moment you were born. Your mama *insisted* that eyes were always on you."

Maze's eyes filled up and her skin prickled before she knew what was happening. "My mama?"

"Yeah," Addie smiled, "your mama."

Maze took a long steadying breath. "Where is she?"

Addie stared down into the teacup for a moment as though she might find the right words in the delicate porcelain. Finally, she turned her big, magnified eyes on Maze and squared her shoulders, "She's dead, Maze. They're *all* dead."

Tears she didn't realize she was holding back began trickling down, finding their way to the pillow smooshed up against Maze's cheek. Dead. Figures. That's the shit show her life had been so far, why should it change? But that was better, right? At least she was dead and that's why no one ever came to find her. That's why things were left up to Addie and Philip, right? Dead.

"My daddy too?"

Addie nodded, "But not without one hell of a fight."

Maze let herself smile a little. "What were they like?"

The teacup lifted from Addie's hands and floated to rest upon the ornate mantle over the fireplace while at the same time a thick, hardback book flew across the room to Maze. The girl sat up and wiped her eyes, positioning herself cross-legged. Pages flipped until coming to the picture of a man and woman. "That's them." The tears filled up and spilled over again. The illustration was in full color and colorful it was. Both had rich, brown skin and their eyes were as bright and alive as their smiles. Maze could see where she got her shape. Her mother was a curvy woman, big chest, broad hips, and round face. Daddy was tall, broad, and built like a club bouncer. The crowns on their heads were covered in jewels and only out shown by their clothes. The low cut dress her mama wore was so colorful it would put Times Square to shame, and her daddy's long coat and fitted pants stood their ground with the dress.

Maze soaked them in and ran a finger over them, tracing their faces over and over. The two held hands, their jeweled fingers interlocked. "What were their names?"

"Mazonne and Marque," Addie said softly, literally hovering over Maze's shoulder.

"I'm named after my mama?"

"You're daddy."

"My *daddy*. Mazonne." Suddenly that name she had avoided all her difficult life meant more than she could ever express. It sounded powerful now, not weird. "Mazonne." She took a deep breath, "How'd they die? Does this book say?"

"That book doesn't mean shit. Bunch of old screwed up and twisted stories written by a couple of fools who have no business doing what they're doing."

Maze kept her thumb on the page where her parents were pictured then turned it over to look at the spine. James and Harriett Daniels. Book six of the United Realms. "Who *are* they?"

Addie was clearly irritated by the topic, but Maze needed to know things now. "I don't know, baby. I tried several times to get in touch with them over the last seventeen years to find out how they knew what they knew, but the damned fools wouldn't return my calls."

"Why didn't you go find them?"

"Baby, I tried the internet, I called their publisher, and I even used the trinkets I have around her," she said with a sweep of her arm, "but they aren't going to be found. I don't know what they have in terms of their own trinkets and safeguards, but they don't want to be found."

Maze opened the book again to the picture of her parents. "Can I have it?"

"Of course. Rip it right on out of there, baby. The Daniels might be shit as writers, but they had one hell of an illustrator. The joy in your mama's eyes," the ghost murmured.

Carefully, Maze tore the page from the book. "Will *you* tell me how they died?"

"I wasn't in the council chamber when it happened; I was already with you and the others, but Philip was outside the chamber door and said your mama started in on the Council of All before any of them had taken their seats. Lashed up one side and down the other, then gave it to them again. It's when she was cut off mid-word and he heard her body hit the floor, he said your daddy bellowed like an enraged bull and the fighting began. Philip ran to the rest of us as planned and we all came here to the Prison."

"The Prison?"

"Earth. *This* Earth."

"Why'd you call it the Prison?"

"Because it is, baby. This whole place started off like Australia, just a place where people were sent to be forgotten and die. But just like Australia, this world turned itself into something. And it grew big, a good place to hide. So, with Power dampened the way it is here to keep the prisoners from using it, we all thought it was the best place to bring the babies and keep them safe."

"But the time for hiding is over," Maze concluded.

"That's right," Addie sighed. "The time for hiding is over. Somebody started something and we're all in it."

A tapping noise startled Maze and she jumped, the book falling off her lap. Perched at the stained-glass window behind her was a black crow.

"Nightfeather," Addie said in explanation, "an old friend."

The crow tapped again on the window insistently.

The window unlatched and swung opened on its own, rather, Addie did it, but that's how it looked to Maze. The crow hopped in and just as it was opening its beak, it stopped and cocked its head to look at the new comer. Something about the black beady eye unnerved Maze. Weren't crows always the bad guys? Always trying to eat the corn in cartoons? Spies for evil witches and shit?

"Well," the bird croaked, "you finally brought the girl here."

"What. The. Hell." Maze heard herself. "That bird just talk?"

"She be as stupid as I thought she would be?"

"Hey," Maze said indignantly.

Nightfeather squawked and flapped as one of its large tail feathers suddenly removed itself from the black bird's backend. "Keep that up, crow, and you'll be as naked as a Thanksgiving turkey," Addie warned. "Now, what do you want?"

"The many squirrel found him. The orange-hair boy? I thought it be dumb to employ them, but you were right. The many squirrel found him in Central Park."

"Orange-haired boy?" Maze asked.

"Stephen, baby," Addie said with the wave of a hand.

A door down one of the hallways off the living room opened and seconds later Philip walked in wearing silky boxer shorts and yawning. "Morning." He raised his cell phone, "I have a meeting this morning in the Square. I gotta get down there."

Addie ignored him, "So the boy has been found. That's good. Did you lead him here?"

"No," Nightfeather hopped to the back of the sofa. "I left him with the girl and her companion."

"What girl?" Addie, Maze, and Philip said together.

"The little one. The little person."

"Oakenroot?" Addie rose higher into the air.

"Yah, yah. That be what the companion called her. Claimed he had her taken care of. He and two big dog. Headed to a building in Times Square. Tourist trap," the crow snipped.

Philip yawned again, "Meetings at the B&B with the agency, I'll just be a bit. Contract review, no big deal."

"B&B. Yah, that be the one. I pointed them that way. The little one be strong. Looked good to me, and I left the orange-hair boy with them. And it be a good thing I did too. The crowd out your building do no look terribly good."

Philip, very alert now for as bleary as he had been moments before, leaped to the window and looked out. "Oh, shit."

Maze scrambled to the window. Down below stood hundreds, maybe thousands of people, and every single one of them stared slack-jawed back at Maze. A few bystanders on the fringe took pictures of the massive gathering of the city's apparently dead homeless. Dumb asses probably thought it was some sort of performance art or protest. Shit like that was always going down in the city.

"They can't actually see us," Addie said, hovering at Maze's shoulder.

"Then why are they looking up here? I mean, they're looking right at us," Maze said quietly.

"Whoever is behind all those eyes knows enough about me to look in the right direction, but trust me, no one can actually *see* us."

"They know this is Addie's building, they killed her, so they've been onto it for a while," Philip looked as though he were counting the Shells below. "It's probably been watched for a long time now. When you and I showed up, the troops were called in and now we're trapped. I can't fight through that by myself."

"I'm a big girl," Maze said, "I can take care of myself."

Philip shook his head, "No. Not in all that. They'd swarm you the moment you cleared the door."

Maze studied the sea of upturned faces. Despite the diversity of skin color and age, the men and women down below had one thing in common: they all carried the weight and wear of homelessness. Those people down there were *her* people. “Can’t we do something?” Maze asked.

“Yeah,” Philip said as he jogged back to the room he’d slept in, “we can get the hell out of here.”

“How?” Maze asked, unable to take her eyes off of the people below. She was sure she recognized some of them and there was one old face she was praying she wouldn’t see staring back.

“We’ll take the bathroom,” Addie said with resolve.

“What?”

“We’ll take the bathroom,” Addie repeated as she floated away. “Get the teacup off the mantle and come on.”

“Okay, people, I mean it, what the hell? Someone needs to start talking in words that I can make sense of, and not just bathrooms and teacups.”

The crow made a sound as though clearing its throat and spoke in slow, measured words as though he were talking to Crazy Eddie on 5th and 57th. “Pick up the tea cup on the mantle. That be the shelf over the fireplace. It be called a mantle.”

“I know what a mantle is, god damn it,” Maze snapped at him. “I just didn’t know why the hell I was getting it and heading to the bathroom.”

“Big hume girl would be good to follow an order and keep beak shut.”

Maze’s eyes widened, “Did you just call me fat?”

Nightfeather cocked his head, “You be a big hume. Big.” He cocked his head again, “Big of hip. Big of breast. You be big. Yah, you be a fat hume.”

Maze took a hard swing at the bird, but he flapped out of the way easily.

"And you be a lethargic hume. Now come, follow instruction. Pick up the teacup and go to the bathroom."

Maze grumbled all kinds of combinations of swear words as she swiped the teacup off the mantle and stomped down the hallway. Philip was dressed in the clothes he wore last night, with the addition of a slender sword he was in the midst of belting around his waist. The buckle was golden and ornate, like something from a big budget pirate movie. Addie hovered down the hallway toward them with a large purple purse floating in front of her. "Put the teacup in there, baby, and carry my bag for me." Maze did as she was told to avoid further rebuke from the jackass of a bird. "Now close the door." She did. "Knock . . ." the ghost paused.

"Knock . . . ?" Maze asked after a moment.

"Hold on, I'm thinking. I've never actually had to use it." Addie's big eyes were searching her memory and her lips moved as if she were reciting something. "Six times in even succession. Six? Or was six the police station?"

"I don't know about you, but if six is the police station, I'll take my chances."

Philip shook his head, "No police. They'll slow us down. How many knocks, Addie?"

"Wait, I'm gonna knock and then what? Somebody gonna yell, 'occupied'?"

Philip responded as though the answer was obvious, "Then you open it."

"I swear I'm gonna bust you up," Maze said with a clenched jaw. "What happens when I open the door?"

Addie answered this time, "It's a communicating door. An escape. I rigged it when I moved in here fifteen years ago, but I've never had to use it. Okay, try six. If that's not it, we'll try again. Go ahead, baby."

Maze knocked six times, slowly and in a steady succession.

"Now, open it, baby."

Taking a deep breath, Maze did as she was told. At first, as the door swung open, she thought she had opened the door into nothingness, but as her eyes adjusted, she could see the rails on the ground. "Is this the subway?"

"Yes," Addie said with relief as she floated through the door first. Her lavender color shifted to a bright blueish white, lighting about ten feet around her. "I'll go first, I'm already dead. Philip—"

"I'll take up the rear," he said firmly.

"Good. Baby, you stay between us."

Nightfeather perched on her shoulder, the bird's touch startling her at first. "You better not do nothing on my shoulder. You got me?"

"That do be repulsive."

"You're a bird."

"I do no hold being *hume* against *you*."

The group stepped into the dark tunnel, Addie's light casting shadows all around them. Philip closed the door, a sturdy metal door on big hinges, behind them quietly. "If they do happen to get in, Adelaide, will the door lead them here?"

Addie shook her head, "No. One time use per knocks. It's a little, nautical themed guest bathroom again."

Philip nodded. "Where exactly are we, Adelaide?"

"It's an abandoned tunnel about three blocks off the Harold Square Station. We come out of that station—"

"Then head up to Times Square and the B&B where we find Oakenroot and Stephen. Lead the way," Philip said firmly.

Addie floated down the tunnel, the shadows shifting as she went. Gripping the purse tightly, Maze followed, the pinch of the crow's claws a strangely welcoming comfort. The air was terribly still and it smelled horrible, like piss and rot. Now and then she could hear rumbling from a distant train and that took some getting used to.

She wanted to panic every time she heard it, thinking a train would be bearing down on them any moment. Her feet eventually fell into a rhythm with the tracks. At first she stumbled over them, either stepping between them or partially on them, and once she fell, banging her knee pretty hard. The bird scolded her, but she reached up and threatened to pull out a tail feather, and the scolding ended abruptly.

Like everyone else, Maze had heard stories of pockets of homeless who lived in abandoned tunnels. They were secretive groups even in the homeless community. Lola joked about trying to find them, but Maze wasn't interested. If they wanted to be hidden so badly, they could *stay* hidden as far as she was concerned. If the urban legends were true, she imagined the things done down here in the dark where police weren't a threat, were far worse than the those done up above in the light. It was bad enough sometimes sleeping in a shelter with a known pervert a few cots away. Down here . . .? Maze shuddered.

"How much farther?" Maze whispered.

The ghost responded, "I don't know, baby, can't be too far."

Maze had kept her eyes down on the tracks insuring she wouldn't fall when she realized Addie had stopped.

"What is it, Adelaide?" Philip asked, his hand on the hilt of his slender sword.

"I'm not sure," Addie said quietly.

Maze peered into the darkness just beyond Addie's light. Was there someone there? It felt like it, but the dark was blacker than night and she couldn't really tell. Addie floated forward and as she did a silhouette became visible. Short. Slim. A girl? The light exposed her and Maze's throat caught.

"Lo-," she worked at the name. "Lola?" Maze finally choked.

Her friend's head tilted slightly.

Maze rushed forward despite Philip's warning to stay back and the bird's flapping protests. "Lola? Lola! Girl is that you?"

Glassy eyes stared back in response.

Maze took her all in. It was her. Just as she always was. But something was frighteningly off. "What's the matter with you, Lo? What's going on? Why you down here? Please, Lo, talk to me. You're scaring the shit out of me! Lo?"

Maze reached up and touched her friend's unresponsive face. It was cold. Too cold. "Addie," Maze turned to the floating spirit, "what the hell is wrong with her?"

Lola's hand snaked around her throat and closed tight. Maze heard Nightfeather cry out and flap away as Philip lunge forward, freeing the blade from its scabbard. The hand around her throat was strong and the fingers were digging into her neck. But she wasn't scared. Instincts jumped in, instincts that had been born and bred on the streets. She grabbed the skinny arm in both of hers and thrust her considerable backside out while pulling forward with her upper body. It was something she had learned at a shelter one night and the instructor had been impressed, saying Maze was built to defend herself. Lola flew over her shoulder and landed on the ground hard, her head knocking against the train track.

Philip raised his sword.

"Philip," Maze shouted! "No! She's my best friend! She ain't right! She's out of her head!"

"She's not your friend, Maze. She's not just out of her head, she's not even in there. She's Vacusai. Someone else has her."

From above, Nightfeather cawed. "There be more, Addie. Look!"

"I see them, bird," the ghost answered. Her voice was tight.

Lola pulled herself up. Her head tilted to the side. "A spirit, a talking crow, a man with a blade, and . . ." her eyebrows raised, "you must be one of the Six." That wasn't Lola's voice. The voice, the sound was right, but the way the words fit together and the . . . the accent? The accent sounded like the Count on Sesame Street. It wasn't Lola. "Why are you in my tunnels?"

Addie floated near the crowd of Shells. "Who are you?"

The crowd spoke in sync with Lola this time, "Why are you in my tunnels?" All of them bore the same chilling accent.

Philip raised his sword and slid into a strange guarded stance, "We don't answer to you."

Lola spoke alone this time, "Why must we proceed so aggressively? Answer my question and I'll produce another. I'll continue to press until I feel you've answered adequately. I must confess, the members of your party have piqued my interest a great deal."

Maze was struggling with seeing her friend like this. "If we answer your damn questions, will you give me my friend back?"

"This is hard for you?" Lola asked.

Maze could only nod as tears threatened to break loose.

A short, pudgy man in a long coat stepped forward. "Is this one easier?" he asked.

Maze let out a breath she didn't know she was holding and nodded again.

Addie hovered near the new mouthpiece of their mysterious interrogator. "We're on the run."

"From whom?" The little man asked curiously.

"I'm not certain. Could be you for all I know."

"Your pursuer has engaged Vacusai?"

Addie didn't respond.

Guardedly, Philip approached her, "First World?"

"It looks that way," Addie replied softly.

"Did the Vacusai follow you here?"

Addie shook her head, "Impossible."

"You of all people should know how possible impossibilities are, Adelaide Penitrail." The short man grinned. "Weaver of Winds. Truth Whisperer. Witch."

"Who are you?" Addie's voice was firm.

The short man laughed, "You don't recognize this scruffy one?"

"Should I?"

The man shrugged, "It's been nearly ten years since I sent this one. I'm sure many faces have come and gone in that little office of yours in Brooklyn. How about any of these?" The man gestured behind him and several more Vacusai stepped forward into Addie's light. This time recognition was clear. "Ah, so you *do* recognize them. It's good to know you haven't lost your touch. What use would you be to the princess there if you had?"

Philip hissed, "Who are you?"

"I've enjoyed your work on stage, Mr. de Grande," a woman said from outside the light, her voice carrying the same accent as the others. Tall, voluptuous, a pale-skinned woman with rich, red hair stepped forward. Philip's eyes widened.

"Emily?"

"Most of the time," she replied. The woman was gorgeous and Maze thought she was out of place compared to the others who looked as though they belonged on the streets or these tunnels. "Come with me," Emily said.

"What do we do?" Philip asked the ghost.

"You come with me." The crowd said together.

"Addie?" Maze asked, her hands shaking.

The ghost sighed, "We go with her . . . him— them. Damn it, whoever the hell they are."

Turns, doors, turns, junctions, and forks, the small party followed the crowd who all shared one voice. Lola walked beside Maze the entire time, which was both a comfort and torturous as they toured the dark, rumbling tunnels. When did this happen to her? *How* did this happen? She had only been away from Lo for a day. Was it just a day? Was it more? If Maze hadn't disappeared into all this trippy shit with Philip and Addie, could she have saved Lo?

The short, balding man approached a door with a wheel mechanism like a safe in the movies. He turned the wheel opening the thick door and as he did, warm, welcoming light spilled into the dark tunnel. The group was ushered forward through the portal as another train rumbled in the distance. Once in, Emily pulled the door closed behind them and locked it. The room was an eclectic collection of old and new, much like Addie's apartment, but more rigid and studious. Maps covered the wall, of subway systems and the world. Another wall was covered in pictures of people with notes written beside them in a spidery, scrawling hand. Furniture filled the room, however most of it looked like it had been discarded as garbage but repaired with other pieces. And so many plants. Plants everywhere of all kinds. Plants bearing fruit, flowers, even small trees and planters growing vegetables along the walls. The room was giant and full, but comfortable and warm, lit by Edison bulbs and candlelight.

As the group filed in, the crowd, including Lola, dispersed through doorways leading away to hallways filled with much of the same from what Maze could see. She desperately wanted to catch Lola and pummel her with questions, but at the same time wasn't sure she wanted the answers.

"Forgive my methods," a voice said, the same accent Maze had heard from the crowd, but in a rich, smooth baritone. "I'm protective of my sanctuary and there has been much in the way of trespassers of late." Emerging from the crowd flowed a man. Unusually tall and pale. His face was beautiful, but hard, lined deeply, on the verge of gaunt. He wore a dark silky robe that hung open down to his all too visible ribs and bony hips. The man looked sick, like he was dying.

Addie kept her distance, "I never expected to find one of your kind here."

"You should, Ubeir."

Her ghostly spine stiffened and her color darkened, "Don't call me that."

"What did he call her?" Maze whispered to Philip.

"It's a— um . . . Dark Sister. Witch."

"Is she?"

"No," Addie said firmly, "I'm not."

The weary man smiled weakly and slid to a rigid looking chair and sat, easing his body onto it. "Then why else have you been banished here? What was your crime?" He turned his sunken eyes on Philip, "What was *your* crime?"

"We're here by choice."

The man laughed, a thing that was full but ended in a coughing fit. "No one comes here by choice. Even if you are her Pair, you did something to deserve this hell."

"Why do you have my friend?" Maze blurted out. That's all that mattered. All this stupid talk and squaring up, playing games. It was all bullshit. What mattered was Lola and why the hell she was down here.

The man turned his eyes to her, measured her. "I have her because I can't release her. Try though I have, I can't. All of them, my . . . friends? Patients? At one time or another, each of them on the brink of death, and I reached out my hand to them. Brought them back. I shouldn't have, I know that now, but I did." He shrugged, his sharp shoulders raising in the old robe, "It's who I am. Who I was, rather. Was. I am no longer what I was."

Maze crossed her arms, "And what the hell are you or *was* you?" She raised a quick finger of warning, the middle one, to Philip whom she had heard draw a exasperated breath behind her.

"Maze, you shouldn't—" Philip tried to caution instead, but she didn't give a good goddamn.

"No," Maze threw up a hand, "I am so damn tired of all this bullshit. Buuuullshiiiiit. I want answers and I want them now. Everyone in here got me? Right fucking now."

She had miss-stepped. She knew that. But she was done. Her best friend, her sister, wrapped up in some kinda weird voodoo cult was the cherry on top of a stupidly shitty sundae. All eyes stared at her, Addie through her big glasses, Philip wide-eyed, and the poster child for heavy drug addiction in the silky porno robe. But the creep in the robe was the first to respond. He broke out into rich laughter, again ending in a dry coughing fit. "Yes! You! Entuziasm!" He pulled himself up, a glimmer of regality. "I will match yours. I, princess, am Mikhail. Vampeir."

"Vampire?" Maze blurted.

"Vampire," the sickly man spat. "Tales to twist and create fear. It is what is done in this Prison. Yes? Make you afraid of good? Bloodsuckers? Undead? Even Vacusai are a perversion of the beauty that is the intricacy of life and the bond. No. I am a healer. *Was* a healer. Once a servant to the All, now banished and disgraced. A rat hiding in the dark. Playing with puppets, a Crowd of Mutuos, the Shared, my little adopted family. Of which your friend is a precious part."

"How? How is Lola a part of *this*? When? We were only apart for a day."

"Princess, your friend has been a part of my family for many years. Many, many. 1983? Overdose of drug. Found in an alley in the East Village. Beautiful girl."

"What the hell are you talking about? 1983?"

Mikhail nodded gravely, "Da, yes. 1983, back when I didn't know."

"Didn't know what?" Addie demanded.

Mikhail spread his hands, "Didn't know simple practices do not work so simply here. At home, I could revive and release. Here, this damned Prison, I can't let them go. They *tie* to me. And if I cut them off, they perish like rotting fruit. I can't bear to see them perish. Therefore, I cut myself off from *them* up there, stopped wandering the streets because there is so much dying and I can't give anymore of myself or we will all perish, my family and me."

Maze worked on wrapping her mind around the cryptic revelation. No, this wasn't possible. She knew Lola. The two were sisters. They shared everything with each other. Maze said as much.

Mikhail waved a hand, "She goes out from here, *they* go out from here and live. When they run low, they come here to... *refresh*? *Rejuvenate*?"

"But in the tunnel, there, you were controlling them!"

"Only when my home is trespassed upon, Princess, only then do I play that little parlor trick." Mikhail gestured to the nearby chairs, "Please, where are my manners, sit. I'll have my family bring refreshments."

"No," Addie said, "We have others to find. At least two. Probably more."

"Others?" Mikhail asked, his hand going to his emaciated chest. "Others of the Six? Which ones?"

"The Daughter of Dree and the Speaker." Philip pitched in.

Mikhail was startled, "*All Six will join and journey home . . .*" He looked from the ghost to the swordsman, "Now? It happens *now*?" With obvious pain, the gaunt man pulled himself up from the chair. "Then yes, you *must* go. If Vacusai have found the Princess, they'll find the other two. But not through the tunnels. Too many places for wretched things to hide. Do you know where to locate the Speaker and small one?"

"Times Square. B&B," Nightfeather spoke up for the first time.

"Times Square? Hmph, da, good," he waved a long fingered hand. "Good enough. Safety in numbers."

"Are you coming with us?" Maze asked.

Addie shook her head, "No, he would slow us down."

"Yes," Mikhail agreed. "I'm in no shape to be useful." He grinned painfully, the lines in his face deepening grotesquely.

"I'll go." Lola was standing in the doorway. It was *her*. The voice Maze had known for so long. Their eyes met and her friend smiled reluctantly. But she wasn't *just* Lola now. She was something unfamiliar and Maze wasn't sure she could handle it, or even wanted to.

Emily stepped into the room too, "And me. And Bernard."

"Like hell!" came the pudgy man's voice from down a hallway.

"Bernard," Mikhail said softly, "you're needed. You'll go."

Bernard rushed into the room, "'You always have a choice'. That's what you tell us, we have a choice. Now I don't?"

Mikhail shrugged, "You can go on your own accord or I force you. There's your choice. Pleased?"

The squat, scruffy man pulled a burgundy sock cap on his head, "I sure the hell am not *pleased*. But fuck it, right?" Bernard pushed through the others to the vault door. "Times Square? That's where we're goin'?"

Addie shook her head, "This isn't necessary, we don't need an escort."

"We'll be fine," Philip agreed, his hand resting on his sword hilt.

Mikhail held up a crooked finger, "They will escort you *through* the tunnels and *beyond* the tunnels is their choice."

"Oh, so we *do* have a choice?" Bernard started, but clammed up when Mikhail twitched his finger.

Emily gracefully turned the wheel and pushed the door open, "Come along, sweeties."

CHAPTER TWENTY-FOUR

An Odd Escort

It was always like this. Children's clothes. It was embarrassing. And not just children's clothes, but *large* children's clothes, like for . . . overweight kids. She didn't even bother trying to go to the women's section. She would have if her Mam was there to tailor her clothes down to fit her perfectly, but she wasn't. Her Mam was in Oregon. Her Pap was in Oregon. *Everyone* she knew and loved was in Oregon. And Hedy was in New York City.

Her Pap had told her to get to the Bull and Badger building to hide out until they could get to her. How long was that going to take? How long did it take to fly from Oregon to New York? She imagined her Pap and Mam, their shorts legs racing through PDX to catch a flight, and it brought a smile to her lips. Even sillier to her was the thought of them with Ubby and Sunnie, all of them in their faire clothes. She added more of her friends to the frantically running herd, until she came to Marla and Old Millie and even Denny. It wasn't silly anymore.

Bogart bought them the clothes with the cash he found under Millie's bed and they changed in the store. She found the least childlike clothes, a pair of jeans, a t-shirt and denim jacket. The clothes still fit her oddly, not like the custom-made ones Sunnie had made her. No, the people intended for these clothes didn't have boobs yet. But with a roll of a pant-leg, a tuck of the t-shirt in front, and flip of the jacket cuff, Hedy made the look work for her.

They walked out of the store and Stephen stood up from the sidewalk. Polly and Brutus sat with their butts against the wall, their thick leashes laying on the ground beside the red-haired boy. He had insisted on staying outside, something about fresh air, though the smell of Manhattan was anything but fresh, especially compared to the woods she was so accustomed to. The redheaded boy smiled. "I like your clothes. They're nice. You like mine? I'm not wearing underwear."

"They're very nice," Hedy agreed awkwardly.

He wasn't easy to get used to. The strange boy had appeared suddenly in the doorway of Millie's RV with a silly grin on his face, in a trench coat and ski cap. When the rat popped its head out of the pocket the first time, she had nearly screamed. It wasn't the sight of a rat, just the size of it. Hedy had seen dogs smaller than that thing. The redheaded boy, Stephen, called it Jacob but said he hadn't found a suitable name for the little squirrel yet that liked to race back and forth across his narrow shoulders. His speech was immature and fragmented, like a six-year-old, but he appeared to be good natured and genuinely thrilled he'd found them. Obviously, something wasn't right in his head. He felt . . . broken. But as broken as he might be, he was sweet. Kind. And coupled with Bogart and the dogs, Stephen made her feel safe.

"Where to now?" Bogart hefted the bags with their faire clothes.

"I suppose we need to follow my Pap's instructions and figure out where the Bull and Badger building is."

Bogart nodded. He was in jeans and a Star Wars t-shirt that hugged his belly and a bulky pair of tennis shoes. She missed him in his puffy-sleeved shirt and cloak, he had looked so chivalrous. But the warm smile was still there and that's what comforted her. "Guess I should ask directions," he suggested. After the purchase of a dozen hotdogs and a brief conversation with the vendor, Bogart had it down. "We're on 5th Avenue," he explained, slipping a hotdog to Polly, "if we keep going down that way, we'll come to 47th and then we turn right." Brutus nuzzled his hand for his own hotdog.

"This one's right," Stephen held up his left hand. Bogart and Hedy raised their eyebrows. Stephen looked down to the rat in his pocket and quickly changed hands. "*This* one's right," he said with more confidence.

"That's right— I mean, correct. You're correct, that's right." Bogart tried to clarify. He was like that. He didn't correct Stephen, he didn't patronize him, he genuinely tried to appreciate him. It was endearing.

Stephen grinned from ear to ear.

"So, if we turn right," Bogart raised his right hand and Stephen approved, "onto 47th, we'll eventually come to Times Square and the B&B, that's what he called the Bull and Badger building, it's right there at the heart of Times Square." Brutus gobbled down an offered hotdog, his counterpart stomping her feet impatiently for another of the vendor's delicacies.

Hedy took a deep breath, "We'd better get walking, yeah?"

Bogart tossed the two beasts another hotdog each, the treats gone in a flash of teeth and slobber.

The trio plus two maneuvered the streets, following the hotdog vendor's directions. 56th. 55th. 54th. 53rd. This wasn't a place Hedy had ever wanted to see. It just wasn't natural. Too many buildings, too many people, too much noise. It was all overwhelming. She could feel her agitation growing as she was jostled and bumped into. It was hard enough being her size in normal circumstances but put her in the middle of this mess of people, and she felt like she could get crushed at any moment.

52nd. 51st. 50th.

Whether it was out of self-preservation or her "like" for him, she took Bogart's hand in hers. It must have been new to him too, because he jumped a little and looked down but quickly recovered with a smile. "Are you okay?" he asked.

"I am," she smiled. "We're going to be okay." She held Polly and Brutus' leashes lightly in her hand. They really didn't need them, but she figured the sight of two dogs that size without their leashes might make a few people nervous. They were good babies and wouldn't hurt anyone. Not without cause anyway. She saw Polly with Denny's throat in her jaws and took a deep breath.

"We're going to be great," he squeezed her hand. "I'm with you. We're going to be great."

49th. 48th.

Stephen followed behind them, humming to himself, a song she assumed, but she couldn't catch the tune of it. It may not have been a song at all, just a random string of notes and rhythms. He kept his left hand in his pocket, the pocket where the rat moved now and then. Did anyone think they were as strange a group as she did? Did they stand out? No one seemed to be watching them, staring at them. She supposed the constant bumps from passersby proved that no one was paying attention to them whatsoever.

Bogart was right. This was going to be great. They were going to be fine.

The walk became easier, or she grew used to it. The odd troupe turned right on 47th and the throng of people thinned out some. The blocks were longer this way. Hedy allowed herself to smile and enjoyed the warmth of Bogart's hand and the odd melody hummed behind her. They would reach the B&B and probably be checked into a hotel, watch television, maybe order some room service, and her Pap and Mam would be there in no time.

6th Avenue.

The blocks were so much longer this way. Up ahead, she could see Times Square and all the people. So many people again. Her stomach dropped. More jostling, more bumping. Hedy tightened her grip on Bogart's hand in preparation and steeled her determination. Stephen was now on her right, humming his disjointed tune. She felt protected between the two of them and the dogs in front.

The walk sign had just swapped to the blinking stop hand at the corner of 47th and 7th Avenue. “Come on, we can make it,” Bogart urged.

They hopped off the curb and quickly rushed across the street.

CHAPTER TWENTY-FIVE

Still a Sister

Twists and turns, tunnels and doorways. The escorted group made their way through the subway system without incident. Maze expected the worst every time they rounded a corner, a horde of Shells waiting, or worse, their guides would turn on them. Lola walked beside her the whole way and she could feel her friend's eyes turn to her several times, but Maze wouldn't return her looks. Was it Lola looking at her or the one behind her eyes? Had *Mikhail* been her friend the entire time? And was Lola even her friend? Even her name? Everything felt like a setup. Addie and the welfare office, Philip and the cash and tickets, and now her best friend, her sister. What was really *hers*?

Emily walked beside Philip and the two talked in hushed whispers. Maze imagined he was struggling with the revelation his colleague and— and something else, lover? — struggling with the revelation she was more than she appeared.

Addie provided light as before, but Bernard often walked ahead of it, swearing and muttering to himself. That was comforting, in its own weird way. Crazy people on the streets were at least something normal for her. He led them to a door with a crash bar and stopped. "So, we're goin' through here and we'll be at the far end of a platform. When the train pulls in, we'll go through and blend in with everybody else." And moments later, the sound of rumbling could be heard on the other side of the door. Bernard held up a finger, waited a moment, then opened the door. Just as he suggested, the train was emptying of pedestrians, and the little group merged. It being New York, no one paid much attention to the girl with a crow on her shoulder, but several took notice of Philip and the red head with him, snapping pictures on their phones.

Addie! Maze looked around her, but the ghost was nowhere to be seen. "I'm here, baby." Her voice came from the bag where the teacup was kept. "New York City might be accepting and numb to most weird, but I don't think they're ready for spirits-weird."

Up the stairs and out, Maze was met with fresh city air and took it in deeply. Well, as fresh as the air in Midtown could be. The sound of honking and sirens was a welcomed relief to the silence of the tunnels. Down the block to their right, people swarmed the sidewalks of Harold Square, going in and out of stores, texting and walking, stopping to take pictures of the Empire State Building. Maze could breathe deeply again. Emily took the lead, Bernard slipping to the back of the group, as they walked up 7th Avenue.

Lola took her hand. Maze tried to yank it back, but the woman held it tightly. "Girl, stop it."

"Me stop it? I don't even know who the hell you are."

"I'm me. You're friend. Same person I've been."

"Are you? Cause I just found out you been around since the eighties. Like, you were *this* old in the eighties! *And* there's someone else rollin' around in your head!"

"Shhh . . ." Lola hissed.

"Don't tell me to be quiet. Is he listening? Did *he* just tell me to hush?"

"No, that was me, bitch."

"Oh, you did not just . . ." but it was real. That was her friend. That was the Lola she knew. That one endearing word.

"He's not always in here. I know when he is and I know when he isn't."

"How?"

Lola shook her head, "I don't know. But he leaves me be. It's usually just down there when I hear him in here." She tapped her forehead.

"And he makes you do shit?"

"Only when he needs to, but he lets us know first." They walked along in silence another block and then, "I'm sorry, Maze."

"Okay, Lo."

"Just like that?"

"Oh, you still freak my shit out, but yeah, just like that. For now," She squeezed her friend's hand.

They walked on for a while, crossing street after street. 37th. 38th. 39th. Philip had pulled away from Emily and was walking behind Bernard now. His sword was still on his hip, and it drew some attention, but most just pointed and laughed. You could see all sorts of things in Manhattan and Maze figured most people assumed it a prop or fashion/political statement. Gun carriers in Texas, sword carriers in New York.

40th. 41st.

"The B&B is up ahead," Philip pointed.

The red-haired woman came to a stop, "I'm letting you go from here. I've had run-ins with those people and I'm not interested in entering their lair again."

Philip laughed, "They're good people, Em."

Emily shrugged, "Maybe to you, but that woman with the golden eyes is a bitch. I'm an actress and I know bitches and she's on a whole new level."

Philip squeezed her hand, "I'll get in touch when we're done."

The woman gave him a kiss on the cheek and stepped into a crowd headed in the other direction, disappearing immediately. One more of the vampire's puppets gone. Was he watching them now through Lo? Was there a way to separate her from him without killing her like he claimed? Was that a bluff? If there was a way, she was going to find it.

CHAPTER TWENTY-SIX

Unexpected Touchdown

He had failed and he knew it.

Ben sat in the room he'd been escorted to by the B&B security. They hadn't been rough with him by any means, but following them hadn't been an option, that much was clear. If Veronica Carrington, the other twin, was here, he needed to get to her before the Gohlem could. And a Gohlem being a Gohlem, it could be anywhere at any time, *anyone* at any time. He had learned that from the stories his Da told his sisters and him around the fire at night, stew bubbling in a pot. Gohlem were cunning and manipulative, as natural at shifting their tactics and loyalties as they were at shifting their shape. Ally, friend, lover, they could take on any of those roles.

The room was sparsely furnished, obviously not intended to be welcoming. Ben stood and wandered over to the window. Looking down, he could see people milling about in the square. How proud would Coach be now? He had touched down in the middle of the night just inside of Central Park. A few trees and bushes masked his landing from anyone who might have seen. However, it was late and no one was around except for a guy sleeping on a bench under a thick blanket. The trip had been dizzying, but he was good. He'd made it. Because of where he landed, he knew Charlie must have been nearby, though he had no idea where. Too many buildings full of too many apartments lined the street facing the park. And what if he wasn't in one of those at all? While he was certain Charlie was here in the city, after all, the blood had brought him here, but he could be a mile away.

The plan. Ben knew he had to stick to the plan for any of this to work. Finding Times Square was easy enough once he found someone sober enough to shoot him in the right direction. At first, he thought he'd approach one of the many officer's he saw patrolling, but he knew the torn, blood stained shirt might cause suspicion, so he ditched the idea in pursuit of another. The kind couple he had found pointed him in the way of the dazzling lights and his heart soared. Ben never had any aspirations of coming to NYC, his place was with Coach and the Pack, he had a sworn duty, but this city was phenomenal. At home, his *real* home, nothing like this would ever have crossed his mind. He couldn't have fathomed it. While in Farnsworth, Texas, NYC felt as mythical as Camelot, one of his favorite stories from lit class. Now he was *here* and he realized he was *still* struggling to fathom it.

Once he reached the heart of the Square, he closed his eyes and centered himself. It wouldn't do him any good to be a moonstruck farmer boy in the middle of this city, not with the plan to enact. His eyes closed, Ben placed his palms over his heart. With the lights shut out, he hummed a tune, a tune his Ma sang while pulling the fruits of their labor from the earth, to fill his head with the voice. It was a daily drill for the Pups in Coach's house. Before they left for school, before they started practice, they cleared their thoughts, listened for the voice, and focused in. And in the middle of Times Square with the plan on his shoulders, Ben needed to hear the voice more than ever.

Peace.

Resolve.

Move.

He felt the tear of the shirt under his hands. First things first, and quickly, Ben needed a change. He had his pick of stores that were still open late into the night and Coach had given him cash to take care of himself until the rest of them could arrive. Ben chose a store that looked trendy enough and boasted of a big sale. Be smart, be wise. The men's clothes were on the third story and he quickly mounted the escalator steps. Finding a good pair of jeans and a simple t-shirt, he purchased the clothes and changed in the dressing room. Before trashing Charlie's clothes, he had torn a swatch of the bloody shirt and stuffed it into his pocket. He hadn't been sure if Gladys would still need him to be in possession of it in order to locate him, and he didn't want to take any chances. Strategy.

In a hurry, he was back on the street with a clear view of the B&B building, its illuminated crest dancing and flashing with the rest of the Square's signage. Ben mounted the steps of some slick, red bleachers oddly positioned in the middle of the bustling life. He sat with his back against the rail and started his surveillance of the building and the people who passed it. The crest flowed from picture to picture and soon he had the whole thing memorized. Hours passed and he remained put. He was determined to succeed, to prove himself.

But why?

Not a soul at FHS had a problem with him. Ben Hartling, that was the surname Coach had given him, was undeniably loved by everyone. He was kind to everyone and purposeful about it. While he wasn't the top of his classes, he worked hard and his teachers praised him for it. The Pack admired him for his work ethic and he quickly earned Coach's trust, carrying more responsibility than the rest of the Pups. Socially, he looked out for everyone, not just those in his circle. Obviously, he couldn't say he was friends with each and every person on campus, he still treated them all with the respect they deserved simply because they walked the planet. His Da had taught him that.

But there was more to it, wasn't there? When he lay in bed at night, when he was quiet and listening to the voice, he realized he felt sorry for them. Ben felt sorry for every person he saw walking the halls of FHS, driving down the streets of Farnsworth, Texas. Why? Because they didn't know. They didn't know their entire existence stemmed from men and women sentenced to this world for questionable actions. Yes, most of them heinous, but like Ben, many were here for a difference of perspective and heart. Trouble. Rebels. Abominations. And even though his peers weren't directly sentenced, those who came before them, who turned this world into what it was, all suffered like he had, and that knowledge tore at him.

The night passed and Ben listened to the voice. Sometimes it was direction, other times it was encouragement. Coach had never identified what the voice was, but they all heard it, and it wove them together. More than their sentencing, the voice bound them. And every person who heard it struggled to explain it. David called a compass of right and good.

When the sky turned pink and the sun peaked between buildings, Ben had allowed himself to buy a breakfast sandwich and cup of coffee from a fast food restaurant next to his perch. He could still see the B&B as he sat perched on a stool by the window and munched on his egg sandwich. Hours passed again and Ben was about to buy another cup of coffee to keep his eyes from closing when a long black car pulled up to the building and the doorman helped a young woman out. Her pale blond hair spilled down her back and Ben's pulse zoomed. It was her, the woman in the picture, Veronica Carrington. The other twin.

Looking back, he could have handled himself better. Coach told him time and again, as sharp as he was, he was also too impulsive. Convinced that plays were right, he'd been known to make a call on the field that cost them ground. The tongue-lashings that would follow were enough to cause the rest of the Pack to tuck their own tails and avoid him until they were sure he was back in Coach's good graces. But neither Coach nor the Pack had been there to keep him from racing across the streets and flinging himself into the building to grab the woman's arm. Security crushed him to the ground like a well-oiled defensive line before he could get a word out and he was sure his arm had been broken at first. The alarm in the woman's golden eyes and heat in her silky voice ranked up there with Coach's own and Ben's stomach dropped when he realized what he had done. His urgency to warn her of the Gohlem had gone severely awry and now he found himself locked in a bare room high above the Square.

He could have railed against the door, beaten at it, yelled warnings, and raved like a madman, but it would have cost him yards. Sit tight, the voice said, so he did. When the door opened the next time, the startled woman, just a girl really, was clearly unaware the room was already occupied. Ben assumed she was an assistant of some sort, her professional attire said as much. "Do you have an appointment?" She asked.

Be calm. "You're damn right I do," he said with an aloof confidence, "with Veronica Carrington. I've been in this fucking room for an hour now!" He hated that word, hated it when the Pack used it, but he had a part to play. New strategy. "I was going to leave, but they locked the damn door. Fucking locked me in here like a fucking criminal! I could sue your ass! You know that? Sue your fucking ass! You and everyone in this goddamn building!"

It was working, the woman's eyes widened, "Sir, I'm just an intern, I don't know who put you in here. No one tells me anything. I'm sorry you were locked in, I think the door just does that? I'm sure it wasn't on purpose. If you can tell me what the nature of your—"

"Fucking representation by the fucking agency, you dumbass!" He felt like he was going to throw up. He wanted to apologize right then and there a million times over.

"I will let Ms. Carrington's assistant know you're here right away. Again, I'm so sorry." She glanced out the door as though trying to make a decision, "I hate to ask this, but would you mind sharing the room? I don't want to impede on you, but I was told to . . . um . . ." The poor girl was obviously torn between her responsibility and the asshole she had just been accosted by.

He had to give her a break. "Whatever," he sighed dramatically and turned to go look out the window.

"Thank you so much," she let out a breath. "If you could just wait in here," she directed to someone outside the door. "We're short on waiting rooms at the moment, so many of our floors are under renovation. Crazy, right? Big building like this?"

Ben heard three people enter behind him. No, three people and, what, two dogs? "Thank you," another woman said, "this is just fine."

"Certainly," the intern replied, a note of relief in her voice, probably glad she wasn't being verbally accosted again by the blond asshole. "I was told one of Mr. Carrington's assistants was ordering lunch for you. Is there anything else I can get you?"

"No," a man responded, "this is perfect."

"Thanks again," the woman said on the man's heels.

"Of course," the intern said and the door closed.

As soon as it did, Ben turned to see who his new cellmates were. He wasn't ready for it. Couldn't have been. A little woman holding the leashes of two giant dogs. A skinny, pale boy with bright red hair who looked to be his own age. And— "Bogey?"

The curly-headed boy's eyes widened in recognition. "Ben Hartling?"

CHAPTER TWENTY-SEVEN

The Bull and Badger

Spence was gone when Charlie woke up. Spence was gone, but the hangover wasn't. His head was pounding and he felt sick to his stomach. He wouldn't drink today, he needed a break. He stretched his big frame the entire length of the huge bed and sighed. For a moment, he pretended as though this sweet room was his. Big bed, cool stuff around. He could get used to it. Swinging his legs around, he stood and sleepily ambled to the closed curtains and threw them open. Though the sudden sunlight was blinding and didn't help his hangover, the scene outside was magical. Sprawling as far as the eye could see were rooftops of skyscrapers. And if *he* was seeing the rooftops of skyscrapers, that must mean he was in the tallest one around. Directly down below was a forest, he guessed it was Central Park. Giant apartment on an upper floor of a building next to Central Park. This place was money.

Charlie smiled to himself. This was all right. Today would be all right.

Turning, he saw clothes laid out on a tall, black lacquer chair that screamed rock and roll. Nice jeans, a plain white v-neck t-shirt, colorful underwear and socks, and a pair of designer sneakers. It all looked like clothes he could get at a local store in Farnsworth, but he was sure he was looking at several hundred dollars in clothes. On top of that, it all looked like clothes he would actually wear. It felt like ages since he had worn anything "normal." Bogart's clothes were too baggy, Spence's tight. Just a pair of normal jeans and a t-shirt. Normal like him.

The silver cuff laid on the lap of the jeans. Whoever had laid out the clothes must have assumed he'd want it. Charlie had to admit, now with a slowly clearing head, it was a strong piece. Manly. He'd seen guys at school wearing similar bracelets. Surely, he could separate the gift from the giver, right? Or did he have to? How much of an ass had he been? He really couldn't remember. Picking up the cuff, Charlie ran a finger over its smooth face. Nothing fancy. He slid it onto his wrist and his body came alive again just as it had last night and he closed his eyes soaking it in. Immediately, his head was clear, the throbbing gone. Just like when he was touched by her. His heart missed her. If he apologized, would she take him back?

In the sleek bathroom, Charlie undressed and slipped off the cuff. The moment he did, the room went cold and gray. No, not gray, but lifeless. Definitely lifeless. He put the cuff back on and his bodied hummed, the room went full color. Nothing remarkable about the simple metal band to the eye, but what it did to him was indescribable.

The shower was perfection. Shower heads sprayed him from all directions and he soaked up the hot water. This was good. This was how his life should be. Things were going to be better. He would find Meg, or she would find him more likely, and he would apologize. They would get back on track. Or was *this* on track? Maybe he was supposed to be here. Meg left him here after all, so she must be good with it. The shampoo bottles were all shampoo, both relieving and disappointing, he admitted to himself. He needed his head on straight, so it was all good.

Charlie dried off and wrapped a towel around his waist. When he walked back into the bedroom, he almost yelped. Veronica was lounging in the tall chair engaged with her phone, the clothes unceremoniously moved over to the bed. "Hey there, puppy," she purred, her voice silky and inviting.

His heart was pounding in his chest from the scare, "Hey, uh . . ."

"V. That's what my friends and Spence call me. V is fine." Her eyes were looking him over and he felt less like a puppy than a mouse being watched by a hungry cat. He eyed the clothes unsure of how to go about getting them on his body. "You like them? I picked them out from daddy's goody closet. That sounds dirty to someone who doesn't know the business. It's just where he keeps pieces designers send him. I guessed your sizes. Go ahead."

He picked up the underwear and glanced at them then back at the bathroom door. Why was this so uncomfortable with her? Had it been Meg, he could have just turned around, dropped his towel, and put them on. But Veronica was different. Very different. And why didn't he just go back into the bathroom? Was he trying to prove something? Be a man? Not be frightened by a girl? She wasn't just a girl, he was sure of that. She was powerful . . . and hot.

"Go ahead, puppy, get dressed." He couldn't help but hear the amusement in her voice and simultaneously felt a strong compulsion to follow the instruction.

Emboldened by the suggestion, he still had enough sense to turn away from her when he dropped his towel. He heard an approving, "Mmhmm" behind him and what sounded like the click of a camera. Face burning with embarrassment, he yanked things up quickly and turned around just in time for her to click the camera on her phone again with a smirk. "My Vollowers will like those."

"Did you just—?"

"Post pictures of that tight ass? Yes, I did," she purred. "You love it."

Charlie was at a loss for words, the heat in his face settling quickly and his pulse slowed. It'd be okay. People did that kind of thing all the time, right?

She laughed. "Where are you from? You're hilarious. So conservative."

He eyed the rest of the clothes on the bed, "Texas. A little town in Texas."

"Ugh, Texas. I hate it there. So hot. Boring. Even Austin is lame compared to this gorgeous city."

"Yeah," he smiled nervously, "it really sucks."

V stood, "He may be a world class bullshitter but Spence can do *one* thing well and that's find pretties. God, puppy, your body is enchanting." She glided to him and placed her hands on his chest then ran a finger over the stitched gash across this chest, "This is unfortunate, but it could be your *thing.*" As tall as he was, she was only barely shorter, and when she raised her face to his, he noticed how easy it would be for him to lean down and meet her lips. She laughed, "I don't think so, puppy." He didn't realize it, but he must have been acting on the inclination. "I'm not the *easy* Carrington. Spence is in the kitchen if you're wanting a morning make-out session."

He was horrified, "No, I don't— I mean, we didn't—"

She raised her hands playfully, "I don't need to know all of my brother's little secrets and positions. What happens in Spencer's bed, stays in Spencer's bed . . . and floor, and pool, and ugh, my car that one time." She laid a hand on the doorknob. "Get yourself dressed, puppy. Daddy wants you to come see him in the office today." She looked him up and down one more time and slipped out the door.

Did she really think the two of them had . . .? They hadn't! They had both just slept. "Careful of the company you keep," he could hear his mother warn, "you don't want their *dirty* laundry getting mixed up with your *clean* clothes." It had never actually been an issue since he didn't have any friends. Keep yourself isolated and another person's reputation wasn't an issue. And just how clean were his 'clothes'? He knew the teenage thoughts that ran through his head. He knew he liked liquor. He knew what he had been willing to do with Meg had their moment in the pool house not been crashed . . . and just now with Veronica. But was all of that really *dirty*? His parents would say so. They'd certainly label it as inappropriate. Indecent.

Charlie did his best to dismiss the shame wiggling its way in and pulled the clothes on, surprised at how well they fit. He felt good, like himself finally. It had been quite a while since he had felt that way. Exactly how much did the jeans cost? Or would they cost if they weren't a freebie in Carrington's closet? At home, his parents just bought him what fit. It didn't matter the brand; if it fit and looked good on him, that was enough. "Inflated price tags are only for inflated egos," another of his mother's sayings played in his head. But there was clearly something different about these jeans, they felt so good and hung on his hips just right. And the shirt! It was just a t-shirt, but none of his t-shirts felt this soft. Well, the worn-out shirts felt like this, but that took years of work and by the time they were just right, he would either outgrow them or Harriett would turn them into dust rags. The socks and canvas sneakers finished off the look and what Charlie saw in the mirror was exactly what he was hoping for. He looked *right*, like himself, or the self he had always *wanted* to be. The self he would be now.

Spence was in fact in the kitchen, cooking. "Hey, big guy, what do you want in your omelet besides me?"

Veronica sat at the large island touching up her makeup. She smirked.

"I— just some of whatever you're having, I guess." As good as he'd been feeling a moment ago, he was back to feeling awkward.

"I've gotta get to the office, Spence," Veronica put her things away and stood up. She was so incredibly hot. "Can you get puppy to Daddy?"

"Yeah, whatever," Spence said over his shoulder as he worked the skillet with his spatula.

"Spence, it's a big deal. Can you do it?"

"Yes, V. Shit. I'll get him there. I found him, didn't I? I'm not going to screw it up. He'll be there."

"What time?"

Spence groaned, "11:00."

"AM or PM?"

"Holy shit, V. 11:00 fucking AM. He'll be there."

V turned and grinned. Charlie had seen enough of this sort of thing in school to know the woman loved every bit of the power play, thrived on it. She winked at Charlie and poked him in the chest, "I'll see you there, puppy. Don't let him get you all dirty."

Charlie's face burned.

She left.

Charlie sat on a stool at the island while Spence finished up. "She's such a bitch," Spence finally said. "Such an absolute bitch. It's always like that. Why do you think I live in Cali while she and my dad make camp out here? I mean," he wilted a bit, "my dad's not so bad when she's not around, but when the two of them get together, the crosshairs fall on me and they just verbally beat the shit out of me, you know?" He finished up the omelet and slid it onto a plate. "There's some salsa there if you want it, big guy. That's what you people from Texas do, right? Slather everything in salsa or ranch dressing? You could slather me up—"

"Could you not?" The words were out of his mouth before he knew it.

"What?" Spence's back was still to him as he started on what Charlie assumed was his own breakfast.

"Stop with all the hitting on me. I'm not— I don't— just stop."

Spence shrugged, "Don't knock it 'til you try it, big guy."

Charlie just took a bite of his omelet and dropped the subject altogether. And the distraction was actually delicious. He let Spence know as much. "Yeah," Spence said with another shrug, "culinary school was one of my many vocational stints. And," he sighed, "like every other one, it didn't stick."

"Why?" Charlie said around another mouthful.

Spence slid his own breakfast onto his plate and tossed the small skillet into the sink with a loud crash. The slight guy sat down on a stool and cut into his food. "I don't know, man. Nothing really sticks with me. Nothing feels right, you know? Like, I'm supposed to be doing something and none of this shit is it. I used to try to tell my dad that, but it always ended up in, 'you need to keep looking, Spencer,' or 'if you could commit to something, you would eventually find satisfaction.' Jobs, relationships, I get bored with it all eventually."

Charlie could hear his own thoughts and frustration in those of the guy sitting across from him. When Charlie was little, anytime anyone asked him what he wanted to be when he grew up, he would tell them, "a superhero!" On their campouts, his dad would tell him the stories of Hercules, Galahad, or d'Artagnan of the Musketeers. He would even tell him stories about men like Sitting Bull, William Wallace, and Martin Luther King, Jr, men in the real world who stood up for justice against all odds. Charlie wanted to be those men and those stories stoked his desire to be someone more than some guy in a small town in Texas, dissatisfied with the status quo. Was it his dad's fault he found himself a self-made outcast? He took another bite of his breakfast. "I get it," he admitted.

Spence barked a laugh, "the hell you do, man. The hell you do."

"I get it," Charlie said adamantly. "I don't know what the hell I'm supposed to be doing with my life. I spent the majority of it thinking I was gearing up for something, only to realize a couple of days ago that I've really just been wasting time. My parents didn't prepare me for anything. Dragon hunts, campouts, it was all a waste of time. I can't put that on a college resume. I'm screwed."

Spence nodded, "Yeah, you are."

Despite himself, Charlie smiled. "Thanks."

"Hey," Spence spread his hands, "you can be my knight in shining armor."

"Veronica already thinks I am."

Spence shook his head, "I told her nothing was going on between us, she just likes to play that shit."

"And you don't?"

It was Spence's turn to grin and it actually met his silvery eyes, "touché, big fella."

They finished eating and Charlie cleared their plates to the sink. Spence slipped away and came back with a pair of aviator sunglasses. "Here, Chuck. From the goody closet. Can't be a hottie in NYC without a good pair of shades. With your complexion, I was going to go gold for you, but that cuff you're wearing is silver, so silver it is."

Charlie had forgotten he was wearing the cuff left by Meg. The humming sensation was growing on him. When he thought about it, he could feel it coursing through him, but the moment he shifted his thoughts, it just melted into the background like white noise. He took the sunglasses and slipped them on. Somehow he felt like those completed the new him. This was who he was supposed to be.

The two hit the pavement and strolled down 7th Avenue toward Times Square where the B&B building stood. Spence had asked him if he wanted to walk it or have their driver take them, but Charlie had been too drunk and angry to appreciate the city the day before and wanted to take it in. Spence pointed out different sites along the way and the two fell into an easy rhythm, something Charlie hadn't expected could be possible between the two. Once the other guy let the asshole persona drop, he was actually a pretty decent person. True, he swore more than the entire student body at FHS collectively, but Charlie got used to it. Something about Spence's story rang all too true with Charlie's own and he couldn't shake it. That feeling of purpose and not being able to find it. Knowing there's something big, but not being able to see it. And to hear it come out of someone else's mouth made Charlie feel like he wasn't as big of a loser as he was afraid of being.

At some point between blocks, Spence nudged Charlie's hand with something. Looking down, the bigger guy realized it was a flask. The skinny guy raised an eyebrow. Charlie shrugged and took a few sips from it before passing it back. The liquid burned and coursed its way through him, and thanks to the cuff, Charlie could feel it *all* the way down. This was good. This was going to be good. Charlie reached up and squeezed Spence's shoulder resulting in a grin from the other guy as he popped a pill in his mouth.

The insanity of Times Square was everything Charlie had hoped it would be and he pulled off the sunglasses so he could fully take it all in. The signs flashing and beckoning him caught his attention immediately, doing the job they had been assigned to. Musicals, movies, stores, television channels, they were all represented in flashy, monstrous ads. Charlie loved it.

And the people. People everywhere. All sorts of people from all over the world. Languages he recognized and languages he wasn't even sure were real. In Texas, if you were white, you spoke English. Here, someone could be white and from anywhere in the world. But there were people of all colors, something he was completely unused to and it was beautiful. Charlie loved it.

And past the people, was the weird, the costumed people. Ratty versions of what Charlie assumed were popular children's show characters, taking pictures with tourists and demanding money in return. A dude in his underwear with a guitar, cowboy hat and boots. Vegas showgirls with feathered headpieces and body paint. Charlie had never seen breasts before, and now he had. Spence had gotten a kick out of his reaction and pulled him along when Charlie had become frozen in place.

This is where he wanted to end up. California's beauty and chill had been nice, but New York City was his speed. All the people and flash. Farnsworth, TX, was suffocating, but this place, though it certainly had its smells, was fresh air. All around him, people pulsed to get where they were going, cars honked and passed, the city lived. However he had to do it, this is where he was going to land. Sorry, California.

Rising from the beating heart of the Square was the B&B building, a beacon of modernity. A giant crest was situated in the middle of the building, spanning the entire width of it, images of a rearing bull and proud badger glowing brightly in the center. As Charlie began to look away from it, the image changed to movie posters, television show ads, and talent the Bull and Badger agency represented. The only thing Charlie actually recognized was the title of a play Charlie had attempted to read in school, *A Raisin in the Sun*. He hadn't understood the story at all, it just didn't mean much to him, a white kid in Texas, but his English teacher had insisted it was among the most important pieces of literature to originate in America. "Tony Award winning Philip de Grande's greatest performance," the image boasted. The image soon shifted again, a giant B&B spray painted across the ad and the original bull and badger charged and scampered back to their places.

"My sister says that show is phenomenal. I haven't seen it yet. We represent Phil." Charlie's confusion must have been clear, "My sister runs the agency that represents Philip de Grande. Like, *she* works to get *him* work, auditions and shit. Your parents have an agent?"

Charlie shrugged, "I don't think so. I mean, they have an attorney and a publisher, but I think they just handled most things on their own."

Spencer looked impressed, "Not how it usually goes these days, especially on the level your parents played. Good for them. Cuts out some of the bullshit."

Charlie's parents always had a head for business. Somehow they got what they wanted and steered clear of what they didn't. Charlie clearly hadn't learned that art. Or at least, if he had, he never could get it to work on them. But maybe the problem was the apprentice attempting the craft against the masters? Whatever it was, now was the time to step it up.

A doorman welcomed *Mr. Carrington* and Spencer just grinned and shook his head when Charlie raised his eyebrows. Later, he told Charlie he'd never seen the new doorman before. The new guys were given flash cards of the VIPs and could get their asses fired if they didn't address someone appropriately. Water splashed nearby in a gigantic fountain, the centerpiece of the sleek lobby. It danced and spilled. Mesmerizing. A couple of receptionists, one a girl and the other a guy, but both pretty, welcomed *Mr. Carrington* again as they walked through. Spence stepped up to an elevator set apart from the others and whipped out a keycard and swiped it, "Access to the top floor, daddy's office." He mimicked V perfectly.

He couldn't admit it to Spence but that elevator was the second Charlie had ever stepped foot in, the high-rise apartment being the first. There were no elevators in Farnsworth, no need for them. Well, aside from the handicap one at school, but it was an immediate detention if you got on it without permission. Charlie was too much of a rule follower to risk it while he'd heard rumors of other kids having sex on it. This one moved fast and Charlie could feel it in his gut. The numbers zoomed past and before he knew it, they stopped on the 86th floor. Charlie's stomach eventually caught up.

Spence slipped the flask into Charlie's big hand then fished in his pocket and pulled out the prescription meds container, deftly popping another in his mouth before tucking the orange container away again. He knew better than to offer one to Charlie. Charlie took a few nips from the flask. So much for swearing off booze today.

The doors opened and they were met with light. So much light. Windows everywhere. Actual walls didn't exist, just windows. In fact, Charlie could see a toilet and sink a few rooms away and must have been wearing his confusion openly. Spence laughed and slapped him on the back, "the shitter's walls turn into a two-way mirror when you lock the door. You can still see out which really freaks people's shit out. Like, you're standing there pissing and you can see everyone around you, but they can't see you. Takes some getting used to. I couldn't piss for a week in there and had to go downstairs anytime I needed to take a leak."

"How'd you get over it?"

Spence shrugged, "Whiskey and painkillers."

Eric Carrington hung up his phone and turned a welcoming, fatherly smile to them through the clear wall of his office. He beckoned them in. "Let's go see daddy," Spence muttered.

A glass panel slid open as they approached it and Carrington met them with an outstretched hand, "Mr. Daniels, I trust you slept well?"

"Yes, sir," Charlie replied, pulling his sunglasses off.

The powerful man made a sour face, "First rule of the city: don't say sir or ma'am. I know it's how you were raised on the farm and it's all well and good in Texas, but here, people think you're calling them old. Mocking them."

"Oh, no s—" Charlie caught himself, "No, I didn't mean it like that."

Carrington laughed, a warm thing, "It's all right, Charlie, we'll turn you into a Yankee yet." Carrington turned to Spence and pulled him into a hug. Spence reciprocated without hesitation, a sentiment that surprised Charlie for all his talk of angst toward the 'monster.' Families were complicated. What he wouldn't give to hug his own dad right now. Charlie took a deep breath that he hoped went undetected by the other two. "Thank you for bringing him, Spence. Right on time. Well done."

"I can read a clock, dad."

"Of course you can. Of course you can." The older gentleman made a sweeping gesture toward his office, "Please, Charlie, make yourself comfortable, have a look around. Can I get you a drink? Soda? Beer? Scotch?"

Charlie glanced at Spencer for help and the other picked up his cue, "Scotch for the both of us, please."

"You got it." Carrington set to pouring their drinks.

Spence wrapped an arm around Charlie's shoulders and led him to the window. "Check this shit out."

"Spencer."

"Sorry, dad." The apartment view had been amazing, but this one was mind-blowing. Below them, people crawled over Times Square like ants and before him the city stretched out forever. "There's the Empire State Building," Spencer pointed out, "the Chrysler Building, 432 Park is our building right there at the foot of Central Park, and down the other way is the One World. Pretty sweet, huh?"

Carrington pressed Charlie's drink into his hand, "It isn't much, but we call it home, huh?" He laughed to himself, but Charlie was sure he detected a touch of weariness. For all of Spence's talk, Charlie couldn't help but like the man. But that's how parents were, right? One minute, you're being yelled at, but as soon as the phone rings, it's all calm and poise. Charlie always hated it when his mom did that to him. Sometimes when he was getting yelled at, he wanted to pick up the phone and call her to finish the conversation minus the shrieking. Now, he'd give anything for her to yell at him. Charlie took another deep breath and a gulp of scotch. Not right now. He couldn't deal with that right now.

"I'm sorry to hear about your parents, Charlie." Carrington squeezed his shoulder reassuringly. Had he been playing those thoughts across his forehead? "Do the authorities have any idea what happened? Of course they don't. Nothing against small-town officers, but how could they? I've seen the news footage. Unearthly."

Charlie took a sip of his drink and nodded. Obviously, he had no idea what the 'authorities' were thinking. He had no idea what *anyone* was thinking for that matter because he got the hell out of there before he knew what was going on. *Meg* got him the hell out of there. Meg. He had half expected to run into her on the street. Maybe she'd shift out of being a mailbox or one of those weird costumed photo traps. Or one of the Vegas show girls? "No, I don't know anything about it, honestly. It all happened too fast."

Carrington gestured to a sitting area with comfortable looking black leather armchairs, "Have a seat, boys." They did and so did he. "Just terrible. Just terrible." The older gentleman took a sip of his own drink and let out a deep sigh. "If you don't mind my prying, what brought you here after their disappearance? It seems like an odd choice."

Charlie wasn't sure how to answer. He'd had no intention of coming to New York, no intention of leaving home at all, well, where home had been. Maybe it would have been better to stay, find out what the police actually thought. Charlie hadn't been offered a choice though, had he? Meg was on the scene with Bogart when he awoke and she pulled him away insistently. Positive more Shells would show up to finish the job. So how was he supposed to answer? How ridiculous did the whole thing actually sound? Sure, Spence could back him up, but what good was the word of the addict even if the addict was the man's son? The whole thing seemed like a weird dream. He opened his mouth to say something to that effect when the door slid open and Veronica swayed into the room.

"Sorry, I'm late, daddy," she said as Carrington rose and Charlie followed suit.

Spence stayed planted where he was, "Well, look who *wasn't* on time. 11:00am, wasn't it, V?"

Veronica kissed Carrington's cheek, "Spence, sometimes *work* interrupts plans. You know what work is, right? That thing the rest of us do so you can fuel yourself up on booze and prescription pills?"

"Veronica," Carrington chided.

"Sorry, daddy." She winked and kissed Charlie's cheek. "De Grande is missing. Didn't show up for a meeting this morning. Not like him. Doorman said he left last night with a young woman in tow and then this morning, a guy left claiming he had slept *naked* in Philip's bed." She rolled her eyes at that last bit.

"Fascinating. I didn't know Philip was gay," Carrington said with a raised eyebrow.

"Well, everyone does *now*," Veronica said with a sigh and flashed her phone at her father. "I guess the doorman posted it on social media because there's a picture of the guy standing at the curb. Not bad looking, but I wouldn't think ginger would be Philip's flavor. However, I didn't think Philip's flavor palette included men either. Morning shows have been calling all morning for confirmation. Typical response, 'what Mr. de Grande does on his time is his business. We applaud him for his bold choices in life as much as we applaud him for his bold choices on stage. Yadda, yadda, yadda.' "

Carrington took Veronica's phone and swiped through the pictures, "*Our* doorman did this?"

"That's what the article claims," Veronica said.

Carrington shook his head disappointedly, "Have him let go."

"Oh, that's already been done. As soon as I saw it, I called and reported him. Probably got a pretty penny for the info and I'm sure he'll get a few interviews. Hope it'll last him." Veronica arranged herself and smiled, "Now, where are we?"

"I was talking to our guest about his parents and their tragic disappearance." Carrington was grave and sympathetic again.

Veronica frowned, "I'm so sorry, puppy. I saw it on the news. Terrible."

"Thank you," Charlie said. "It all kind of feels like a nightmare. Not entirely sure where to turn. I mean, I don't really think I'm equipped for this, you know?"

"Who is?" Carrington said and took a drink. "Look, as far as we're concerned, you have a home with us for as long as you need it. But I think you'll find your financial needs are well taken care of. Your parents' books are doing well the world over. You won't be begging on the streets, that's for sure."

"Thank you," Charlie said.

"Now," Carrington continued, "it's no secret those books are a hot commodity and the entertainment world has been burning up to make them into a film or television series."

"Dad," Spence tried to interject.

Carrington held up a hand and continued, "No, Spencer, let me continue." Setting his drink on a glass coaster, Carrington sat back and crossed his legs, "Bull and Badger had been courting your late parents for the film rights to the *United Realms* series for years to no avail. I get it. Many authors want their works to remain on the page and play out in a reader's imagination. Sure. But times are different, especially with stories like these."

"Daddy," Veronica interrupted, "maybe now isn't the best time."

All three of them were watching Charlie intently and for his part, Charlie wasn't sure what to think. Was he trying to get Charlie to sell the rights to his parents' work right then and there? James and Harriett had been adamantly against the idea. Always had been and always would be. "My parents wouldn't like this."

Carrington nodded, "I think you're absolutely right, Charlie. They wouldn't like it and *they* wouldn't be sitting in my office right now." He laughed to himself, "They wouldn't set foot in this miraculous city, would they?"

Charlie knew they wouldn't. Ever. "The only people who live in that city, Charlie," his dad once said when Charlie told him he wanted to visit it one day, "are people with mixed up priorities."

"It's a city of opportunity," Charlie had fired back, "Immigrants flocked to New York from all over the world to make something of themselves."

"And we've made something of ourselves right here in small town, Texas, Charlie," his dad shrugged. "Place doesn't make a man. A man can make his place wherever he is. It's about character and choices, not geography."

Charlie took a drink, finishing it off. Spence rose and refilled it. "Hey, boss," Spence said, "you don't have to make a decision about this right now. It's too fresh. Bad timing," he said directly to his dad.

"Actually," Veronica interjected, "it's *perfect* timing." She laid a hand on Charlie's knee sending goosebumps all the way up his neck. "Charlie, right now the news is still fresh. Book seven is about to be released and the fans are going to be both elated and devastated by the news of the deaths of their favorite authors. They're going to be looking for *hope*. This is how we give them that hope. *You* give them that hope," she purred. "While they've experienced the loss of their storytellers, we'll give them their stories brought to life. A film a year, spinoffs, and a television series. Your parents' legacy will continue."

The truth of her words tickled through Charlie's head. The sentiment seemed right, felt good, so much so he might have signed something right then and there. Yet, he knew how his parents would respond to it, but they weren't here now to make that decision. He also knew how much they loved their fans. They would spend entire weekends responding to letters and signing autographs, dumping thousands of dollars into the local post office just to make their readers happy. "We'd be nothing without them," his dad would say with a warm smile.

Charlie looked down into his glass and swirled the melting ice around. He didn't know what to do.

"Veronica, Spencer, would you give us a moment?"

"Sure, daddy."

"Yeah."

Charlie didn't look up as they left. His head was swimming, and this time it wasn't from what he was drinking. Veronica's words lured and pulled him. He focused on the hum from the cuff on his wrist, letting it soothe his thoughts, bring them into focus. What would his mom and dad do right now? Did it matter? This was on *him*.

"Charlie," Carrington's voice was warm, the weariness underlying, "I know who you are."

Charlie looked up.

Carrington's blue eyes regarded him gently and he offered a reassuring smile. "I know who you are, Charlie, and I know who my children are. And Maze. And Stephen. And little Hedy." The older man smiled reassuringly. "It's all been very confusing, Charlie, and there was no reason for it to be. Someone has started moving pieces on the board, employing Vacusai, Shells. Meg did as I asked and did it well. And I'm sorry about James and Harriett. So *very* sorry. I wish I could've been there for them. I wish they'd let me." Carrington took a deep breath and let it go. "I have answers, Charlie. No more secrets. No more mysteries."

No more secrets? No more mysteries? He was going to give the answers. *He* was going to give all the answers. Solve all the mysteries?

The man across from him hit a nerve Charlie didn't know existed. The anxiety Charlie had been feeling over this colossal issue of licensing dissipated only to be replaced by a familiar anger. *He* was going to give Charlie all the answers? All his life, Charlie had wanted to talk, to hear what he needed to hear. About women, about life, about being a man, about himself. Answers had been what he hungered for, even from Meg in the last few days. But most importantly, it was *who* he wanted the answers from: his dad and mom. James and Harriett. Charlie wanted *their* thoughts, not some guy in a skyscraper in New York, as well-intentioned as he may be. He wanted to sit at the kitchen table and hear it from *them,* whether they were really his parents or not. And if those books were what Meg and Bogart believed them to be, actual stories and histories of whatever the hell world he was from, then *they* had those answers too.

Anger roiled inside him and his body almost vibrated from it. The old man watched him from across the table, his blue eyes keen on him. "Charlie?"

Charlie barely trusted himself when he felt like this and now was no different. He took a deep breath and let it out slowly. "No."

"I'm sorry?"

"No."

Carrington frowned. "No, to what?"

"No to all of it," Charlie said firmly. "I don't want anything you have to offer. Your money, your answers, or your bullshit sympathy."

"Charlie," Carrington leaned forward, "this is a big deal. I understand how you must—"

"No, you don't," Charlie stood. "You couldn't possibly. My parents are dead. My home is gone. I've lost everything. You couldn't possibly understand."

Carrington locked onto him. "I couldn't?" Carrington rose to his feet. "Stripped of what you know, the home you have, and thrust into a world that makes no sense?" Carrington spread his hands, "How do you think I came to be here? Put it together, Charlie. The very ones who slaughtered your family and the families of my dear children and the other three, the Council of All sentenced *me*! I was one rebel against a Council of rebels, but the Council had the power to do it to me! I don't belong here either and I want to go *home*!"

It was silent.

"I have searched and collected. I've spent fortunes on relics only to find them twisted or dead. I've hunted this entire world over, following trails and myths only to come up empty-handed. Then fifteen years ago a sudden influx of refugees hit the ground and bit by bit, I pieced it together. They dared confront the Council and the Council took swift and decisive action, ruthlessly cutting down anyone who stood in their way, rooting out anyone who might stink of thoughts differing from theirs. Many more than just the few who whisked you and the other five away have used the Sentencing as an escape route to come here. So many terrified refugees. A camp of them in the northwest passing themselves off as a faire, enchanting the locals. A pair of *court historians*, the very man and woman who called themselves *your parents*. So many." Carrington paused and drew a steadying breath, his shoulders slumped. "Charlie, more than anything, I want to return and put an end to the atrocities the Council against us and our true home."

Charlie regarded him. The older man, his lined and weary face, tired from the hunt. He spoke of another world, a whole other life— a home Charlie didn't know and cared nothing for. Whatever *this* world had been intended to be, it wasn't that anymore. It *was* his home. This was where his parents had raised him. This was where he hunted for dragons in the attic and trees with his dad, ate the meals his mother cooked him, and had loved them both deeply. Carrington confirmed James and Harriett weren't his parents, a punch to the gut. Charlie took a deep breath and stored those thoughts away for another time. Whatever battle Carrington was gearing himself up for with this Council, Charlie wasn't interested. It was time to pull himself back together and return to his home: Farnsworth, Texas. It was time to find Meg and Bogart, look at square one, and put this thing together. It *would* be best to quit running and go back home, work with the authorities. Whatever he had to do, this business with Carrington wasn't it.

Charlie shook his head, "No, I'm sorry. I don't know what your battles are, but I'm not a part of them." He turned and headed toward the sliding glass doors and ultimately the elevator.

"Not only are you part of them, Charlie," Carrington said firmly, "you are the *reason* for them."

Charlie kept walking. "Bullies will say anything to keep their power," his dad would say.

The glass doors slid open and Charlie walked straight for the elevator. He didn't have a keycard and prayed it still worked without one.

"You wouldn't leave a friend behind, would you?" The tone was taunting.

Just keep walking.

"A little glowing friend?"

What? Charlie couldn't help himself. He turned.

Carrington hadn't moved. He still stood his ground, but now held a glass vial in his hand and inside the vial was a small, yellow glow. The same glow Meg had shown him beside the pool beneath the blue Californian sky.

"Meg?" Charlie asked.

The little glow pulsed.

"Give her to me," Charlie demanded. The anger that simmered below the surface throughout the entire damn conversation with Carrington was beginning to boil. His hands, his chest, his face, his entire body humming with it.

"In the business world we trade, Charlie. It's called the art of the negotiation. I haven't arrived where I am today by handing over valuable commodities freely. Are *you* ready to negotiate?"

A few strides was all it took and Charlie covered the space between them. His body was humming loudly now, vibrating, his head pounding. "Never negotiate with bullies," his mom had told him. He saw that kid in high school again, the one he punched. The only time he'd given over to the anger when provoked. "Give her to me," Charlie demanded again.

"You will help me return home," the older man demanded in return.

Impulsively, Charlie's shaking hand whipped up and took Carrington by the throat, the pounding in his head reaching a deafening noise. It was soothing, relieving, giving into the anger and feeling it. Carrington's eyes, once so aloof and confident, bulged with fear and mouth moved with gurgling pleads, but Charlie couldn't hear him, wouldn't hear him. The cuff was no longer humming through him but causing his whole body to buzz and burn. Better than the booze, stronger than his kiss with Meg, the rage seduced him. He easily raised Carrington into the air and pressed him against the glass wall, spidery fractures spreading from behind the old man's head. "Give her to me," Charlie whispered through clenched teeth.

Carrington's face was turning purple in Charlie's grip, eyes bloodshot, but the older man still held tight to the vial trapping the little glow. Charlie pulled Carrington close, and with a final surrender to the anger raging through him, squeezed Carrington's neck with a satisfying crunch, then thrust him against the wall of fractured glass a second time causing it to give way, showering around the two of them in shards. The vial tumbled from Carrington's limp hand, landing amidst the broken glass. Charlie dropped the old man, his body crumpling to the ground. The vial was whole, Meg's glow pulsed erratically. Charlie scooped it up in his big, shaky hand.

"What the fuck have you done, man?"

Spence stood a few feet away, the elevator door closing behind him. Carrington lay bleeding on the ground, his eyes gazing emptily at the ceiling.

CHAPTER TWENTY-EIGHT

One Down

Tourists packed the streets of Times Square and it drove Maze insane. These five blocks made her want to scream at every dumbass tourist she passed during the day. At night, the place was lit up and beautiful, a beam of hope and dreams, her eyes too busy looking up to take notice of the idiots surrounding her. But during the day it was packed with tourists who didn't know how to cross a damn street. The worst were the gawkers who suddenly stopped in the middle of the sidewalk to take a selfie, no warning, and bam, you were busting into the back of them. What they found out later was that sudden stops cost them their wallets. Coogey had taught her that one. "Assholes gonna stop, assholes gonna get slicked."

But there hadn't been time for the slick. Maze had counted twelve opportunities to slip a hand into a purse, three back-pocket wallets, and nine backpacks. Philip was pushing them up 7th Avenue to the B&B building, where they would find Stephen and someone else now according to the bird. *According to the bird.* That was a phrase she never thought would pass through her head. How many times had dumbass tourists snapped her picture in the last fifteen minutes as they worked their way up block after block? She knew she was all over social media by now. White girls posting pictures of the big black girl with the big black bird on her shoulder. Should charge their asses like that guy with the cat on his head in the West Village. That crazy white boy would get pissed anytime somebody snapped a picture without his consent. What did he think would happen? What did *they* think would happen?

The B&B was gigantic. Maze saw it every day, "the crown jewel of Times Square," the tour guides would tell their photo happy herds. Buncha bullshit. What they didn't know was the majority of the building was empty. You learned stuff when you listened. Monika, a big mama in the shelter, had made her way onto a cleaning crew that serviced the B&B. Said it was an easier job that she thought it would be because only a few damn floors in the whole eighty-six got used. The rest are under renovation, or so she said. Most buildings like that have the one big name on front which takes up a good part of the space inside, then the leftover floors are rented out by leaches who like the fact their little business is attached to the big fish. This fish had a shiny face, but the rest of it was mostly bones. Maze wasn't a business tycoon, but even *she* knew it was a waste of potential.

Philip bypassed the front desk and security, but no one paid him any mind, just a couple of "Good morning, Mr. de Grande"-s, the huge ass fountain splashing in the background. Waste of space and money. The doorman did a double take at the bird, but no more than that. "Act like you're supposed to be here and no one will think twice," Philip instructed as they approached the building. He was preaching to the choir. Act confident was a rule she lived by and it *always* worked. Most people were afraid of confrontation; Maze wasn't a fan of it, but she'd use people's fear against them.

Addie didn't make an appearance until the elevator doors had closed behind them. She was lavender again. "What's the plan?" she asked, her magnified eyes blinking. Did ghost's eyes have to adjust when they appeared?

"How far can you roam?" Philip asked her.

"Free reign in a building where my anchor is. The first year of being dead, I poked about in the apartments below mine and saw things I can't ever unsee. I stayed put from then on."

Philip nodded, he looked like he was gearing up for a fight. "So I take Maze and this one—"

"Lola," Maze interjected. "She has a name."

"I take Maze and Lola with me and find my agent, no big deal. You do what you can to find Stephen and Hedy."

"And then?" The ghost raised a skeptical eyebrow.

"Then we hunker down and figure out what's next. This place is safe. V will let me use an office or conference room."

The elevator chimed, 54th floor, Addie vanished, and the doors opened. A young receptionist sat behind a rounded, sleek white desk with the Bull and Badger crest 'spray painted' across the front. Her eyes were too done, Maze thought, she looked like a bitch. Probably was if she worked here. Looking up from her computer screen, her eyes slid over Maze and Lola quick enough but paused a moment on the bird. She smiled. Yep, she's a bitch.

"Mr. de Grande!" she said when he stepped out from between them, "Miss Carrington will be so thrilled to see you! She said she's texted you over and over. Should I tell her you're here?"

"No need, Cynthia," The fighter was gone and mister slick and smooth was in control. An office door opened and a tall Asian woman, at least Maze thought she was Asian, stepped out. It was her, the woman who handed her the handkerchief at Philip's show. Maze would never forget those eyes. Golden. Unsurprisingly, the woman didn't appear to share the recognition. "Why the hell haven't you been returning my calls?" Despite her frustration, she stepped forward and kissed him on the cheek. Golden eyes glanced at the sword hanging from Philip's fine hips. "Preparing for another role? Or did you just come in from Queens?" She tittered at her own stupid joke.

"It's been a morning, V."

"I'll say," she said, pulling her phone out. "Your new boy-toy has made quite the splash on social media. Who knew? I certainly didn't and that's my job."

"What are you talking about?"

The tall woman glanced at the receptionist who was taking it all in. With a raise of a well-manicured eyebrow from her boss, the girl got back to work. That's power right there, Maze noted. She's *head* bitch. "Come on in, Philip." She appeared to notice Maze and Lo for the first time, "Who are these people?"

"My niece and her friend are in from Connecticut. I told my sister I wouldn't let them out of my sight. Maze wants to be an actress, so I thought it might be interesting for her to see how the business works."

"Fine," the woman sighed, "I guess she can see the ugly parts too." She turned and they followed her into her office.

It was the view that took Maze's breath away. All her life she had clung to the streets. Paying money to ride an elevator to the top of one of the city's skyscrapers was a waste of well-earned cash. Of course, she had seen pictures on postcards, but that was a lifeless photo. This was alive. Helicopters flew by in the distance and pigeons glided below her. Even further down was *her* place, the streets, and from all the way up here, the people who wandered those streets were nothing. Smaller than bedbugs. Smaller than pinpoints. From up here, she and her people were less than nothing. Maze stepped away from the window, that was enough of that.

"Would you girls like something to drink? Water? A soda?"

"You could at least offer them the good stuff," a voice scoffed from the corner. Maze hadn't even seen him when they walked in, but a guy was lounging on a white leather sofa, scrolling through his phone.

"Forgive my brother," the woman smiled, "he's an imbecile."

"You got Sprite?" Lo piped up.

"Ginger ale?" The woman offered.

Lola shrugged, "That's fine."

"I'll have one too," Maze said.

Philip offered his hand to the guy, "Philip de Grande."

"Veronica's brother," the guy said ignoring the hand.

"Don't be a dick, Spencer," Veronica shot at him.

"I'm going to check on our buddy upstairs." Spencer stood and slipped out of the room.

Awkward silence hung in the room for a moment, but Veronica handed the girls their drinks and broke it, "Philip, you've made quite the stir online."

"Yeah," he said suspiciously, "what's going on?"

Veronica sighed and seated herself behind her desk, "Our doorman had a run in with your. . . whatever-he-is this morning."

Philip sat down across from her, "What are you talking about?"

"I don't know, Philip, and that's what's so damn annoying. Your boyfriend? One night stand? If he's an escort, I hope you didn't pay much. Listen, I don't care what part of yourself you're exploring, but could you give me a heads up so I know how to spin these things?"

"I don't have— I'm not— What did Oscar see?"

Veronica slid her phone across the sleek desk, "That guy claimed he slept naked in your bed last night."

Philip swore under his breath the moment he saw the picture, "That's not what's going on."

"Then what's going on? How do I fix this?"

Philip glanced at Maze, "He's a guy we found last night. . ."

"How's that, exactly?"

"Lola found him. At a club." Lola started to say something, but Maze put her hand on her leg and squeezed. The other girl sat back. Was it right to call her a girl? Technically, she was, but she was an *old* girl. She was at least in her fifties now, wasn't she?

"Wait," Veronica squinted at him, "you took two underage girls to a club? I mean, I *am* assuming they're underage. How old are you two?"

"We're old *enough*," Maze said defensively.

"'Old enough' means you aren't. God, Philip, you're worse than my brother. What is it with men and their inability to adequately judge age?"

The phone on the golden-eyes' desk chirped. She pressed a button, "Yes, daddy?"

"V!" It sounded like her brother, "I need you up here."

She frowned, "What is it?"

"I *need* you up here *now,*" the urgency was impossible to miss. So was the fear.

Philip must have heard it too. He stood up, "He okay?"

Veronica pushed back from her desk and rose, clearly annoyed by the interruption, but maintaining her poise. "Who the hell knows? Daddy's working on a deal, a deal I think you would be perfect for, by the way. Put that sword to use. It's a silly medieval, fantasy thing. Spence probably screwed it up and now he's in trouble. I'll be right back."

"I'll go with you," Philip insisted. "If I'm perfect for it, maybe I can help land it."

"Fine by me."

Philip gestured for the girls to follow him.

The elevator doors opened on the 86th floor and it was the shattered glass Maze saw first, then the body on the floor in the midst of it. A hulking guy sat in a chair by the window, rocking back and forth, hands covering his mouth. He was freaked. And judging by his size and the damage, he was the one who did it. Spencer was pacing between the big guy and the body, "I came up here and . . . and . . . and—," he said as soon as he saw his sister.

Veronica had frozen, but Philip rushed to the body, feeling the neck of the old man for a pulse. When he didn't find one, he shook his head, "He's dead." Maze held Lola's arm. She'd never seen a dead body before. Yeah, they were all over TV and the movies, but this was for real. And she was here. And that was bad. Someone of her status didn't do well in this sort of situation. She'd seen too many of her friends take the fall for things they hadn't done. Her kind, black and homeless, were an easy target who couldn't afford decent lawyers, and she was sure B&B had the best the city could offer.

"What happened?" Veronica quietly demanded. Even though she didn't direct it to anyone in particular, Maze knew it was intended for her brother.

"I don't know," he said in a panic, "I came in and Charlie was kneeling beside him. I don't know! It was like this when I came in! It really was! I don't know what happened!"

"We gotta get outta here," Lola said. She must have been thinking the same as Maze, the same scenario playing through her head. It was good to know that part was still Lola.

"No one's going anywhere," Veronica snapped and Maze felt the need to stay put. The golden eyed woman folded her arms and approached the body of her father, glass crunching under her designer shoes. She was too calm and that scared Maze even more. If she'd been blubbering, wailing, or even passed out, that would be fine, but this wasn't right.

"Veronica," Philip said gently, "we need to call the cops."

She shook her head, "Not yet. Not until we know how to play this."

"'Play this'?" Spencer shouted, "He's fucking dead! What, he tripped and fell through the window? There are marks on his neck where this asshole strangled him to death! No amount of *playing* is going to work!"

Maze looked at the big guy in the chair. He hadn't moved except for the constant rocking back and forth. His arms were huge and if he stood up, she knew he'd tower over her. Had circumstances been different, she'd take her time looking him over. She even liked his long shaggy hair. But he messed up. Messed up bad and wasn't getting out of it.

Veronica knelt by the body, her fingers touching the marks on her father's neck. The room was silent, each person mulling the whole thing over as hard as Maze was, she was sure of that. How would this whole thing play out? Were there cameras? Surely, in a place like this there would be cameras. Looking around, she didn't see any. Maybe men like him didn't have cameras in their office. Maze was about to ask when things hit a whole new level of crazy ass shit. She didn't see it happen, but Lola's scream and Philip's shout pulled her away from her search for security cameras.

Veronica was still kneeling over her father's body, but her hand was now at her own throat where a long shard of glass pushed all the way through and out the back of her neck. Her blood spilled down the length of glass and the hand holding it.

Eric Carrington pushed his daughter over to the ground and coolly stood to his feet, pulling the bloody shard free. With his clean hand, he adjusted his tie and straightened his suit. He pointed the makeshift weapon from his son, to the big guy now standing in shock, to Maze, who's heart was trying to beat its way out of her chest and the room. "Who's next?"

CHAPTER TWENTY-NINE

A Face in the Ceiling

Right ear wiggle. Left ear. No. Not yet.

Way high up and no one speaking. Quiet. Too very quiet. On the streets, they had all been talking for their needs. *Must find food. Must find shelter. Must find mate.* But the closer he walked to the big building with his new friends, it just got quiet. One side of his brain liked the quiet. No noise. His own thinking could be heard loud. His and Jacob's. And Little Girl. That's what he decided to name his little squirrel friend from the big park. He smiled to hisself. Squirrel friend sounded like girlfriend. Stephen never had a girlfriend. Not yet. Lots of girls were pretty, but all the girls he had known were broken in the head too and he didn't want a broken in the head girlfriend. He wanted a good girlfriend who could help him think right.

When they found the yelling man in the room with yellow hair, he had got excited after the door closed. The nice boy with glasses knew him and he knew the nice boy somehow. And it wasn't just the nice boy he knew, he knew the short girl, even though she didn't look like she knew him, and he knew Stephen also. Stephen really, really didn't know the yellow-haired man. He thought he was a man, but it felt like he might be younger than Stephen. Or older than Stephen. How many years people was was hard.

At the sound of the yellow-haired man's excitement, Jacob poked his head out the big pocket he'd been hiding in. That made the man get all the more excited. Stephen liked excited.

Ask him how he knows us, my lord.

"Jacob asks how you knows us?" Stephen asked timidly. He wasn't real good at talking to people he didn't know. People were harder than little animals.

"Descriptions, sir," the yellow haired man-boy explained. Stephen was having a hard time with how many years he was. "It's one of the first things Coach taught us. All of your names, descriptions of you, well, and there were pictures, kind of. David, one of the Pack is really good at drawing, so he drew pictures of you based off of what Coach said and, I have to say, they're pretty close, yeah?"

"Coach?" The nice boy asked. "Who's Coach?"

"Tark. Coach Tark? He's— oh my God, there's so much, isn't there? But you can take it, right? You're all about this! I mean, you found *her*, right? And *him*!" The yellow haired man-boy's eyes looked like they were going to cry. He rubbed them with his hands before they cried.

The nice boy smiled real, real big, "Yeah, I did. I found her in—"

"Oregon," the man boy said real fast.

"One mustn't interrupt when another is speaking," she said.

Stephen looked around for her. Behind him.

Just you and myself now, my lord. Jacob always knew when he thought he heard her.

Stephen nodded his head.

"So, *you're* the third pair of footprints, Bogart, the ones that disappeared at the tree in the field!"

"Yeah," nice boy said. "Me, Charlie, and Meg."

"Who's Meg?"

"The girl who helped Charlie when his house vanished."

"The Gohlem?"

The nice boy frowned, "She's not a . . ." His eyes got big, "Oh, mierda."

The short girl raised her hand, "Okay, hold on. Who are you and what's going on? I don't understand any of this."

And that's when they started talking over each other, the yellow-haired man-boy and the nice boy with glasses. It was like listening to the rats. All talking on each other, not listening, just talking. They talked a lot and Stephen stopped listening. Too much things to remember and remembering to tie his shoes was hard. He sat down in a corner between the window and the wall and pet the big dogs. He liked the big dogs a lot. Little Girl climbed on top of the boy dog's head. Jacob listened to all the talking, his ears and nose twitching. He kept asking Stephen to say things for him, but Stephen didn't want to. He just wanted to pet the dogs. The dogs couldn't talk and that was okay. They talked enough with their faces.

"Tark and Gladys the bus driver are his Pair? Ay, dios mio!" The nice boy said real loud.

"Right," the yellow-haired man-boy said. Ben, he said his name was Ben. Ben, Bogart, and Hedy. Ben, Bogart, and Hedy. Polly and Brutus. Jacob. Little Girl. And Stephen. Left ear. Still no wiggle. Left ear. He scratched the white hair around his left ear.

"Who are my Pair?" Hedy asked.

Bogart's eyes looked to Ben's eyes. Names. "People have names," *she* said. "People aren't just descriptions." Stephen took a deep breath. You and myself.

"Your aunt and uncle," Ben said, his face confused, "right?"

It was little Hedy's turn to have a confused face. People's faces said more than their mouths. "I don't have an aunt and uncle."

Stephen saw the face in the ceiling before anyone else did. The face with glasses. He smiled. Ceilings didn't have real faces, but sometimes he could make them have faces when the dots made shapes. Like clouds. But this face was wearing big glasses and was light purpley. Stephen waved at it. Polly growled and so did Brutus. Little Girl jumped back onto Stephen's shoulder.

The light purpley face was connected to a light purpley body that floated down out of the ceiling. The dogs were growling strongly at it, the hair standing up on their backs, so Stephen knew she was real and actual and not because of the medicines *she* made him take. No more medicines. Jacob said he didn't need them. His head was good, but it wasn't. Not like everyone else's. "Oh, thank the lord," the light purpley lady said and scared the others.

Little Hedy screamed and a knife was in her hand real fast from nowhere. That was a neat trick. Ben and Bogart jumped in front of the little woman. Stephen sat on the floor. Little Girl sat up, her nose sniffing. *What is it, sun-haired hume? It has no smell.*

"I don't know, but it's real and actual."

It's Adelaide, Jacob said. His voice sounded funny. Kind of scared and kind of happy. *My lord, I must insist you speak for me.*

"When addressing others," *she* said, "you must stand and . . ." No. You and myself.

Stephen stood up and as he did, Jacob crawled up to his other shoulder. "Jacob is asking where yours is?"

The purpley lady looked at him. Stephen didn't know what he was asking, but Jacob knew and he thought she would. "Up on the next floor. She's with Philip. And Veronica."

Ben made an excited sound, like Stephen when he sees waffles, but Bogart said the words, "the Elyf twins?"

The lady squinted her giant eyes at him, "Yes."

"If there's five here, what are the odds. . .?" Bogart said.

"That there's Six?" Ben said after him.

Someone screamed in the hallway. Then someone else. And a lot more.

The building suddenly wasn't quiet at all.

CHAPTER THIRTY

Squeezed

Charlie laid the lifeless body of Veronica on the dusty conference table in a huge room on the abandoned 77th floor of the B&B building. The windows had been blacked out, shrouding them in complete darkness. Fear induced adrenaline coursed through him, amplified by the cuff vibrating on his wrist. The big black girl was sobbing on the floor beside him, holding her purse to her chest. He wrapped his arm around her shoulder, hoping to console her, but she only leaned in and shook harder. The vial with Meg's glowing . . . soul? Essence? What had she called it? Heartsoul? Whatever it was, it was in his pocket and he could feel it moving as though she was fighting her way out. He had considered unscrewing the top, but didn't. Spence sat on the table beside his sister's body, his legs crossed, scrolling through his phone with one hand and holding her lifeless hand with the other. Every now and then he would wipe at his eyes with the back of his phone hand, refusing to let go of his twin. Charlie imagined the pills he had popped the moment they found the room had deadened his anguish. The crow perched on the back of a tall chair at the head of the table, just visible in the light of Spencer's phone.

He couldn't get Spencer's wail out of his head, the gut-wrenching sound had filled the room when Carrington slid the shard of glass into his daughter's neck. It was shocking enough that Carrington was on his feet after so clearly being dead moments before, but Veronica's bleeding and struggling body on the floor was too much. Philip drew his sword and leaped at Carrington, but the older man was more than he'd been moments before, or at least his true nature was now on full display. The old man dodged and sidestepped all of the swordsman's lunges and strikes as though he were playing with a child. For every twenty of Philip's attempts, the godlike Carrington would strike Philip so hard it sent the swordsman crashing through glass. Charlie was scared one of those hits would send him through an exterior window and plummeting to the concrete below. But time and time again, Philip would rise and attack again. Relentless.

"Fly! Fly!" The crow was circling through the office, crying out. Nothing was strange anymore. In fact, a talking bird barely registered on Charlie's weird-scale now. No one was moving though; the big black girl and her friend were arguing for some reason and Spencer had fallen to his knees at his sister's side. Only the swordsman and the amused Carrington were in motion. They all had to go. Now.

Charlie ducked low and ran to Spencer's side like a man in battle attempting to avoid stray bullets. He took Spencer by the upper arm and pulled, but the skinny guy pulled away. When he tried it again, Spencer shouted at him, "I'm not leaving her!"

"She's dead!" Charlie hissed back.

They both ducked as glass shattered somewhere in the sprawling office. "Are you done yet, little mosquito?" Carrington laughed, his voice echoing strangely.

"Dammit!" Charlie scooped Veronica up in his arms and when he did, a fresh gush of blood erupted from her neck and down the front of him, warm and slick. He forced himself to think past it, focusing on the hum vibrating through his body. Those expensive clothes were worthless rags now.

Charlie kicked the elevator call button, hoping the man with the sword was holding Carrington's attention enough for the others to escape. Something collided with him from behind, rather, someone. "I will find you," the skinny black girl was telling the other. "I promise you, Maze, I will find you."

"I ain't leaving you, Lo," the bigger girl was saying forcefully through her tears, gripping a big purple purse in her hands.

"Shut up and go, fat hume," the bird cried loudly as it landed on Maze's shoulder.

"I swear to Jesus," Maze said through gritted teeth. With a kiss on Maze's cheek, the smaller girl bolted, and stooping, she picked up a shard of glass and ran toward the fight.

Maze started to yell after her friend, but Spencer slipped a hand over her mouth, "Let her go, you idiot," he hissed at her, "she's doing this for you."

The girl nodded with a furious look in her eyes.

"Are there stairs?" Charlie asked quickly.

"Yeah," Spencer answered, "come on."

The little group ran stealthily, rounded a corner, and Spencer flung open a door leading into a stairwell. They ran down the stairs, the crow flying ahead of them, circling down floor by floor. Despite carrying a body in his arms, Charlie made fast work of the stairs. How many floors did they have to go? Eighty-six? Could Maze make it? Is it possible they could run down several floors and then find an elevator?

Seventy-seven.

She was already slowing down, but not near as bad as Spencer. He was struggling down the stairs, stopping to take in gulps of air. Swaying. Charlie waited for them both. The other guy was pale and sweating profusely. He gripped his chest and his side, his breathing ragged. Charlie knew exactly what it was. However long he'd been destroying himself with booze and pills, it was taking its toll. "Are you going to make it?"

Spencer rubbed his silver eyes and shook his head, "Probably not, but what choice is there?"

"Back up!" the crow cried from somewhere down below, "back up! Back up!"

"What the hell?" Maze held the purse to her chest and looked down between the circling stairs. "Oh shit! It's those things! The zombies!"

"Shells?" Charlie blurted. "Where?"

"I don't know, like, twenty floors down? Ten?" Maze said in a panic.

"That's a hell of a difference," Spence wheezed.

An echoing laugh reverberated through the stairwell from below.

"What the hell's that?" Maze asked, her eyes wide with new terror.

"It's them. All of them," Charlie offered, his own fear stoked.

The laughing continued, bouncing off the walls, pounding in Charlie's head. Spencer seemed most affected by the horrible sound. Many voices mingling into one. The laughing gave way to words, "the pests were adorable. Quite fun to play with. Haven't stretched my legs like that in quite some time. Mr. de Grande is quite the swordsman. Had his skills with a blade matched those he engaged on stage, he might have lasted longer. Did I say *is* quite the swordsman? That isn't proper grammar for the situation. *Was* quite the swordsman."

"No!" Maze screamed gripping the railing, tears threatening to break free anew, and finally finding their release.

The laughing exploded from down below, Charlie shuddered.

"And that slip of a girl? Do you think the size of the splat on the sidewalk below is as small as she was? Crash through the window, splat on the ground," it chuckled.

Maze's scream was guttural and she would have collapsed down the stairs if Spencer hadn't caught her. Somehow he forced her to her feet with what little strength he had, "He's a liar. He's a fucking liar. They're fine. They're fine! Probably knocked out and tied up, but they're fine."

“Oh, my sweet boy,” the voices cooed, “I’m many things, but I’m not a liar.”

“Shut up!” Spencer yelled, “Just shut the fuck up! Why are you doing this?”

“I don’t need the others. They’re superfluous. Just you Six. I’m going home.”

And now they hid in the dark. How long did they have until they were discovered? How long had they been hiding in the room Charlie found? Spencer’s silver eyes reflected the light of his phone. He’d been glued to it since they settled in, scanning screen after screen. At one point, he breathed in sharply and looked to Maze who was crying too hard to take notice. Charlie didn’t want to know what he’d found, but he was sure he could guess.

Hedy had been holding his hand the whole time. Not the hand her heart wanted to hold, but the hand that needed to be held. Stephen was terrified when the screaming started, he kept claiming he knew the building was bad, too quiet. The large rat and tiny squirrel scurried their way back into the large pockets of his coat, but the man— the boy had frozen. When Ben and the ghost tried to lead them all from the room, the room that was certain death if they stayed, the skinny boy couldn’t move. Coaxing him along by the hand was the only thing that worked. So she was still doing it, though she knew her hands would be of better use if they were holding her daggers.

The lavender ghost flew far up ahead of them with Polly taking the stairs without a problem. And Bogart, despite his size, was moving up the stairs quickly. Funny what the added urgency of a horde of Shells could do to motivate a person. Ben insisted on bringing up the rear with Brutus and she was glad of it. The blond boy and the big dog walked up the stairs backward, always keeping an eye on the Shells below. The creatures weren’t moving like those in the faire grounds, but they were moving all the same, like slow rising flood waters. They had started on the 54th floor and were now reaching the 71st. How far up did they have to go?

Bogart was stooped over the banister, catching his breath. He was sweating profusely, his breathing labored, but the determination in his eyes was clear. "I'm all right," he said between breaths. "I'm all right. Are you all right?"

Her knees ached as usual, and so did the knuckles of her left hand from her grip on the one dagger she could have while leading Stephen by the hand. The blade was near useless, she had seen those things take beatings and keep moving. What was the use of one pointy piece of metal? "I'm good," she nodded.

Stephen wasn't good, she was sure of that. The boy hadn't said a word the entire time, but still followed all the same, his distant eyes locked on each step before him and free hand tugging at the white hair around his left ear. Hedy was sure he kept saying things under his breath, but she hadn't been able to understand a word of it. But his grip was tight which meant he was still semi-present. She would take that as a good sign.

When they'd broken from the tiny waiting room, the 53rd floor was pure chaos. Beautiful people were torn apart, their pieces flung against walls. Shells fell from the ceiling tiles overhead, crashing into the helpless and the desperate trying to get away, but pinning them to the floor before mutilating them. Unlike the faire, they didn't seem to bother turning them, just utter destruction. And the Shells themselves were mixtures. Dried out skeletons, fresh men and women in rags, bloated naked bodies with stitches down their chests and jaws hanging open. The ghost had managed to create a wall of some kind between the small party and the Shells. They pressed against it with their bodies, but didn't look as though they were putting up much of a fight to break through it. Within minutes, all of the yelling and screaming ended, all of it except for their own. Like a house of horrors, Shells kept leaping from behind corners or dropping in from the ceiling. Those that bothered to drop. Hedy could often hear them running above her, skittering, crisscrossing. It was unnerving. And every time one leaped out, she would scream, Bogart would shout, and the dogs would bark. Stephen only flinched and Ben didn't do a thing. He was different, as though he had trained for this all his life.

Ben found the first stairwell near the main elevators, but the ghost returned through it immediately and said it was full of Shells moving upward. They continued running through the halls until Bogart found the second stairwell near a service elevator. This time the ghost said it was clear and they started their way down it until Polly began barking and Adelaide shouted to turn around and move up.

Up was the worst idea in any situation like this, but it was the only way they could move. Ben and Adelaide had swapped places, and the group continued mounting the stairs, hoping to find some sort of escape, but Hedy knew it couldn't happen. Not moving up. Up was a death sentence. With every floor passed, hopelessness settled in a little deeper. And when Polly started barking from above, Hedy almost broke down.

Maze hugged the big purse with the teacup to her chest.

They were gonna die. She knew that much. They were gonna die and now nobody would miss her. Lo was gone. Completely gone. She knew when her friend pulled herself away from her in the glass office, Maze would never see her again, even though her friend promised it.

"You have to get out of here, Maze," Lola had insisted, tears in her eyes. She had never seen Lo cry before and still wouldn't. She was the strongest person Maze ever met in her whole life. As skinny as she was, she was strong. And it didn't matter anymore. Whatever that man in the subway had done to her didn't matter anymore. Lo was Lo and that was that. And she was never going to see her again.

The arm around her was heavy and comforting. No one had ever put their arm around her, touched her like that in a comforting way. Especially not a boy. And it wrecked her. Everything was gushing into her brain and she couldn't handle it. All she could do was cry and she felt so stupid which only made her cry all the harder.

The Asian boy sat beside his sister on the table. She thought she saw him pop another pill, but couldn't be sure, it was too dark and her own head wasn't right. She was sure of the flask in his hand though. It gleamed in the light of his phone.

Maze took a deep breath. "What are you looking at?"

He looked up, his silver eyes swollen, "What's going on out there."

"What is it?" She asked after another calming breath.

He shrugged, "All the major news outlets are out there, it looks like. Interviews with security guards who were stationed on the ground floor. Said their radios exploded with panicked calls from people on the 53rd and 54th floors, then went quiet. Nobody really knew anything until a window blew out and . . ." he trailed off.

Maze didn't think she could cry anymore but proved herself wrong.

Right hand.
One.
Two.
Three.
Four.
Five.
Left hand.
One.
Two.

Three.

Four.

Five.

She held it. The small lady. Hedy. He never held a girl's hand before.

Right ear.

Left ear. No. Left ear. Wiggle now. No. He pulled left ear with his other hand. The one not holding a girl's hand.

We will live, my lord.

"No," he said very, very, very quietly, "no, we won't, Jacob."

What is they? Little Girl asked. *Humes?*

Not humes, Jacob told her. *Something very bad.*

We go back to the trees now? Little Girl asked.

"No," Stephen told her very, very, very quietly, "not now. Later." He didn't want to scare her also. He was so scared. So scared he couldn't move by hisself.

The girl dog up the stairs barked and the purpley ghost came down. "They're up there," she said. Stephen wanted to giggle about her big eyes, but he couldn't. He couldn't laugh. He was so very, very scared.

"How far up?" Hedy asked as she pulled his hand up the stairs to the landing. The door had a big 75 on it. He knew his numbers good because of the puppet show on TV.

"78th floor," the purpley ghost said, "and just standing there."

The boy dog and Ben were still down under them. He could hear the dog growling now. The scary things were closer.

Bogart took a deep breath. His face was bright red. "We're being squeezed," he said like a hard-breathing dog. "If they're still up there and moving down there, we're being squeezed. Just like in Star Wars." He breathed in hard again. "The trash compactor scene? I hated that scene. It made me. . . it made me so . . ." He was having a really, really hard time breathing. The sweaty, nice boy pulled something out of his pocket and stuck it in his mouth and sucked from it. A boy at the home had one of those. One time he didn't and almost died. Stephen didn't know what it did. "It made me so claustrophobic."

The boy with the yellow hair and the big dog were now coming up their stairs. "Move up!" He yelled at them.

"They're upstairs too!" Hedy yelled back at them.

"We're being squeezed," Bogart yelled to Ben, "they want us to *go* somewhere and wherever that is, it can't be good!" He coughed.

"I don't want *all* of you to go there," the words filled the stairwell, "just two of you."

The voices were a lot, but they all said the same thing at the same time. Stephen squeezed Hedy's hand hard. She squeezed also.

"You can't have them!" The ghost shouted, her voice big in the stair room.

The voices laughed. A big scary laugh. "Oh, Adelaide. I already have them."

Ben and the dog were with them now. And so were the monsters. Their faces dead. Some were skeletons already. This is why the building was so quiet. Why the small voices didn't speak here. They knew to stay away.

"You will not have them!" The ghost shouted and when she did, some of the monsters close to Ben fell backward like someone hit them hard with a fist.

But they stood up again and kept moving.

"Delightful trick, Adelaide," they said, "but you only have so much of that, don't you? And then, poof!"

The ghost lady's face looked mad and she turned darker purpley.

"So keep moving up, please," the voices said.

"We don't have a choice," Ben said very quietly.

"We're being squeezed," Bogart said.

Hedy squeezed Stephen's hand, "Come on."

Left ear. No.

Her crying went from stifled sobs to momentary shudders. Charlie didn't really know what to do for a crying woman. He'd never seen his own mother cry, though he was sure she must have. Asking himself what his dad would have done led him to putting his arm around Maze in the first place, but past that, he was lost. James and Harriett may not be his actual mom and dad, but they were definitely his mom and dad.

If Spence had offered to share the flask, Charlie would have taken it. He knew he would have. He probably would have finished it. Maybe that's why the other man didn't bother to share. How many pills had he popped now? Was it two or three? Every time the bottle rattled, Charlie looked up. Spence never met his eyes, just popped the pill and went back to looking at his phone. He wanted to yell at him when he said what he did about the window shattering. Maze had almost been settled until then, and it only served to confirm what she must have feared. What they had all feared on some level. No one was safe.

The vial in his pocket hadn't stopped moving. He didn't know what Meg was doing. Did she have any idea what was going on? Where she was? What Carrington was doing? What Charlie had done to him?

With his arm still around Maze, Charlie shifted to his side and pulled the vial out of his pocket. What harm could it do to add another light to the dark room? Spence had been on his phone for a while and nothing terrible had happened. Meg's yellow glow was still for a moment. Could she tell something had changed? A little cap at the top of the vial was screwed into place. Clearly she was unable to open it. Had it been a cork, she might have been able to push it out of place, but the simple screw-on cap had her trapped. *Carrington* had trapped her in it. And if Carrington had trapped her in it, who was Charlie to *keep* her in it? If he let her out, was there anything she could do to help them as a, what, wisp?

According to his mom, wisps weren't terribly helpful. In the stories she told him, they floated about their own business, sometimes luring curious people into trouble for the fun of it. "If you ever see a bobbing light in the woods," she would warn, "steer clear of it and let it be. Wisps are no man's friend."

But Meg wasn't a wisp. She was a person. A person who had lost her body. A Gohlem. But a Gohlem who had lost her Gohlem body too.

And why? What had she been doing with Carrington? What had *Charlie* been doing with Carrington?

The little glow floated up and bounced against the cap. And again.

Gently pulling his arm from around Maze, he gripped the cap and unscrewed it. Immediately, the glow flew from the vial and up into the air. It hovered for a moment in front of Charlie's face. He followed it with his eyes. Maze had stopped crying and was looking at the glow, her eyes wet and puffy. The crow cocked its head and watched it with a beady eye. Spencer, too, broke away from his phone and was watching the glow. "Wha is it?" He asked, his words slurred.

"It's Meg." Charlie said softly.

"She a ghost too?" Maze asked.

Charlie shook his head, "I don't think so. Maybe, kind of."

The glow hovered near his face a moment longer, then came closer, touching his nose. Despite his current situation, Charlie smiled and tried not to cry. Someone had to keep from crying. "Hey," he whispered.

She hung in the air.

"I'm sorry," he whispered to the glow. He took a deep breath and let it out, steadying himself. "I don't know what you can do like that, but we could really use some help."

The glow simply floated. Did she understand him? He was about to ask her to respond in some way, but before the words could come out of his mouth, the little glow darted away through the room and under the door. Charlie leaped to his feet and crossed the room. He threw the door open, Spencer protesting behind him, but the protests were unnecessary. As soon as the door was open, Charlie was met by bodies and stench. The bird cried out in alarm. Spencer flung his light around and Charlie saw the Shells blocking his path. He jumped backward, expecting them to advance, but they made no move to pursue him. The dead simply blocked the only exit.

Charlie could see Meg's glow dipping and flying between Shells, manically lighting empty face after empty face in her warm yellow glow. "Meg," Charlie choked through his fear, "come back, please."

She hovered in the air amidst the Shells a few horrible seconds longer, then reluctantly returned to float by Charlie's shoulder. There was comfort in that, if only a little. She *could* understand him.

Spencer stumbled forward, lifting the light. Charlie could see body after body filling the hallway outside the conference room. None of them moved or appeared to take notice of them.

Maze trepidatiously approached the door too and whispered, "Why aren't they doing anything?"

"I don't need to do anything," they responded as one in Carrington's familiar arrogant voice, causing those trapped in the room to jump. "I have you where I need you."

"Wha for?" Spencer blurted out.

"I told you, I'm going home." The Shells turned their heads as one to look at Charlie, but it wasn't Charlie they addressed. "Hello, little Meghan."

"Don't talk to her," Charlie demanded.

The Shells up front grinned. Charlie assumed they were *all* grinning, all the way down the hallway, dead faces smiling horrifically. "Meghan and I are old friends. Aren't we?"

Meg's glow moved behind Charlie's shoulder.

"We had a deal, didn't we, my little friend? You find the boy, bring him to me, and I help you find this."

There was movement among the Shells, a rippling through the ranks, and eventually the front line parted and a small Shell stepped through. It was her. Meg. A withered version of the spunky girl Charlie knew at least. Eyes dull, skin gray, hair disheveled and brittle. As much as Charlie wanted to take her in his arms, cradle her, he was just as repulsed by her. She was one of them. *It* was one of them. What would Carrington do if he got too close? His first victim, his own daughter, still lay on the table behind them.

The glow timidly moved forward, touching the face, *her* face. Meg moved about as though inspecting herself, and as she did, Charlie saw she dimmed noticeably, as though hope was dying.

"Okay," Charlie said, "you have me now, so give her back. That's the deal, right? You're a man of your word, right? You don't lie? So, give her back."

The Shell with Meg's face looked up into Charlie's eyes. "You're right, Mr. Daniels," the little Shell said, "I'm a man of my word."

Hands reached through the door and took Charlie by the arms and pulled him in, the fingers digging into his biceps, his neck, twisting his shirt. And at the same time, the small Shell slipped past him, and at a full run, threw herself against the blackened window. The glow intensified and flew toward her body, zipping around it frantically. Again, the small body threw itself against the glass, its head beating hard against it. Charlie opened his mouth to cry out, but dusty fingers slipped in, stretching his mouth back painfully. He pulled against them, but there were too many even for him. The fear that engulfed him in his first encounter with the Shells exploded throughout him, paralyzing him.

Spencer watched in horror and Maze was petrified against the wall, the purse on the ground and a teacup in her hands, rubbing it as though it were a magic lamp, her lips moving. Only the bird had taken flight to stop the small girl, but despite its flapping and cawing to stop, the little body continued to bash itself against the window, skull and glass cracking.

Carrington's familiar laughter filled the hallway as the glass finally buckled and fell from its frame, "I'm a man of my word, Meghan." The battered body of the little girl turned toward Charlie and stood still for a moment, one side of its head crushed. The body itself seemed to glow framed by sunlight. In silhouette, she looked almost whole, alive. And as the hands holding Charlie finally released him, she leaned backward, toppling through the shattered window.

The little glow followed.

She had made a deal.

"We'll go on up, if you'll let the others go," Hedy had said to the air, unsure which direction to look. Up or down? Did it matter? They were well and truly surrounded. Ben. Polly and Brutus. Bogart. "Just let them go. You don't want them."

"Very good, little Daughter of Dree," the multitude of voices said together, the title echoed in the stairwell.

"No!" Bogart shouted. "No deal!" He took her other hand. "You can't make that deal."

She squeezed his hand and spoke to that multi-bodied presence, "You clear a path and they walk down the stairs on their own. They walk through the doors at the bottom, hale, whole, and healthy."

The voices laughed, "I can't work miracles. The fat one is anything but healthy."

"Hale, whole, and healthy. As they are now," Hedy said firmly. It was like making a deal with a Jynn. Her Mam had told her stories of the Jynn. Not terrible people, just masters at wheeling and dealing. If there was a loophole, the Jynn would find it and exploit it. Hedy would lay in bed playing the stories through her head, working through how the deals should have been negotiated until she couldn't see a loose end. Sometimes, the simplest words were the best.

"You can't let her do this," Ben pleaded with the ghost. "You have to stop her."

"I can do no such thing, baby," Adelaide said heavily. "She's saving you."

"Do we have a deal?" Hedy demanded.

"Aren't you afraid you're pushing things too far, Daughter of Dree?" the voices asked. "What's to stop me from tearing them apart right now?" The fingers of the nearest Shells twitched.

"If you wanted to," she said more boldly than she felt, "you would have. Instead, you've just herded us like sheep. Do we have a deal?"

Silence hung heavy. Finally, the voices spoke, "And the ghost goes with them."

"Like hell," Adelaide said through gritted teeth.

"The ghost goes with them or I tear your companions to pieces before your eyes." Dry fingers twitched and cracked.

"The ghost goes with them," Stephen said. He looked down at Hedy and nodded. She wasn't in this alone. He was there. Actually, there. She squeezed his hand.

Below them, the Shells began to part making a path. Hedy's stomach twisted. Was simplicity enough? Had she said what needed to be said? In her mind, she saw them filing down the stairs only to be enclosed upon and pulled to pieces like the poor people on the 53rd floor. Or maybe they would be turned into Shells and used against her and Stephen in a sick turn of events?

"I sure hope you know what you're doing, baby." Adelaide said as she floated past the foremost Shells.

"I have no idea, honestly," she said.

Ben stiffened and turned his back. He was angry. Very angry. He'd been so thrilled to find her and Stephen and now she was taking the win from him. It was for his own good, though. She knew it. At least, she *hoped* she knew it.

"Go on," she directed Polly and Brutus, "go on down. Stay with Bogart." The name almost caught in her throat.

"I can't go," the curly haired boy said. "This isn't how this goes."

"It's how it goes *this* time," she said with a sad smile.

"You're very brave," he said and bent low, kissing her on the cheek. "You're all I hoped you'd be."

Any other time, the tears threatening to break loose would have been happy ones after a moment like that. Now she wanted to cry because this was the end. She released Stephen's hand and gripped the front of Bogart's shirt, pulling him down and kissing him on the lips. If she was going to die, she would at least get a first real kiss. He kissed her back, those lips every bit as wonderful as she had hoped.

"Go before I change my mind," the voices said ominously.

Hedy pulled away, letting the boy go. Bogart took a deep breath and adjusted his glasses, "Adios, mi amor."

"Bye, Bogart."

He turned and followed as the others walked single file down the stairs between the flanking Shells.

Charlie at the shattered window through which Meg and her body had disappeared. Seventy-seven stories high, he couldn't see the moment when she hit the ground. He was grateful for that. He watched her fall, becoming a small dot among other dots. Her glow vanished from sight long before, a yellow glow lost in the bright sunlight.

He wanted to rage, wanted to shove the conference table through more windows, chuck chairs out one by one until the room was empty. He was still tempted to do it, but Veronica's body laid out on the table kept him from it. Her still, pale body, except where blood had spilled down her, staining clothes and skin. Staining his clothes. Again, blood. This time someone else's, not his own. He could still feel the tightness in the stitching across his chest. He'd almost forgotten about it. Meg had taken good care of him.

Charlie wanted to surrender and follow her.

Meg.

The crow had calmed itself and landed on another chair at the other end of the conference room, a good distance from the Shells filling the doorway. "You could go, you know," Charlie said to it. "You're the only one who can." He rubbed his temples, trying to loosen the rage and despair.

The bird turned a black eye on him, "And abandon post? It may do for hume, but not crow. We do be vigilant. We do take care." The bird cocked its head at Maze who was still rubbing the teacup with her thumb. "And too," the bird croaked, "Adelaide would pluck me bare."

Despite the throbbing heart pain, he felt a glimmer of amusement. Charlie was holding a conversation with a bird. It was a welcome distraction from what Charlie knew was certain death. They would all end like Veronica. Or Maze's friend. Or Meg. "Who taught you how to talk?"

The bird blinked. "The Teacher."

"This Adelaide? The feather *plucker*?"

The bird cocked his head. "No, ignorant hume. Adelaide do no be the Teacher. She can no teach like him. Hume are all too stupid."

Despite the insult, Charlie couldn't help but smile. "So the Teacher isn't human?"

The crow puffed its feathers, "You prattle about thing you do no know when death do be near."

"It's the theme of life, right now." Charlie chose not to look back out the window. What happens to them now? How *would* things end?

Spence had crawled back up on the table, his sister's hand once again in his own, silver eyes locked on his phone. He assumed he was keeping up with the outside world's reports on their situation. What did it look like from the outside? Two bodies had fallen now, colliding with the ground below. Were any bystanders hurt by them? Charlie had seen for himself how the police had set up a perimeter. Hopefully, when Meg's body had fallen, pedestrians had already been cleared. It felt cold to think of her as a falling object, but what fell, it wasn't her. Not anymore. That hadn't been the girl he knew.

One slim girl, falling backward. Toppling through the window.

The Shells at the door parted and Charlie took a deep breath. He knew what was coming. He knew he would be faced again with the actual presence of Carrington. What he didn't know was how he would react. The swordsman hadn't been able to touch him. Surely Maze's friend hadn't been any more successful. And both of them were dead. Isn't that what awaited them all? If he needed the Six of them alive, Veronica would be among the living, wouldn't she? No, he was sure they would all wind up dead.

But it wasn't Carrington who entered the room. It was a— what was he supposed to call them? A little person? A little woman? And a very skinny, red-haired man. Five and Six. All Six. Spencer looked up from his phone long enough to see them, but immediately dismissed them.

"Hi," Charlie said, unsure of exactly what else to say. What do you say in a situation like this? I'm sorry? Welcome to the party? Sucks to be us? "I'm Charlie," was all he could come up with that seemed appropriate.

"Hedy," the fierce little woman said. Her ferocity was palpable. Where Charlie wanted to come unhinged, wreck the room, he could tell she was studying it all. Her eyes darted from person to person, and if she was afraid, her eyes didn't betray it. She held a dagger of some sort in the hand not gripped by the man in the long coat. "This is Stephen."

That guy, Stephen, was a completely different story. Charlie couldn't read what his eyes were saying at all. They said way too much all at once. And sometimes not the same thing between the two. His age was elusive too. On the one hand, his full red beard and sunken cheeks made him look like he could easily be in his twenties, but the timidity with which he stood spoke of a boy, younger than Charlie. His free hand kept running over the bulging pockets of his coat, tapping one and then the other and back to the first. When he glanced toward Maze, his wild eyes brightened and he gave her a small wave between pocket pats. She responded with a nod and a deep breath. There was something there.

"That's Maze," Charlie said with a gesture toward the girl and her teacup. "And that's Spencer . . . and his sister, Veronica."

"Is she—" Hedy started.

"Dead?" Spencer said, still not looking up. "Yeah, my dad shoved a big shard of broken glass through her neck and killed her. I don't think family counseling is going to help this shit." He looked up with a terrible smile, "So, welcome to fucked, party of Five."

"Okay. Now what?" Hedy asked, looking from person to person.

"As I see it," Spencer said, returning his attention to his phone, "we have three options. One: we all take a swan dive out that window. Two: we see how far we can shove our way through the Hall of the Living Dead. Or three: we wait here for my dad to show up and slit us open like V. Oh, fourth option," he fished in his pockets and pulled out three orange prescription pill bottles, setting them upright one by one at the edge of the table, "and this little gem is my personal favorite, for obvious reasons, we see how many of these it takes to not feel any of this shit."

"I don't personally like any of those options," Maze murmured.

The little woman let go of Stephen's hand and approached the table. She looked from one container to the other, then in one fluid movement had them in her hand.

Spence scrambled off the table and flung himself at her, maybe in some attempt to grab her, but he was already too sloppy to have been effective. Hedy dodged him and deftly flung the pills out the window. "No more option four."

"What the hell?" Spence shouted at her. "What the actual hell did you do that for?"

"How are we getting out of here?" she asked calmly.

"Are you as stupid as you are short, you dumbass little midget?" He grabbed her by the wrist, but it didn't last long. Spencer was flipping to the ground over Hedy's back, landing hard. The woman had a foot firmly planted on his crotch, a fistful of t-shirt, and a dagger at his throat.

"I will *not* go down like this. I have parents out there who love me. A boy out there who loves me. And I *will* see them again." The last was delivered with a clear lump in her throat. She held Spencer's pained and frightened gaze for a moment longer, and with a final bounce on his nuts, stepped off him. "Now," she said, wiping her eyes with the back of her denim jacket, "how are we getting out of here?"

Spencer lay groaning on the floor, moaning about bitches and balls. He deserved it. He *absolutely* deserved it. But Charlie couldn't leave him on the floor. He offered the other guy a hand and was mildly surprised when the offer was accepted. Charlie pulled out one of the dusty chairs for him and Spence dropped into it, his hands gently cradling his wounded manhood and ego, his forehead dropping to the table with a thud.

"You think it's safe to talk about anything with *them* there?" Maze asked quietly with a glance at the door.

Charlie crossed the room and slammed the door in the face of the slack-jawed Shells. It was a little act of rebellion, perhaps even a feeble one, but it felt good when the walls rattled, took some of the edge off. "The hallway and stairs are off the table," Charlie said softly. "I'm assuming the elevator would be just as useless."

Maze walked over to the table and sat in the chair with the bird perched on its back, the teacup cradled in her hands, "If we could even get into an elevator, all he'd have to do is press a button on a lower floor and we'd be just as caught as we are now."

"Isn't there an emergency override for elevators?" Charlie asked as he sat in a chair beside Maze.

"If you have a fucking key for it," Spencer said through gritted teeth, his face red. Eyes watering. "I have a key card to get upstairs, but it can't override any of the security systems."

Hedy looked up at the ceiling over the table and pointed at an air vent. "What about crawling through the ducts?"

"This isn't Mission fucking Impossible," Spencer sneered.

"I swear to God," Hedy pointed the dagger at him, "right now you *have* your balls. Keep that up and you won't."

Charlie turned his face before Spence could see his smile. Hedy was fantastic. He cleared his throat to keep himself from laughing. "I could lift you up there," Charlie offered, "take a look at it?"

The dagger twirled and disappeared, and Hedy climbed up on the table, careful not to disturb Veronica's body. Spence watched her closely. Charlie stepped onto the table, the effort much easier for him and his long legs. "I weigh more than you'd think," she said with a grin.

Charlie returned the smile, "I think I've got this." He flexed an arm, earning a laugh from her.

Spence groaned.

Ignoring him, Charlie took her hips in his big hands, "Ready?"

She nodded.

He lifted her easily, though she was right, she was solid. Had to be solid muscle. He was impressed. Hedy pulled the vent cover off and handed it down to Maze who was now standing eagerly by the table. She set it down gently by the wall. Hedy reached into the vent and pulled herself upward, Charlie giving her the extra push. Her head lifted into the dark duct and as it did, a hand darted out, gripping a handful of her hair. Maze screamed and Spence swore, almost tipping his chair backward. Even the bird panicked and cawed as it flew circles around the room. Charlie could feel the hand pulling Hedy up, but she didn't make a sound, not a scream or anything. Her legs had wrapped around his right arm, anchoring her to him. He pulled her down, knowing he was causing her more pain, but he didn't have a choice, "I've got you! I'm not letting go!" One of her hands was gripping the wrist of the hand tangled in her hair and the other was hacking at it with her dagger, stabbing it over and over again. Carrington's cold laugh echoed in the ceiling above and outside the door. The lunatic had been waiting for this. With a few more jabs from Hedy's blade, she was free and falling into Charlie's arms. He jumped to the floor and set her down, steadying her. Hedy's breathing was erratic, her eyes wide.

"That was scary," Stephen said matter of factly, "real, real, real scary."

Maze paced the room taking deep breaths and letting them out in whispered strings of swear words, her fists planted on her broad hips.

Spence glared up into the now quiet hole in the ceiling, the Shell had pulled back from sight.

Charlie gulped for air, his heart beating rapidly in his chest. How were they going to get out of this? How much longer did they have? Surely, Carrington would be coming any minute. Or was he playing them? He had all the time in the world if he knew they were completely trapped.

"Okay," Charlie said, still trying to calm himself, "conventional isn't going to work." He looked out the window just in time to see a helicopter make a distant pass, NYPD across the side of it. Hope. Of course. With two bodies hitting the ground, news crews and citizens down below, the police were making their own moves. How would that work? Could they get something close enough to pull them out? The blades would hit the building. They would have to make the rescue from the top of the building and they had no way of reaching it. Could they lower something from up there? Could they even land on the roof? Would they be overwhelmed by Shells and thrown from the building too? He asked Spencer anyway.

"Yeah," Spencer said, no mark of sarcasm or spite in his voice, the Shell in the ceiling had really scared him. "Yeah, there's a landing pad up there, for dad's—" he swallowed, "for *his* private chopper. But that's, like, ten stories up. I don't know what they could lower down to us."

"My boy is right," a single voice said from the vent above, "and I'd tear them limb from limb the moment they opened the craft's door. But please continue, this is far more entertaining than I ever imagined it would be."

Charlie mounted the table and leaped up to the vent, flinging his arm inside, his hand landing on a dusty, brittle shirt. He gripped it and pulled as he fell back down. The Shell came loose, its noseless face inches from Charlie's. The others pushed away from the table with various shouts or swears, hugging the wall. The Shell grinned as it hung in Charlie's hand. It was the first time he'd seen one show any emotion and he knew it wasn't originating from the corpse itself. He flung it out the window and watched it fly like a rag doll.

"How many times do you think you can do that?" A voice said from overhead. Charlie looked up and found another Shell, a woman with long dark hair, poking her head in just far enough to be seen, to mock. Charlie grabbed the nearest chair and rammed its wheeled base up into the hole, shoving it up over and over until it was jammed tight. The Shell laughed from the other side, joined by its comrades in the hallway. "This building is brimming with my darlings. Do you know how easy it is for people to disappear in this city? You know, don't you Mazonne? Do you have any idea how many people come to this glorious city with visions of grandeur? Actors. Models. Entrepreneurs. Immigrants. Dreamers. Those looking for that one shot. I know. I've collected them for years. And if you're willing to pay enough to the right people, inspectors quit poking around in your building and fill out the paperwork with a blind eye. Eighty floors of Vacusai standing shoulder to shoulder. They don't eat. No waste. And no one misses them. Wouldn't you agree, Mazonne, your Highness?"

Maze had her hands over ears trying to block out the voices, her eyes squeezed shut.

"Sometimes, like your friend Mr. Coogey, they catch on and I just can't get my fingers around them. There wasn't enough of him left after the train decimated him for me to scrape together to make it worth it."

"Shut up!" Maze screamed, tears cascading down her cheeks.

The voices laughed in the hallway and above.

Charlie was sick of being toyed with. The others were watching him. Maybe waiting for him to say something? Lead? He didn't have it in him. He wasn't a leader. But they expected it from him. Everyone had their expectations of him. Tark. The Pack. Bogart. Meg. His mom and dad. And he didn't think he could live up to any of them.

But what did it take? What did it take to be the leader? Five pairs of terrified eyes were waiting for something from the guy standing on the table, the crow included. The guy who had just jumped into action and pulled the creature from the ceiling and sent it sailing out the window. The guy who had killed Carrington, not that it had stuck, but he had done it. And now he'd do it again and again if given the chance. The guy who had *done*. Action.

His life had been marked by inaction, sitting on the stump. Waiting. Preparing. His parents knew it all. They had the scope of things in mind as they wrote their books. They were *for* him, the books and his parents. The dragon hunts, the hide and seek, the exercise and discipline. Whether they were his blood parents or not, they were his mom and dad and they'd been preparing their son for this his whole life.

Charlie looked at each of them in turn. All right. Action. He took a cue from Hedy, "Okay, how are we getting out of here? Because we *are* getting out of here."

The chair rattled from above. Apparently, Carrington didn't like the obstruction.

Maze peeled herself off the wall and took a deep breath, "Only one way I see possible." She wiped her eyes and nodded at the missing window.

Spencer snorted, "Nothing can *reach* us up here."

She shook her head, "No, but I have an idea." She laid the teacup on the table beside Veronica's pale body.

Spence opened his mouth to say something, but with a glare from Hedy, promptly closed it. "Go ahead," the little woman encouraged.

Charlie stepped off the table and gestured for everyone to come in tight. They did. Even Spencer. They did and it felt good. Charlie wrapped an arm around Stephen's shoulders. The other guy tensed briefly, then relaxed, smiling nervously.

"So," Maze started softly with a glance at the chair hanging from the ceiling, "this cup is connected to a lady, a ghost. Her name is Addie."

"Purpley ghost lady with big glasses," Stephen whispered excitedly.

"Yeah, that's her. You seen her?"

"She found us in the waiting room with Ben," Hedy explained quietly.

"Who's Ben?" Charlie asked.

"I don't really know. Bogart knew him though."

Chills ran all over Charlie's body, his eyes teared up. He was surprised by the effect that kid's name had on him, but there wasn't time to dwell on it. "Bogart is here?"

Hedy's eyes searched his, "Yeah, well he was. He's gone down with Ben and the ghost. Hopefully they've made it out by now. Hopefully."

"Hey, hey," Spence pulled them around, "what's the plan here?"

"Addie can't leave the building," Maze whispered and pointed at the fragile cup, "she's tied to this thing."

That information got a reaction from Hedy. Fear? Whatever it was, she didn't go into it.

"Now," Maze continued, "I've seen her do some crazy shit. Like, throw books around a room, lift a whole sofa. So, if she's still here somewhere and can lift things like that, maybe she could catch us if we . . ." Her eyes shifted to the hole where sunlight poured in.

"Oh, shit," Spencer breathed.

No one else said anything. If they were like Charlie, the whole event was playing through their heads with a gruesome ending. What if it didn't work? What if the ghost didn't appear? Even if she *did* appear, what if she couldn't hold them all? What if she *could*, but couldn't slow them down fast enough? How long does it take to fall seventy-seven floors?

"Ten seconds," Spencer whispered, holding his phone up, "she'd have less than ten seconds to catch us before we . . . you know . . ."

"What's the alternative?" Hedy asked. "There isn't one, right? We wait here for whatever's going to happen to us or we don't. If this building is as full of Shells as Carrington claims, and he's a self-proclaimed Honest Abe, then there's no chance in hell we're making it to the roof. So . . ." That last word was delivered with a meaningful look to the gaping windowless hole.

Charlie looked at Veronica's still body, her skin waxy, eyes lifeless. Not much different than the bodies standing in the hallway. There was no better option. It was a risk, sure, but anything else was surrendering to the man who killed his own daughter.

Charlie nodded.

Hedy nodded.

Maze nodded.

Stephen nodded, though Charlie wasn't sure if he knew what he was nodding for.

Spencer's silver eyes were full of doubt. He looked from one to the other, eventually mouthing his favorite expletive and nodded.

They all moved in silence. Maze picked up the teacup and cradled it to her chest. Hedy took Stephen by the hand and led him to the window. Charlie joined them, the breeze slipping up his blood-stained shirt, mussing his hair. Spencer stood by the table.

Charlie raised an eyebrow.

Spencer gripped his sister's arm.

He wanted to take her with them? She would literally be dead weight. Charlie shook his head, mouthing *no*.

Yes, Spencer mouthed.

No, Charlie repeated and pantomimed trying to hold her and her weighing too much, then splatting. He felt like he was playing a morbid game of charades.

In turn, Spencer pantomimed a zombie rising, his eyes rolled up in his head, jaw hanging open.

Hedy held up her arm and tapped her wrist, *running out of time.*

Why not? They were probably going to die anyway, what was one more body hitting the pavement at terminal velocity? Charlie hurried to the table and scooped the body into his arms. Satisfied, Spencer joined the group. Maze was tearing up again, but her jaw was clenched tight. Hedy and Stephen held hands, the boy's other hand resting on one of his pockets, patting it. Spencer unscrewed the flask and took a swig, then tucked it away. So this was it.

Charlie was trying to imagine how to take the first step, when the door opened behind them, a familiar voice breaking through his thoughts, "Children," Carrington said jovially, "I thought it was time to set things—"

No one heard the rest of the sentence. As soon as Charlie saw the man in the doorway, he turned to the others, and with determination and brute strength, he used Veronica's body to shove the others through the hole in the wall and out into the empty air.

CHAPTER THIRTY-ONE

Chaotic Eruption

The sight of the man in the doorway was what she'd been dreading, enough to make her body freeze in place when she saw him all slick and shiny in a clean suit. Smiling. Maze had been so confident in her theory about Addie and the teacup she was fully prepared to take the leap. After all, she had witnessed with her own eyes a living room turned tornado of books and collector's plates. Addie could do this, right?

It wasn't just seeing Carrington again, a re-living monster dressed in an expensive suit, it was seeing the man who had killed her best friend. Her sister. The man who had killed her mentor, as short-lived as it had been. And now he claimed to have chased Coogey onto the tracks. Over and over again, while waiting in the dark room, she secretly played through scenarios in her head where she killed the murderer with her own two hands, viciously getting revenge for Lola and Philip and Coogey. All of her people, the homeless and unwanted, the forgotten on the streets. All of them picked up by this monster. However, when actually faced with him, she couldn't move. And it wasn't until her feet were tumbling over themselves backward that she was aware of her new situation—free falling toward the pavement of Times Square.

Maze tried to scream, but nothing would come out of her gaping mouth, everything was lodged tight in her throat. She couldn't even tell what direction she was facing, everything toppled and flipped around her, air rushing up against her, her expensive weave flapping around her head. Some of the color blurs had to be the other free fallers, but she was spinning so fast she couldn't make anything out for certain. Someone was yelling or screaming or something, or maybe that was just the sound of the howling air around her head.

And then she knew it. She had been wrong. They were all going to die.

Gripping the teacup, she prayed to whoever might be listening in her head. Surely, someone could hear her in there. *Please, don't let us die because of me. Please, don't let us die because of me.*

Her words were gurgles and moans, like a baby. Was she even crying anymore? Maze tried so hard to get the words out past her lips, forcing herself to concentrate.

"Addie!" The word finally dislodged itself from her throat and she screamed it. She screamed it again and again and again.

And that's when she died. She never felt the impact of the ground but guessed she wouldn't have time. Too many times she'd lost friends who had in turn lost themselves to depression and desperation. Far too often word passed around a shelter that someone had finally broken so far they flung themselves off a building. Most of the time they died on impact, sometimes they didn't. But for the ones who did, Maze couldn't help but lay in a cot at night and wonder if they even felt it. Was there time to register the pain of the hit or was it all immediately over? She always thought herself too chicken shit to do that. No, it wasn't just that, she'd always been too *hopeful* to do that. Life couldn't always be awful. It must have a break somewhere. It had. His name had been Philip. Her break was over.

But hanging in the air, the world slowed, people were staring up at her, pointing. Could they see her spirit ascending? Would she be heading to the light now? Where the hell was the light anyway? She took a deep breath and . . .

. . . took another one. She was alive. Dead people didn't breathe. It didn't take a high school diploma to know dead people didn't breathe and she *was* breathing. Beside her, Charlie was scrunched into a tight ball, his arms tightly wrapped around the dead girl's body, his legs pulled up like he was doing a cannonball in a public pool. Spencer hung limply upside down, his eyes closed, Maze assumed he must have passed out. And Hedy and Stephen were hugging, the little woman just now daring to open her eyes too.

Maze turned her head and about six feet below them, a crowd of onlookers and emergency responders were just as perplexed and confused as those hanging in the air in various states of awareness. The floaters were actually, what, maybe twelve feet from the ground? No one moved, and Maze thought it was possible she *had* died after all and this was some sort of weird afterlife thing, like maybe you hung in limbo in the moment you died. That would really suck. Stuck in limbo with Spencer. Shit. At least he was out cold.

A familiar face popped in front of hers, eyes bulging more than usual behind big glasses, Addie's face dangerously purple. "Baby, I can't hold you for long! What the fu—" and she disappeared. The Six of them fell the rest of the way, hitting the ground hard. It knocked the wind out of Maze, and she lay there gasping and croaking for air, until finally her lungs kicked in proper. Men and women she could only assume were paramedics rushed forward and cheers erupted around them. The people of Times Square were always up for a good show, and Maze was sure this one would get phenomenal reviews. A skinny Hispanic woman with her hair in a bun rushed to Maze's side encouraging her to lay back down. When had she sat up? Maze complied and as she did, she saw the hole in the side of the B&B from where she and the others had just fallen. And a little further up, another hole. Tears hit her hard.

"Shhh," the paramedic whispered as she nimbly went about her professional business, "you're okay. We have you now. You're okay. I don't know how, but you're definitely going to be fine."

Charlie looked up and saw the skyscrapers reaching up overhead. As they'd been plummeting to the ground, he instinctively curled himself around Veronica. He didn't know why, he couldn't protect her, she was already gone. But it somehow made the fall easier to cope with. When they came to a strange stop, he couldn't force his eyes open. He was terrified. He was afraid he might have pissed himself and prayed it wasn't true. Someone nearby said something and suddenly they were in motion again, crashing to the ground in a quick second.

But he was alive. He was alive and no worse for the tragic fall they'd all taken.

Veronica was still dead, but Charlie was alive.

Charlie gently released the body in his arms and laid her on the ground. He stood to his feet and looked around. His hands shook hard. Eyes wide, his body hummed and tingled from adrenaline intertwined with the cuff. He looked down and his crotch was dry. From the other side of police barricades, people were cheering and taking pictures. Paramedics came rushing forward, some were pushing stretchers. He couldn't get his hands to steady. An older man with a beard in a navy paramedic uniform asked Charlie to have a seat, but he shook his head. How were the others? Were they okay? Maze lay on her back, crying. That was a good sign. Hedy was sitting up, taking in the scene around her. Stephen cradled a rat in his hands, petting it. Where had he gotten a rat? *And* a squirrel? What the hell? Spencer didn't look well. He lay on the ground, an oxygen mask over his nose and mouth. Eyes mostly closed. Charlie stumbled over to him, "Is he okay?" He felt drunk. Did he sound drunk? He could really use a drink. Charlie thought about searching Spencer's pockets for the flask. His hands wouldn't stop shaking.

A young paramedic was shining a light in Spencer's silver eyes, "Dunno, man. Guy landed on his head when he fell the rest of the way." The paramedic looked up at Charlie, "What the hell *was* that, man? I mean, we all thought . . . And then that purple, what, smoke? Light? And then bang, you all hit the ground." He turned his attention back to Spencer, "That was some crazy shit, man. This is gonna be on the news for days."

Charlie forced the words out, "Is he alive?"

"Yeah," the paramedic nodded, "he's alive. He's gonna have a hell of a headache, but he's alive. Guy's probably pretty concussed. You his friend?"

Charlie nodded hesitantly at first, then more emphatically, "Yeah, we're friends. He's my friend." He patted Spencer on the leg, "You're gonna be okay. You handle concussions well." He felt the flask in the other guy's pocket and slipped it out.

The paramedic gave him a look then nodded, "Yeah, man, have at it. That was some bonkers shit."

"You've no idea." Charlie guzzled whatever the hell was in the flask and dropped it empty on the ground.

Someone took Charlie by the arm, pulling him around. It was an NYPD officer, a bald man with a tattoo peeking out from his uniform collar. "Can I ask you some questions? You seem to be the only one in decent enough condition to do so. That okay with you, Mr. Daniels?"

Charlie nodded, "Yeah. Yeah, I can do that." He wished he had another flask. Or maybe even the shampoo bottle. His hands kept shaking. Was he in shock? Is this what shock was like?

The officer led him over to one of the squad cars. Charlie couldn't even imagine where to start. He hoped the officer was good with questions. He tried to straighten his clothes up, look presentable, but Veronica's blood covered him neck to toe. His hands wouldn't stop shaking.

Hedy and Stephen had landed on their sides, their shoulders and hips taking most of the hit. She'd taken hits before when training with her Mam and Pap. They never held back, so a little bit of pain was nothing. But what was pain when you were *alive*? She was alive and for all practical purposes, should be a small splat in the middle of Times Square. She sat up slowly, pushing herself up with a hand. Stephen was already sitting up, legs crossed. The big rat peeped its head out of the coat pocket. The boy laughed and yanked the rodent out the rest of the way and kissed its twitching nose. To her surprise, the rat returned the affection, nuzzling its head under Stephen's red-bearded chin. The little squirrel was much quicker, climbing up the boy's shoulder and taking in the scene around it. He smiled at Hedy, "I'm okay. We's okay."

"Your head okay?" Her voice was quivering.

Stephen knocked his skull with his knuckles, "My head is broken already." He smiled a big toothy grin.

Emotion threatened to overwhelm her, but she steadied herself with a good deep breath. News cameras were focused on the scene, reporters talking into microphones at frantic speeds, pointing to the hole in the side of the skyscraper and then sharply dropping their hand, only to pause it for a moment, then drop it. Hedy assumed they were describing the event she and the others just lived through. She kept scanning the crowd, looking for a certain face, a round face with curly hair.

"Hedy!" The very voice she was hoping to hear. "Hedy!"

Wobbling to her feet, Hedy turned to find Bogart. She couldn't see him in the sea of faces, but she could hear him. "Bogart!" she called out. "Where are you?"

"Hedy! Hedy!" She heard him again, but this time realized it was coming from behind her. The little woman turned unsteadily toward the B&B building and smiled to see him running toward her, arms stretched out in front of him. Elated, she started stumbling toward him, her knees and hips hurting more than usual. But his open arms started waving, "No, Hedy! Run!"

She stopped. His glasses were missing, and the side of his face had blood running down it. Ben was limping behind him as fast as he could, his shirt ripped open at the neck and right arm hanging at his side awkwardly. Bogart grabbed her by the arm and yanked her into a run, but she pulled him to a stop. "We have to run!" he insisted. "They're all back there! They're coming! Adelaide disappeared when we were coming down the last flight of stairs and . . . and they all went crazy, just psycho. The dogs . . . the dogs kept . . . fought them off of us . . . But . . . We have to go!"

Polly and Brutus! Where were they? Twenty feet behind Ben, Polly and Brutus were jumping at the glass doors, leaping at them. They didn't know how to open the doors, trapped. Hedy pulled her arm free of Bogart and took off for the doors, her body sore, her knees aching, but she couldn't leave them in there. They had saved her life in the trailer when Denny had attacked. She wouldn't let them die. Bogart was calling her and Ben tried to grab her with his good arm as she ran by, but she side-stepped him easily. The dogs barked frantically, jumping and throwing themselves at the doors. Through the glass, she could see hordes of Shells spilling into the giant lobby, pouring out of a distant doorway. In a few more steps, she reached the doors and with all her strength, pulled one of them open. The door swung open slowly, and the dogs shoved their way through almost knocking Hedy to the ground. They were covered in gashes and blood, breathing hard, drooling white ropes, but still breathing. Once Brutus cleared the door after Polly, Hedy turned and ran.

She didn't see the first of the Shells burst through the glass, but she heard it, and an explosion of glass showered past her.

Jacob asked a lot of questions. He was scared. Stephen kept trying to make him calm when he heard about the plan to jump out the window.

It's too risky, my lord!

Don't let them do it, my lord!

Speak up for us, more lord! Say something!

Little Girl didn't understand any of it, but was happy when Jacob didn't kick her out of his pocket.

Stephen wasn't scared. Stephen had met the ghost and knew the ghost would catch them. Maze was smart and right. He wanted to be smart and right like Maze. He also wanted to be strong and kind like Hedy. When she stepped on the penis of the guy with the silver eyes, it was funny. That guy wasn't nice. Stephen couldn't step on another boy's penis. One of the men in charge at the home hit boys in the penis if they didn't obey. Stephen got hit in the penis a lot because he didn't obey fast enough. He couldn't hit another boy in the penis.

Falling through the air felt like flying. Not real and actual flying, but pretend flying. Jacob had been scared. But not Stephen or Little Girl. She giggled the whole way down and as soon as they plopped onto the ground, Little Girl wanted to do it again.

Stephen did also.

Not Jacob. Jacob's eyes looked even more bigger and googlier than always.

Nice people in important clothes ran to help the others. No one helped Stephen yet and it was okay. He didn't need any help. He was busy helping Jacob.

We are alive, my lord?

"Yes," Stephen said softly and smiled.

How are we alive, my lord?

"The light purpley ghost," Stephen said, his skin getting goose pimples. "Maze was right. She's real, real, real smart."

We fly again? Like birds? We fly again? Little Girl climbed up his shoulder and circled around to his other ear. Her little feet tickled his neck.

No, you stupid little thing.

"That isn't nice, Jacob. Say sorry to Little Girl."

Deepest apologies, my lady. Stephen didn't think he meant it.

He almost said it when Bogart and Ben came running through the doors. Hedy was happy to see them. Stephen was real, real, real happy to see them too. He wasn't happy to see the scary bodies that crashed through the glass. Stephen pulled Little Squirrel off his shoulder and grabbed Jacob in his hands. He curled into a tight ball making sure his small friends didn't get hurt by all the glass pieces.

The entire way down the stairwell had been uneventful. In fact, the Vacusai had turned to face away from the descending party. Maybe the Vacusai's Dominosk was attempting to ease the group's fear? Ben was positive it was some sort of strategy. "Everything is a strategy," he heard Tark say. "An enemy never gives ground. An enemy lures you into false safety. Never drop your guard. You drop your guard and you lose yardage. You drop your guard, you die."

Ben wasn't dropping his guard. He didn't have weapons on hand, but he was skilled enough with his hands to know how to protect himself and Bogey. *Bogart*. His name was Bogart. Bogey is what the others called him at school. In class. In the hallways. The others, even most of the Pack, even David, were relentless in shaming the kid, but Ben wouldn't do it. He tried not to at least. It slipped at times. Popularity was intoxicating and somehow he'd gained it. Girls tried their hardest to get him, and every now and then he would allow them to. He would pretend to enjoy it when they "took care" of him after a game, he would slip away to have sex with one at a party. But his heart wasn't in it. It was all subterfuge. Distraction from the truth. Strategy.

The order of the group descending was important. Adelaide in front. Polly next. Bitches were ferocious animals when their young were threatened and Ben knew that dog would rip Shells to pieces when it came down to it. Bogart followed the female with Brutus behind him. And then Ben.

Leaving Hedy had left Bogart raw. The other boy had cried for the first twenty or so floors and Ben couldn't blame him. He'd never blame another man for crying. Ever. Ben had muttered words of comfort as they descended, "She's going to make it. They're all going to make it." He wasn't sure if the words were meant for Bogart or himself. Both.

Just as they passed the second floor, Adelaide vanished in a blink. Ben's heart dropped.

As one, the Vacusai appeared to inhale and then bellowed, "Betrayer! Traitor! We made an agreement!" As they shouted, the sound deafening in the stairwell, all hell broke loose. Vacusai began turning and grabbing at them. The dogs snapped into action, ripping at the throats of their attackers. One after another, the empty fell to the hulking pair, whose mouths were foaming and dripping blackened ooze. At times, one or both of the dogs would lose its footing and plow down the stairs like a linebacker before they could find their feet again. To his credit, Bogart pushed his way through, taking the arms of Vacusai in his hands and bending or twisting them until they snapped, no longer able to pull at their victims. One of them caught him in the side of his head, knocking his glasses askew, and leaving a large gash. But the boy shoved through, his will a remarkable strength.

Ben was struck from behind several times in the back of the head, with each blow, his vision blurring, dazing him. Break the arms. Crack the wrists. Ben pushed his way through, fighting when he had to. Bogart shoved through the door at the bottom of the stairwell, the dogs holding the Vacusai at bay as Ben pressed through. Just as his foot touched the ground floor, his right arm was yanked up behind him and he felt his shoulder pop. Searing pain ripped through his focus and he cried out. He felt his knees go weak and even though the door was so close, he was afraid this would be it. Two tanned hands reached back through the door and grabbed the front of his shirt, tearing it, but yanking him free as he fell forward to the first stage of freedom, toppling over Bogart who still held his shirt in his fists.

The dogs struggled out of the door, jammed open by the Vacusai. The entrance to the building was well past the jumping fountain and felt like it was at the other end of a football field. But the quarterback had done *that* before and he could do *this*. He pulled Bogart up with his good arm and pushed him forward. "We're going to make it, Bogart! We'll make it!"

As they crossed the empty floor, the security desk abandoned, Ben couldn't help but spare a thought for Adelaide. What happened? Where had she gone? Why had she abandoned them? She must have known what would happen if she turned back, didn't she?

Keep your eyes ahead, the voice directed. Coach had often chastised him for losing sight of the play when it wasn't going well. "Stop watching the failures and problem solve!" he would shout. The door. The door was the touchdown. He could hear the dogs barking behind them, their nails clacking across the tile.

Finally, Bogart burst through the door, and to Ben's amazement the Six were there.

There wasn't time to celebrate the touchdown.

The screams of pedestrians erupting from the subway stations were only seconded by the screams of the pedestrians being blasted by shards of glass and descended upon by the living dead. The officer at Charlie's side had pulled him down and shielded him with his body against the shower of glass. "Keep yourself down, Charlie," the officer said firmly, "we can't lose you in the middle of all this. We're here. Lots of us." The officer pulled at the collar of his uniform to reveal a black wolf's paw tattoo. The Pack? Here? Charlie's head was swimming from the sudden revelation. The man had called him Mr. Daniels earlier. He had known his name.

The flurry of people was so intense that no one paid any attention to the dozens of NYPD officers pulling medieval weaponry from the trunks of their squad cars. In the chaos, Charlie looked around at the Pack officers leaping into action to pull the other five away from danger. They didn't fight like officers, or like Charlie thought officers would fight. They knew what they were doing against this enemy, breaking joints, dismembering. One by one, the Six were guided into the back of an ambulance with an unconscious Spencer. They laid Veronica's body inside, zipped up inside a body bag. Even Bogart, Ben, and the dogs had been ushered into the emergency vehicle. The two big dogs insisted on positioning themselves on both sides of Hedy. It was a tight fit, but he felt safer. His hands were still shaking.

The door was slammed behind them. Charlie sat near the entrance to the cab and could see people running and screaming outside. Shells jumped into the air and fell upon victim after victim, often smashing their head into the pavement until it was an unrecognizable mush. Charlie realized every now and then, a particularly decomposed Shell would brutally kill a pedestrian, only to see the Shell collapse from the person's back and seconds later, the freshly dead pedestrian would rise from the ground having become a Shell itself. They were transferring, Charlie decided. A never-ending army.

The ambulance was just as swarmed as everything else in Times Square, Shells running over the roof and hood, feet landing on top only to jump away a moment later. The officers, both from the Pack and civilian, were valiantly fighting. Gunshots rang out and Shells would fall, but wouldn't stay down. But soon, those officers wielding guns took note of the Pack's strategy and were aiming for legs and arms, some armed with nightsticks, beating the Shells until they were too broken to move.

However hard they fought, Charlie could tell it was still too much for them.

The ambulance lurched and everyone inside braced themselves as well as they could. It rocked again. "It's going to turn over," Ben said. And it did. They all tumbled over each other, Spencer thrown with the stretcher he was strapped into. Medical paraphernalia spilled from cabinets making it hard to get clear footing once the ambulance came to a rest. They all worked to upright Spencer who was still out cold. Charlie envied him.

"Son of a bitch!" Maze screamed. "Get it the hell off me! Get it the hell off me!" The body bag with Veronica inside it had fallen on top of the panicked girl, who was trapped like a turtle on its back amidst the sideways mess. She was thrashing about as though she was drowning and Hedy and Bogart did their best to free her, but it was a difficult job since they had to add dodging clawing hands and kicking feet to the task.

Veronica's body was moved and situated by her brother as the ambulance continued to rock, jolt, and spin. It had been tight before, but now they all perched where they could, the dogs struggling to find footing among the scattered medical supplies.

Maze tucked herself into a corner and worked at calming her nerves with deep breaths and fanning hands. Hedy rubbed the girl's shoulder, trying to soothe her. Stephen held his hands over his pockets, his eyes wide and lips moving. Bogart and Ben simply listened and waited.

Spencer's eyes fluttered and he moaned. He looked around groggily, eyes cloudy, words working their way on his lips. After a couple of silent attempts, he finally got them out, "What the fuck?"

Despite their current situation, Charlie smiled weakly and gripped his friend's shoulder. "Glad to have you back."

In all of the commotion of untangling Maze from Veronica's body bag and welcoming Spencer back to the land of the living, it took Charlie a moment to realize while there was something worth celebrating inside, everything outside had stopped. It was still.

Completely still. Nothing rocked. No one screamed. Gunshots had ceased.

It was silent in Times Square and Charlie knew that wasn't good.

CHAPTER THIRTY-TWO

Emergency Huddle

Thankfully, it was quiet now. That had to be good, right?

Maze was holding it together. Barely. She could feel the threads of her emotions stretched tightly and losing the battle. It felt like she only just managed to pull some of those strings back together when that damn body fell on top of her. When had she become so damn weepy and skittish? Her whole life she'd been the strongest person she knew. Others might break down, but she didn't.

It was that damn play. Ever since she saw it, she cried. Cried at the play when the dead bitch gave her a handkerchief. Cried when that crazy ass white boy jumped her in the alley. Cried at Addie's apartment when she saw the picture of her mama and daddy. Cried when she realized she lost her only friend. So much crying.

Yes, Maze had lost her shit when the dead rich bitch in the body bag had fallen on top of her, but she was with it now. No time for crying. No time for freaking out any more even though every bit of her wanted to. She was terrified. She hated scary movies and refused to watch them even when Lola begged her to. No. Why fill your head with that shit? Life was scary enough without adding extra. She didn't need to see no serial killers when she was sure somebody in the shelters she frequented *was* a serial killer. She didn't need to see no demons possess people when she'd seen enough crackheads wobble their way down the street talking to people who just weren't there. And she sure as hell didn't need to see no zombies ripping into people.

But now she was *living* that shit. It was *real*. And even though Charlie had blocked most of the activity outside the ambulance with his big body, she still caught glimpses of the real-life horror movie going on. It was the fear in people's eyes she couldn't handle. Why?

Because she couldn't do anything about it. A mama ran by with her baby in her arms, and a Shell jumped her out of nowhere taking them both to the ground and out of sight. It was hearing the baby's cry for a second and cut off that was really messing with her. That suddenly muted cry might not ever leave her ears.

The damn teacup! Maze had managed to keep hold of the teacup even when the officer tried to get her to let go of it, to just set it down. She didn't know where Addie had gone, but she might come back, and if she did, Maze wanted her to come back to *her*. But when the ambulance had turned over, she lost her grip on the delicate little cup. Of all the damn things in that woman's house, why a little, fragile cup? Why not a fork? Or a butcher knife? A butcher knife would have been *practical* too! No, it was a little damn teacup and Maze couldn't find it.

"It's quiet," Hedy said after they had cleared a little space and situated the twins, one on the stretcher, the other in a bag. Maze had seen those bags too many times, usually after someone was discovered dead in a shelter, overdosed in the middle of the night on drugs they snuck in. Why did they keep lugging her dead ass around? Bitch was done. They needed to be focusing their energy on the rest of them. The big guy was covered in her blood from neck to foot. She'd be throwing up if that shit had been all over her.

Spencer had woken. Maze wished he'd just stayed asleep or in a coma or whatever the hell he'd been in. Better yet, and she knew she was going to hell for thinking it, but maybe they could just zip him up in that bag with his sister. She knew addicts and she had no space for him. At least he was quiet right now.

"This is bad," the tubby Mexican kid said, "this is so bad. Things never go that crazy and then suddenly stop because the good guys won, you know? I mean, it's always 'cause the invading forces have stamped out the resistance and know they've won, so they're just waiting outside for their quarry to peek their heads out the door, then they'll get them. Us, I mean. They'll get us. And me and Ben, we're not even *important*. They'll kill us right away, you know? I mean, we're extras. I mean, we're not even supposed to be a part of this. Us and the dogs. We're done for." He wound down and took a puff off his inhaler.

The others watched him for a moment. Maybe waiting for more? Maze knew he was right, so what was she supposed to say? He sighed and shook his head, fiddling with his inhaler.

Charlie reached up and tucked the privacy curtain into a niche on the ambulance's wall, closing off the cab from the back of the ambulance where they were all pressed in. There was no room to move, no room to sit, they stood or squatted on medical instruments and supplies, shoulder to shoulder with the twins in the middle.

"Okay," the little woman said, "how do we get out of this?" Everyone took a deep breath. Maze admired her. If Hedy was afraid, she wasn't showing it. And with those few words, she had calmed them all and brought them into focus. "We *can* get out of this. So, how do we do it *this* time?"

Charlie spoke first, "Bogart, why does he want *us*? I mean, we're the Six. I get that. But . . . what . . ." he paused for a moment and took a deep breath, to what, not cry? "What does it say in the books?"

All eyes turned on the Mexican kid again. His in turn grew and he stood taller, if that was possible in their cramped quarters. "Okay, so . . . yeah, there's a ton in the books, you know? I mean, it's kind of what they're all about. I mean, where do I even start? A lot of fans say book four, *Fields of Foretelling*, had the meat of the clues to the prophecy, but—and no offense to your parents, it was the least satisfying of all the—"

"Come on, man," Maze blurted, "we got an assload of zombies out there and—"

"Shells," Bogart mumbled.

"I will call those shitheads zombies if I want to call those shitheads zombies. I don't think they're gonna get offended, do you? Shells? Zombies? They ain't gonna get any more pissed off than they are. Got me? They're zombies. Shit! You know what I'm talking about, Taco Chunk. So get on with it and cut to the necessary shit. Jesus knows how much time we have left in here before the *zombies* peel open the walls and pluck our asses out like a can of Vienna sausages."

Spence laughed a little . . . then winced. Good.

Stephen smiled and giggled to himself, his eyes on the floor.

"What are you laughing about, Looney Toons?" Maze demanded.

"I like you," he smiled. "You're funny."

Crazy white boy.

"Go ahead, Bogart," Hedy urged.

"Yeah, so, there's a lot of theories, which I won't go into," the boy said quickly with a glance at Maze, "but the prevailing one has to do with your blood. All Six of you. '*All Six will join, make journey home.*' For a long time, the assumption was that you would come together as a group and somehow a . . . a, uh . . . portal or something would open and, you know, you'd all . . . *whoosh* . . . go back to the United Realms and save the day or something. But . . ."

"No portal," Ben said.

"Yeah, no portal," Bogart agreed. "So, this other theory is more about you *joining*. Some perverts in the forums suggested a . . . you, know," Bogart's face turned bright red.

"*Intimate* joining," Ben offered.

Bogart nodded and the others had their own reactions, Spencer raised an interested eyebrow. Only the ginger looked like he was still confused, but Bogart went on, "But I, and many others, think it has something to do with blood, you know? Each of you, your blood . . . joining."

"Dead or alive," Charlie looked to the body bag, "it doesn't really matter."

"And then?" Maze asked warily.

But before Bogart could give an *and-then*, before the idea could settle in, the ambulance shook. They all braced themselves and the dogs growled. With another violent movement, the tumped over ambulance started rotating. Maze's heart raced and she thought again of that damn teacup. Where the hell had she dropped it? It had to be crunched to little pieces under all these feet. And if it was, was that the end of Addie?

Scrabbling could be heard outside the doors, many hands touching, pulling, hitting. Then *click*.

One door fell open and the other was lifted by two particularly imposing and dead looking members of the NYPD. Maze didn't trust the police before, but this was on a whole new level. Beyond them, a path lined with Shells old and new led from the toppled ambulance to the steps in front of the B&B building where Carrington stood waiting.

CHAPTER THIRTY-THREE

Shattered Promise

She had followed herself all the way down.

All the way down the side of the building.

All the way down as the sidewalk and spectators below rushed upward.

All the way down to the end.

Her dry, brittle body shattered like the dirt clods her brothers used to pelt the looming city wall with outside of their cramped little home. She could barely remember their faces. Or her daddy's. Or mama's. And now she could barely remember her own sometimes.

Meghan only had eyes for her shattered form shrouded in a cloud of dust. She wanted to scream, but had no mouth to scream with. She wanted to cry, but her tiny floating self couldn't cry. Everything she'd done. All those times she made a promise to that man and immediately started working her way out of it for the good of those he was collecting. All of it was for nothing. Her promised reward was nothing.

Futilely, she attempted to fuse with her pathetic body, but the moment she reached out to it, she sensed nothing. Again, she pushed within and was met with blackness, the world around her fading away, blurring. Gathering herself, she peeled herself away, wanting to sob, rage. But she had nothing to sob and rage with.

Carrington had promised her, the moment she blinked into this world, somehow ripped from her body, he promised he would restore her if she would just help him too. Every time she asked about her body, he said he was gathering the necessary instruments to make her whole again. He would gently smile and reassure her that once she helped him gather the Six, he would be ready to make her whole.

It had taken years, but Meghan tracked them all down. Those still in the system were the easiest to find, of course. Carrington had been so drawn to the twins, he adopted them for himself. That was their danger, even at birth. He should have known that, but the allure was too strong even for him.

He was content to leave Stephen and Maze where they were, but something was wrong with Stephen and she desperately wanted to connect with him. Meghan had walked the halls of the home with him, no one noticed the extra boy who wandered the halls with a dull look on his face, his hair bright blond, his eyes blue and distant. She had almost lost herself in that *home,* almost crossed the line when she discovered what the orderly was doing to Stephen. No one knew about it, and therefore it kept happening. The woman, half of Stephen's Pair, didn't do anything. Did she know? Over the years she watched him crumble.

Maze had been a different story. Meghan admired her strength and humor in the worst of situations. It was easy to follow Maze through the city, no need to shift from her true self. In the city, no one cared about a blond-haired girl in garish clothes. She had checked in with Adelaide regularly, it was easy to pretend to be a fellow social worker in that building. Just another face. But they had relaxing conversations, until the woman suddenly disappeared. Philip was useless.

And Hedy. Sweet Hedy. Meghan couldn't bear to interrupt her life, so she put off reporting the little girl for as long as she could. But Carrington eventually pressed her, dangled her heart's desire in front of her, and Meghan broke. Soon after, he *purchased* the faire. Did he know what he'd *actually* bought? She heard their conversations, the things they said when they didn't think anyone was listening. A camp of exiles is what they were. A camp of sentenced exiles intent on protecting the little girl in their midst, her very own aunt and uncle, her Pair. But Hedy didn't know and Meghan never wanted her to find out.

Charlie. Her heart twisted in anguish because she would never truly feel him. No flesh to feel his warmth now. No buds to taste his kiss. No heart to skip a beat at the sight of him. Never. She wanted to scream and weep, but she had nothing to scream and weep with.

Meghan found him last, tracking papers, files, and dead ends. James and Harriett didn't want him found, but that wasn't up to them. They never should have been there in the first place. How had they even come here? She still hadn't figured that one out. But Charlie was theirs and they were ferocious in their protection of him. Cautious. Isolated. When Bogart showed her the books, Meghan had pretended not to know anything about them, but she knew. At night, she sloughed much of her size and slinked around in the night as a little gray fox. Curious creatures and beautiful, just like the ones at home. As a little fox, she would slip around the house at night, peer into windows, taking in as much information about the "Daniels" as she could. And she would watch *him*. Charlie had taken to sitting on the roof outside of his room several years ago. She watched him grow bigger, stronger, just like all of his kind. He had no idea what he was. It broke her heart.

She had discovered it all for the man who promised her a reward.

And that reward was scattered and broken.

He was a liar.

A cheat.

He wasn't kind.

He wasn't gentle.

Eric Carrington was a monster.

And so was she.

And it would take a monster to kill a monster.

Someone in uniform draped a black blanket over her broken form, paying no mind to the glowing speck hidden in the dull blonde hair.

She was grateful for that, at least someone cared. But no one would mourn her. Her body would be a mystery and eventually forgotten.

Screams erupted from the crowd and the spectators pointed up. Meghan flew up and attempted to catch the falling Six, but she'd no strength to give and none of them even realized she was there. Not even Charlie, his eyes squeezed shut, gripping Veronica's lifeless body in his thick arms. And as they fell to the ground, after a brief catch from a suddenly appearing and disappearing Addie, she zoomed around them trying to get their attention, warn them that he wouldn't be done with them. He wouldn't let his quarry go so easily. Eric Carrington would come after them.

And he did. Bogart and the dogs, and a boy with a wounded arm she had never seen before, rushed from the building only to have chaos explode around them. Chaos everywhere. The streets were awash in blood and fear, gunfire and destruction. In the midst of it all, Meghan had lost sight of her charges, charges she had found for him all based on a lie. She told herself they would be safe with him, and now one was dead and she was positive the others would be too.

Meghan had to find him before he found them. She zipped to the giant building, doors she had walked through in many different forms now gaping holes in a polished wall. From here to there she skimmed through the foyer, the enormous fountain still spraying its aquatic dance into the air as though nothing was happening outside, not even missing the throngs of people who filled the sleek lobby on a daily basis. *Ding.* The elevator opened, and there he stood all alone in a crisp, clean suit, unafraid. The monster was confident and cold, his eyes as empty as those he controlled, but for an entirely different reason. Eric Carrington had sold himself a long time ago, a process she herself had started as a common girl looking for power in an overpopulated city where she and her family were forgotten. Carrington and she weren't too terribly different. Meghan would have vomited if she'd a stomach.

As he stepped from the elevator, adjusting the cuffs of his suit, she zipped to his face, flew around his head, threw herself against his forehead, but he only smiled, a hideous thing.

"Hello, little bug," he said, his voice strong and smooth. "I thought you would be catching up with your body, reminiscing about the good old days."

She flew about furiously, bouncing off of his eyeballs, willing herself to be sharp. But she couldn't, not like this.

He only smiled, "Just go die now. Slip into those old dusty rags, release, and die. It's all you have to do, little bug, and you can be finished. Job well done. Or go look for your old clay Gohlem costume. It's up there somewhere. But this will all be over by the time you search eighty-six floors. I don't lie. It's up there." He stepped past her, his eyes locked on the devastation multiplying outside. It didn't matter what she did, she couldn't deter him. She was nothing. He lured her from the moldable body she'd been manipulating for years when she came to tell him Charlie was now in the city. It was the body he trained her to use. Clay. He told her shedding it was the first step in regaining her true self. She foolishly trusted him. Then with lightning speed he captured her in a vial and stuffed her in his pocket. That's when she knew. When she first knew she wanted to kill Eric Carrington.

Helplessly, the little glow watched as he stepped outside. Just passed him, she could see an ambulance tumble to its side amidst the violence, violence which was slowly coming to an end and not for the better.

What could she do? Meghan knew she must stop him, she didn't know where the Six were, but if *he* was still here, *they* were still out there. Somewhere. In a growing panic, she zoomed about the lobby looking for anything she could use to form a body. The potted plants were fakes, like most things Carrington involved himself in, and contained no soil to pull together. As she zipped past the fountains, she briefly considered trying to pull the stuffing from the cushions in the waiting area, but what would a fluffy doll do against anyone? She could hear his derisive laughs.

Silence had fallen outside. Nauseating silence, if she'd had a stomach. Carrington stood with his back to the building and her, his empty eyes fixed on the overturned ambulance. *All* empty eyes were turned on that ambulance. Was that where they were? Trapped inside? The only sound was the water in the fountain splashing down into itself.

If Meghan had breath, it would have caught. If she'd had a heart, *it* would have caught. The water. Water. She'd avoided it for so many years now because her adopted body would have dissolved, but she didn't have to anymore. Water.

Meghan hovered over the surface, her little light reflecting in the rippling pool. Slowly, she dipped, touched, and pulled back. She was still whole. Another dip, longer this time. Still alive. No need to breathe. She had never manipulated water before, only earth. She wasn't confident she could do it. Water was so loose, it didn't have edges like dirt. Beyond that, she was still so scared of it.

Outside, she heard metal wrenching and one of the doors on the sideways ambulance fell open.

Meghan dove into the water.

CHAPTER THIRTY-FOUR

Too Many for So Few

"Come out, my children." It wasn't a request. It wasn't an option. The thousands of Shells filling Times Square made it clear those three words weren't up for debate. Hedy looked up to the others crammed in the back of the overturned ambulance, rubber tubes and chords dangling like vines. The Shells had wrenched open the doors and now the dead lined a path leading from their hiding place to Carrington standing before his fortress, the Bull and Badger building. The building was supposed to be her safe haven, but had only turned into a terrible nightmare. If she walked down his path, she would never see her Pap and Mam again, Ubby or Sunnie. Would Marla meet her on the other side of death with a pastry and an off-color joke? Even Old Millie?

What would happen if she refused to go? She knew what would happen, those things would grab her, lift her in the air, and carry her like a child. If there was one thing her people hated, it was being treated and handled like a child. If there was one thing she couldn't stomach the thought of, it was humiliation before death. No, she would honor herself and her Pap and Mam. When they're told how she died, they'll hear Hedy Oakenroot walked with honor and took the power of her own death. Carrington could take her life, but her pride belonged to her alone.

"Come on," she said and stepped through the doors between the two ravaged NYPD Shells holding the door aloft. She didn't look back, but could hear the others moving, she prayed they were following her.

"I can't get the stretcher out . . ." she heard one of the boys mutter quietly.

"Take him off it," another one said.

“I can walk,” words were mumbled.

“Do we bring *her*?” Was that Bogart?

“I’m sure as hell not touching that bag. Bitch can walk herself out of here.” *That* was Maze.

“My sister’s coming,” he mumbled firmly.

“I’ll get her,” Bogart again. “I said, I’ll get her, okay?”

Carrington was waiting patiently, his hands folded before him. As she passed Shell after Shell, none of them acknowledged her. Their empty eyes looked off into the distance. What was going on in there? Was there any piece of who they used to be tucked away in a corner of their minds? Were they caged within, watching the terrible things they were puppetted to do? Would she soon find out?

The few steps leading up to Carrington made it appear as though he stood upon a dais from which he ruled his decomposing subjects. Overhead, the crow circled and perched upon one of a few street lamps still standing. In the chaos, she had forgotten the bird. She was glad to see he was safe. Could *he* do something to help them? Hedy doubted it.

The Shells backed away from the steps leaving a wide space for them to all stand before him as they came near. Polly and Brutus flanked her and she saw Bogart to her right as he stooped to lower the body bag to the steps with Stephen on the other side of him. The red headed boy was smiling and his lips were moving. He wasn’t well, but maybe that was good for the time being. Carrington appeared to consider him for a moment, then turned his attention to the other end where Charlie stood with an arm around Spencer, holding him up, Maze and Ben beside him.

They were all here. This was the end.

“I’ve waited for this moment for so achingly long, children,” Carrington’s tone was solemn, and what, apologetic? Hedy clenched her jaw. “I didn’t want it to be like this,” he said with a sweeping gesture to the multitude behind them. “There was no need to involve anyone else in a matter that only pertained to us." And now it was disappointment? Like a father admonishing his children. Was he laying this at *their* feet? Putting the burden of the bloodshed on *their* shoulders? Like hell. But she wouldn't give him the satisfaction of an argument. He was a smart man, smooth with his words. Hedy was better with her blades. She prayed it would come to that and she watched for the opportunity.

"You know what a man who has everything wants?" he asked, turning his attention from one to the other down the line. "Do you? He wants home. That's what he wants. That's what *I* want. I want to go *home*." Carrington spread his hands innocently. "Is that so much to ask? I just want to go home and deal with the creatures who put us *all* in this mess." Hedy watched as the man seemed to transform before her. Nothing dramatic, it was subtle. He was weary. Exhausted. "And I was prepared to take you all with me. It was going to be a simple transference, an easy process, but you all went and made it so damn difficult and ugly. Certainly, I was dramatic in my approach, but forgive me, I'm an entertainer. I like the spectacle. I've built an empire on it. An empire I was going to— no, an empire I *am* going to sacrifice in order to go home. Unfortunately, *without* you all."

"You killed your own daughter!" Charlie shouted at him. Hedy shook her head. You don't give people like this fuel, her Pap taught her that. Don't ever heckle the professional performer reigning on his stage. "You're a lunatic! How the hell could we trust you?"

Carrington only took a deep breath and released it, "Charlie, could you possibly believe there are things I know that you don't? Many things. I offered them to you, but you denied me rather violently." He gave a slight smile and pointed at the tall boy, "Now, you're parents, well, James and Harriett, they also knew things. They knew so many things. Too many things. Secrets they never told you."

Spencer simply stared at the ground. Hedy couldn't imagine what he might be going through. As much as the guy got under her skin, she felt for him.

Hedy was suddenly aware that Stephen was outright laughing as though someone had told him a joke he kept playing on repeat in his puzzling head. Bogart was elbowing him and mouthing for him to stop, but the pale boy was paying no attention to him, in fact, he only laughed all the harder, his shoulders shaking. It finally caught Carrington's attention who pulled his eyes from Charlie to the boy in laughing fits.

"Is it too much, my boy?" Carrington asked sympathetically. "Is all of this too much to bear? It could have been easier, not scary."

Stephen waved a hand as he tried to catch his breath, his face was flushed and tears trickled down his cheeks, "No."

The older man watched Stephen curiously. Hedy glanced over at Charlie who was still helping Spencer stay on his feet. Charlie's face mirrored her own. Complete perplexity. Maze was even leaning forward to get a look at him. "What is it, boy?" Carrington asked, a hint of irritation in his voice.

"You has to—" Stephen was working hard to stifle more laughing and covered his face with his hands, "you has to say the . . . the word."

"Stephen," Hedy said gently, but firmly, "this isn't a good time for games."

Carrington shrugged, "Why not? My children can tell you I've always had a good sense of humor." He glanced at the silent Spencer and the body bag, "Maybe not now, but they could have told you." He turned his attention back to the red-haired boy who was barely holding it together, "What is the word, my boy?"

Stephen took a deep breath and wiped his eyes, "Say cheese."

The older man grinned in strained good nature and took a deep breath, "Very well. Cheese."

Hedy couldn't say exactly what was happening, but immediately, Shells began dropping to the ground as though their legs had given out. Stephen was laughing uproariously and clapping in delight. Carrington's face clouded and stormed, turning red, anger seething openly. But Hedy still couldn't see why the Shells were collapsing, until one went down near her and then she saw them. Rats. Lots of them. Hundreds of them, probably thousands, in clumps gnawing through the heels of the brittle Shells, felling them like lumberjacks in the deep woods, then working to tear away hands, arms, fingers. All around, pockets were opening in the multitude of Shells.

Carrington began to fight back. The fresher Shells were near impossible for the rats to pull down, tougher to chew through, the flesh and muscle still strong. They began to stomp, squeals and screeches filling the air as rats were crushed under foot. Hedy could see it all now, the pandemonium was everywhere. Shells would fall to the ground and rats would work at incapacitating them, but many were splattered, blood spurting.

Stephen wasn't laughing any more. His eyes were clearer than Hedy had seen them since knowing the broken boy. "You can't has this city," Stephen said. "They says this is the rats' city. Not your city. The rats' city."

"Call them off," Carrington shouted, eyes flashing and spittle flying from his lips, "call off your fucking rats!"

Stephen shook his head, "Rats isn't mine. Rats isn't anyone's."

A knife flashed in Carrington's hand and in two steps he held Stephen by the throat, the point of the blade inches from the boy's stomach. "Call them fucking off, or I kill you right now!"

Stephen didn't budge, he met the man eye to eye and didn't waver, his toes barely touching the ground.

But Carrington cried out in alarm, shoving Stephen back and flailing his hand, the knife clanging to the pavement. Fastened to his wrist was Stephen's giant rat, its teeth sunk deep into Carrington's flesh. The man stumbled back and tripped over his own feet, falling to the ground, the rat losing its hold and rolling away. Stephen rushed to it, scooping its body up and cradling it in his arms. A tiny squirrel crawled out of the other pocket and climbed up the boy's coat to its furry friend, nosing and working its small paws through the rat's fur.

Carrington regained his composure and the knife, his eyes still wild. Blood ran down his hand, staining his cuff and dripping on the ground at his feet. "Enough!" he bellowed, "Enough!"

But it wasn't enough, Hedy realized. It couldn't and wouldn't be enough. The air crackled around them, electric and metallic. Hedy's arms goose-pimpled, her scalp prickled. It was only beginning. The beginning of hope.

The yellow school bus fell from the sky with a crash that should have shattered its windows and buckled its axles, but the cushioning Shells saved it and the passengers within such destruction. Those not in the bus dropped from the air and fell upon their victims with blades already drawn.

The Pack had arrived with a howl.

Charlie had never been so happy to see those guys, *ever*. But they weren't the same Pack he had avoided in the halls of Farnsworth High School, nor was it just them. He recognized Mr. Hall, the short man who trimmed Charlie's hair once a month at the insistence of his mother, now wielding a pair of long daggers. When needed, his dad took his car to the bearded beast of a man who was now pulling a giant battle ax down from over his head, effectively separating Shell heads from their shoulders, then cleaving off their arms. And the list of familiar faces went on and on. Boys he sat with in pre-cal wore their shoulder pads and FHS helmets, but swung swords and thick warhammers in their fists. The tattooed wolf's paw on their bare chests made so much more sense now. This whole time . . .

The bus doors opened and those who'd been inside poured out in a second wave upon the Shells, taking them down with ease. Here and there, a Shell would leap onto the back of a Pack member, but unlike before, it wouldn't stay for long. Another man would tear the creature from his Brother's back, smashing it to the ground. The Shells that had been so effective against the civilians and even the very few NYPD Pack members were out matched against a hundred or more members of the Pack, young and old. But was the combined effort of the Pack and the rats enough?

Tark was set on another task. The moment he had stepped from the bus doors, the brawny, mustached coach seemed to have been drawn to the NYPD officers, not just those whom Charlie expected to have the black paw on their chests, but any who wore the uniform and were desecrated by Carrington. He pushed through the throngs and cut them down, simply and with grim determination. Charlie imagined it was a solemn duty, one Tark took no pleasure in, but would not lay at anyone else's feet.

In the midst of the onslaught, a Pack member in a Texas police uniform and a few others made their way to the steps where Charlie and the others still stood with an enraged Carrington shouting and swearing. As much as Coach Tark and the Pack had turned the tide, there was still an unbelievable tide roaring against them. And like the ocean itself, the Shells seemed to keep rolling in. Now and then a member of the Pack would lose his footing and find himself consumed by a wave of Shells. Carrington had stopped trying to turn the bodies to his side, now he simply destroyed them. Blood would go up in a spray and pieces of the fallen would be thrown about as though Carrington wanted his opposition to bathe in their loss. But it only worked to stoke the controlled frenzy of the Pack, their howls growing louder, fiercer.

Charlie decided it was time. He eased Spencer to the ground between Pack members who had cut their way to the Six, two boys from his social studies class and a man he'd seen repairing roofs in town. They nodded to him and he knew Spencer would be safe with them. It was time for Charlie to take action. He was part of this, he was one Sixth of the cause of this. The time for sitting on the stump had ended in Carrington's tower. All of the drills his dad led him through with sticks and pipes, all of the weight lifting and gaining strength, even the cuff pulsing on his wrist was ready to be put into play. All his life his parents required him to put fetters on his curious strength and he did. He hadn't wanted to hurt anyone or draw unwanted attention, but the moment to remove the restraints was now. Charlie had been a leader on the 77th floor, now he'd be a warrior. He turned his attention to Carrington. Or he would have, but the man was no longer there, he'd vanished. Charlie used his height to his advantage and looked out over the crowd, even still, he couldn't find the bald, older man. Had he slipped back into the building? No, fighting had spread there too, Carrington couldn't have slipped past it.

"Have you seen Carrington?" Charlie shouted to Hedy over the den of clashing and howling.

Then he felt it again, the tingling feeling that filled his entire body in the seconds before the bus had crash landed in the middle of Times Square. Charlie looked to the sky.

But the new arrivals didn't come from the sky this time, they were there among them. And quite a picture they were too. Charlie squinted at the motley crew, all of them like characters from his parents' books. Color and flash, armor gleaming and necklines low. However bright their clothing, the gleam in their eyes was brighter. Men, and a woman, on horseback held the reins of their snorting, stamping beasts. Mixed throughout the garish party were more of Coach Tark's Pack, Marrs and Hawkins at the front, their faces streaked with black paint and the paw prints visible on their chests. A giant of a man, his skin radiantly dark, lifted a bearded little man to stand on his shoulders, who scanned the crowd of Pack and Shells, all frozen in place for two very different reasons. Wherever he was, Carrington was obviously stunned by the appearance of the new group.

"Hedy Oakenroot! Where are you, my girl?" the little man bellowed over the crowd.

For her part, Hedy stepped forward and wiped tears from her reddened face. She smiled a smile that must have bloomed from her heart. "I'm here, Pap!" she shouted back. "I'm here!" For his part, Charlie immediately lifted Hedy onto his own shoulders, reminded of her solid build.

But it wasn't just the man she addressed as Pap who responded with a guttural roar, the whole clan, because they must have been a clan, erupted in a deafening cacophony, the Pack among them joining in with bloodthirsty, celebratory howls. "Hedy!" he called again, "draw your blades my girl, *woman* of Dree! Dance the dance!"

In a flash, two daggers were in Hedy's grip and she threw her head back and cried to the sky from atop Charlie's shoulders and so did everyone around her.

Charlie joined in the battle cry, surrendering to the pulsing through his arms, his legs. The lust for a good fight filled his mind and he finally, for once in his life, quit holding back. Hedy had barely touched the ground before she dove headlong into the surrounding Shells and Charlie was quick to follow suit. Charging in, he didn't know exactly what he was doing, but he must find Carrington and end it all. But how? The man had already risen from the dead right before his eyes. Charlie had already killed him once. Now what? He would have to figure it out when the time came, but for now he turned from one Shell to the next, pulling them apart with his hands. Battle churned around and within him. Now and then he would catch a glimpse of rats running about his feet; a lithe woman in a snug pair of medieval breeches using cutting shears to slice into a Shell;

Gladys standing atop her bus, smoking a cigarette and surveying the scene; Maze and Bogart kicking out at Shells that got too close; a crow circling overhead.

What stories would New Yorkers tell of this day? If they didn't win, would there be anyone left to tell the stories? What was winning? While Charlie's body swung and pulled and threw, his mind was busy asking questions and sometimes answering, and that was something altogether new.

Absolutely, there's a win.

But what does it look like? How many people will die before someone wins? What was it he was fighting for?

To stop Carrington.

From getting what?

From getting you, the Six.

What if he gets us?

He'll bleed you.

Dry?

I don't know.

Why not?

You haven't asked.

Charlie shook his head. This was stupid, the head talk and the road it was going down. Carrington was a maniac and had already proven it by killing his own daughter. The only thing that could stop the mad man was destroying him.

Or was it?

More Shells poured into the already demolished Times Square. Every time Charlie caught a glimpse of the city around him, it was shattered and wrecked. Street lamps and traffic lights were toppled, store windows were either turned into spider webs of cracks or gone entirely, and most of the advertisements had been put out of commission by flying debris. And no matter how hard the Pack and the faire folk fought, the Shells just kept coming.

They needed something.

And they got something.

The sound of grinding and groaning metal filled the air, squealing and popping. Everything paused as those fighting for the Six and the one fighting against worked at locating the source of the bone-shuddering sound. But there was a familiarity about it to Charlie. Noise of all kind had filled the Square, but this was different. "It's the bus!" Marrs shouted from nearby, "What the hell is happening to the bus?"

It *was* the bus. It shook and rumbled, swayed from one side to the other, the sound terrible and skull grating. And through the dingey front windshield, Gladys could be seen, her round shoulders slumped, her eyes drooping. Nothing about her appearance suggested anything out of the ordinary was happening. But when the bus lurched and the front began to twist, the sides ripped open and the back end split and tore, Charlie realized what he was seeing. The bus was taking on the form of a person, a person rising a good forty feet into the air, and droopy Gladys sat in its windowed head, a cigarette hanging from of her lips.

When one of the formed arms with a tire at its end swung down and wiped out a mass of Shells, a renewed cry went up from the troops down below. Hawkins beamed, "That damn witch never ceases to amaze me!"

That damn witch never ceased to amaze him. Tark stood just as stunned as any of the other gawking onlookers. What had she done? Every ally whooping and hollering around him didn't get it. To them, she had won the battle. A metal monster swinging its arms and clearing out pockets of Shells in a fraction of the time the Pack and the faire folk could. Yes, that part was all well and good. But none of them were asking *how* it was happening. As the metal Gohlem's body twisted into shape, so had Tark's stomach. He was certain *he* knew how it was happening, but not *exactly*. He had to get closer.

The Shells immediately resumed their battle with frenzy and the Pack had begun a new strategy, herd them together into a mass and let Gladys sweep them away or crush them underfoot. Herd and sweep. Herd and crush. Tark admitted to himself, regardless of how the Gohlem came to be, it rallied the troops and gave them renewed hope for victory. The faire folk had begun to sing a tavern song, one he knew all too well from home, and his men joined in. Soon, the song was filling the Square and swipes and slashes were falling to rhythm.

Tark finally pushed through to the other side of the battleground where the school bus was busy crushing Shells while Gladys rode behind the wheel, smoking a cigarette. She looked completely unimpressed with herself. Knowing the woman like he did, he could say she was just doing what needed to be done. A woman of duty and practicality. It's what landed her here in the first place. "Our connection was gone," she told him dully one night over beers while sitting at the grimy kitchen table in her modest apartment. Every corner was full of books, anatomical charts, and overflowing ashtrays. Instead of emptying them out, she simply moved them aside and started on a new one she'd bought at the gas station on the corner. Ashtrays everywhere. "Our connection was gone and we'd discovered a way to get some of it back. It wasn't perfect." She would take a gulp of her beer between thoughts. "It wasn't perfect, but it worked well enough." She shook her droopy head, "We weren't ever going to get *perfect* back. We're not *ever* going to get perfect back."

Tark didn't say a word. The old woman never went on like this. Did she even know he was still there? How many beers ahead of him was she? Her watery hound dog eyes stared off into nothing.

"Blood is pure enough. It's the essence of life. The building block of life. That's why it's so potent. It wasn't *meant* to be used, but we were severed. We had to look somewhere. Blood works."

Blood works. Tark knew blood all too well. And he saw blood, lots of it, dripping from the underside of the school bus turned Gohlem towering over him. Blood. Seeping. Dripping. What had the witch done? How had she come by so much?

And it hit him. He knew exactly how. *He* had supplied her with every drop. What did she do with all of those men who had appeared in his backyard but were too untrustworthy to add to his Pack? He didn't know then, but he knew now.

Movement on the other side of the lumbering Gohlem caught Tark's attention. The old man who'd been gloating over the Six, the one Tark presumed was the Dominosk of the vast army of Vacusai, the one who had smiled from framed pictures in the Californian mansion, boldly knelt by a puddle of blood dripping from the beast overhead. Tark moved too slowly, he couldn't get to him before the man had dipped his finger in it and placed it on his tongue. In a blur, Carrington stood, shifted, and was gone. What had this man turned himself into and what had he just done?

The blur—that strange scattering the Council had taught themselves. Why was so much of this crashing down on him now? Gladys working the blood. The Gohlem that had tracked Charlie. And now Carrington behaving openly like those who had tempted Tark. The Council practiced in secret. Many of them. And when Truvion had made him the offer, Tark felt real fear for the first time. He ran and hid like a coward. Volunteered with the underground and ended up no longer a General, but a Coach. Now *there* was trickling into *here*. It was only a matter of time before he'd get sucked back in.

All too soon, Tark had his answer for Carrington's strange actions. The Gohlem ground to a halt. Looking up into the cab of the bus, the creature's head, Tark could see Gladys moving and fidgeting with levers and knobs. He knew she must have been mumbling and swearing to herself as she did on the rare occasion when the drooping woman was flustered. A rare thing indeed to see Gladys flustered. Whatever she was doing must have worked, because the metal beast kicked back to life, a cloud of smoke and spray of blood from the exhaust pipe. Raising an arm, it looked like it was going to take yet another swing at the Shells below, but it didn't. Instead, it shoved its clawed hand through its windshield and pulled the scrambling witch out by the head through the broken glass. Her legs kicked and her hands pulled and beat at the big fingers which held her in a vice. Tark could only look on with horror, he couldn't get to her. No one could. The drooping woman was screaming, an agonizing sound. The Coach never heard her scream before and he was afraid he would never stop hearing her scream. The truly terrified scream of a friend, because Tark did consider the old hound a friend, was something that rattled a person forever and etched itself into his skull.

But mercifully, the screams ended abruptly as a red spray exploded from between the Gohlem's fingers. Gladys was dead and her Gohlem was no longer hers. It was his. Carrington's. And now it fought for *him*. Its two giant arms swung down and slammed into a group of Pups, flattening them to the ground, bodies breaking.

Tark howled and his Pack answered.

Carrington must be taken off the field.

Maze stood side by side with the tubby Mexican kid, kicking and shoving away any Shell that might get too close. The weirdest part about it was they didn't seem to notice her before or after the well-placed foot. Stephen stood nearby cradling his giant rat in his arms as scores of smaller rats ran about his feet, acting as his little security squad, but it wasn't needed. Not a single zombie looked his way. Every now and then, Hedy would pop into view with those two dogs on either side of her chewing up anything that got too close. She hacked and slashed her way to the people Maze assumed were her mama and daddy, so while the little woman wasn't fighting for her own survival, she was definitely fighting tooth and nail for those she loved. The zombies weren't after the Six, Maze concluded. Not at all.

Regretfully, Maze wished she'd been able to fight for her best friend the way Hedy did for her parents, but Maze had just been too scared. Now Lola, what was left of her, lay under a blanket about twenty feet away, the cloth covering the slender body but not the splatters around her. Maze's imagination filled in what she must have looked like under the shroud and her eyes teared up and stomach twisted. She'd been too afraid to stop it. Too afraid. Too afraid in the ambulance when the body bag fell on top of her. Too afraid.

Shit. That's not who she was. She wasn't too afraid of anything before all this started happening. She was a street girl. Lived through some fucked up shit in foster homes. Not all fosters were bad, most of them were good, but somehow she kept getting the bad ones. Horrible ones. Mamas who would slap her if she looked at them wrong. Drunks sitting in their recliners saying shit about her, how fat she was or how big her titties were. And the last hellhole she lived in? That boy. He had no right and deserved the beating she gave him. Whooped his ass with the ironing board. She never went back to a foster after that.

No, she wasn't a coward. Maze took a deep breath and balled her fist. She smacked the next zombie that got too close, its neck cracking and collapsing to the ground. "That's right, bitch."

Ben, the pretty, blond white boy was standing next to her, his arm dangling at his side. "Nice one," he said. He sounded impressed, but she didn't need it.

It was about that time the bus had come to life, a victory that melted away to horror almost as soon as it had started. Now the thing was stomping its way through the crowds, crunching zombies and those fighting for the Six all the same. Maze wanted to run, take off down the streets and subways she knew all too well. But it wouldn't get her anywhere. Sure, she could get some distance, but Carrington would find her again to get what he wanted.

And what had he wanted? Home. To leave this place. Maze had known a lot of con men and liars in her time, hell, she was one of the best. But when Carrington said all he wanted was to go home, he was being for real. He was just going to go home and take them all with him. Those were his words. Home. She'd never had a home. What would it have been like? What *could* it be like? It was still on the table, right? It could still happen? Damn right it could. And it would stop all of this.

"Hey, Mexican kid."

"Um, my name is Bogart, and I'm actually from the US, though I do have Mexican heritage," he said uncertainly.

"M'kay, Bogart," she'd let him have that. "What was it you were saying in the ambulance? About our blood?"

"Oh," he perked up, "lots of people think that if your blood is mixed together, something will happen. But it—", he flinched at a particularly loud crash from the school bus Transformer. "But it isn't proven, you know? I mean, no one actually knows what would happen, if anything."

Maze counted. One, two, three, four. Her, crazy white boy, concussed Asian guy, dead Asian bitch. Two more.

"Crazy!" Stephen looked her way, "get over here and have your rodents keep an eye on these two."

Ben grabbed her with his good arm, "Where do you think you're going?"

"I suggest letting that go before lefty is hanging at your side too." She gave him the eye. The eye always worked in the shelters with assholes who tried to take her cot.

It worked here too. He let go, but wasn't happy about it. "Where are you going?" he pressed.

"I'm bringing this shit to an end." She took a deep breath, adjusted her bra, and stepped out into the crowd. She *wasn't* afraid. She *wasn't* a coward. These things weren't going to hurt her and that thing marching its big, rusty, yellow ass through them all wouldn't hurt her either. If Carrington wanted her dead, it would have happened. No, she was going to be just fine. Hedy was easy enough to find, her people were in the craziest clothes, like the cast of medieval *Godspell* knotted tightly near her. The two big dogs' mouths were dripping with drool and blood. A few of their wounded were nearby being tended to by a big, black, bald man, his touch surprisingly gentle. Her mom and dad were holding off any zombies that came near, but Maze knew they couldn't last long, especially if the magic school bus from hell turned its attention on them.

"Hedy!" Maze yelled at her. "Hedy!"

The small woman turned her tired eyes to her. It was clear she wasn't going to last much longer either. The fierce woman was giving it all she had and she was just about out of it. "What?" Hedy called back through her obvious exhaustion. Somewhere a horse screamed and was suddenly quiet. Maze couldn't think about that.

"I need you to come with me!"

Hedy swiped out at a passing walking skeleton, "I can't! I have to take care of my people!"

"You're going to!" Maze yelled back. Here it was. She knew Carrington was listening. "We're giving in!"

Hedy was stunned, but her face darkened, "I'm never surrendering! Not happening!"

Uncomfortably, Maze realized a few zombies nearby had stopped in their tracks and were watching her. She imagined Carrington somewhere close, listening intently. Time to try out those acting skills, "Hedy, please, it's the only way we can end this thing." She pointed at the bus that was busy trying to catch another rider trotting around it. "We can't stop that! It'll come over here eventually, and when it does all your people are dead! You wanna protect them? We quit this shit!"

Maze could tell the other woman was now in a different kind of fight. Hedy looked to her mom and dad, at the hulking man doctoring those who had been hurt in battle, and finally those who had already fallen.

"It's the only way," Maze pleaded. She didn't plead with anybody. Hopefully Carrington was enjoying the show. She was getting an agent when this shit was over and becoming a Broadway star. If Broadway was still around. If *she* was still around.

With a deep sigh, Hedy nodded. She turned to her dad, "Pap, I'll be back."

The bearded man swung a club at two decomposing men, crushing knees and bringing them to the ground. Her mom, every bit as bold as the man at her side, brought her knives down with precision, lopping the heads off of the fallen Shells and with a swish, their hands too. There was a breath of space in which nothing was ambling their way, a momentary break in the action around them. "Hedy, you stay here with us," her mom said firmly, brushing hair out of her face with the back of her hand.

Hedy shook her head, "No, Mam, I'll be back. Maze needs my help."

Her dad eyed her, but nodded, "Take the pups."

"Yes, Pap," she agreed. "Polly. Brutus. Come."

Maze let out a breath she didn't realize she was holding. She got *one*. Now she had to get the other. Where was he?

To her dismay, the way opened up. All around her, the killing dead had stopped their fight and stepped out of the way.

Carrington *had* been listening.

"Do you have a plan?" Hedy asked quietly.

"Other than give the man what he wants?" The two were walking past zombies, the dogs growling, snapping at anything that got too close. It was just like when they'd left the ambulance, except on the other side of the zombie path, the football warriors and the circus people kept fighting for their lives. The bus continued swinging and crunching, so Maze decided to try something. She stopped and looked one of the dead in the face, a woman, who judging by how pink her skin was, hadn't been dead for too long. "We're surrendering. Please put the brakes on the bus."

And it did, squealing to a halt like so many buses she'd heard in her city.

He really was listening. Listening and willing to work with her. Okay, *now* a plan would be good.

The way forward kept opening and the two women kept following it. Hedy never put her knives away and Maze couldn't blame her. Carrington didn't seem to mind either. The way the zombies were fighting had changed too. They weren't fighting to destroy; they were only defending. Toying. Disarming. Pushing back. And the battle was slowing. Maze could see past the Shells every now and then through little windows, and wished she couldn't. Bodies lay everywhere, so many of them unrecognizable as having been human or rat. That metal monster had wreaked more havoc on those trying to defend the Six in the short time Carrington had controlled it than the brief time that saggy woman had sat behind the wheel. That's why this had to stop. How many more would have to go down?

Maze assumed when she found Charlie it would be in the same state she found Hedy, fighting with everything he had, tearing apart the dead with his bare hands, wearing down. But he wasn't. He was knelt on the street over a body, a big man who was bleeding from a gash in his stomach. "All right, Coach," Charlie was saying, "I promise." Charlie had taken off his shirt and was pressing it to the other man's wound. Two other men, one olive skinned and the other black and cute, were at the Coach's side, both of them with their fair share of cuts and bruises, both with big black paw prints on their chests.

As Maze and Hedy neared him, Charlie stood up and faced them. She'd forgotten how big he was, and with his shirt off, he was far more of a man than a boy. Had the circumstances been different, he might have been enough to make her consider a white boy. But circumstances *weren't* different and there was no time for that. Probably never would be. Plus, Charlie was covered in blood. Seemed like he had been this whole time. When he carried the Asian girl's body, it had spilled down him from the wound in her neck. The wound Carrington had given her, his own daughter. The other five wouldn't survive this.

Charlie looked down at the two men now tending their leader, "Coach Marrs, call the Pack off. We can't lose anymore." The olive-complected man hesitated, but with a nudge from the other, nodded and stood, howling into the air, a powerful thing, but solemn all the same. And the fighting stopped. Maze noticed Hedy's people were quick to follow suit, what few of them were left.

Silence fell again in the Square.

CHAPTER THIRTY-FIVE

Off the Stump

Had the three men found Charlie or had he found them? He couldn't remember, all he knew was he'd slipped into a frenzy and forgotten himself. One minute he was trying to work through the problem of ending this thing when the bus had turned against them, then he lost his mind. It went red. Everything just went red. Charlie had heard of people blacking out and of others seeing red, but this was something altogether different. He knew he'd lost his mind and the whispers from the cuff were all he could remember. Whispers or humming? He couldn't remember anymore.

And then he came to his senses. Coach Tark was on the ground, blood pulsing from a rip in his side. Charlie pulled what was left of his shirt off and held it on the wound hoping to save the man's life, but he didn't know if that was enough. Hawkins and Marrs were there immediately, and Charlie was relieved, but when Charlie tried to stand to give the other two room to tend to the mustached man, Tark held Charlie by the arm and pulled him close. "It was always the plan," the man whom Charlie had feared for so long whispered to him, "it was always the plan, just not with *him* in it. We didn't know anything about *him*."

"Carrington?" Charlie mouthed and the other confirmed with a nod and a wince from his pain.

"She knew," the man went on in a nearly inaudible hush. "Gladys knew how important this stuff was." He raised a hand and weakly dragged his finger across Charlie's chest coming away with sweat and blood. "That's how, Charlie. She knew. It's why they assigned her to you," he grimaced in pain. "Dabbling in blood had sentenced her, but she was willing to do what it took. She wasn't afraid to have it on her hands."

Blood. Bogart had been right when he said that about the Six in the back of the ambulance. His brilliant friend said it was only a theory by some of the Daniels' fanboys, but Tark confirmed it.

"This wasn't *his* plan, Charlie, it was set in place well before him. He's only hijacked it." Tark winced again and swore under his breath with gritted teeth. "Take care of it," he finally said. "It's on you."

Charlie made the promise, but they were words he didn't know how to fulfill.

Walking with the two women, they followed the path the Shells had cut through the crowd. Now that silence had fallen, Charlie could hear Tark wasn't the only one suffering from the battle in Times Square. Hidden from his view, others cried out for help, groaned from their pain, wept, and little voices squealed. All of this for them. For Six people. One already dead.

No more.

Charlie could still feel where Tark had wiped his finger across his chest, across the wound that still puckered from what seemed like weeks ago in the backyard of a Californian mansion. He touched his chest and looked at his own finger, flecks of dried blood, Veronica's blood, on his fingertip. How did this work? What was he supposed to do? What would happen when he did it? *If* he could even do it, whatever *it* was. And what would happen on the other side? Carrington had suggested vengeance on those who sent him here. Maybe even sent them *all* here. And if that were the case, wouldn't that mean they were on the same side in all of this? No, Charlie could never adopt the mad man's tactics. There was a line.

The crow called out over head and Charlie looked up at him, circling freely above them all. It looked as though something was clutched in its claw. He couldn't help but feel jealous of the bird. It could get away anytime it wanted, fly away and be done with it. The Shells couldn't reach it. The metal Gohlem couldn't reach it. Safe and clear. But it didn't go. Nightfeather had a sense of honor. If

Charlie were the one with wings and feathers, would he leave all of this behind?

The Shells opened before them and they were back where they had started, at the expansive foot of the Bull and Badger building. Its front doors a jagged, gaping mouth where the Shells had poured through, shattered glass bursting out and showering upon the defenseless spectators. All of those spectators and first responders Shells now and many of those in twitching pieces on the ground. Water was spilling down the steps, likely the result of the damaged building. It cascaded around the shrouded bodies of Maze's friend and Meg, even Veronica hidden within the bag and Spencer sitting at her side, not minding the pooling water.

In a blink, Carrington blurred and shifted before them, water lazily flowing by his polished shoes. It made him look like some sort of savior, standing on its shimmering surface. No doubt it's how he pictured himself in his mind, saving them all from those who had *really* caused all of this. Saving them even from themselves. He said *they* made the whole ordeal harder. Had they? How many would still be alive if the five of them had surrendered from the beginning?

Carrington looked upon them all, discarding the visage of the maniacal murderer and resuming the role of the disappointed father. His wound from Stephen's rat was wrapped, but that wound served to remind Charlie that the man could be caught unaware. Despite whatever speed he possessed, he could still be surprised.

"Remove my daughter from the bag." The command wasn't domineering, it was soft, almost gentle. He wasn't attempting to crush them. No, they had been crushed and it would only require waking up his Gohlem to finish them off.

Gohlem. Charlie wished he had his own. He wondered where she was. If she was safe.

Surprisingly, Maze had stepped forward to open the body bag, but Charlie held out a hand, "I'll do it." She was clearly relieved.

Charlie knelt and unzipped the bag, Veronica's death-pale face meeting his, golden eyes mostly closed. They hadn't taken any steps to staunch her wounds, she was handled hurriedly by the emergency responders, and her blood now smeared her face and congealed in her platinum hair. Charlie reached in, his hands meeting her cold blood, and he withdrew her.

"Lay her before me," Carrington directed with a touch of sadness in his voice.

Spencer made to protest, but Charlie did as he was told. He lay her gently at the mad man's feet.

The father looked down at his daughter. "None of you know. You think I did this lightly. Out of madness? You don't know." He had claimed this before, claimed to have an understanding of which the rest of them were ignorant. He raised his eyes and looked out over the battle ground. The brokenness, the destruction, the moaning wounded. And he shook his head. "None of this had to happen. You brought all of this senselessness. When anyone asks the question *why,* the answer is *you.*" He looked upon the five who could look back, met each one in the eye, the only sound was that of trickling water. When he came to Charlie, he felt as though those pale blue eyes delved deeper, probing his mind. Could he? No, Stephen had proven that. The mad man could be surprised.

"A dagger," he held out his hand to Hedy, "Daughter of Dree."

"Hedy, no!" A man shouted from behind them somewhere. "Don't listen to—," the shout ended in the sound of a struggle.

A woman screamed out, "No! Braeden! Leave him be! Please, leave him be!"

Hedy's face paled and she produced the knife in a flash, "Please, leave them alone! Leave my Pap alone! Please! Here!" The blade lay across her trembling, open palms.

Carrington nodded solemnly, "Very well, child." He took the blade from her hands and looked upon it. "And the other two."

Hedy slumped and two more blades appeared in her shaking hands. He nodded. Taking them from her and immediately tossing them behind him, the metal clanging, splashing, and skittering well into the building and out of their reach. He wasn't afraid of them. He showed no fear of foolishness from them. They were wholly defeated.

Carrington turned his tired eyes upon the crowd, the survivors. "Lay down your arms," the Shells spoke as one in his same tenderly firm tone. "Lay down your arms or I do this cruelly, however, in my heart of hearts, I want to do this gently, but I will suffer no more distractions, defiance, or misplaced acts of heroism." To punctuate his meaning, the looming metal beast turned and looked down upon them all, its joints groaning and squealing.

"Lay them down!" A voice called out. Charlie was sure it was Hawkins, he recognized it from the many days of PE when the man had shouted out directions to run another lap or do twenty more pushups.

"Do it!" A woman called out, the same who had pleaded for her husband's life.

The air was filled with the sound of metal meeting the concrete. The sound of metal scraping the ground was heard next. Charlie turned and watched as the Shells picked up the discarded weapons. Even if someone here or there had kept something hidden, they had no hope against the now fully armed Shells.

Carrington took a deep breath and released it, the burden of holding an army at bay becoming that much lighter. He even smiled. "You're going to love our home, children," he said reassuringly. "Your hand, please, Daughter of Dree." She held it out boldly.

Bogart took her other hand in his.

"This doesn't concern you, boy. You can walk away."

Bogart shook his head, "No . . . sir."

Charlie couldn't help but wonder who the boy had become.

The older man studied Bogart for a brief moment, then smiled. "Charlie, you should teach your little friend the first rule of a boy from the south coming to the big city." Carrington directed his attention down the line as he held Hedy's hand in his. "You see, each of you holds the key," he lowered the blade and pulled it deeply across Hedy's palm. For her part, Hedy bit her lip but showed no other sign of pain. As blood seeped to the surface of the cut, Carrington gently pulled the flat of the blade across it. Holding it up, the blood ran down the blade onto the hilt, dripping to his knuckles.

One.

Carrington, splashing lightly through the water, approached Stephen, a group of rats defiantly arching their backs and baring sharp, little teeth flanked around the red-haired boy's feet. Stephen watched him with curious eyes and without a word offered his hand palm up. "Maybe you aren't as mad we thought," Carrington said soothingly. "That was very smart, Stephen." Gently, Carrington pulled the blade across the boy's hand just as he had Hedy's. Stephen's eyes never left Carrington's.

Two.

As the older man crossed to Maze, Ben glared at him. Carrington stopped before him, "I don't hate you. I don't hate any of you. I watched you ransack my home," he grinned, "yes, I saw it all. Modern technology, no *magic* necessary. I watched as you disappeared from my tennis courts. Your presence at my building was expected, boy. Here," with his freehand, Carrington took Ben's shoulder and twisted. Charlie heard the pop and Ben's knees buckled momentarily, but he regained his footing and stood in silent opposition. The boy Charlie shared classes with flexed his, until then, useless hand. "You see," Carrington continued, "I'm not without mercies. That's why I'm choosing to take them home. I am merciful."

Ben glowered.

Maze thrust her hand out, though Charlie saw tears trickling down her cheeks. She was brave. Bravery wasn't the absence of fear; it was choosing to act past it. That's what his dad always told him. Maze was brave. Unceremoniously, and Charlie thought he detected disdain, Carrington cut into Maze's hand. "Mercy? Bullshit. You're an asshole," she said firmly. "An evil asshole." She gripped the blade in her hand and forced him to pull it out, smearing her blood over it. "But I am Mazonne Marie Archambeau." Another tear slid down her cheek, but it was nothing compared to the pride shining in her eyes.

For his part, Carrington sneered, "You people are next on my list. And you'll be there to watch as I crush them as easily as I crushed all of you today." He spat at her feet.

Maze made as to lunge, but Ben grabbed her arm and held her tight.

Kneeling in the water, Carrington caressed his son's face. Unlike the others, Spencer refused to look at the man. Had refused to speak to him. The father took a deep breath and released it, brushing the hair out of Spencer's eyes. "I'm taking you away from here, my sweet boy. Away from the things that enslave you and make you sick. You'll get a new start." He took Spencer's pale hand in his and drew the knife across it, mixing his blood with the others', then softly closed the skinny boy's hand into a fist to help close off the wound. "It's all going to be fixed soon."

Carrington stood and drew another deep breath. He lifted the dagger before him, admiring the crimson covering it blade to hilt. His own hand was streaked with red, dripping, staining the cuff of his expensive shirt and suit jacket.

"And now," he said as he stood in front of Charlie, "we come to the end." He took Charlie's big hand in his, the hand covered in Veronica's blood, and wiped it over the big man's chest, across the previous wound. "We'll take care of two in one, shall we?" Charlie was ready. He had been making himself ready, watching for any sign of a gate or portal opening, but there was nothing so far. He had braced himself to have his hand sliced open, but it looked like Carrington had a different plan for him. "Charlie, it would be kinder for me to slide this blade between your ribs and into your heart," he said with a touch of sympathy. "You have no idea what you are and what might be waiting for you." He turned the knife and placed the tip just under Charlie's muscle, the tip pointing directly at his pounding heart. Charlie could feel the pressure of the blade, a little more and the blade would cut. "Should I? You've caused me so much trouble and I could bring it to an end." Carrington looked deep into Charlie's eyes again. Searching.

Then he looked past Charlie. "Trouble must be punished." A sudden clattering and clanging of weaponry. Charlie stole a look over his shoulder and saw the Shells brandishing their confiscated weapons and advancing upon what was left of the defenseless Pack and faire folk. Hawkins, Marrs, and Karsark gathered tight around the fallen Coach and, likewise, Hedy's colorfully dressed family huddled close, hands gripping each other. To all of their credit, no one shouted, no one screamed. They raised their heads, ready to face the end. Looming over them all, the bus, what had once been the harbinger of a new school day, groaned and squealed to life.
"Trouble must be punished, Charlie."

Charlie was once again the boy sitting on the stump in the intense Texas morning heat. Sweating. Hoping for something new and different. Going through his days, dodging expectations, but expecting something to happen to change his monotonous path. Shoved into a bathroom wall by a man who had only ever intended to train him to be ready for a moment like this. Prepared with camping trips and dragon hunts, and nightly dinners full of laughter and words of wisdom. Just the boy sitting by and waiting.

No more sitting on the stump.

He'd led.

He'd fought.

Charlie looked down at the knife held against his chest. He felt the hum of the cuff, the buzz that reminded him of the girl who gave it to him. Quickly, Charlie grabbed Carrington by the wrist and pulled the blade across his chest, cutting through the stitches that held the wound closed. Blood spilled and the pain was intense, but Charlie held the blade to it with everything he had, feeling Carrington attempting to pull away. The look on Carrington's face was a strange mixture of incredulity and satisfaction, as Charlie forced the knife against the wound, hoping whatever was supposed to happen would kick in soon.

Then Carrington shifted and leaned in, using Charlie's strength against him. The blade slipped into his chest and suddenly Charlie was fighting to stay alive. He could feel the steel inside his chest, the cuff bringing every new slice of flesh and muscle into brilliantly painful reality. He was scared. His strength pressed against Carrington's, but the man had the advantage of Charlie's fear and shock.

Even so, it started.

Whatever *it* was, it was starting. He felt the lurch, the spin, the sickening whirl. This wasn't like before with the orb, this was slower, churning, but no less powerful. Carrington held the blade in place with gleaming satisfaction. "Thank you, my boy. Thank you most sincerely." As the wound in Charlie's ribs burned, he could feel his legs weakening. Had the blade gone too deep? Had Carrington managed to pierce his heart? He could feel the blood like fire, flowing down his side in pulses, his hands numbing. Gratification in his eyes, Carrington jerked his arm and blade free of Charlie's languishing grasp.

The others shouldered past Carrington and rushed to Charlie's side, Ben and Bogart easing him to the ground beside Veronica and Spencer, the latter quickly helped guide him to rest on his back.

Hedy pulled her jacket off and like he had done for Tark, she pressed the cloth to his chest trying to staunch the bleeding. Maze held his head, urging him to hold on as Stephen looked on, concern deep in his eyes. Wind whipped around them all, a deafening sound.

Above them, Carrington stood arms spread and victorious, face turned to the sky. Charlie watched him dizzily. The mad man had won. After all they'd been through, they had lost and the mad man had won. He looked down on them arrogantly, "It's time we all went home, children!" The world was twirling and slipping, sliding and shifting, blinking in and out, from the city to vacillating colors. Carrington watched it all with wild-eyed wonder. Those around Charlie even watched the tornado of color and light swirling about them, fear and worry plain on their faces. Even the dogs whimpered and nuzzled Hedy and Bogart.

Charlie realized he was beginning to lose his grip on reality as he lay there, the blood like fire on his skin. His head lolled to the side and all he could see were Carrington's shoes and pant leg, and the water flowing up them. Water flowing up them. Up them. Charlie's eyes followed the little stream and the small glowing ball traveling up the stream. And his skin prickled. He knew that glow.

Charlie gathered himself with a groan and lurched to his side, then unsteadily onto his hands and knees, despite Maze's protests. His head swam and he fought to regain focus. But it was her! He knew it was her! And that pushed him up to his knees where he reached out and found Ben's hand. He locked eyes with the boy and pulled. Ben responded by helping him to his feet, but Charlie almost collapsed again, the wound near his heart agonizing. But he had seen her. In the water.

In the chaos of the undulating colors, flashing world, and now whipping wind, Carrington had taken no notice of the stream creeping up his trousers to his waist, but Charlie watched it. She continued to make her way up and up. "Carrington!" Charlie yelled over the din, the effort causing him immense pain, so he pulled on the hum of the cuff to focus himself. No, not humming. Whispering.

Fire flashed in Carrington's eyes and his gloating exultation turned to hatred. "When will you admit you've been defeated? When will you simply surrender to what is inevitable and good?" He adjusted his grip on the dagger and lifted it, pressing the tip to the bleeding wound. Charlie cried out in pain. Just the touch of the dagger was excruciating. And when Carrington saw it, he pushed it further, the steel slipping deeper into the wound again.

That's when the water gushed, raged, and flooded up around Carrington, flowing up to his head and encasing him in a strange bubble of living torrents, the little glow Charlie knew as Meg, zipping through the water in streaks of light and flashes. In the distraction, a pale hand gripped Carrington's wrist, fighting to pull it from Charlie's chest. Spencer, swayed on his feet, yet resisted his father with everything he had left. Charlie took a deep breath, listened to the whispering urging him on, and thrust his hand through the tumultuous water, gripping Carrington by the throat one more time.

Maze and Stephen lent their strength to Spencer and together they managed to wrestle the dagger away from the surprised Carrington, who's attention was turned to his own fight for survival, his free hand splashing frantically through the water surrounding his head. Charlie could feel things cracking and popping in the man's neck, muted by Meg's fluid assault. Behind Carrington, the world Charlie had known was gone, in its place flashing light and deafening roars. This was nothing like when he'd journeyed with Meg before. Her sweet voice always reminding him to keep his hands and feet inside the swirling colors. Stay inside. He had. But what if he hadn't?

With a final surge, Charlie shoved Carrington to what he hoped was the edge, hoping Meg would be okay. Before Charlie could wonder if anything was happening, he felt a grinding reverberating through Carrington's body, the man's water magnified eyes opening impossibly wide, mouth gaping, fingers now digging into Charlie's arm. Charlie himself could feel a strange pull, his body leaning forward, following. The water surrounding Carrington's head began clouding with red and Charlie kept pressing forward, the vibration growing and jarring Charlie. Pieces of Carrington's scalp and skull floated in the bulb of water like a gruesome snow globe. "Meg!" Charlie yelled, the pain in his chest pulsing and his own consciousness beginning to ebb, "Meg! Let him go!"

The water crashed to what might have been the ground, but Charlie didn't know if where they were even had a ground. Carrington's high pitched tortured screams filled their space, echoing around them as his head continued to be chewed away from behind by the swirling torrent. Charlie was weakening rapidly, the effort taking its toll, and he could feel himself being pulled off his feet, ready to tumble with Carrington into nothing.

Arms, many of them, reached around Charlie and pulled him back. "Charlie!" A voice called out, "You have to let him go!" Was it Bogart? "I mean, you have to push him away, all right?"

And Charlie did. As his own last shreds of cognizance slipped away, Charlie shoved Carrington through the edge. With a look of shock on his face, the man tumbled backward into an explosion of expensive clothes and flesh and bone.

Charlie buckled and fell to the ground, the world fading into white around him.

Peaceful.

Restful.

Welcoming bright light.

CHAPTER THIRTY-SIX

Home Again

Maze's head throbbed. She felt like she wanted to throw up, but the breeze was soothing. It felt good on her body. All over her body. She sat up and rubbed her eyes and squinted against the bright sunlight. Her muscles ached and her head throbbed painfully.

Sunlight?

Forcing herself to open her eyes, she looked around. Hills. Green. Grass. Trees in the distance. The sky blue. The suns bright and warm.

Suns.

"What the hell?" she slurred, her head pounded.

She looked around her.

Ben laid on his stomach snoring, his face turned toward her. His bare ass visible through long blades of lush grass.

Stephen lay on his back, arms and legs sprawled. Naked. His giant rat curled up beside him, resting. A little squirrel snuggled on his chest.

The little woman was standing between her dogs, the male licking himself, the female sniffing the air. Hedy covered herself with her hands. Her tubby Mexican boyfriend naked and asleep on the ground beside her.

The skinny Asian guy lay beside his sister. Her golden eyes unseeing. His closed peacefully. Both bare.

The sound of flapping wings, and something landed beside her.

"You be naked, hume. And fat. You should cover."

Nightfeather stood beside a teacup, his head cocked to the side.

Maze rubbed her eyes. "What the hell is going on, bird? Where are we?"

The crow cocked his head again, "You be home, idiot hume."

In the distance, a very naked Charlie ran to a house, a tall, green house that looked like something out of a storybook. Strange trees cut in half long ways standing sentry around it, their green leaves rustling in the breeze.

ABOUT THE AUTHOR

Kirk Holland lives in Shanghai, China, where he teaches theatre at an international school. At fifteen, Kirk started working at a small bookstore in a mall in Fort Worth, Texas. It was then he was introduced to the fantasy genre and fell in love with the adventures and endless possibilities. He earned his undergraduate degree at Texas Christian University in theatre and television with a focus on script writing and later his graduate degree in theatre education at the University of Houston. Telling stories on stage has been a passion of his for over twenty years that he shares with students as he leads them into their own discovery of their storytelling voices.

Made in the USA
Las Vegas, NV
03 May 2021

22402132R00219